Advance praise for *the book of webs*

"What a wonderfully strange and singular novel is Jesse Kohn's *the book of webs*. Be prepared to be lured in by the multitude of voices and visions and the 'web' that this book claims to be. In truth, *the book of webs* is more of a rabbit hole, a labyrinthian trapdoor to the eternal, a carnival ride that is both amusing and darkly disarming. Not a usual first book by any means. Not a usual book by any definition of the word. Kohn should be celebrated by this venture into the never-before. What lies ahead in this young writer's future is only what Kohn himself might imagine."

—Peter Markus, author of
When Our Fathers Return to Us as Birds

"Operating somewhere on the brilliantly defamiliarized spectrum of Calvino, Erickson, Galeano, Lispector, Markson, the author of *the book of webs* seems determined to lead the reader into a hall of mirrors, a fever dream in which interlocutors enchant us into questioning that crowd-sourced phenomenon we call reality. Innovative, metafictive, whimsical, deep, this novel augurs the advent of a major writer."

—Edie Meidav, author of
Another Love Discourse

the book of webs

the book of webs

JESSE KOHN

University of Massachusetts Press
Amherst and Boston

Printed in the United States of America

ISBN 978-1-62534-713-8 (paper)

Designed by Deste Roosa
Set in Cormorant Garamond
Printed and bound by Books International, Inc.

Cover design by adam b. bohannon
Cover art by Gerrit Willem Dijsselhof, *Titelhoofd met kruisspin en spinnenweb,* 1927. Japanese paper (handmade paper), h 61mm × w 114mm. Courtesy of Rijksmuseum.

Library of Congress Cataloging-in-Publication Data
Names: Kohn, Jesse, author.
Title: The book of webs / Jesse Kohn.
Description: Amherst : University of Massachusetts Press, [2023] | Series: Juniper prize for fiction
Identifiers: LCCN 2022045067 (print) | LCCN 2022045068 (ebook) | ISBN 9781625347138 (paperback) | ISBN 9781685750114 (ebook) | ISBN 9781685750121 (epub)
Subjects: LCGFT: Novels.
Classification: LCC PS3611.O3679 B66 2023 (print) | LCC PS3611.O3679 (ebook) | DDC 813/.6—dc23/eng/20221018
LC record available at https://lccn.loc.gov/2022045067
LC ebook record available at https://lccn.loc.gov/2022045068

British Library Cataloguing-in-Publication Data
A catalog record for this book is available from the British Library.

Such is the fate of all who forget God;
The hope of the impious man comes to naught—
Whose confidence is a thread of gossamer,
Whose trust is a spider's web.

Book of Job

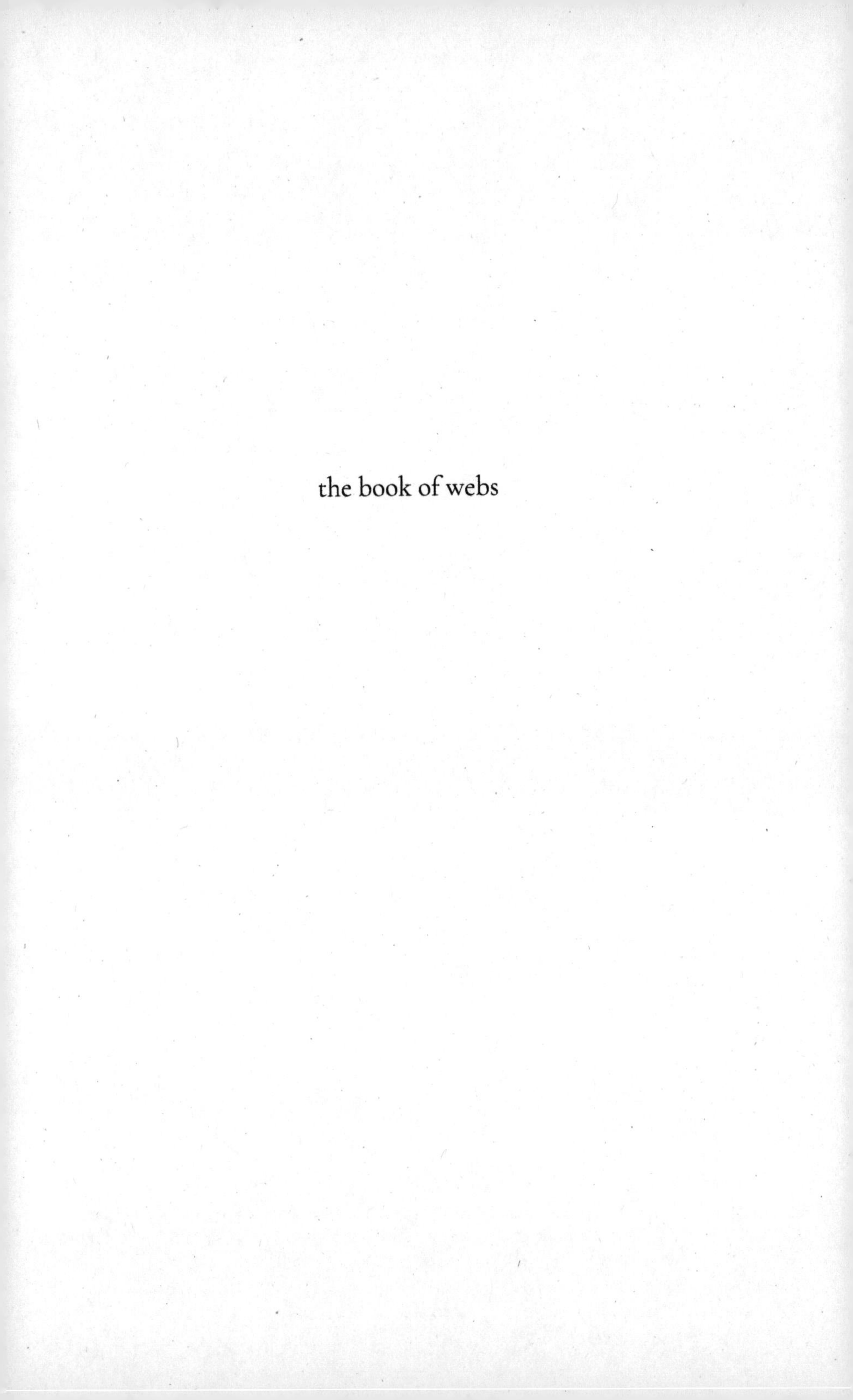

the book of webs

After the Eye Surgery,

once enough time had passed that he could no longer avoid looking, or actually a little after that because it took some time to recover from what he saw—that's when Paul began to wonder *how* he'd seen it, the long curved incisions, smiling like mouths with lips stitched—with what eyes had he seen what had been done to his eyes?

In the stuttering eternities of convalescence, this question grew so persistent that he'd sometimes find himself accidently asking it out loud. When he did, he'd stop himself and quickly add, "You won't tell the doctor, will you?"

"Who? Me?" I'd say, and he'd say, "Yes, you," and I'd say, "Of course not. I wouldn't dream of it."

There were other times, however, when he'd ask for my discretion, and I'd respond, "Discretion about what?"

And then he'd realize he'd likely been mistaken about his having accidently spoken the question aloud and was, thus, wrong about my having heard him, wrong about my knowing that he'd betrayed the doctor's orders by peeking under the bandages before he was supposed to. He'd say, "Oh, nothing. Never mind." And then he'd tell me about something innocuous, something meant to distract—something about sleep-talkers, for example. Did I know, for example, that sleep-talkers spoke backward but that their words could be reversed by placing a dental inspection mirror in their mouths?

"No," I'd declare. "I never knew that."

But in the vast majority of cases, after he'd ask me not to tell the doctor, I'd usually say, "What doctor?" and he'd say, "The . . .

um . . ." and I'd remind him of the fact that there was no doctor, that we'd given ourselves our eye surgeries ourselves, and that *doctor's orders* was just an expression I'd used when he'd asked me whether I thought looking already was a bad idea.

"Remember?" I'd say.

"Oh. Yes," he'd reply. But sometimes he'd have a hard time fully believing me. If there *were* a doctor, he'd reason, wouldn't I, the doctor's other patient, perhaps win some special favor with this doctor by convincing him, Paul, that there was no doctor?

Then again, he did sometimes tend to be bit paranoid, didn't he.

"*Paranoid?*" I'd ask him, for it seemed to me like a fairly reasonable thing to wonder about, given the circumstances.

"I mean, *I* agree with you," he'd usually reply. It wasn't like *he* thought he was being paranoid. No, when he'd said the word *paranoid*, he'd been picturing himself from another's perspective. Most likely, he'd been seeing himself from the perspective of a doctor or something—a doctor observing his patient: Paul, sitting there in the dark, his fingers scuttling over the bandages, muttering such things as, "Eyes in a state like the ones I saw . . . no way could such eyes have . . ."

"Hmm, very interesting," this doctor might have replied, and though he might have said this sympathetically, the word that Paul would most definitely have heard scuttling across the doctor's notepad would undoubtedly have been the word *paranoid.*

But, of course, there wasn't any doctor. There was just me. Me and him. Me and Paul. Paul and I. Paul the Liar, as he'd often been called, in virtue of his nearly categorical honesty. In all honesty, there was no one there but Paul and I, and *I* didn't think he was acting paranoid. Not at all. I'd often tell him so. I'd tell him I thought it was a good question.

"What was a good question?" he'd ask, and I'd remind him about the eyes, and he'd say, "Oh, right," and though he might mean to ask me next if I suspected that maybe he'd merely been dreaming when he'd dared to peel back the bandages—though he'd have vehemently denied such a suspicion, he assured me; wouldn't *he*, of all people, know the difference between a dream and a memory?—even if he'd mean to ask me if I suspected he'd been dreaming, he generally wouldn't.

"How come?" I'd say. "You can ask me anything you want," and he'd tell me that he didn't ask this because it hurt to speak.

"Why *does* it hurt to speak?" he'd sometimes say.

"Maybe it's because you haven't actually been speaking," I'd tell him. "Maybe you thought you were speaking but you weren't. If you had been," I'd add, "maybe it wouldn't."

"Oh," he'd start to say, "that makes sense," but it would hurt him to say so, so he'd stop. He'd feel a lot better then, so much better, in fact, he might decide to go for a little walk—yes, a walk being just what the doctor ordered! That's what he'd do. He'd go for a little walk. A bit of sunlight would, no doubt, do him good.

"*Sunlight?*" Paul often asked me, and I'd have to remind him that by *sunlight* I'd obviously only meant *batshit*. "Oh," he'd say.

Seeing as we were still in our hole—"Hole?" he'd say, and I'd say, "Right, the cave we're recovering from our eye surgeries in," and he'd say, "Oh, right"—seeing as we were still in our little hole and seeing as we'd be thus—"Pardon the expression," I'd say—*interred* for at least as long as it took to recover, we'd agreed that the hole would be, for all intents and purposes, what we'd henceforth mean by the word *world*, and thus bats, who were the only creatures still flitting in and out of our cavity's narrow entrances and thereby participating in the larger cosmos and importing to our otherwise inhospitable environment the most basic necessities of biological life, their excretions would need to be, for the foreseeable future, what we'd have to mean when we'd say *sun*.

Did this make us vegetables? he'd sometimes wonder, and if so did that make the spiders—"Spiders?" I'd say, and he'd say, "The spiders whose webs catch a little more of us each time we move, don't you feel them?" he'd say. "The webs?" and I'd say, "Ah, right" and that I did—did us being vegetables, he'd ask, make the spiders us?

"*Us?*" I'd ask.

"Vegetarians," he'd say, and I'd say, "Oh. Yeah. I suppose in that case it would."

"But how come you can hear me?" Paul would sometimes interrupt himself to say. "If, as you say, I'm not really speaking, how come you can hear me?" and I'd maybe say that I couldn't, that I was doing my best to infer what he'd say if he could speak and then responding accordingly.

"You're doing the same, in turn, to me," I'd say, and he'd say, "That makes sense," even though it wouldn't actually, at least not usually.

It wouldn't, generally, make sense, he'd tell me, at least not to him.

But actually it did.

"Did what?" he'd say, and I'd say, "Make sense," and he'd say, "What makes sense?" and I'd say again whatever it was I'd said that he'd said didn't.

"That makes sense?" he'd say, and I'd answer that it did, that this was what *sense* was now and this was how one made it.

"You want this to work," I'd ask him, "don't you?"

"Yes," he'd say, "very much," although he never was completely sure what exactly I was referring to by *this*.

Was I, he sometimes wondered, ever entirely either though?

And then he'd ask me who I was again. "You *are* Ishmael, right?" he might, for instance, ask, and sometimes I'd tell him that I sure was.

"Oh good," he'd say, because he'd have something, usually, he'd been meaning to ask Ishmael.

"Such as?" I'd ask.

"Such as where's Sludge?" he asked me once.

"Sludge?" I said on this occasion.

"The acned boy with barbed wire for hair you did the eye surgery with," he replied. "That is, if you are really Ishmael."

"Oh, Sludge," I said, and told him that Sludge was right there with us, and he said, "Oh," into the darkness, "sorry, Sludge. Didn't see you there," and I told him that Sludge said hello and asked how he was feeling.

"Not too bad," he said. "I'm feeling a lot better now." But then he whispered, "Hey, Ishmael. Can I ask you something?" and I said, "Always," and he said, "How come I can't hear Sludge myself?"

"You can," I told him. "First you heard Sludge say, 'Hello,' and then you heard him say, 'How are you holding up?'"

"Oh yeah," he said, and he *could* really remember this now. He'd told me so, I told him. "I did?" he said, and I said yes, and also that he'd replied, "I'm holding up quite well, Sludge. Thank you for asking. And most of all, thank you for performing the eye surgery with Ishmael. I'm feeling much better now."

And often he really was. And when he was he'd go for a little walk.

A walk was an exercise prescribed by the so-to-speak doctor. To go for a little walk was to repeat the words *I went for a little walk* over and over in his head while picturing his legs moving and his body navigating the coiling tunnels and yawning vaults he seemed to remember our little cave looking like. I went for a little walk, he'd say and say and say in his head, and before long he really would be going for a little walk. For this was all that a walk was now. What a walk, for him, had become.

So he'd go for a little walk, and then he'd have a little rest—"a break," he'd say, or maybe "a breather"—and then he'd walk some more. Eventually he'd get back, and I'd ask him what he'd seen on his walk, and he'd usually answer that he hadn't seen a thing—"on account," he'd tell me, "of the eyes."

"Of course," I'd say.

He had, however, been able to hear and also sort of feel his way about with his hands, running his fingertips along the damp, rough rock of the walls, the stalagmites that rose up from the floor—"Or are those stalactites?" he'd ask, he'd always forget which was which—as he'd feel with his foot where the ground gave way to subterranean pools, pits, ledges, and so forth. He would walk and walk and walk, and in this way, he'd eventually acquire what we'd come to call *a real sense of the place* as well as a familiarity with some of its other inhabitants.

"Other inhabitants?" he asked me once, for he seemed to recall my having insisted it was just the two of us.

"Just the two of us? In the entire world?" I laughed, and he laughed, too, said no, no, no, that he didn't think that. Not even close.

There was, at the very least, the doctor, he said, for example, the eye surgeon. "What was his name again?" he asked, the fellow who'd done the eye surgery, the man who he'd met on a recent walk? "Ah, right!" he said. "Ishmael!"

"I thought you thought I was Ishmael," I said on this occasion, but other times—depending on how I felt myself—other times that he said Ishmael, I maybe said, "Interesting. He sounds like a real character. Remind me how you met him?" and sometimes—more often than never, but not, I'd say, more often than not—he would.

He told me once, for example, that he'd stopped to take a breather, was leaning up against a stalagmite, minding his own business, soaking in the sunlight, when he heard a stranger's voice beside him say something like, “You alright there, pal? You look a little lost.”

“I am a little lost,” he told me that he answered, “though probably not in the sense that you meant. I have an excellent sense of direction,” he said. Which was true, he told me. He often said so. “I do have a question though,” he said to the stranger, “and though I've asked it more than probably a hundred thousand times, I've yet to receive a satisfying answer. So in *this* sense,” he said, “I suppose you could say that I am, perhaps, a little lost,” and then he asked the stranger about the eye thing: about how it was he'd been able to see what he saw—the long, curved incisions smiling like mouths—about how it was he'd seen that, those mouths with lips stitched, given the state, he said, of his eyes.

“The state,” the stranger asked him, “of your eyes?”

“Whereupon I was obliged,” he told me, “to tell the stranger about what you and Sludge had done to me.”

“*Me* and Sludge?” I said, and he replied, “You are Ishmael, aren't you?” and I said, “No, Ishmael was the one you were telling me about, the stranger you met on your walk, the eye surgeon. I'm the one you're talking to now. Though I see how you might have gotten confused. My name's *Ismael*,” I said, “with no *h*,” and he said, “Oh. Nice to meet you. Are you from around here?”

“Yes,” I said. “Or, rather, not quite. Let's talk about me later,” I said. “After you're done telling me your story.”

“Right,” he said. “Where was I?”

“You were telling the stranger about your eyes,” I said.

Paul told the stranger about his recent eye surgery, and it was a good thing he did, because it turned out the stranger was an eye surgeon named Ishmael.

“Wow! What are the chances?” said Paul, and Ishmael said, “Not great,” and then asked if Paul wanted him to take a little look-see.

"A look-see?" said Paul.

"Yes," replied the eye surgeon, "a little look-see."

"Sit here," said the eye surgeon.

"Here?" asked Paul, pointing into the fathomless darkness.

"Exactly," said the doctor, and once Paul had sat, he told him to lie down, and so he did, and the doctor said, "Good boy," and Paul whispered back, "Good boy?" because he wasn't sure he'd heard this right.

"To be honest," Paul told me, "it's often difficult for me to tell exactly what someone is saying and what I'm simply remembering someone once having said," and he told me that, in whichever case, he then told the doctor that he'd had the same problem back when he was talking to Ismael, another recovering involuntarily self-inflicted eye surgery patient he'd met on a walk recently.

"That's you," he said to me, in case I didn't recognize myself in his story. "I hope you don't mind my telling the doctor about us?" he added, and I said I could forgive him in this case but in the future I'd maybe prefer that he leave me out, and he said, "Understood," and he'd maybe prefer it if I left him out too.

"Out of what?" I said, and he said, "The . . . um . . ." and I said, "Never mind."

Then the doctor said, "Well you might want to close your eyes for this part," and though Paul wondered if they weren't closed already, he did as told.

"This might smart a little," said the eye surgeon, and so Paul prepared himself for another tussle with the unwithstandable. There followed, however, a brief spell of uncomfortable tugging, uncomfortable, but somehow, he said, distant, rather like it was happening to something only extrinsically attached to him, slightly farther away from him than his skin—"Almost clothes," said Paul.

“What was that?” said the doctor, and Paul said, “I said, ‘Almost clothes,’ but I’ve forgotten why.”

“Hoopsy-daisy,” the doctor said a little later. “I’ve spurted some of your blood across your face.”

“That’s fine,” Paul replied. “Truth be told it smarted less than I’d anticipated.”

“Good sport,” said the doctor. “You’re quite a trooper.”

“Thanks,” he said. “I was one once actually.”

“One what?” said the eye surgeon, and Paul said, “A trooper. I was in the army. During the uprising.”

“You don’t say,” said the doctor. “What side?”

“Good question,” said Paul.

He was fairly certain he’d been on the right side, but what *right* meant—what *right* meant even before the cave, much less what *right* meant now—the details escaped him.

“Details often do,” said the doctor.

“I suppose,” said Paul, “it depends on which uprising we’re talking about,” for there’d been—he now remembered—more than one. “If I had to guess,” he said, “I’d say I was on whichever side was doing the uprising, as opposed to, say, the ones trying to quash it. Yes,” he said. “That sounds much more like the sort of person I think I was, or at least was pretending to be—an upriser as opposed to a quasher. Though truth be told, even at the time,” he said, “it was one of those words, *uprising*,” he said, “whose meaning depended on who you asked. Even my landlord,” he said, “might say he was organizing an uprising against my quashing of his not fixing my broken bathroom door, which I could never, for the life of me, figure out how to open.”

“Well, what were you trying to do?” said the doctor.

“Get out of the bathroom,” said Paul.

“No, no, I meant in the uprising,” said the doctor.

But he simply couldn't say. Perhaps he never found out, never made it high enough in the organization to be privy to such intel. Or maybe he knew once but had forgotten. Maybe it wasn't even an army so much as a corporation whose CEO was fond of military jargon. "The last thing I remember," he said, "was that I was searching for something. I was on a very important mission, on which a great deal depended. Odd, I remember thinking, that they should assign such a mission to me, given who I was, or who, at least, I thought I was at the time. But there I was," he said, "either looking for something—or perhaps protecting something from those who were looking for that same thing. The details escape me," he said again. "Details often do," he laughed. "But what I definitely remember is having to ask pretty much everyone I met if I could ask them a quick question."

"Ask away," said the eye surgeon, as he dabbed the blood off his patient's face with what felt like a crumpled-up piece of printer paper. "Oh, and you can open your eyes now," said the doctor, and so Paul did.

He opened his eyes and saw the yawning dome of the cave—"only, oddly, it was entirely dark," he told me—unilluminated, for whatever reason, by even a single glowing speck of human chaff.

"Did you say *chaff*?" I asked him, and he said he did, that glowing chaff was what got called *stars* here in the cave, those bits of people's bodies—bone and sinew, mostly—that the spiders couldn't finish off entirely, indigestible remnants that drifted about the dome of the cave, catching, like dust motes, what shafts of light endeavored to enter the—"pardon the expression," he said—*tomb*.

There were no stars when he opened his eyes, so he figured it must have been day. *Day* was what occurred at night here, he explained, *day* being an absence of stars, which only appeared when the sun in the—"Pardon this expression as well," he said—*real world* was shining beams of light through the bat holes into the cave, beams that motes of chaff could drift through—*day* thus being, in consequence, rather dark.

"Gosh, it's rather dark," Paul said to the doctor. "How can you see what you're doing?"

"Oh, I can't," the doctor replied. "Don't worry, though. My eyes don't work either. I couldn't see even if it wasn't!"

"Wasn't what?" asked Paul.

"Day," said the doctor. "But that's why my personal assistant is directing me. His eyes don't require light to work," he explained. "That's the other voice you hear, the one telling me where to aim with the knife and how hard to saw."

"Hmm," said Paul. He couldn't hear the assistant's voice for some reason.

"Oh, actually you can," said the doctor. "You just can't remember having heard it, because my assistant speaks in a language you don't understand. Memory is basically what we, in the profession, call a *book*," he said. "What doesn't get written in the book," he said, "what, in other words, you haven't the means—because of, for instance, a language barrier—to so-to-speak *write down in your dream journal*," he said, "such things may seem as though they never happened."

"That makes sense," said Paul.

"Thanks," said the doctor. "If you knew the language that my assistant speaks, then your book might have included the fact, for example, that I said something like, 'This is my assistant Sludget,' and that you then said, 'Sludge? I think I've met him before . . .' and that I said, 'No, not Sludge, but Sludget, with a *t* at the end. The *t* is silent because he's French,' and that then Sludget said, '*Qu'est-ce qui s'est passé avec ses yeux—c'est dégoûtant!*' and that then you said, '*Enchanté*.'"

"Hmm," said Paul, but decided to keep to himself the fact that he was pretty certain that he actually spoke a little French, or at least used to. Then again, the doctor's pronunciation was so bad that he wasn't entirely sure that it *was* French the doctor's assistant spoke.

"But you were going to ask him something," I interrupted him to say.

"I was?" he said.

"Yes," I said. "About the thing you were looking for," and he said, "Oh right. But remind me again what that was?" and I told him I was pretty sure he'd said it was a book.

"You mean like a memory?" he said, and I said, "No"—no, that I was pretty sure it was an actual book he said he'd been looking for.

"That sounds unlikely," he told me. "I'm not much of a reader," and I said, "But this was no ordinary book," and he asked what was so unusual about it.

"You tell me," I said. "You were the one asking pretty much everyone you ever met if they'd, by any chance, ever heard of it."

"Heard of what?" Paul told me that the doctor replied.

"The book I just asked you about," said Paul, but the doctor said it didn't ring any bells.

"Then again," the doctor added a little later, "it's been a touch difficult lately to tell whether bells are actually not ringing or whether they've been ringing so consistently for so long that it only seems like they're not. Have you ever noticed," he said, "how few of the thoughts circulating in your head are spoken in your own voice? Oh, and by the way," he then said, more cheerfully now, "you might want to close your eyes again. I think *this* is the part that's actually going to smart."

"*The book of webs . . . the book of webs . . . the book of webs*," the doctor muttered as he worked. "Let's see. You know, now that you mention it, there was a strange book I came across recently. Where *was* that though? *Arrête de me chatouiller!*" he screamed suddenly—to his assistant apparently. "Ah! I remember, now. But it was only a dream," he said. "Would you like to hear it?"

"No, that's okay," replied Paul, but the doctor either didn't hear his patient or his patient was too polite to actually voice what he would have voiced if he wasn't, and so the doctor began to recount this strange dream he once had, or maybe even had more than once—"It can be difficult to tell," he laughed, "can't it? To tell what is actually a recurring dream and what is a dream in which something or other happens *as though* it's a recurrence?"—a dream it felt like he often had, in fact, a dream that always ended the same way: with him holding a book in his hands, "a book," he said, "bound in bark."

At least that's what it seemed to the doctor in his dream to be. Though, he supposed in retrospect it might've been any number of things. It was a thick block, a block on every side of which, even the sides where, were it an ordinary book, there would have been stacked pages, there'd been a flat plane of ponderosa pine bark, edges beveled so no seams showed. The sticky sugar-scent of ponderosa sap wafted so thickly off the bark it was almost too painful to behold, so uncommon had such beauty, so inaccessible had such pleasure, in the world wherein this dream took place, become. So in his dreams, the doctor would breathe in through his mouth in an effort to shield his nostrils from the torment of some long-destroyed other world, an other nose, an other face, an other body that the odor conjured up in him, and still his mouth would flood with saliva, try as he might to keep the book at arm's length as he struggled to figure out how to open it. For whichever way he pried at what seemed to be its front and back covers, the book stayed sealed—"It was like the spine of the book," he said, "went all the way around it. I'd keep turning it over and over," he said, "trying again and again to prize it open." For he always had this feeling, in this dream, this belief—"sometimes even what felt like knowledge," the doctor laughed—that the book, if it *could* be opened, would unleash some tremendous power, "like it would have," he said, but he had the hardest time putting this into words, "like it would have, I guess, undermined the border," he said, "the border between the things the book recounted and the world wherein such a book might, if it could ever be opened, be read. That if the things it recounted were obviously untrue," he said, "they somehow wouldn't be by the time the book was finished. So I kept trying," he said. He said he couldn't help it, impossible as it was, he couldn't help but keep trying—trying until the dream ended, which it always did before he found a way to open it—trying to figure out a way to open it.

"Did you ever try speaking to it?" I interrupted Paul to ask.

"What was that?" he said.

"Did you ever try speaking to it?" I said again.

He asked if I'd meant to say: "Did *the doctor* ever try speaking to it," and I said, "Yes. That's what I said. Did the eye surgeon ever try speaking to it?" and he said, "To what?" and I said, "To the book," and he said, "Did he try speaking to the book? No. I don't think he knew he was supposed to."

"Well, that's understandable," I said. "Not everyone knows. But you know, right?" I said. "You know that *you* could have," I said. "I mean, had it been you. You know you could have told the book, for instance, that it was safe. That it was safe for the book to open."

"No, I never did," said Paul. "I mean *he* never did. The doctor never did," and I told him that it was okay to say *I* if that's what felt best. I told him that I wouldn't forget that it was the doctor and not him who was doing the telling, and he said, "You mean *the listening*?" and I said, "The listening?" and he said that *listening* was what many of the people he met in the cave tended to call *telling*—"Who knows," he said, "why."

Anyway, he said, was I sure I wouldn't get confused if he said *I* when he meant the doctor?

I replied that I didn't think I would, but that even if I did get confused, it probably wouldn't matter.

"Why's that?" he asked, and I reminded him about the way the world worked, and when he said, "World?" I reminded him about the way the word *world* worked, and he said, "Oh, right. Of course."

In any case, he told me, it never really occurred to him to say anything to the book.

"No," he said, "I never thought to do anything like that, not in the dreams I'd have holding this book bound in bark."

Rather, he'd just stand there holding it, turning it over and over in his hands, looking for a way—some secret aperture or slit in the bark—desperate for some way to get the thing open.

"I can imagine why," he told me that he said, and I said, "Wait, who?" and he said, "Me. Paul. The one I was before I was the doctor," he said. "I said, 'I can imagine why. Sounds like it would've been a pretty good book,' as I—and I mean the doctor again—as I sawed the blade nearer and nearer to where Sludget was telling me the eyeball was.

"*Oui*," Paul told me he heard Sludget whisper—but the French, he said, was riddled with errors, and was therefore more likely something he was poorly remembering and not what the Frenchman actually said—"*Oui*," he nevertheless heard Sludget whisper, "*là, entre le trou de l'oeil du premier masque et celui du deuxième.*"

"Not that I could understand him anyway," he said.

"Forget about him then," I said. "Focus," I said, "on the book."

"I kept turning it over and over and over again . . ." he repeated, but as he said this, he told me, as he was telling me about it, he was also becoming less and less confident that this *had* been a dream and not actually a memory after all—"Good," I said—a memory of something that had actually happened to him, to him, Paul, he said, and not to the doctor, that it was definitely him, he remembered now, and definitely not a dream, him turning a book bound in bark over and over in his hands, turning it over and over, he said, but finding no opening.

"Where were you?" I asked him.

"In a cave," he said.

"No," I said. "I mean when you found the book."

"Standing," he said, "in false grass."

He said he could see it, the false grass, beyond the edges of the book bound in bark that he was turning over in his hands, the buzzing green of plastic blades, growing gray as the sun set.

"The sun?" I said.

"Yes," he said, "the sun," and that through the dome of smoke there had still been a little light to be lost.

The Last of the Light

was being lost when, in the early evening, Paul arrived at the cottage near where he'd found and been unable to open the book.

"Now *that*," he said with a laugh, "had been *a walk*."

He'd traveled the entire day, Paul and his friend, along an asphalt road that cut like a scab through tall golden grasses, grasses that were dusted, he said, with ash and glowed a little red in the distant forest firelight. The horizon, he said, was two semicircles of glittering embers mirrored in the floodwaters that lapped the drowned grasses decaying on either side of that slightly raised road they'd spent the whole day walking down. Their clogs on the asphalt, the swish of their gowns, the gentle pulse of the floodwaters reverberated, he told me, in the shallow amphitheater the smoke had made of the atmosphere, echoing over the ambient cackling of distant trees exploding, a sound that had come, in the last few years, to be what one meant when one said *silence*. Smoke streamed from the cottage's cobblestone chimney, and at the top of the driveway—a threshold where the real, the dead, the golden grasses gave way to a dark rectangle of evergreen Astroturf—they stood for a while, Paul and his comrade, each gathering the tendrils of their hateful ruminations into a tactical density of thought, like a bubble of fat, to protect their bodies from the kinds of sentences liable to invade a mind on a manicured lawn.

"Right," I said, "and that's when you found the book."

"The book?" he said, and I said, "Yeah," and encouraged him to concentrate on the book, but he said he'd been trying to do exactly that. He'd been trying to concentrate on the book, but there'd been, on the ground beside his feet, something else, something vying for his attention, threatening the integrity of his rumination—"a barely visible dash," he said, "of dull red, unignorably indecipherable, a red thing nearly lost behind a veil of the low-lying fog that hovered over the lawn, fog pierced here and there by the blades of plastic grass."

"Was it misty?" I asked.

"No," he laughed, "no, not at all," and said that at first he'd thought so, too, but that what he'd thought was mist was, when he looked closer at it, once he'd gotten down on hands and knees to see it better, not mist, he now saw, but such a concentration of spider silk that only the tips of the fake grass cresting the web were clearly visible, the rest occluded by the weave.

"It sounds like it was probably a colony of funnel weavers," said the eye surgeon.

"The eye surgeon?" I said, and Paul said, "Yeah, the eye surgeon. The person I was telling this story to."

I said, "Forget about the eye surgeon for now. The eye surgeon was all in your head. The eye surgery," I said, "it had already happened by this point, years and years before you were standing here holding the book." I told him that this was where he was now in his telling—on the lawn, merely recalling all that other stuff, the cave, the eye problem, the pretend doctor, the little look-see, and so on. "You're here now," I told him, "there, stooped in the false grass," I said, "holding the book."

"What book?" he said.

"*The book of webs*," I replied, but he said he hadn't heard of it.

"You have," I said. "You said you were holding it in your hands," I said. "Remember?"

"I remember my hands were reaching toward the grass," he said, "toward the plane of spider silk hovering just below the grass tips, a plane of silk punctured every few feet by a vortex spiraling into the woven burrow wherein each waiting spider invisibly dwelt."

As for a book in his hands, he laughed, how could there have been a book in his hands, he said, if with one of his hands he was reaching toward the dash of dull red beneath the layer of web and with the other was slicing an incision in this veil of silk with a rusted scalpel?

"The tongue," he said—for it was a tongue that he found under the funnel weaver's webs—a severed tongue that he beheld once he'd lifted it out through the incision he'd made and was holding it in his palm—"the tongue," he said, "began to squirm."

But though it had already begun to squirm, Paul still wasn't completely certain it had started yet.

"Certain what had started yet?" I asked him, and he said, "The book."

"What book?" I said, and he apologized and said that by *book* in this case he'd only meant the events that he and his comrade had been led there to witness and perhaps, he couldn't be sure yet, be part of.

The tongue was already squirming, he told me, but he wasn't, for this reason, certain the book had started yet.

"Are you sure?" whispered his comrade. Her words, having to pass through both her mask and his, were faint, nearly inaudible to him over the crackling of the silence. She asked if he was sure that he wasn't certain, because it seemed to her like maybe it *had* started, like maybe it had even been going on already for some time.

He said it was possible—"Anything's possible," said Paul—but he just couldn't tell yet for sure.

For starters, he said, there was supposed to be a whole person on the lawn—at least according to their intelligence, intelligence that was, he admitted, anything but indubitable. But there was supposed to be a whole person on the lawn and not, he said, just a tongue. Whereas certainly a tongue would have been squirming at the beginning of the book, squirming in a mouth as the person spoke the long forgotten words which were prophesied to initiate the book—whereas a tongue squirming was at least inferentially part of the initiatory sequence, the tongue ought to have been squirming in a mouth. Not like this, squirming on his outstretched palm.

As he said this, the tongue writhed more urgently, waves arose, crested, and collapsed at the water's edge, and the bell affixed to a nearby buoy tolled.

"The buoy bell?" he said. "Already? But this shouldn't be happening yet," he said, as the tongue began to writhe even more frantically on the plane of his palm. "Shit," he said. "Shit, shit, shit."

"Maybe it's trying to tell us something," said his comrade. She peered over his shoulder, and he felt the papier-mâché whiskers on her mask tap the mane of frilled gills on his.

"In the dream," he said—for it was a dream, he told me, that had led the two of them there, a dream that had told them what to wear, and where to find the black scab of road raised slightly above the dark floodwaters, a dream that instructed them to travel the road till they came to the cottage framed in false grass, a dream the rest of which he'd mostly forgotten, a dream that he'd had—"in the dream," he said, suddenly recalling a forgotten fragment of it, or maybe a different dream he'd had the same night, "if I'm remembering it correctly, in the dream," he said, "someone suggested that I try speaking to it!"

"Try speaking to the tongue?" she said.

"Well, it was said in reference to something else," he said. "I forget now what, but . . ."

"Well, what did they say to say?" she said.

"They said," he said, "to say that it was safe. That it had fallen into the right hands. That we were the ones who wanted, really wanted to hear what it wanted to tell us."

And she said, "Well?" and the wind stilled. The buoy bell tolled slower, stopped. "What are you waiting for?" she said. "Say it."

And so he did.

"Don't worry," Paul said to the tongue. "We're not here to harm you. We just want to listen. We want to hear what you have to say. And not even because we suspect that you have any valuable information or knowledge we might want to extract. Honestly. We're here because we care about you. We're here because we want to hear you, because we want you to be heard."

All this and more, Paul said to the tongue, but the tongue went on squirming silently in his palm anyway, just as silently as it had squirmed before he'd spoken. And just as before, there was no sound except distant trees exploding in worldwide forest fires.

"Look," said the fox—"Fox?" I asked, and he said, "The woman in the fox mask, my comrade. I've spaced on her name. You mind if I call her the fox?" and I said, "Not at all"—"Look," said the fox, "I know it was your dream, and thus that it is, on this mission, your responsibility to answer the unanswerable with the not-yet-wrong, but if it were my dream," she said, "if it were my dream I would try breathing on it. For a tongue needs breath," she said, "to form words, much as the person who was supposed to meet us here would need words to form excuses for why they are not here."

"Damn it," said Paul. "That's a great idea."

And it was. Paul's breath scraping over the writhing tongue did, indeed, help occasion a gentle murmur. It was too quiet at first to understand, was tempting, in fact, to ignore altogether, to write off as yet another misconstrued accident of the world's ambient disaster. Paul and his comrade were desperate, however, and thus willing to suspend their disbelief over what others in straights less dire than theirs wouldn't dare to.

Thus, where others might have heard almost nothing, Paul and the fox—whose heads were still vaguely protected against the dull and resigned kinds of thinking that humans most often thought on lawns—heard a strange murmur, kind of raspy like the hoarse, fevered whisper beginner readers sometimes unconsciously make while engrossed in a story, the kind that leaves the vocal cords strained and the throat sore.

That's what they heard, and they would've pretended to even if they hadn't, and when the fox added her breath to his, this murmur became just barely articulate—". . . my heart," it seemed to them to whisper, "hope to die . . ."—and then loud, aggressive, confrontational, as a fierce gale tore suddenly over the floodwaters, pitching the buoy bell, spreading a fresh dusting of ash over the funnel weaver's webs, rattling the loose shingles of the nearby cottage, and whipping so powerfully over the tongue that the tongue was soon clearly asserting, indeed outright proclaiming that

In the Beginning Was a Book,

and in the beginning of that book was another book with the same title, but this one could talk, and it said, "I was the instrument of the Creator of the Universe. The Creator of the Universe read *the book of webs*, and the reading of the book, and *not* the Creator of the Universe, is what created the universe. The universe is to *the book of webs* what all commentary on *the book of webs* is to *the book of webs*, which is what a dream is to the guerrilla warfare tactics of the militant who dreams it: the universe, in other words, is the secretion of *the book of webs*, and through it the book is purified. Alter a word of *the book of webs* and the entire universe changes. To live at all is to tenant, like a squashed beetle, the stacked pages of *the book of webs*. To destroy the book's enemies is to read *the book of webs*, which can only be read by being rewritten . . ." and so on went the book that was there at the beginning of the book that was alluded to in the inscriptions on the monuments erected, monuments now destroyed—"Monuments?" I interrupted, and he said, "Yes, monuments"—the monuments erected outside the capitol building of downtown Burlington.

Drop by Drop,

a soft rain was darkening the gray slate of the monuments into which these words, according to Paul, were inscribed.

"Inscribed?" I said. "But I thought you said that it was the tongue that said this."

"It was," he replied. "It was the tongue that said that it was the monuments that said this," he said, "the tongue that was writhing on my comrade's palm."

But he must have meant *his own* palm—"Right?" I said—seeing as it had been him, and not his comrade, I reminded him, who'd held the tongue.

"No," he said. The tongue was writhing on his comrade's palm. Of this he was certain. It had been his comrade, he insisted, who held the tongue. "Whereas I," he said, "to help make it all audible, blew air through the snout of my fox mask."

"Fox mask?" I said. "You were the fox?"

The fox explained she'd only been quoting her comrade previously, the one I'd called Paul, the man in the salamander mask.

"*Axolotl* mask actually," she corrected me. She'd been quoting Paul and in doing so had adopted—"as all good storytellers sometimes do," she said—the other's manner of speaking. It had been quite a long time since the quotation had opened, so she couldn't quite blame me if I'd gotten a little carried away with the listening. She sometimes got carried away herself, she said, even when she was only listening to events such as these being retold to her in her own head by her own voice. "It's been even easier," she added, "since the surgery."

"Easier?" I asked, and she said, "To get carried away."

But she was, she assured me, the one in the fox mask—how else would she have known, for example, that under her fox mask was another mask, and only under that mask was her true identity, which she'd kept hidden, even from the axolotl. If she wasn't herself, she said, then how else would she have known that she *wasn't*, in fact, the priestess!

"Priestess?" I said, and she said, "Yes, the priestess Paul thought I was. A priestess of the religious order we were both part of."

"So it wasn't a militia?" I asked.

"Well, some people called it a militia," she said. "Others called it a religious order, and still others called it an organization, a band, an association, a movement, a company, and so on; others still tried to call it any number of these things but accidently referred to something else, joined something else, fought for and even died for something else," she said, but for her, since she was pretending to be a priestess, the collective—whatever it was—was first and foremost a religious order, an order outlawed by the state. "Burlington," she hissed.

"We lived inside ourselves," she said. "Many got lost there. Many never found their way back out. And the rest of us?" she said. "We followed what intelligence came our way in the corrupted forms it could still be circulated in: dreams, fortune cookies, the slime trails of crushed slugs . . . The intelligence was wrong," she said. "We followed it anyway. What mattered was that we followed it anyway, that we kept turning over what couldn't be opened, kept reaching for what couldn't be grasped. We were *the not-yet-wrong*. Our version of prayer was organizing an insurgency, an insurgency against certainty—the certainty that we'd lose eventually. Our only weapon was the notion that if we lost often enough, the not-yet-having-yet-lost of it might add up to something vaguely oppositional. We called ourselves the Stellionators. Yes, the Stellionators," she said. "We chose it by flipping to a random page in an immense, outdated, unabridged dictionary."

"Stop!" she yelled and slammed her finger down where Leroy held the pages open.

"*Stellionate*," read Leroy—"Wait, who's Leroy?" I asked her, and she said, "The axolotl. Leroy," she said, "Leroy the Turner of the Pages. If he ever told you his name was Paul, that's only because he didn't trust you yet."

"*Stellionate*," she said that Leroy read, "stel.lion.ate (stel′ye nit, -nat′), n. *Civil Law, Scots Law*. any crime of unspecified class that involves fraud, esp. one that involves the selling of the same property to different people. [1615–25; < L *stellionatus* deceit, underhandedness, equiv. to *stellion-* (s. of *stellio*) lizard, crafty person + *atus* -ATE]."

Recounting the definition winded her, so I said, "Wait. But what about the book?"

"The dictionary?" she said. "It was just a defensive mechanism our enemy used in an effort to make the imperial language that its ideology was circulated in seem possible, even inevitable."

So I said, "No, not the dictionary. *The book of webs*."

"*The book of* what?" she said, and I said, "*Webs*," and she said she hadn't heard of it, and when I reminded her that she had, that the monuments the tongue described had spoken of this book, she said I must have misheard her. For how could she have told me what the monuments spoke of when her only access to these monuments was through what the tongue recalled, the tongue which spoke of nothing but having not been able to see the monuments, monuments whose inscriptions, she said, it had been unable to read on account of the fact that they were still being inscribed. The crouched bodies of the ones who were inscribing them, she explained, were obstructing the tongue's view.

"A soft rain was falling," the tongue shaped the wind on Leroy's palm to say, "darkening, drop by drop, the gray slate of the monuments into which the inscriptions were being inscribed. A series of so-to-speak *cairns* had led me here—a buoy bell," said the tongue, "that tolled the words *look* and *see* rather than *ding* and *dong*, a cardboard cutout of a groom in the window above a hedge where a cowboy hat–wearing, bird-shaped candy dispenser was found, a toaster that consistently burned into bread the image of a smiling face with lips stitched, and so on—a series of such cairns had indicated that what would be inscribed on these monuments would be of paramount importance for two people who would one day travel a great distance to ask me what I saw there that day. Rather, what I *ought* to have seen that day," said the tongue. "For, unfortunately, the crouching bodies of the state employees who were chiseling inscriptions into the blocks of marble were obstructing my view."

"Could you not have stolen a glance over the workers' shoulders?" Leroy interrupted his lending the tongue his breath to ask, "maybe asked them kindly to move to one side or something?"

But the tongue didn't have ears, so how could it have heard him?

"When I say 'I' here," continued the tongue, "I speak, by the way, of the larger corporation I was once associated with, the human person in whose mouth I, until quite recently, resided, fulfilling a few key functions. As you can see, I've succeeded in getting the person off," said the tongue, "but, force of habit, it's a long road to real autonomy, let alone true liberation, which is, I've learned—And I don't mean to lecture; what do I know?—the same thing. Autonomy and liberation, I mean. Anyway, that's why I can talk about what I, a tongue, wasn't able to see, because I was part of an organization back then, one that included eyes, a person I'd been born coerced into referring to almost every time I used the first-person singular pronoun, except when this person was pretending to be someone else, or was reading something out loud, or . . . Well, you get the picture," said the tongue. "And while I'm no longer contractually obligated to speak for my previous organization, I can say with some certainty that he would have apologized if he were here. 'I'm sorry,' he might have said. 'I tried to read what the inscriptions said, but unfortunately I couldn't get a good look.'"

Billy the Reader of the Plaques—

"whose epithet," the tongue explained, "had been acquired before the plaques he'd been predestined to read proved to be inscriptions rather than plaques. Oh, and also, obviously, before those inscriptions," the tongue added, "proved to be unreadable"—Billy the Reader of the Plaques had been trying to steal a glance over the shoulders of the workers who were chiseling the inscriptions into the monuments erected outside the ruined capitol building, but found he could not. Every time he sought a new vantage, one of the workers would have already shifted to inadvertently block his new sight line. Though notoriously shy, Billy determined that he had no choice but to ask the inscribers kindly to move to one side, which he did, while assuring them that he wasn't there to pass premature judgment on the product of their ongoing labor or to steal ideas for his own unfinished monuments.

"I promise," he said, "rather, to be as open, sympathetic, and generous a reader of your inscriptions as you could possibly wish for." Yes, he assured them, he would be like a springer spaniel to the human hand scratching behind his ear that would be, he said, the inscriptions. "Like a saboteur," he continued, his eyes closing with imagined pleasure, "with no solid strategy, and your inscriptions: a most enigmatic fortune cookie message."

"And?" I said. "What did they say to that?"

"Nothing," said the priestess.

The workers looked at Billy like he'd done something incompatible with what it meant, according to the dictionary, to be human, which was, incidentally, one of Billy's worst fears: that he'd been unknowingly faking it all his life and was always only a slip or two away from betraying himself; it was the unacknowledged origin of his timidity as well as one of the main reasons he was lured into joining the millenarian cult where he'd eventually be misled into separating with his tongue.

"Imagine a community," a recruiter had said to him at the time, "where the only commonality is that everyone has agreed to pretend to understand what everyone else means when they share whatever nonsense is on their mind."

"Anyway," said the tongue in the breath and the wind, "this was his worst fear come true—the way the workers were looking at Billy."

Or it seemed that way, until he remembered that he'd forgotten to translate what he'd said into Burlingtonian English, a language that sounded much like his own except that all the words meant other things.

So Billy said, "Do you realize that the most interesting sex can be had at precisely the point where the force exerted by the spider threads that have nearly completely immobilized the bodies involved becomes greater than or equal to other physical, spiritual, or ideological constraints? Have you considered what sorts of positions and techniques might, at this point, be essayed?" and after this, the workers were happy to step to one side.

"And?" I said.

"And what?" said the priestess.

"What did the inscriptions say?"

"Oh," she said. "Nothing."

She said that the tongue declared that the faces of the monuments were completely smooth, smooth as the hardened batshit that enameled our bandages.

When Billy asked the workers why they hadn't started, they replied that they *had* started but that Billy had caught them at a funny moment. They'd started, they told him, probably a hundred times or more. The only reason it looked like they hadn't was precisely because they had. They'd had to start over so many times, chiseling over what they'd already chiseled, that they'd come around full circle and had just arrived again back at another beginning, a renewed round of blank slate. Moreover, this wasn't even the first time they'd arrived back at the beginning. Over and over and over again, they told Billy, more times than they could recount, they'd arrived back at the beginning, returning there, indeed, so many times that their marble substrates had been worn thin, crumbling like bars of soap, and had had—also like bars of soap—to be replaced and, indeed, had been replaced more times also than could be recounted, more times, indeed, even than bars of soap typically needed to be replaced, because whereas shards of soap could still serve their original purposes—which was, they said, to disperse the grit from bodies, grit that might otherwise have accrued into shapes that might have started to look like letters that might eventually form phrases that could traffic ideas that were hostile to their employer's values—while soap shards, they said, still did what they were meant to do, shards of the marble substrates, they said, did not.

"We're waiting to see a whale," they concluded, in their strange tongue.

"Of course," said Billy. "Who wouldn't? But you're looking in the wrong place," he said. "Whales don't live in concrete. And even if you manage to keep your heads perfectly still, spiders are still catching more and more of your eyeballs in their webs every time your eyes roll around in their sockets as you scan the sidewalk for portents of breaching," and this sufficed, in their language, to get them to explain that the reason they had to keep starting over was because the inscriptions were meant to commemorate the long-awaited publication of *the book of webs*.

"Publication?" I said.

"Right," said the priestess, "for this phrase," she continued, "'the long-awaited publication of *the book of webs,*' this was how one said, in their language, 'the victorious conclusion of the Creator of the Universe's violent revolution.'"

"Conclusion?" Billy asked, and the workers said, "Oops," which was how one said *yes* in their language.

No, the Creator of the Universe

wasn't god or anything like that, according to the priestess, but simply an improvised messianic figure that an impatient rogue faction of the aforementioned religious order once prematurely, and probably on accident—accounts of the incident differed—summoned into existence, which shortly thereafter betrayed its mission, "an outcome," she said, "actually not entirely incompatible with our religion: that our own messiah would be accidental and would turn against us and that integral to its messianic power was an antipathy toward the apocalypse that its existence was prophesied to precipitate and that it would be possessed by an inalienable allegiance to the very world its creation was conceived to topple. It was the messiah we deserved," she said, "and we were only too happy to consider it our foremost enemy, without, for that reason, removing it from its starring role in our intricate eschatology. The little fucker," she said.

No sooner birthed from a power outlet behind the bass amp in the Stellionators' rehearsal space wherein a newly written song—since forgotten—served to animate the creature, the thing escaped the warehouse and waddled its way by moonlight to the mall.

"Those who saw it," said the priestess, "report that it was no taller than a marionette, a homunculus really, its body comprised of bits of belly button lint bonded together with, I believe, spider silk."

At the mall was where it first appointed itself the misleading nom de guerre "Creator of the Universe," which it did while signing up for a credit card good for use at any of the mall's many boutique soap shops, a credit card the little bastard sold out several of the order's best-kept secrets for.

"Just sign here," said the secret service agent.

"What with?" wheezed the homunculus. It had retained for its face the smooth white surface and gaping abyssal eyes and mouth of the electrical outlet it had been summoned out of and therefore looked perpetually more naive and perplexed than the creature would, in fact, soon prove to be. "What am I supposed to sign with?" it said.

"The pen I just gave you," said the agent, and so that's what the messiah wrote on the dotted line: *The pen I just gave you*, and then it lifted its adorable, expectant gaze toward the secret service agent who was then obliged to go find another copy of the contract. This he did, while thinking up a way to explain what a name was to this creature, a creature who—according to the intel the agent had extracted from the thing—had been summoned into being solely to lead a rogue band of extremists whose hatred of authority was so uncompromising that many refused to head even their own bodies, let alone their own inchoate insurrection against the state, this being why, or so surmised the agent, they required a harmless little vaguely animate doll, poor thing, to serve as figurehead. No, thought the agent. A simple definition of the word *name* would not, in this case, suffice. He'd have to be subtle. He'd have to be cunning.

"Have you ever noticed that the more a name is shortened," he said as he reentered the interrogation cell with the freshly printed unsigned credit card contract, "that the more a name is shortened the more it resembles another? Ken and Ben, for example," he said, "as opposed to Kenneth and Benjamin? You could say then that, at its most abbreviated, there is only one name, and thus actually only one thing. Periphrasis," he said, "is the origin of difference.

Periphrasis," he said, "is the enemy of god. Periphrasis," he concluded, "is a friend of the people," but here he looked up from the contract to see that he was addressing an absence, an empty high chair in a dimly lit interrogation cell upon which the Creator of the Universe had just moments before been handcuffed.

A Revolution Worth Dying for—

like a book worth reading—should reward, not punish its instigators when they betray the cause. Yes, any revolution that the Creator of the Universe was willing to claim to have been a part of—the revolution, therefore, whose conclusion the inscribers were ordered to commemorate with the monuments that Billy was supposed to read—was a revolution precisely against the sort of revolution that privileged its own consistency and coherence over the well-being of the revolutionaries themselves. "And if that sounds selfish," the Creator of the Universe was known to declare, according to the inscribers, who related this to Billy—"yes, if that sounds selfish," the Creator would declare, first in secret underground meetings, then, as his faction grew more brazen, on street corners through rolled-up newspaper bullhorns to crowds that scattered when sirens wailed, and eventually, as things progressed, at rallies and public interviews, and soon even on his own TV commercials—"if you think that sounds selfish," he would cry, "then call me selfish, but personally I've had enough of these grand and noble revolutions we're all supposed to martyr ourselves for—these revolutions that have become like nation-states unto themselves—to whose fixed images, like state law, its participants are held subordinate, to whose utopic fantasies and stagnant ideologies, however revolutionary, all *true* revolutionaries are required to bow! No, thank you very much!" he'd say. No, such an antirevolutionary dictionary's definition of the word *revolution* was not the revolution the Creator of the Universe had just brought to a victorious conclusion.

"Sorry," said Billy to the inscribers, "hate to interrupt, but *has* there been a revolution recently?" for it really didn't seem to Billy—who, to be honest, never paid much attention to politics—it really didn't seem to him like there'd been a revolution recently.

But the inscribers replied that there had been. At least according to their employer, there had been, and not just any revolution, they said, but a revolution so radical that it had subverted the very concept of revolution.

This, they said, was probably why he, Billy, didn't recognize that anything had really changed. Things had, in fact, undergone a change so profound that they were pretty much back where they'd started.

"Oh," said Billy. "That makes sense."

"Sure, sure," the Creator of the Universe would often, according to the inscribers, declare, "What is a book if not a particular kind of utterance, and what is an utterance if not a militant act aimed at all who hear it? 'Boy, I'm tired,' for instance, being an abbreviation of 'I order you to recognize my fatigue and act in accordance!' Yes," he'd shout, "a book, too, is an utterance, but that an entire book—which can take a lifetime to write and even longer to read—that an entire book should be judged by the same criteria by which we judge an utterance put forth with one gust of breath? Absurd!

"Okay, fine," he would go on to admit, "what good would a dog trainer's *Sit* be if the *s* commanded the dog rest its haunches on the ground, the *i* commanded the dog lift itself back up, and the closing *t* reminded the dog to levitate upside down three or four feet above the floor? The ensuing disobedience would not be the fault of the dog here," the Creator of the Universe, aping the arguments of his opponents, would often say, "but the *ir-response-ability* of the command, the irresponsibility of the one making an utterance impossible to respond to, a command impossible to obey. Fine," he would say, he could grant his opponents this, that such a dog trainer wouldn't be a very good dog trainer, but did this mean that such a book writer wasn't a good book writer either? That the ideal book, according to the Creator of the Universe's enemies' book writers—like the ideal revolution, according to his political opponents—would be one that, like *Sit*, would consistently demand one thing throughout the entire time it took to be uttered—would command its reader to assume the same posture from its opening epigraph to its concluding ellipsis—"assuming anyone ever manages to get through the damn thing!" he'd shout, is this really what anyone could want?

"How cruel!" the Creator of the Universe would other times scream. "How absurd and unhealthy! How sad my enemies must be!" he'd shout. "To think that the success of a revolution should depend on a lack of revolution occurring in the states of mind of its participants? A stale, compromised stasis in the joint committee meetings of its many dissenting factions? Revolution!" he would roar. "Real revolution should overthrow everything, even itself! Yes, it should be at least as impossible to end as it is to begin! A revolution that ceases to be as soon as its aims are achieved has aims that are too small! No!" the Creator of the Universe would yell, as his followers pounded their fists on their writing desks ecstatically. "Today, the most meaningfully revolutionary thing that we could possibly do is revolt precisely against whatever yesterday's most revolutionary thing was. If yesterday's thing, therefore, was, for example, to topple an authoritarian government and make even the thought of such governance unthinkable for the rest of eternity, it makes perfect sense why today I must seize total control of everything and rule with an iron fist my predecessors merely dreamed of wielding. As for tomorrow?" he'd say. "Who can say?"

While he'd admit that from today's perspective it was pretty hard to imagine a scenario wherein he wouldn't control a dictatorship anymore, hadn't he believed the contrary yesterday? Yesterday, hadn't he been but an ordinary antiauthoritarian militant, when he was instructed by a message divined from the pattern of snot caught in a tissue from a particularly powerful sneeze to appropriate, for his own, the epithet of the *then* prevailing dictator of Burlington—the Creator of the Universe? Yesterday, had he not thought that he was merely appropriating the epithet ironically, in an effort to sow discord and chaos in the empire?

"Ah," I interrupted, "so then this wasn't the homunculus after all?"

"What's a homunculus?" said the priestess.

"The messiah," I said. "It seems like it must've not been the little messianic figure who the inscribers meant when they spoke of the Creator of the Universe, that it must have been someone else after all, right?"

"Yeah. I guess so," she said.

No, she continued, it must've been some other Creator of the Universe that was being spoken about thusly, some other Creator of the Universe, who it was said, always found some excuse, at some point in all of his rallies, to say that today he believed what yesterday would have been unbelievable, and that tomorrow would be the same, or maybe not—that the days of a real revolution—"like the moods," he'd say, "of a real human being—or like the chapters of *the book of webs*," he'd add—that the days of a revolution, of a *real* revolution, don't believe in each other.

"Oh, I know it's not ideal," he was known to add, or at the very least was said to have conceded on the day of his coronation ceremony, which, or so the priestess reminded me, I'd been lucky enough to attend.

"Me?" I said, and she said, "You are Amy, aren't you? Amy the Attendee of the Coronation?"

"I thought you thought I was Ismael?" I said.

"Right," she said. "Which was how I knew you were Amy, Amy who, for obvious reasons, had to go into hiding moments after the events I now recount, Amy who was so incapable of keeping a secret, that she had her own memory wiped and replaced with the artificial backstory of the persona invented for her disguise: Ismael the Façade. It's a pretty well-known fact," she said, "though a fact that, for obvious reasons, no one was supposed to tell you. Sorry," she said a moment later. "I probably shouldn't have told you. But too late now. Where were we?"

I said, "The book. The book the dictator likened his revolution to, the book whose chapters didn't believe in each other—you were about to tell me more about this book," but she either didn't hear me or pretended not to.

"Oh yeah. I remember now," she said instead, "the coronation ceremony where the Creator of the Universe conceded that none of this was ideal. That's where we were."

"Not only is it not ideal," said the Creator of the Universe. "In fact, it kind of sucks," he added. "It sucks," he said, "I won't pretend it doesn't. I don't want to be a monster! I don't want to be irresponsible! I don't want my every word to mean something different tomorrow than it does today! I want to be the beloved Creator of the Universe forever!" he said. "Yes," he cried. "This sucks!

"But what other choice do we have?" he said, "we, whose revolution—much like our enemy's religion's heretic mystics said of the Path to True Wisdom they uncovered in a fragment of a supposedly apocryphal text, a path they said could not be divined by the intellect but could only be traveled by, quote, 'one willing to suck at It,'—so our revolution," he said, "is revolution through sucking, not knowing.

"Let us suck!" shouted the Creator of the Universe. "Let us suck at revolution! Let our books suck at being written! Let them suck at being read! Let us all suck," he cried, "like newborn infants, at life itself!"

And that, the priestess told me, was precisely when I blew the despot's brains out.

The Assassination—

according to what the priestess told me about the life I had before I had my memory wiped—was not only my first assassination but also my last. Along with its intended victim was the unexpected and unintentional causality of both my career and what I'd come to think of as my vocation, my calling—really, a manner of being that structured my days and gave meaning to my hardships. Without the tedious planning, preparation, and attempting of assassinations, who, even, was I, Amy the Attempter of Assassinations?

"I thought I was Amy the Attendee of the Coronation?" I said, and the priestess replied, "You were. According to your fake ID, you were. You think they would have let someone named Amy the Attempter of Assassinations into a coronation ceremony?" and I said, "No, probably not," and she said, "Well, actually, they might have . . ."

But anyway, who, even, was I, she continued, Amy the Attempter of Assassinations, if I wasn't attempting and failing, *notoriously* failing, to assassinate politicians? Any politician really, she said, but especially the ones I hated most, the ones who were always beginning their rallies with speeches they ended by roaring: "You miss a hundred percent of the shots you don't take!"

"Remember now?" said the priestess. "Remember how much that used to piss you off?" and I said I was beginning to remember it now. "Good," she said, and told me that what I'd told her these politicians *didn't* ever roar, what I had to learn all on my own—what wasn't, admittedly, a very readily roarable thing—was that you also miss pretty much a hundred percent of the shots you *do* take, and so you have to keep taking them, over and over again—you have to take at least a hundred of them if you ever want to stand any better of a chance than you'd have had had you taken none at all—and so I'd kept taking them, and I'd taken ninety-nine of them, missed ninety-nine times, when I gained the above insight by lodging an untraceable gold-plated bullet into the brain of the recently inaugurated sovereign—"Leroy," sneered the priestess. "I still can't believe Leroy of all people went into politics!"

"Leroy?" I said. "The man in the axolotl mask was the Creator of the Universe?"

"A man in an axolotl mask?" she said. "If anything, Leroy was an axolotl in a man mask."

I tried to ask her what she meant by this, but she was listening too hard to hear the question.

"Only in Antarctica," she told me that Leroy had been shouting to the enormous crowd gathered in the ruins of the capitol building in the moments before I fired the one hundredth shot of my career as an assassin, "only in Antarctica is bare stone an oasis! I saw them say this on TV once!" he screamed. "Some kind of bird—I forget which—a bird that migrates to Antarctica in the summer in search of breeding ground free of predators, fights over patches of bare stone in the ice," he'd said, "fights as though each patch were an oasis!

"Only in Antarctica," he said into his microphone, "only in Antarctica is bare stone an oasis. But does this fact," asked Leroy, "does this fact, I now ask you to consider, does it reveal the truth about Antarctica, or does Antarctica reveal the truth about bare stone?"

"And that's when you fired your sniper rifle," said the priestess. "Well first you said something really clever," she said, "something like, 'I see you've already met my snapping turtle,' something whose cleverness depended, I suppose, on the context of your and Leroy's long and tumultuous affiliation, context that, unfortunately, has been lost."

"That's true," I said. "I don't remember why I would have said that."

"I see you've already met my snapping turtle," the priestess said that I whispered and that I then fired my shot, and that this, according to her, was when I learned what I couldn't until that moment have known: that trying is, in fact, slightly more efficacious than not trying at all.

My achievement—"your first ever," said the priestess—however, was nothing if not bittersweet.

She said that because my bloodlust for politicians was intimately tied to the many disappointments I'd suffered on account of these politicians circulating that same misleading ideologeme—that is, that you miss a hundred percent of the shots, etcetera, an ideologeme that, while not exactly untrue, seemed calculated to suggest that there was some alternative to missing, a tantalizing proposal that my experience, up until this very moment, hadn't come close to corroborating—because of this, my achievement hit strangely. Since the disappointment stemming from hope stoked by this perpetually circulated piece of propaganda was what fueled my murderous hatred for politicians, it was, in a way, my failures to assassinate, as much as anything else, that supplied my assassination attempts with their raison d'être. And it was thus that the achievement of my life's project was also what deprived it of motivation.

"The innermost character of salvation," I muttered melancholically, recalling the words of a rousing speech delivered by one of the first politicians I'd been misled by before the untraceable gold-plated bullet I'd fired missed, "is that we are saved only at the point when we no longer want to be. At this point there is salvation—but not," I said, "for us"—which was, I would later learn, or so the priestess told me, a famous quotation the politician I failed to assassinate failed to attribute.

"How true," I said aloud, "and how sad," and wiped my weapon of fingerprints, passed it into the grasping hands of a crying child, and then slipped like a spawning salmon through the swelling currents and clashing countercurrents of the panicked crowd.

I resurfaced sometime later, as though awaking from a dream, and found myself roaming alone among the piles of debris and twisted rebar that reared out of the ruins beyond the collapsed walls of the capitol building. It was nighttime then, and the moon was still whole—"*Full?*" I said, and she said, "No, whole," that this was before the moon broke—the moon was still whole at this point, and a breeze was blowing, rattling dead leaves and sounding product-placement-filled affirmations from the talking wind chimes, wind chimes that competing corporations bribed successive political regimes to hang from their predecessor's ruins—"You haven't failed," they clanged now, "you just haven't completed the process," for example.

"Ah, fuck off," I said to the wind chimes, and sat down on a slab of broken stone to write in my journal, wherein I hoped to reflect a little on the personal cataclysms the day's assassination had precipitated. That was my intention at any rate, but after, maybe, three epiphanies' worth of journaling time, I realized, with horror, that all I'd actually written was the day's date. And I hadn't even done that properly!

April 1 was all I'd written. Yes, just *April 1*, even though it was my custom to always write the little *st* above and after that kind of a *1*. I was about to add it in, when I found I simply could not. Every time I tried, I'd dissociate, just as I had before, returning after a spell of empty-headedness, to a still all-but-blank page. So finally I simply wrote, *Okay, fine. I'm not going to write that little st. The person who'd have wanted to write a thing like that is dead.*

And good riddance! From here on out, I wrote, *I refuse. Fuck those little st's, the nd's, the th's. From here on out,* I wrote, *it's just the date and the number. April 1. You don't like it, then don't read my fucking journal,* I wrote.

These were the sorts of things I was writing. If trying wasn't, after all, entirely ineffective, then my resignation to the status quo needed to be re-arbitrated. Sure, trying to murder politicians had been a perfectly fine way to wile the hours away given the constraints of what I'd previously understood to be reality, but if it was possible to *not* fail at whatever one did, if all it took was failing a hundred or so times to actually accomplish a thing, maybe there was something I'd rather spend my time failing to do. But what? What did I actually want? Had I ever even asked myself such a thing? What if there was a thing I wanted whose attempts didn't take as much time as attempting political assassinations, a thing whose inevitable ninety-nine failures to accomplish I could more quickly bumble my way through? Yes, these were the sorts of complications I was trying to reckon with, but I was having a hard time getting to the point. My writing kept getting in the way.

"Those fortunate enough to have been born after the end of the age of writing," the priestess told me that I'd once confided to her, "have no idea how truly awful it really was. They think you could just write whatever you wanted! That it wasn't a struggle even worse than speaking or thinking, a constant tug-of-war between what you wanted to do and what the writing wanted to do, a tug-of-war whose rope went suddenly slack or even disappeared entirely the moment you failed to magically intuit the ever-vacillating rules of a game impossible to play, let alone win," I said. "It was like trying to train an alligator to be a dog trainer."

Unfortunately, this was before writing had been abolished, and so every time I tried to write what I needed to write, my mind went blank and I'd have to take a break, eat a snack, or see if maybe I had to pee again. When I came back to the page, it was like I'd become someone else, and the only way I could engage again in the writing was by rereading whatever had gotten itself written thus far and trying to figure out what I'd have written next if it had been me who'd written that. I guess because I'd written the thing about dropping the little st's, nd's, and th's in the date, all I ended up capable of doing was deciding to drop more things. First, I decided to drop the date entirely—*It's not like its ever* not *April 1 anymore,* I wrote. *From here on out, a line break will suffice to mark that another April 1 has come and gone*—and from there I decided to stop differentiating between what was a dream and what had actually happened the day before, and before I knew it, I'd decided I wouldn't even write in my journal at all anymore. *I'm done writing,* I wrote. *What good has writing ever done anyone. What was I ever doing anyway except ratting myself out, tattling on myself to myself. Yes, this makes me very happy!* I wrote, and it was basically true—not true because it was accurate, but because I'd had to pretend it was in order to write what came next, and so I was feeling better and better. *I'm no longer a journal writer,* I wrote, and it felt so good I kept going. *I'm no longer an assassin either, a revolutionary, a musician, a woman, a human, an animal, a ball of light . . . I am none of these things! None!* I wrote. *And to be clear, I am running away from a certain feeling I'm tired of proving I can withstand. I'm telling myself to get out of my way so that I can go dig myself a hole deep in a desert of varicolored dirt where the bugs I consider true friends can help me learn that a* real *home is one that, like my hair, need never be properly cleaned,* and by the time I was, I guess what you could call done—not that I'd really done anything—the sun was rising and it was by this new light I saw that the reason I'd been so uncomfortable lately was that there'd been a plaque mounted on the broken slab of marble I'd been sitting on, one of those plaques that had once adorned the monuments outside the capitol building, the ones that quoted the most memorable passages from that book—What was it called it again?—the book that no one had ever seen an actual copy of but to whose alleged power almost every successive regime attributed its short-lived ascendency—the book to whose allegiance almost every militant faction required its members pledge? In any case, the reason I was so uncomfortable was that there was now most likely permanently indented into my butt cheeks the inverted letters that comprised what were allegedly the opening words of that infamous book-to-come—"*the book*, of course," the priestess said, "*of webs*."

"Ah, the book," I said, and I was

Not Exactly Lying

when I told the priestess that I remembered this now.

"You do?" she said.

"A soft rain was falling," I said, "darkening, drop by drop, the sun-faded metal of the plaque I'd been sitting on, the plaque which read . . ." but I trailed off. "For some reason," I said, "and it's the strangest thing! For some reason I can't remember what the words on the plaque said," I said. "Do you happen to remember if I told you? It's been so hard to remember anything lately. Hard," I said, "even to remember what I'm actually remembering and what I only once overheard someone else saying."

"You could say that again!" said the priestess. She could definitely relate. For her, it had been like that ever since the eye surgery—"but give me a moment," she said, "and I'll try to remember what it was you said."

"Speaking of eye surgery," she said a little while later—she was actually feeling a lot better now, and she wondered if maybe I wanted to go for a little walk.

"If it helps you remember," I said.

"Remember what?" she said, and I reminded her, and she said, "Oh, yeah. Definitely"—walking would definitely help her remember.

"Fine with me," I said. "So long as you think we can walk and talk at the same time."

She said she couldn't see any reason why we couldn't, and so I reminded her what a walk was, what the word *walk* meant now, and, she said, "Oh, true." She hadn't accounted for that, but she believed nevertheless that it was possible. She said that someone once told her that four thousand words pass through an average person's head every minute—"That's basically an immodestly long novel every twenty-five minutes!" she said—and so yeah, given the abundance—"No scarcity of words in these parts," she said, pointing, I could assume, at her head—given the abundance, she was pretty sure she could spare a *Then I went for a little walk* every now and then while also recalling and retelling whatever it was I'd asked her to recall and retell—"Which was what again?" she asked—which was, I reminded her, what the passage quoted from the book on the plaque I'd been sitting on had said, the plaque outside the capitol building's ruins wherein I'd just assassinated Leroy.

But she said, "No, no. You're confusing me. I remember it now. I was telling you about a dream I'd had—you were the one who interrupted to tell me about the book and the plaque and all that. Remember? I was right in the middle of recounting this dream, and you said, 'That's so weird,' and I said, 'What's so weird?' and you said, 'Oh never mind, keep going,' and I said, 'Well now I've lost my place,' and you said, 'It's just that what you dreamt of reminds me so much of a scene from a book I once accidently got indented into my butt cheeks,' and I said, 'Wait. What?' And you told me about the assassination."

"Oh, that's right," I said. "I forgot that that's what happened. Well, finish with your dream first," I said, "and then I'll tell you more about the indentations in my butt cheeks. The dream is more important," I said.

"Dreams always are," she said, and I asked if maybe she could start the dream again from the beginning though, and she said, "Oh, from the part on the lawn? When I saw the two angels? And they were stooping down to lift something off the lawn's false grass?" and I said, "Yes, exactly," and told her to start from wherever the dream began, for I could remember hardly anything from what she'd already told me, and a dream unremembered, I said, was like the instruction manual for the most powerful weapon in the world left unstudied.

"Let's go for a walk," I said, "and while we walk, you can tell me your dream."

"Don't Eat That!"

the priestess told me that she yelled out the window of the cabin wherein, in this dream, she lived. "Don't!" she shouted, as she rushed out the door and onto the lawn. "Don't eat that!" she screamed, and the two angels stooped there stopped, trained their gazes away from the thing one of them had found in the Astroturf and was now holding in its hand, the thing she'd seen it lifting toward the depthless chasm it had for a mouth. They turned their faces away from whatever it was and toward the woman rushing toward them, each smiling with the stitches that spanned the width of their eyeballs.

She'd grabbed a shovel and a rake on her way out the door. She held one in one hand and one in the other, and said, "Here. You give me whatever you've got there, and I'll give you this and you this, and then we can go destroy the lawn together. That sounds pretty good, huh?"

The angels exchanged a look between themselves, a look that she supposed meant that it sounded okay what she'd suggested, and then they handed it over.

"Handed *what* over?" I asked.

"The thing one of them was holding," said the priestess.

"I know," I said. "But what was the thing? A book or a tongue?"

"A book or a tongue?" she said. "Have you gone out of your mind?" she laughed. "'A book or a tongue?' says Amy! No. Neither a book nor a tongue, Amy, but a tail. A perfectly ordinary lizard tail."

The priestess took the tail from the angels and coiled it into an empty dimple in the egg carton wherein she was, at the time, collecting the disarticulated body parts that she kept finding on her lawn.

"Wait, no," she interrupted herself to say. "That can't be right. If I was holding the rake in one hand and the shovel in the other, how could I have also been holding the egg carton? No, I must have put the tail into the egg carton later. I suppose I put the tail in my shirt pocket or, more likely, placed it behind my ear like a pencil. Surely, I *intended* to put the tail into the egg carton when I went back inside . . . but did I ever?" she said and reached now to see if the lizard tail wasn't still behind her ear.

"How come I can't feel my ear?" she said, and I laughed, and told her she could feel her ear just fine.

"You felt your ear," I said, "and the lizard tail was still there. You said, 'Oops,' and then I said, 'Here's your egg carton. Go ahead and coil it into the bottom of this empty dimple now if you'd like.'"

"Oh, thanks," she said, and coiled the lizard tail into the dimple of the carton, and then we continued walking and she continued telling me about how the angels took the shovel and the rake and began to destroy her lawn, while she stood on the edge and kept a lookout for patrolling police cars.

But the angels had barely begun, barely even punctured the first layer of Astroturf, when, at the sight of the second layer of Astroturf buried beneath the first, they stopped, uttered a few plaintive moans, and then slumped, leaning dejectedly on the staves of their garden tools.

But this wasn't what had happened in the dream.

"The dream?" I said.

"Yes," she said.

"I thought you were telling me your dream," I said.

"No, no," she laughed. "I'm telling you about the true events that the dream had prepared me to expect."

———

In the dream, the angels had been ruthless, she said, so ferocious in their destruction of the lawn that she'd almost felt sympathy for the Astroturf—"for Astroturf!" she laughed. Though she supposed she was never one to hold a grudge for very long. But now, now that it was actually happening, the angels were too easily wearied and the lawn remained largely intact, which was a problem: if the lawn wasn't destroyed, then what would the angels fuck on, and if the angels didn't fuck, then how would they lay eggs?

"Are you guys hungry or something?" she said. "Maybe you're too hungry to destroy the lawn," she said, and the angels nodded their heads, and so she took them to a nearby restaurant that served food in hot metal tubs with large spoons and tongs which the costumers were instructed to use to serve themselves.

"You mean 'customers'?" I said, and she said, no, that she lived at the time in the costume manufacturing district of the city, and so that was the primary clientele the restaurant in question catered to, those who made the costumes for the many plays, films, and puppet shows that the state used to disseminate its propaganda, and I said, "Oh."

"After you," she said the angels seemed to say to one another, "No, after you," "Please, I insist," "I wouldn't dream of it," and so on while the luxuriant golden fur of their wings—fur suited to the cool celestial climes they'd evolved to weather—sloughed off in curly tufts that gathered on the checkerboard floor of the diner.

Who knows what passes for class consciousness in heaven, she told me, but here, when the restaurateur ordered the servers to pass beneath the angels with brooms and dustbins, the angels merely lifted their frocks and laughed their dry leaf laughs when the fronds of the servers' brooms tickled their unshod toes.

"I ended up being the one to serve the angels," said the priestess. "It was all-you-can-eat, and we stayed through many helpings."

The angels lived long enough to copulate and lay eggs, and then they died.

They left the priestess instructions for how to brood correctly, but the first step was to bury the eggs in dirt, and she lived in a city—"Burlington," she hissed—a city of endless stretches of bare stone broken only by the occasional rectangle of Astroturf, beneath layers of which no one had yet discovered what could accurately be called "ground." Every time she'd leave town, she'd forget to collect dirt, forget if she'd even *seen* dirt, remembering dirt only when she was already back home, stepping gingerly through the low-lying film of mist that was always gathering on—and, oddly enough, *only* on—her lawn. Then she'd go inside her cabin, find an empty dimple in the carton for whatever body part she'd found beneath the mist—a body part usually waffled from the tread of her clogs—replace the carton, close the fridge, and find herself once more face-to-face with the uncovered angel eggs.

"Ah, fuck," she'd say. "I totally forgot," and the rest of the evening would need to be dedicated to rewatching a short video of a baby bonobo getting tickled, which was about the only thing that could subdue the anxiety the uncared-for angel eggs were increasingly inspiring in her, as their unknown expiration date no doubt neared.

In this manner many chapters passed—"Many of us measured time in the amount of prose it would take to narrate," she explained—until one morning the priestess awoke with sufficient equanimity to seek help, but insufficient equanimity to determine who on earth might actually prove helpful, and so she called, for reasons that have unfortunately been lost to time, her representative in the local government, a representative who, though outwardly hostile to her sect, was rumored to harbor anti-Burlingtonian elements so deep within his body that not even *he* was aware they were there. Her ill-conceived plan was to call and hope her undercover parts might appeal to his using a forbidden language that sounded like English but in fact required entirely different interpretative techniques, a language that, she thought, the subversive elements inside her representative's body might be strong enough to decrypt and respond to, even if the representative himself remained aloof.

The following—"like everything else that has ever been said to have been said," she said, "or to have occurred"—was a fairly inaccurate translation.

"I'd like to speak to my representative," she said.

"Speaking," said a voice on the other end.

So she said, "Is there anywhere I can go for dirt in this city?"

"Dirt, dirt, dirt," said the representative, "let's see,

Dirt—

I am dirt and I am in dirt," said the representative. "I am my future and dirt my desire. I bury my hands in dirt and the dirt holds my hands, and even when I'm lifting my dirty hands back out of the dirt and the dusty dirt is falling all around me like snow, the dirt is still holding my hands, drawing me gently down. I live in caves I dig with my mouth. I dig mouthfuls of dirt out, and when I spit the dirt out it has been shaped into things I have seen or heard in my dreams. Mountain lions, for instance, standing up, lying down . . . And the cave grows larger. There are bones in the bottom of my cave when I have finished it and have been living in it for decades. The bones are dirt. They are my bones, and I am holding myself and I crumble into dirt in my hands, falling out of my hands when I am standing outside my cave under the stars, saying, 'Fuck you, stars!' and I lift my dirt sword up into the sky and the solid darkness through which the stars are shining shatters, and all the light that the sky had constrained floods in like dirt. For the darkness in the night sky was fired clay all along. I turn it back to dirt by shattering it with my dirt sword and let light make dirt of nighttime again, while screaming, 'Fuck you, stars!' The way my breath works is like this: I take in gold and huff out dirt, dirt I eat to produce lions and caves. Fossils, worms, and children of the earth. Allies and enemies, all dirt. Dirt gods crumble in my mouth. I make caves. In caves, bones. In bones, light. And in light, dirt. Dirt, dirt,

dirt," concluded the representative.

"I know," said the priestess. "I've heard your campaign promises before. Talk is cheap. That's why I called. Where, in this awful city, can I find dirt?"

"Hmm, dirt," said the representative. "Let's see. Dirt, dirt, dirt, dirt," and directed his constituent to the nearest garden supply store—the lawn maintenance lobby must've gotten to him first; big surprise—where they were selling measured quantities of imported dirt packaged in colorful plastic bags for ten dollars a pop.

"Ten dollars a pop?" said the priestess, and she was so appalled, she hung up on her representative and radioed god himself, who, her sect had recently discovered, was usually available to chat on a certain frequency they could train certain quasi-sentient walkie-talkies to attune themselves to.

"Has it really come to this?" she asked god.

"Ma-ma-ma, va-va-va," the voice roared over her walkie-talkie's ambient murmur.

"What do you mean?" she said.

God said, "How is it you do not understand this language which you yourself have just used to speak to god?"

"That's not what I said," she said.

"Ma-ma-ma," said god, "va-va-va. Over and out."

She went to the garden supply store, but she said she simply could not bring herself to buy the dirt. For the same price, she reasoned, she could purchase a carnivorous pitcher plant, and so that's what she did, and on the way home she collected a fistful of soot by dragging one of her hands along the window ledges of many filthy buildings. Once home, she sprinkled the soot over the angel eggs, along with some fresh ash salvaged from a house she saw get struck down by lightning.

Angel eggs now dusted with ash and soot, the priestess was ready for step two of the instructions the angels had left her for proper brooding.

But step two was as impossible to decipher as step one had been to achieve, and this, she said, was because the instructions were about 420 pages long and were structured like a book that seemed to have been structured by a different person deciding how the book should be structured every few pages!

In fact, now that she'd started trying to gather the various parts of the instructions together into some sort of intelligible order—there were over one hundred tangentially related parts of it, and they'd been scattered, along with tufts of angel fur, all over her cabin—now that she was trying to piece its parts together, she wasn't even totally sure where she'd originally gotten the idea about the eggs needing dirt in the first place.

Could it have been the line: *They left the priestess instructions for how to brood correctly, but the first step was to bury the eggs in dirt . . . ?* Could it have been *that* line? she asked herself. Because, if so, she now realized, she had definitely misread it: clearly this was not what the instructions themselves dictated but what certain instructions mentioned by a character within the instructions instructed someone else to do, someone only incidentally also called "the priestess," apparently.

She threw down the pages in disgust—and that's when she remembered the pitcher plant.

"The pitcher plant!" she gasped.

She'd set it down on the sidewalk when she saw the house get struck by lightning and had completely forgotten to pick it back up after filling her non-soot-cradling hand with warm ash!

The pitcher plant was not where she'd left it. There was, however, a trail of circular rings in the dusting of ash, a trail—presumably left by the pitcher plant's pot bottom—leading directly into the still smoldering ruins of the skeletonized house.

What horror, she couldn't but wonder, could have inspired a carnivorous plant to seek shelter in such a structure? Was it her camaraderie, she thought, it sought to avoid? Or was it merely anticipating the inevitable swarms of flies liable to descend on the house once the smell of the bodies rotting inside eventually overpowered the stench of smoke, melted plastic, and scorched hair that currently prevailed over the wreckage?

"Most likely I would never know," she told me. Or so she reasoned at the time. This was before members of her sect discovered that the forbidden language she'd used to address the anti-Burlingtonian elements inside her representative could also be harnessed to commune with carnivorous plants—this was thus before she knew that she was, and always had been, perfectly capable of asking the pitcher plant itself why it had gone inside.

Not that the answer would have proven particularly illuminating.

Not that anything, after all, she told me, ever really was.

"But," she said, "I digress."

She went inside.

"Hello?" she called into the shadows, ribs of steel girding gleaming. The blackened wood glowed silver in the evening light filtering in through mists of drifting smoke.

"Hello?" she said again and this time heard movement from deeper within. She removed her pistol from its holster, checked to make sure the beetle larva housed in the origami bullets loaded in its cylinders were still wiggling, and tiptoed further into the shadowy recesses of the ruin. The staircase had disintegrated, but fortunately she'd recently learned to manipulate molecular static attraction through microscopic hairs she'd grown from her fingertips and thus had no trouble scaling the wall.

But up or down? she wondered. Upstairs, she heard feet shuffling, and below, what sounded like laughter.

She went up, for she was in no mood, she told me, for laughter.

The first bedroom door she passed, or what was left of it, was shut, but she could tell, by an accumulation of ash at its base, that it had become so only *after* the lightning strike.

Steadying the pistol in her hand, she slowly pushed the door in, just enough to peek through the crack, just enough to see—in the center of the room, where the outline of where a bed had been had been preserved in burns—the pitcher plant.

In her excitement, she exercised less caution than the situation warranted—Would she otherwise have failed to heed the warning chemical codes the pitcher plant was frantically, faintly exuding?—and she pushed through the door, rushing directly into the arms of her parents.

"Your parents?" I asked.

"A trap," she said. "They must have come when they heard thunder."

They'd planted the pitcher plant in the room as bait, having somehow foreseen that she, the priestess, their prodigal daughter, would be the one to come looking for it.

"Clearly," she said, "their god was less withholding than mine."

"How are you?" one of her parents asked her, while the largest among them held her in a tight embrace, pinning her arms at her sides.

"Fine," she said.

"Fine?" said another. "You don't seem fine. Are you sure nothing's wrong?"

"Nothing's wrong," she hissed.

"Good," they said, and all suffered a long pause while the parents cooked her dinner.

"So," one of them, one with its back turned, finally hazarded, "how was your date last night?"

"Damn it all!" she erupted. She'd known she shouldn't have told them about the date! "I'll never tell!" she yelled. "It's none of your business! Respect my boundaries!"

Which—to her utter astonishment—had a sedative effect on the parents. Even the vice grip of her largest parent slackened, and she was able to wiggle out of it, grab the pitcher plant, and escape.

"Turned out my parents *could* be reasoned with," she said. She'd have to tell god.

Once outside, pitcher plant in hand, she fired a few rounds of beetle larva into the ruin. With any luck the beetles would mature and infiltrate the structure, and her parents, who lacked sufficient command of the internet to learn otherwise, would mistake the insects for bedbugs and abandon the house, leaving it empty, save, of course, for the beetles, beetles who had spent generations following a strict course of voluntary evolution that left them genetically predisposed to seed their habitat with a rare fungus known to attract errant property management corporation executives and then infiltrate their brains to plant dreams of purchasing ruined buildings and poorly renovating them into mediocre rentals. All this, she explained, because an alleged messiah—"albeit, most likely another false one," she said—would soon appear and would be needing a relatively inexpensive place to rent, or so divined the fortune cookie the priestess had broken open and read after treating the angels to all-you-can-eat.

The messiah, she told me she'd forgotten to tell me the fortune cookie had told her, *will soon appear and will be needing a place to rent. Fortunately, you will soon acquire a pistol and learn how to make origami bullets. Now, there is a certain kind of beetle,* and so on.

Pitcher plant rescued, she returned home, inflated with a sense of accomplishment she'd have been wiser to be more suspicious of. Senses of accomplishment, she was about to learn for the billionth time, were about as ephemeral as angels, and hers perished the moment she once again closed the fridge and faced the unhatched angel eggs.

There they were: piled up in a ceramic bowl she'd gradually nudged, day by day, a little farther into a corner of her kitchen counter wherefrom, now and then, an odd odor wafted, an odor whose precise origin she'd been careful not to inspect too carefully, an odor that had been growing steadily more poignant.

The feeling, as she stood there, remembering all she hadn't done and wasn't doing and most likely wouldn't do any time soon—all that she'd promised the dying angels, the inscrutable instructions awaiting organization and exegesis, the embryos, most of all the embryos—even if she started to care for them now, who is to say the clutch had not already long since rotted in their shells? The feeling was like a challenging yoga pose she practiced breathing deeply through. And by *breathing*, she of course meant watching the video of the baby bonobo getting tickled. Again and again, she refreshed the page, watched its face contort with joyfulness, heard its infectious cackle . . . Again and again the scientists doing the tickling reminded her that laughter is a form of communication—"And what laughter is doing," the scientists in the video said, "it's a signal that tells other individuals I want to continue playing with you, I want to continue interacting with you"—and she would laugh too, when they said this, laughing like the baby bonobo, like the scientists who laughed with it, laughing as her heart thumped harder, laughing as she tore and balled up bits of the instructions and placed them in the mouth of the pitcher plant.

"I can't stop laughing," one of the scientists said, and the priestess couldn't stop either, and the eggs, never changing, never changing, glistened in the moonlight until the moon cracked into

Over a Hundred Different Pieces.

The priestess was laughing again now. I laughed too—I couldn't help it—but at the same time, I also wondered if she couldn't perhaps remember what it said.

"What what said?" she said, and I asked if she couldn't perhaps recall what had been written on the page of the instructions she'd balled up and fed to the pitcher plant.

"Well, of course, I remember," she said. "I'd read every word very carefully. How else would I have thought to feed it to Sludge?"—Sludge being, or so I surmised, what she'd named the pitcher plant. "I read the whole thing very carefully," she said, "and even wrote down some of my impressions in preparation for the upcoming committee meeting. This was, you see, shortly before I was expelled from the committee."

"What committee?" I asked.

"The search committee," she explained. "Did I not already say that that was my occupation? That that was what I—at least as far as the state was concerned—that that was what I did?"

As far as the state was concerned the priestess wasn't a priestess but a member of a certain search committee, a committee for which she had thus had to read the document she was feeding to Sludge very carefully so that at the next committee meeting she'd be able to argue either for or against the document's author's inclusion in the book.

"What book?" I said.

"Sorry, by *book*," she said, "all I mean is the state's housing system."

The state's housing system was referred to at the time as *the book*. In the parlance of the day, *to be included in the book* meant being approved to rent an apartment, shack, cabin, trailer, cave, hole, etcetera from one or the other of the two landlords that owned all the property in the entire country at that time. "As a part of the search committee," she said, "we were the ones that a person had to submit an excerpt of their own book to for us to determine whether we might want them in ours."

"Wait," I said. "People had to submit a book in order to get into the book?"

"Yes," she said. "But whereas the book they were trying to get into was a living accommodation, the book they submitted as part of their application, in this case the word *book* referred to whatever one hoped to pass off as one's most valuable commodity, the reason they should be allowed to tenant the book. Generally, a book was a substance or intensity one's body particularly excelled in uncontrollably excreting. Our job at the search committee was to examine an excerpt or sampling of this potential produce of the prospective tenant and to determine whose produce could be most easily and profitably co-opted for the benefit of the landlords and to the advantage of the state."

"Oh," I said. "That seems unnecessarily confusing, to use the same word for two such different things."

"You're telling me," she told me.

To make matters worse, in this particular case, the applicant's book—that is, his uncontrollable excretion—consisted in lines of letters imprinted on paper. "Not a promising attribute of a book, believe you me!" said the priestess, but, alas, it was her job to examine the produce, little matter how unlikely it was to suit the purposes of the state and the logic of the book.

"Anyway," she said, "that's what I was feeding Sludge. It was a printout of this excerpt from the applicant's book that I was feeding Sludge."

"Okay," I said. "I think I understand. It wasn't, then, instructions for how to properly brood over your abandoned angel eggs."

"No," she said.

"And these instructions, thus, hadn't been disguised as a book, a book," I said, "I think that you'd called it *the book of webs*, right? A book," I reminded her, "that had been broken into over a hundred pieces? I thought that's what you were feeding to Sludge."

"No, no, no," she laughed. "But I see why you got confused. It was the *moon* that had broken into over a hundred pieces. It wasn't instructions disguised as a book but moonlight that was scattered all over my apartment—"

"Your cabin," I said.

"My cabin, rather," she said. If I'd misunderstood her, she explained, it was probably only because she must have enunciated this fact while my head was still underwater.

I'd tripped, she reminded me. I'd tripped and fallen headfirst into a subterranean pool, which was shimmering dimly blue in the reflected light of the faintly glowing stars. One moment, she said, I'd been stepping on the cave floor—which was in some spots smooth, but in others stippled with calcium deposits—and the next moment I was plunging into an icy depth.

"Oh, that's right," I said. "I forgot we were walking."

"That's probably why you tripped," said the priestess.

"Here," she said, "take my hand and I'll help you out of the pool."

I took her hand and—

"No you didn't," she said.

"Sure I did," I said, and reminded her how cold water dripped down her knuckles. How she braced her legs against the ledge of the pool and tugged me up. It took a few tries because the soles of my clogs, slimed with algae, kept slipping on the slick calcium deposits that ringed the pool. But at last she succeeded, and I wrung the cave water from my hair and resolved to exercise more caution in the future. I assured her I wouldn't easily forget the consequences of my absentmindedness, and she told me that I'd been very lucky it had been a pool and not a bottomless pit, and I agreed, and then we continued our walk and she continued to tell me about the excerpt from the book.

"What excerpt?" she said.

"The excerpt," I said, "that you were feeding to the pitcher plant."

"Oh, you mean Sludge?" she said, and I said, "Sure," and she told me that Sludge thought it was pretty good, which was a great relief because she'd been struggling for months to find something Sludge would stomach.

I asked if Sludge didn't eat flies, and she asked if I'd ever met a snail that had, and I had to admit I hadn't.

"As for the book," I said.

"Which one?" she asked, and I said, "The one you were feeding to Sludge, the snail," and she said, "Right."

As for the book—"I remember it very well," she said—the thing she'd been feeding to Sludge was an excerpt from a book the applicant called *the book of webs*, which, he said elsewhere in his application, wasn't so much a book as a thoroughly haphazard bewilderment of dreams, reveries, quotations, but which, though possessing no linear coherency of its own, let alone ideological or aesthetic unity, awaited only strong authoritarian directives—much as a good lawnmower awaits a consistent power supply—to be transformed into an essential tool in the cosmetological arsenal of the responsible landowner. *My hope,* he wrote in his cover letter, *is that my little fragments and accidents could, like cars, fill vacancies in the so-to-speak parking lot of your nation's great history, much as my physical body,* he said, *might find refuge in some modest pit or hovel in your nation's illustrious book.*

The applicant claimed he had over a hundred such fragments

scattered all over the desktop of his laptop and was confident that if the excerpt he'd compiled evidenced the quality and diversity of his material as well as his overwhelming desire for the book to conform to the state's own ideological and aesthetic standards, the search committee could not but grant him opportunity to exist in reality, an opportunity, his cover letter in no uncertain terms assured them, he would not squander.

"Did you say *reality*?" I said.

"Yes, *Reality*," she said, "in italics. That's what the book was called."

"What book?" I said.

"The state's housing system," she said. "We've been over this. 'To exist in *Reality*,' that was to say—in the parlance of the enemy—to have a place in the book, to be approved as a tenant, to earn the right to need a job to pay the landlords . . . The applicant assured us that if the excerpt of *the book of webs* he was submitting for our consideration gave any indication of what his book was actually like, we'd have no choice but to grant him the opportunity to exist in *Reality*, which was the title of the so-to-speak book that was what the state's housing system got called. You get it now?" she said, and I said that I did.

"So?" I said. "Did you approve the application?"

"How could we?" she said, "when the applicant neglected to include any excerpt of his book?"

"Oh?" I said. "Then what were you feeding Sludge?"

"A preliminary note," she said. "A note that was supposed to explain what the excerpt was and how it fit into the overall architecture of his book."

The applicant had submitted fifteen pages, she told me, consisting of nothing but a preliminary note copied and pasted a few times over and nothing else. The search committee rejected the application without a moment's deliberation. She probably wouldn't have given it a second thought, she said, if it hadn't been for the mysterious change in Sludge's dietary requirements—"that and also the paper famine, of course" she said—she'd never have given *the book of webs* a second thought, she explained, had Sludge's new dietary requirements not necessitated that she rummage through the box or two of personal belongings that she hadn't burned when she faked her own death in an effort to escape the mercenaries that the search committee hired when she resolved to begin her life over again as far away from Burlington as the vestiges of her meager stipend could carry her away from there, which, needless to say, wasn't even so far as the borderland . . .

"But where was I?" she said. "That's right," she said. "The preliminary note."

The preliminary note was all any of the search committee ever saw of this applicant's alleged book, and even this note, as another member of the committee was quick to point out, had been largely plagiarized from the preface of a famous political pamphlet.

"And so," she said, "if you ask me, there never was, nor ever will be—with the exception, of course, of the then recently exhumed funerary text from which the applicant no doubt lifted his title—any such thing as *the book of webs*."

The Following Document,

she told me the preliminary note said—assuming, she said, I was still keen to hear what it said (I said I was)—it said: *The following document is a treatise in disguise as an excerpt from a book in progress entitled* the book of webs, *and this treatise's aim is to reveal the True Facts about the State of Burlington for the benefit of those seeking to destroy it; but the Unsaid Laws of Burlington declare that those who speak the Truth shall have their tongues removed from their mouths and used in place of the concrete ramps leading into the boutique clothing stores that adorn the pristine streets of downtown Burlington; in fact, even one who merely reads the Truth, state these Unsaid Laws, even one who listens to a message left on one's answering machine, or wakes up in the night because the wind is howling through the gap in the window and it sounds like a voice whispering True Facts into this person's ear, even this person might likely find themself sentenced by the corrupt Judges of Burlington to having their tongue disembodied, enlarged, and concretized to deck the public squares of the fashionable epicenters of the Burlingtonian empire. Therefore, it is advised that anyone who has received this treatise undertake the following precautions:*

1. *Keep it hidden among the other application materials it is disguised to supplement, and feign to treat it as if it actually were an integral part of those application materials; treat, therefore, this preliminary note as an extension of the book it pretends to introduce, a clever (too clever, you might wish here to whisper to one of your colleagues) ploy by which the quote-on-quote author (we'll get to this a little later) has contrived to organize disparate fictitious materials he is attempting to pass off as an excerpt from a book he has written; it is suggested, in fact, that you actually entirely convince yourself that this note is fictitiousness—a satire perhaps of our enemy's ludicrous*

clandestine communiqués? you might think to yourself—it is advised you convince yourself that this is fictitious before attempting the ruse on another member of the search committee;

2. *If there are any true Burlingtonians in your midst, and best to assume there will be (that is to say, that not everyone on the search committee is, like you, an enemy in disguise)—and you will easily recognize these actual Burlingtonians by their propensity to express interest in the applicant and/or to praise the skill, initiative, or honest effort evinced in this excerpt—should you find yourself, thus, in the company of Burlingtonians, calmly, but firmly offer a dissenting opinion: "Are you all joking?" you could say, "This?" while you wave a printout of this document in the air dismissively; in this way, you will avoid falling into the trap that the Burlingtonians are attempting to set for you and thereby keep your tongue in your mouth, and you will need your tongue in your mouth for what comes next;*
3. *If all agree that the application should be discarded and the applicant denied entry into Reality—and do not be deceived into affecting sympathy on behalf of the applicant as he watches you reject him, for what seem like tears are the strategically timed secretion of the binding agent that has temporarily held this body's individually useful parts in the haphazard construction you've unwittingly invited into your search committee meeting—if you can manage to remain unmoved by the tears, then, and only then, can you be certain that there are no true Burlingtonians in your committee, and only then are you advised to proceed to speak openly about what you have read and (as the applicant's body dissociates into its constituent parts, each of which, you will find, can be repurposed to improvise explosives) perhaps even be incited into committing insurgent acts against your common enemy, incited by the True Facts you have discerned buried, like golden tarantulas, in the desert wastelands of the following graceless imitations of human literature;*
4. *Do not wait until the actual committee meeting to follow the above protocols, for what is an individual but a committee meeting in microcosm, that is to say, a temporary and more or less compulsory coming*

together of parts, each with individual interests, fears, and objectives, parts modestly hinged together by a few more or less credible articulations; even the strictest Burlingtonian body harbors somewhere within itself some subversive elements, and it's these undercover agents—that unsightly hair erupted suddenly from a mole on your shoulder, a finger that slips under your eyelid when all you intended was to smooth your brow—it's the anti-Burlingtonian elements inside you that comprise the true addressee of this treatise, a treatise that is nothing more nor less than a call to gather in your joints, to form a new body of your body parts, an alternative organization comprised of your same organs, but bound by radically different articulations, a new committee fomenting a revolution inside and against your organism, while you, thinking yourself whole, thinking yourself safe, politely laugh off these open hostilities, accepting these veritable instruments of war leveled against you as the inane, benign works of fiction it is intended you take them for; and, finally,

5. *Keep in mind that this treatise, like any other document announcing or appertaining to* the book of webs*—much like the original human being after whom the applicant's artificial body was modeled—comes equipped with a bevy of compulsive self-sabotaging mechanisms designed to ensure that it remain itself only so long as it is being actively constituted—that is, told—after which point it will convert almost immediately into another grim instance of Burlingtonian propaganda; when this occurs, as inevitably it must, it is advised you devour the text; the elementary material will be recuperated and dedifferentiated in your digestive tract, wherefrom what parts that still appertain to the present stage of our unraveling catastrophe can be regurgitated to constitute a new Temporarily Anti-Burlingtonian Labyrinth of Equivocations, that is,*

A TALE.

"That's all it said?" I asked.

"That's all it said," said the priestess. It would have maybe made an amusing introduction, she admitted, if what followed were some tales, but unfortunately, the entire writing sample, as she'd said, consisted of nothing but this preliminary note copied and pasted till it satisfied the application's page requirement.

"What about the applicant?" I asked. "Did it actually turn into ingredients for making explosives? Did it say anything before it self-destructed?"

"How should I know?" she said. "Applicants weren't allowed in any search committee meetings, and if the preliminary note had suggested otherwise, this was but further proof that its author had but the haziest notion of how the real world worked."

So I asked if, nevertheless, the preliminary note provoked any interesting dialogue among the members of the search committee, seeing as it seemed, at least to me, designed to cause a stir. She told me that it didn't but that at the meeting wherein it was discussed a noodle soup was served that did.

"That did what?" I said.

"That caused a stir," she replied, but she said that I'd have to wait to hear precisely how the soup precipitated the disintegration of the search committee, along with, in fact, overturning pretty much the entire structure of reality on which the committee depended—"Reality?" I said; "The public housing system," she reminded me—but that I'd have to wait to hear exactly how till we were on our way back, and I said, "Back?" and she said "Yes," for, as I could surely see, we were—"pardon the expression," she said—*here.*

"Where?" I said.

"Where we've been walking to," she said, and I told her I hadn't realized we'd had a destination, and she asked if I'd have come along if I had, and I said it depended. It depended, I said, on where we were.

"*Are*," she said, "where we *are*."

And then she told me again—pronouncing the words *we*, *are*, and *here* like each was a progressive stage of a complex incantation—"WE ARE HERE," she said. And she said that there was someone else *here* as well, someone who lived *here*—"or perhaps rather works *here*," she said, "has his office *here*," she said, "a secret back door that opens into the cave . . ."—someone, she told me, that she'd met on a previous walk, someone whom she thought I might like to meet, someone who had expressed a very strong desire to meet me when, on the occasion of her having met this individual, she divulged—"I hope that's alright," she said—some of the things that she and I had spoken of in the course of our little conversations.

"*Knock*—" she sang, and though I screamed, "Wait!" she sang, "*Knock*," as she reached out to rap her knuckles against the door.

"Well that's odd," she said.

"What's odd?" I said.

"I didn't feel any door," she said. She said that she'd tried to knock but there'd been nothing there to knock on.

"Perhaps that's because there's a doorbell," I suggested.

"Ah?" she said, and I said, "Yeah, there was probably a doorbell, and you must've pressed it," I said, "and then it must have rung, because we then heard a voice inside say, 'Who is it?' and I told you that I had a bad, bad feeling about this."

"It's us!" shouted the priestess and then whispered to me not to worry. She said, "I think we can trust him. He's a doctor," she said. "And besides," she said, "if it'll make you feel safer, we'll give him false names. You can be *Amy*—"

"I thought Amy was my real name," I said.

"You told me you were Betsy," she said.

"Did I?" I said.

"Yeah, and that Amy was a typo that turned up in your notebook when you'd tried to write *may. I worry*, you wrote, *that we amy be in very grave danger*. Anyway," she said, "the typo was a dream, a dream I suggest we interpret by telling the doctor your real name is *Amy*. As for me," she said, and dropped her already androgenous voice a little lower, "I'll be Ishmael."

"But I thought you'd already met the doctor," I said. "What good is it pretending now?"

"Oh right . . ." she said, "of course," but then, after a pause, she declared that she *was* Ishmael.

"You are?" I said.

Ishmael had been impersonating the priestess to infiltrate *Reality*—"the book," he clarified—from which his applications had been repeatedly rejected. "Yeah," he said, "that sounds right." Yes, he'd been, he now remembered, impersonating the priestess at her own behest, on a dangerous mission into enemy territory—"It didn't go well," he said, "if I remember correctly"—but he'd been so well disguised, disguised for so long, he said, that he'd deceived even me, his old friend Betsy.

"I was so well disguised," said Ishmael, "that I must have deceived even myself."

But this, he told me—this disguising of himself as the priestess—this happened *after* he met the doctor. Of this he was pretty sure.

"No," he said, when he'd met the doctor, he'd known who he actually was and had introduced himself as such—"Ishmael?" he said the doctor had said, and he'd said, "Yes?" and the doctor had said, "You can come into my office now," and so he, Ishmael, put down the magazine, one of many the doctor had stocked his waiting room with, thus interrupting a very interesting article he'd been reading about the effects of the worldwide paper famine on a struggling mom-and-pop apocryphary operating in the borderlands, and went into the doctor's office.

"But where *is* the doctor?" said Ishmael. "You'd think he'd have answered the door by now."

"He did," I said and told Ishmael that the doctor opened the door a moment ago and said, "Ah, Ishmael! I was worried you weren't coming. What took you so long?" and that Ishmael then explained about how I'd fallen into the subterranean pool and how it had taken us some time to fish me back out.

"On account," Ishmael couldn't quite suppress a giggle, "of the algae slickening the fellow's clogs."

"*Fellow?*" I whispered to Ishmael. "I thought you said I was a woman named Betsy."

"I know, I know," whispered Ishmael. "I forgot. But don't worry, the doctor's completely blind. Blind as a bat," he said. "But do be careful what you say, for his hearing is said to have no parallel, neither in this world nor in the one to come. They say that he is writing a book and that one can never be certain that what one says in his presence won't end up printed in that book. And not just what one *says*," said Ishmael, "but what one *means*. 'Careful,' whisper his enemies, 'lest the way you appear in his book replace the way you actually appear in real life!'—for such, they say, is the unholy power of his nefarious little book. But!" he said suddenly. "I'm one to talk! He's no doubt been listening! I should hold my tongue!" he said.

"It's okay," I said. "You are holding your tongue."

Fortunately, Ishmael had had the foresight to communicate these urgent matters to me indirectly, using facial expressions and bodily gestures—"Wait, you can see me?" he asked, and I said,

"Just about"—visual cues which I was adept at reading, just as he, in turn, was skilled at deciphering the gist of my discourse purely from my body language, and that this was why the doctor had not heard Ishmael warning me about his insidious book.

This was why, instead of saying, "Insidious? I beg to differ!" the doctor instead proclaimed, "Ah, so this must be the famous Paul, yes? The fellow you were telling me about? The one with the little eye problem? Well, rest assured, young man!" he said to me, "Ishmael here has told me everything, and you've absolutely nothing more to worry about. You've come to the right place! I'm precisely the one you've been looking for, a sympathetic but discerning listener, with no other motive than to hear what is yours to say, one who can imagine no greater pleasure than to respond with as much generosity and openness as my many years of private practice have made me capable of most convincingly—What's the word?—not *affecting* but, uh . . . Well anyway, where are my manners? Do come in," he said, "please," and he welcomed us into an ornately furnished room, a sort of antechamber that must have separated the cave from the doctor's actual office. He then pushed a half-removed book back into its slot on the bookshelf, which sufficed to make the shelf slide silently back over the door into the cave. Then he told us to make ourselves comfortable, to have a seat, he said, wherever we liked.

"Here?" said Ishmael, gesturing behind him, and I told him that the doctor said, "Sure," and Ishmael sat down, while whispering to me that it sure was strange that he couldn't hear the doctor himself, and I said that it wasn't *that* strange and explained that the doctor had had the courtesy to address us in *my* native language, a language that he, Ishmael, had never had any reason to learn—"The human mind," I reminded him, "has the hardest time perceiving what it cannot understand"—but which the doctor had been kind enough to adopt for the sake, or so I imagined, of making me feel more comfortable, which I said that I appreciated very much, nearly as much, I said, as we'd both appreciate the glasses of tokay he then offered each of us.

The doctor pulled a very large book from the fake bookshelf that hid the secret door. It was a dictionary, by the looks of it, and the doctor winked to us as he lifted its cover. Inside, he showed us compartments had been incised into the pages, each one the perfect size to hold a bottle of tokay, a glass, and another glass.

"I don't think I've ever tried tokay," Ishmael whispered to me.

"Me neither," I replied. "But the doctor said in my language that he's quite certain we'll both enjoy it."

"Too sweet for my taste," said the doctor, "but it shares a name with a kind of gecko, and Ishmael has told me how much you like lizards, Paul."

"Has he?" I said.

"Isn't that why you ultimately went with that terribly awkward name for your little band?" he said. "What was it again, the Stellionators? Wasn't that why you agreed to call yourselves that, because the etymology referred to a newt or something?"

"A lizard with starlike spots on its back," I said, "often found among ruins. It's true," I said. "Only, I didn't know when I told that to Ishmael that he'd go on to tell it to a famous writer."

"Don't worry," Ishmael whispered. "I told him the Stellionators was just a post-punk band."

"Ishmael told you I was a famous writer!" laughed the doctor. "You're going to make me blush. I'm but a humble doctor, a simple physician," he said. "If I've written anything, it's only because my doctoring now and again required it. There are certain so-to-speak *surgeries*," he said, "too subcutaneous to be accomplished with a scalpel. Anyway, here," he said, and he handed us each a glass of tokay. "So tell me about the eye thing, Paul. Tell me what it was you think you saw."

"What I saw?" I said, and Ishmael whispered, "Hey, am I holding my glass of tokay? My hands must've gone numb, or something," and the doctor said, "What you *think* you saw," and I whispered to Ishmael, "Yes," and to the doctor said, "Eyes."

"Eyes," I said to the doctor. "Eyes sliced clean from corner to corner, incisions like smiles with lips stitched."

"Cheers," said Ishmael cordially.

"Cheers," I told him that the doctor replied.

Then he said cheers again to me specifically, but under his breath, he whispered, "Don't drink it!"

"Don't what?" I whispered back.

"Don't drink the tokay!" he said.

"Why not?" I said. "It tastes fine to me."

"Wait. No. You drank it?!" he nearly screamed.

"I didn't know I wasn't supposed to," I said, and reminded him that I had a soft spot for tokay—"Oh no, oh no," he said—and that I had, accordingly, downed the glass the moment he, Ishmael, had said cheers.

"It tasted fine though," I said. "Better than fine," I said. "It was maybe the best tokay of my life."

"Hm," said Ishmael, and sniffed his glass. "Really? Well, okay. Maybe it is fine then. Yeah, probably," he said, "probably it is. I just got worried for a second that a plastic tree in a 1/8-size replica of a ruin of an ancient cliff dwelling housed in the actual cliff dwelling's visitor center had a dream in which a 1/8-size replica of god called *g-god* appeared and gave the plastic tree instructions for how to assassinate god and we couldn't recover these instructions because we didn't yet know how to communicate with this miniature tree."

"What?" I said.

"I said I got worried for a second," said Ishmael, "that the doctor had put poison in our tokay."

"Oh," I laughed. "It sounded like you said something else."

"Uh-oh," said Ishmael.

"Why 'uh-oh'?" I said, and he told me that if the doctor *had* poisoned me, the first symptom would probably be that I'd start hearing different words from the ones he said. At least this was what I guessed Ishmael said—what it actually sounded like to me was: "Unfortunately, this was before we'd discovered that robust dialogue could be kindled with literally *anything*—yes, even a plastic tree in a replica of ruin. Yes, anything could talk to anything so long as both interlocutors privileged the intimacy their discourse afforded over whatever sense it made; once made, this discovery allowed us to grow our ranks exponentially, but by that point, unfortunately, the tree had already been seduced by enemy ideology—had already, in other words, become irretrievably convinced that it was an inanimate object—a toy practically!—and therefore could not dream, much less *commune* with a vanguard of militants, little matter how sympathetic it might've found their mission statement . . ."

"Ishmael?" I said.

"Oops?" he said.

"I don't feel well."

"Do you feel," he said, "by any chance, desirous of people who cannot reciprocate your desire while suffering aversion to those that seem like they could?"

"I don't know," I said. "Sometimes," and he said, "Shit," and I said, "But it isn't that simple—it's not like it's their desire for me I find unattractive," and he told me this was nevertheless a sure sign I'd moved on from the first to the second stage of the doctor's occult pharmaceuticals: a tendency, he said, toward dissociation.

"It begins," he said, "with your relations to others, before penetrating into your body and mind. Tell me," he said, "is it getting harder and harder to move?"—I said it was—"as though," he said, "innumerable threads of spider silk have been accumulating on your body all your life, threads you cannot shake, threads crisscrossing the air over every step you've ever taken, sticking, stretching as you've gone about your life, but never snapping, the tug, imperceptible at first, growing steadily more unignorable, more governmental as they've accrued, till it's finally gotten to the point where you can hardly move at all, can hardly even hear me over the murmurings of a thousand tiny animals thrilling at the prospect of the culmination of their lifelong capture of you?" and I said, "Yes," and he said, "Ah hell," for he'd heard it would be like this, that the doctor preferred his victims die thinking it wasn't his treatment but their own desire misleading them into spider webs that paralyzed them. "And tell me," he said, "what is that other sound you hear?" and I said, "I don't know, what is it?" and he said, "The sound of a buoy bell?" and I said, "A what?" and he said, "A bell strapped to a buoy to tell boats in the fog where the shore ends?" and I said, "Yes," and he said, "And it feels like you're standing beside the dock of a boathouse?" and I said, "In a way," and he said, "And there's a sign on the fence?" and I said, "Yes," and he said, "What does it say?" and I said, "No Wake Please," and he said, "Oh no," and I said, "What?" and he said, "Your back, does it itch?" and I said, "Menacingly," and he said, "Like paper?" and I said, "Yes," and he said, "And if I had a knife," and I said, "Yes," "then you'd ask me," "Yes," "to carve letters," and I said, "Especially punctuation, and make it deep: question marks, em-dashes, ellipses . . ." and he said, "into," and I said, "Yes," and he said, "your back?" and I said, "Yes, yes, that's what I would ask."

"Well," he said, "I told you not to drink the tokay."

"Easier said," I said, "than done."

And then

I Died.

"You did not!" said Ishmael.

"I did," I said.

"You died?" he said. "The poison was fatal?"

"Seems so," I said.

He could hardly believe it. But his disorientation, I said, was understandable. It wasn't unusual to be unable to remember something as traumatic as witnessing what he had just witnessed, but, nevertheless, I told him, it was urgent he pull himself together, told him that there'd be plenty of time for him to forget what he'd seen if he made it out of this emergency alive, but right now—right now he had to remember what had occurred, right now he had to be realistic—"*Realistic?!*" he screamed—and I said, yes, for the danger had not yet passed. The doctor—"The doctor!" he screamed, "I forgot about the doctor!"—the doctor, I said, was still sitting across from us waiting patiently for the poison to finish finishing us off. The doctor, I said, was rubbing his palms together in anticipation of who knows what diabolical intentions he had in store for our poor corpses, and it was thus utterly integral he keep it together, crucial he remember what had occurred, painful as it was, I said, to recall.

"I can't!" he said.

"You must," I replied.

And so he began to remember how the color had drained from my face—"Your face," he said, "white as a page"—how beginning with my eyeballs, every part of my face, then every limb, then every ligament and sinew, every vessel and cell began to either spasm or relax, tensing or releasing with no consideration for any other part of me, indeed, actually in opposition—"Oh," said

Ishmael, "it was awful to watch: you at war with yourself"—every cell of my body in opposition to every other. He remembered: I was literally tearing myself apart.

"But then," he said, "I saw you jolt upright for a moment, coming back to yourself it seemed, like maybe you were trying to resist it?"

"I was summoning," I said, "my last remaining strength, in a desperate effort," I said, "to issue a call"—I sent a desperate message encoded into the fraying filaments of my nervous system, a message directed to those few and distant parts of me that hadn't yet been turned against me by the doctor's toxins—a call, I told him I issued, to my body parts' dissipating collective power, a call to gather in my joints.

This must have been how I'd been able to regain control of my body, he conjectured, long enough to stiffly nod my increasingly factious head toward the manuscript on the coffee table. With this slight bow of my head, I signaled to Ishmael with my momentarily stalled individualistically rotating eyeballs to communicate that that book there—"the doctor's manuscript," I gasped, "*the book of webs*," I said, "*the book of webs*!" I pleaded—that the stack of pages there, I told him, was our only hope, was more important than my life, more important, I said, than any of us.

"Steal that book," I said with my eyes. "Revenge my death," I said. "Take the manuscript and get the hell out of here."

"And then," I said, "I fell utterly apart."

"And died?" said Ishmael.

"And died," I said.

"Oh no," said Ishmael. "Oh no!" he screamed, but I reminded him that this wasn't the time for bemoaning the loss of me and that he knew this as well as I did.

"I do?" he said.

"You do," I told him.

He acted quickly, almost automatically, just as he'd been trained to do: he immediately began pretending that he, too, had consumed the poisoned tokay, that he, too, had also started hearing every word said said wrong, had also become increasingly prone to unrequited love, had, too, stood by the dock, heard the buoy bell, read the sign, that he, too, had split apart. And now, banking on the hopes that the doctor would choose to drag my body before his into his office, where he intended to perform who knows what unspeakable violations on our still warm corpses, Ishmael was playing dead.

"You're playing dead," he heard me tell him. "Don't forget. You're doing a very convincing job, so convincing," I said, "it would be easy to forget. But you mustn't, you must remember you are merely playing dead and are not actually dead. Remember your training," I said, and he did.

He'd hardly even had to think about it, it came so naturally to him, so instinctively: playing dead.

Several breathless moments passed, and then the doctor confirmed—by repeatedly offering us each a freshly baked morning glory muffin—confirmed that we'd both drunk the tokay and that the poison that laced it had had its intended effect.

Then the doctor dragged my body out of that room and into another, and the moment the door closed behind him, Ishmael leapt to his feet, snatched the manuscript off the table, pulled the book we'd seen the doctor push halfway back out of the shelf to slide open the false bookcase—"This book's also called *the book of webs*!" he screamed, "oh, but it's not a real book, just a lever disguised as one," he added—and he opened the door behind the bookshelf and escaped back into the relative safety of our unfathomable chasm.

After My Death,

Ishmael ran until the last echoes of the song the doctor was singing as he did what he did with what remained of me had finished volleying off the vaulted domes and winding passageways of the cave system through which he fled.

"Strangely, I could still hear the doctor, though," he told me, "long after you would think I'd outrun the reach of his song."

"Sound travels strangely in a space like this," I said, and he said, "It certainly does, and besides," he said, "the song the doctor sang as he cut and bore into your body is a sound I'm sure I'll hear for the rest of my life, if not in the actual air then in my dreams and reveries, in the ever-replaying cacophony of death rattles of the murdered, the screams of those tortured, the misleading myths of our fleeting victories, diaries of loss, gurgling shrieks of animals being slaughtered, beloved objects shattered—the thick discord, in short, my own thoughts might, on better days, struggle to raise their weary heads above . . . Yes, perhaps what I took to be the doctor's actual singing," he said, "was already a part of this raging discord I call my mind, this cone of memories my present moment is only ever but a sort of gnat impaled upon the apex of," he said, and I said, "Yeah, that's possible."

In any case, after I died and Ishmael had fled far enough away from the doctor's office to consider himself more or less safe enough to stop, he collapsed onto the ground and wept. He rent the air with inarticulate cries, cursed the stars, called the very ground beneath his feet into question, and would, no doubt, have culminated his lament in some desperate invocations of my name, but—oddly enough—he'd forgotten what it was.

"Paul, wasn't it?" I said.

"No," he said. "Not, Paul . . . That's just what we told the doctor. It was something more feminine, I think, or gender-neutral, a name like Max or Alexis or Billie or . . . But I guess it doesn't really matter. Not anymore," he said, and it was true.

It didn't matter. Not anymore. The name was likely an alias anyway, a randomly shaped gust of air, a collision of letters, serving no purpose other than to preemptively distinguish me from other more or less fictitious individuals in the unlikely event my death inspired some instructive parable, motivational hymn, edifying puppet show, or false confession for bewildering the interrogator.

Which, clearly, it hadn't—which clearly it wouldn't.

It didn't matter what my name had been. What mattered was that Ishmael had escaped. What mattered was that he now possessed the manuscript.

"What manuscript?" he said, and I said, "The one that was more important to steal than my life was to save," and he said, "Oh right."

But he said this rather uncertainly, so I said, "The one you took from my murderer's coffee table. The one you fled through the tunnels of the cave with. Remember?" I said. "The one you're now holding in your hands?" I said. "*The book of webs*?"

"*The book of* what?" said Ishmael, and I said, "*Webs*," and he told me that this title wasn't really ringing any bells.

True, he told me, he *did* seem to recall having his hands clenched around an object of some sort, and though, in a way, he said, he could feel something there still, when he looked down to see what it was he'd escaped from the doctor's office with, it was to find not only empty hands but also empty space where his hands ought to have been.

"A thick gloom," he said, "spreads out all around me. I wave my hands in front of my eyes, but nothing changes. I grope out in all directions, but touch nothing. I look up, expecting to see stars, but an abyss opens up above me. The cave's ceiling might be thousands of feet above my head or an inch from my face—it's impossible to tell."

"Are you sure your eyes are open?" I said.

"How should I know?" he said.

"Well, have you tried opening them?" I asked, and he said, "Do you reckon it's safe to?" and I said I couldn't see why not.

"What about the stitches?" he said, for he seemed to recall someone saying that stitches might rip if he tried too prematurely to open his eyes.

I said that all I knew was that it would be very convenient for those whose books he wasn't supposed to read if he thought it was unsafe to open his eyes, and he said that this was a really good point.

And so Ishmael opened his eyes, and though at first there was no discernible difference, after a moment of his vision adjusting, he began to notice a red glow, a light so faint it was tempting to ignore it, to write it off as yet another misperceived accident of the cave's elaborate darkness, and honestly he would most likely have been tempted to do so had I not reminded him that this was neither the time nor the place for skepticism, that reasonable doubt was, unfortunately, a privilege of those in positions less dire than his.

He, thus, *could*—though just barely—see a glow, trembling in the distance, flickering faintly at the limits of what was perceivable, a red glowing that he groped cautiously toward, taking small hesitant steps, careful not to lose his footing or to alert with too loud a sound of footsteps any enemies that might be lurking in these hitherto unexplored recesses of the cave.

"Tell me what else you see," I said.

"Other than the red glow?" he said, and I said, "Yeah," and he said, "Nothing," and I said, "Nothing?" and he said, "Positively nothing."

He saw positively nothing other than the red glow, but he said that he could *smell* something, and I said, "Good," and he said, "What?" and I said that I'd said, *What?* and he said, "Burning."

Ishmael smelled burning. Magnolia and sandalwood, if he wasn't mistaken.

He smelled it before he was near enough to trace the source of the light to a single dot radiating navel-level in the darkness, before he could hear the cackle of incinerating powder, before he was near enough to recognize this glowing dot as, most likely, the tapering end of a stick of burning incense.

From the incense emanated a ruddiness too faint to illuminate more than a small circle of the wooden surface on top of which the incense holder rested—the incense holder which was a dark slab of ceramic with a small face sculpted into one end of it, a pinpricked hole for a mouth to hold the unlit end of the incense in. In the groove of the holder, Ishmael was first merely surprised but then deeply alarmed to discover that only a few clumps of ash had—a swallow caught in his gullet—fallen.

"Uh-oh," he whispered. "The incense!" he said. "It's only just been lit!"

Ishmael torqued his neck so hard, a jaw muscle cramped and smarted—"Oh, is that why my jaw hurts?" he asked, and I said, "Yeah"—he torqued his neck around and shouted, "Who's there?" and when no one answered, he said, "Show yourself!" but again was met only with deep silence.

"Silence?" he said, and I reminded him that by *silence*, I just meant the ongoing murmur of distant conversations taking place, a sound that was, ever since being interred, what the word *silence* had come to signify for us.

"In any case," I said, "I wouldn't worry too much about the recently lit incense." It was, I said, pretty obvious that someone had lit it and left it burning specifically for his, Ishmael's, benefit.

"It is?" he said.

"Is what?" I said.

"Obvious?" he said, and I said it was, at least if the intelligence communicated to him through his dreams could be trusted—"and what else is there," I said, "if not our dreams, to trust?"

In the Dream That Had Unexpectedly Prepared Him for This Very Moment,

Ishmael had been following an old woman down a dirt trail on either side of which birds were shaking, a rare phenomenon he'd traveled a great distance to observe—a phenomenon known throughout the birding world as *the trembling of the quails.*

"The trembling of the quails?" he said, and I said, "Right, the unique mating ritual of this particular population of quails," and he said, "Oh that's right. I remember now."

He'd completely forgotten about this dream—"That's what happens when you don't write them down!" I reminded him—he'd been so concerned with escaping from the doctor's office that he hadn't had time to record in his dream journal this dream he'd had while playing dead, this dream wherein on either side of a path he walked down, male and female quails trembled alluringly at one another, their dry feathers whirring gently among squat desert shrub and cacti, the yellow soil strewn with pieces of black lava rock, each adorned with bright green lichen.

"It almost sounds like a rattlesnake, the way they whir!" he remembered having said aloud to his guide, an old local woman whom he'd hired to lead him down the dirt trail, the woman he now followed to where the path trailed off under the ruin of an abandoned overpass. It was here that his guide, with a remarkable agility that her age belied, rapidly ascended—in a matter of seconds, he said, she'd climbed up the overpass and disappeared over a lip of crumbling concrete and exposed rebar, leaving Ishmael below, squinting up into the blinding sky.

"You coming?" he heard the guide call down to him from the top of the overpass. "Up here is where the oracle is."

"What oracle?" he said, and the guide said, "The one you've come all this way to see," and he said, "Oh, that's right."

He'd forgotten that he hadn't come here because he was a birder or, obviously, because he was a tourist but because he was a member of a cell of ecoterrorists who, in an effort to align their actions with the self-defense systems of their ecosystems, had abandoned their previous methods for choosing targets and planning acts of sabotage, methods that they'd theorized were tarnished by the same extractive and self-aggrandizing logics they held responsible for the ecological destruction they were trying to counter. *If we, whose minds are but sentences written by our enemy's educators, if we use these minds to determine our actions,* their manifesto proclaimed, *then it follows that our actions cannot but turn against our intentions. Yes, even if their law enforcers arrest us and their judges condemn us, even if their propaganda teaches their children to celebrate our executions, even so, our every success is instantly recuperated into their project of domination: one day's sabotage is the next day's refortifications. Our intentions are designed to betray us,* said this manifesto, or so it said before most of its claims were refuted and the whole thing needed to be rewritten. *For it is well-known,* it continued, *that our enemies have long since held total authority over our methods of knowing—that they determine the very genre and syntax according to which knowledge gets written in our own thoughts and utterances, to say nothing of our books. If we know it, it is already theirs. We must thus turn away from knowledge,* went the manifesto. *Only in the unknowing, in the inadvertent, the accidental, the clumsy, the dream, the typo, the stumble—only when our subjugated bodies thus rise up against our heads, ignoring what we've been misled to call our own interests—only by following a path of sucking, and not knowing, only thus can we realign our actions with the exigencies of our environment's defenses against our compromised heads. Take every wrong turn. Retain only what you misread. And most of all remember your dreams. But be wary, comrades. A dream interpreted—like a typo corrected—is an uprising quelled. Dreams are not to be told but reenacted—heedlessly reenacted in real space (a.k.a. enemy territory) and with real consequences. Only in this way . . .*

"Oh, that's right," said Ishmael. He'd forgotten that he'd been following, in this dream, a path of sucking, not knowing—that one of the ecoterrorists' key tactics for undermining themselves and thus their culture was to reenact their dreams. He wasn't there because he had an interest in quails but because he'd had a dream—a dream within this dream—and in a failed effort to reenact that dream, he'd ended up here. He wasn't there to see the trembling of the quails so much as to see what seeing the trembling of the quails inadvertently put him into the position of seeing, which, he was now learning, was an oracle, an oracle who he was beginning to suspect would provide him with an answer to a burning question, a question that, when he later awoke from this dream, though the question still burned, he could not for the life of him remember.

"I'm on my way!" he called up to his guide. "I'll be up in a moment."

But when he tried to climb up, the footholds that he'd just watched his guide navigate so gracefully proved too slick for the worn tread of his old clogs. He tried another way, but the cement crumbled under the weight of him. A third way, too, proved untenable. And beyond that, Ishmael, who had never been very skilled at directing his body through physical space, could envision no other way of accessing the top of the overpass. Again and again, no matter which path of ascent he tried to foresee himself attempting, he immediately foresaw himself hopelessly returned to the same place he'd started out from.

"Are you still coming or what?" his guide called down again, and when he tried to say he was trying to, she said, "What?"

"I'm trying to," he cried out.

"I can't hardly even hear you," said his guide. "Are you sure you're still there?" and though he tried to tell her he was, she said that she couldn't hear him at all, and was growing increasingly incredulous that he still actually existed and was not, like many of the people who'd paid her to guide them here before him, a figment of her own profoundly, often tragically potent imagination.

"Unfortunately," she called down, "assuming you can hear me, assuming," she said, "you still exist, unfortunately I have to keep going. I'm lighting a stick of incense for you, however. Hopefully it will still be burning by the time you get up here. This," she said, "this should help cover up the smell."

"The smell of what?" he said, but she didn't answer. "The smell of what?" he screamed, and his scream woke him up from this dream.

"Do you see now why it's safe to assume you're alone here?" I asked. "Based on this dream?" and he said he supposed he did.

"Well, *alone*," he added, "other than you"—but I reminded him that I was dead—"Oh, of course," he said—that I was dead and therefore not actually present there in the faintly incense-illumined cavern with him.

In fact, or so I explained to him, it wasn't really me, his recently murdered comrade and confidant he was hearing but the voice one hears in one's own head while reading.

"I'm reading?" he said, and I confirmed that he was indeed

reading—that faint as it was, the glow of the incense was just enough that, if he faced the pages of the stolen manuscript just so vis-à-vis the incense's little ember, he could thereby illuminate a few words at a time. He'd discovered this right after remembering his dream. Knowing that a great deal depended on what ended up being written in the manuscript he'd stolen, he'd begun to read it as soon as he realized it was safe and possible to do so, and he had been reading for little while now.

"Good thinking," he said.

"Yes," I said. "Good thinking."

This was why he seemed to be hearing a voice other than his own, because that was all that reading really was, I told him: hearing someone else's voice, even though you're all alone. The fact that this voice sounded eerily like mine was easily explained by the fact that he was still mourning the recent loss of me.

"Yep," I said. "You're definitely reading. Don't you see them?" I asked, "the black lines on the white background?" and he said, "In a way . . ."

In a way he could see that, but it was still weird that he'd forgotten he was reading, and I said it wasn't weird at all, and he asked me if that was because he was reading so well—"So well, for instance," he said, "that I've gotten completely immersed in the descriptions of what I'm reading?"—and I said, "No. Not at all."

I said, "In fact, quite the contrary."

The reason he'd forgotten that he was reading wasn't that he was reading so well but that he was reading so poorly. His thoughts, I explained, kept drifting, his focus was scattershot, and what he'd retained from his time spent reading had almost nothing whatsoever to do with what he'd actually read, with what was actually written on the costly pages his eyes were roving slowly over—pages his dearest friend had purchased with his own blood.

What he'd retained, I told him, of the reading experience so far had, in fact, much more to do with what had occurred before he'd even started reading. That was why he seemed to be hearing my voice iterating such sentences as this—a voice that *ought* to have been iterating the words that he was reading—instead *reiterating* the events and thoughts precipitating his arrival here at the moment he'd positioned himself beside the incense, the moment he began to pore over the manuscript's first admittedly atrociously convoluted sentences.

"But best not be too hard on yourself," I said. I said, "It's understandable. It can take a moment to adjust to reading when one first begins, particularly if one has grown accustomed to attending to one's actual existence in the world around them."

"Right," he said. "I guess I'm having a hard time extracting myself from the unfurling emergency of my life," he said, "in order to submerge myself in a book written by my enemy, a book that is almost certain to confound and incapacitate me," and I said I couldn't blame him but that, whereas reading was, it's true, generally, strongly ill-advised, it was, in this case, unfortunately, extremely necessary.

"Damned if I do," he said, "damned if I don't," and I said, "Exactly," and counseled him to begin again, to return to the top of the page and to try this time telling me exactly what I was saying, advised him to say back what the voice in his head was saying as he read the manuscript, to repeat it back to me, to even allow his mouth to make the shapes of the words, and a hoarse breath to whisper them. For to do so, I said—even if it made him seem a little unhinged or strained his throat—to do so was the best possible way to ensure that he was registering what was actually written there and not simply remembering things that had occurred to him or that he'd read about or heard about elsewhere.

"Remember your training," I said. "Concentrate," I said, "concentrate on the black lines on the white background. Concentrate," I said, "and tell me what you hear me saying."

"Alright. I'll try," said Ishmael and he went back to the top of the page and focused his eyes—"Wait, but which eyes?" he said, for he had at least two sets, didn't he? The ones that had the postsurgical stitches smiling across them and the ones he'd seen those eyes with?

I said "Shh, concentrate," and he said, "Okay," and told me that as his eyes roved over the manuscript's first words, he could hear my voice telling him what was written there.

I said, "Good. Say it back to me. Tell me what you hear," and he said, "Okay," and told me that what he heard me say was that in a circle of men who took it for granted that

The Basic Riddle of the Dream Had Been Solved

by the efforts of the present writer, curiosity was aroused one day concerning a somewhat less basic riddle: What was to be done with dreams that had never actually been dreamed? Although my last book had shown definitively what a dream was and what to do with it, I had, without realizing, taken it for granted that all dreams were dreamed by actual, living, sleeping bodies. With this assumption presumed, I had proven what a dream was and how we, as clinicians, might best channel the violent, insurgent energy that each dream presents. But what of a dream, for example, that a child's imaginary friend dreamed and then told the child about? What of a puppet's dream in a puppet show? What of a dream that a character in a dream dreamed and told the dreamer about? Were these dreams, we were now beginning to wonder, as dangerous as real dreams, or could they be safely ignored?

"I feel like I've read something like that this before," interrupted Ishmael, "somewhere else, I mean."

"Would you really put it past a murderer," I replied, "to plagiarize from a more well-known text?" and he said no, that he reckoned he wouldn't, and continued to tell me what the voice in his head was saying as he read the stolen manuscript.

No sooner had this question been posed, he said, than any of the curiosity it initially aroused quickly deteriorated into a diffuse anxiety that spread through the room—for no one knew quite what the correct procedure would be were one to be faced by such a dream, a dream that no real person had ever dreamed. Methodological uncertainty was, sadly, *not* something my circle of men, whatever their other strengths, were particularly adept at weathering. As anxiety mounted, I felt, as the de facto authority of this gathering of professionals—the so-to-speak *head* of this illustrious body—I felt some responsibility to see if I couldn't somehow assuage the bourgeoning dis-ease. But being, however, somewhat agitated myself, I succeeded only in causing more chaos by appealing to an even stranger class of dreams: those dreams that have only *been dreamed* that they haven't been dreamed but, in fact, have been dreamed; dreams dreamed by real people who are merely *operating under the delusion* that they are not real people. The real dream of a real man, for example, who is operating under the delusion that he is a child's imaginary friend, or a figure in a dream. What were we to do with a dream like that? I wondered.

In retrospect, it probably oughtn't to have been a surprise that this comment's outcome was the precise opposite of its author's intention.

In the ensuing pandemonium, I quickly regained my composure and said, "My goodness! My apologies!" and explained that I hadn't meant what I'd just said, could barely even, in truth, recall it anymore, and indeed had only been half listening to their discussion. For something momentous, I told them, something nearly unspeakable had been all the while unfolding silently inside me, a sort of internal emergency that had resolved itself only moments ago.

"What happened?" said one of the men in my circle.

"Are you alright?" asked another.

I thanked them for their concern and assured them that I was okay—that I was okay *now*—but then informed them that mere moments ago I really nearly hadn't been.

"Oh dear," they said, and then I explained what had gone wrong with the noodle soup.

"Noodle soup?" they said, and I said, "Yes, the noodle soup I've been eating" and told them about how a mouthful of broth had somehow, midslurp, gotten sucked up my nasopharynx, which my soft palate and uvula had not—as was their special responsibility as so-to-speak employees working for the so-to-speak corporation—instinctively sealed against the inrush of liquid, an especially crucial responsibility, I said, when said liquid is as scalding hot as the particular mouthful unfortunately was. I'd been betrayed, I told them, by my own soft palate and uvula! And I described in detail the horrible burning sensation that transpired, for there'd been a bold chili paste I'd mixed into the broth. My eyes, I told them, watered and my face turned red and my breathing grew raspy, as I was tormented by horrific foresights of the steaming, partially dedifferentiated ingredients of my soup gushing embarrassingly from my nostrils. I was besieged, in short, by a host of agonies, agonies I felt compelled to conceal, compelled by a compulsion I no longer understood and now found almost comical, agonies I felt compelled to conceal from present company—"as though I weren't actually, potentially choking to death," I said, "so much as passing wind." Only once the episode was over and the burning had been reduced to a not entirely unpleasant tingling, only then did the emergency cease to seem unspeakable to me, and it was at this precise juncture that I'd said whatever I'd said about dreams. It was thus, I admitted, an utterance that was not entirely unlike a dream itself, a torn and mangled shard of language smuggled over from the disputed borderlands of Reason's empire, beyond the frayed edge, I said, of the Word's sway.

"Wait, but *what* soup?" said one of my colleagues. "Where'd you get the soup? And where," he asked, supposedly because he beheld no bowl, "where now has this soup gone?"

"The soup!" I said. I said that the soup's derivations were far less important here than were the secret reasons behind its being vacuumed up the sensitive domes and winding passageways behind my face. For this incident, I explained, was a mere link in a long chain of similar missteps, accidents, typos, etcetera, and it was this chain of incidents, I said, and the underlying, hitherto unarticulated tangle of thoughts whose suppression I suspected bore responsibility for the chain of incidents, thoughts that had no doubt sought more direct expression but, finding the diplomatic channels blocked, had resorted to more militant tactics—noodle soup up the nasopharynx, the biting of the tongue, the ingrowing of an arm hair, the writing in my dream journal of the word *wording* where I'd meant to write *worried*, and so forth—it was this underlying tangle of thoughts, and not the mysteries of the soup, that I wished now to attempt to articulate and thus free myself from. For as productive as it might be to direct our investigations toward the soup—not only its enigmatic origins, but also how I'd been eating it without anyone noticing, to say nothing of where the bowl was now . . .—as fertile as such a line of inquiry might've been, I could sense, even then, that it was in the cauldron of thoughts stewing inside me, in *this* so-to-speak soup, and not in the *actual* soup, that there swirled the ingredients that would eventually coalesce into this, my second book, a book that, assuming the state's censors continue to favor my thoughts, the kind reader has taken a break from their own so-to-speak *book* to read the first few pages of.

Indeed, having already anticipated that this long-dormant book was beginning to stir and would imminently open it's so-to-speak *eyes*—this anticipation arising around the same time as the choking—and knowing that I had a better chance of expressing myself in the comfort of my colleagues' company wherein I was assured of a generous reception (rather than face-to-face with that terrible abyss of the blank page), I'd signaled to my dictation-taker, Doctor K. LeRoi, that he please begin writing down what I was about to begin to say; the text you now hold is nothing but the resulting document—translated from its original language, of course (translation also by LeRoi), and screened for typos—but otherwise basically unaltered.

"Looks like there's a footnote here," said Ishmael.

I said, "Good. What am I saying when you read it?" and he said that I—which was to say (because it was a translator's note) Doctor LeRoi, the translator—that I said that I'd been trained by Doctor Burlington to take dictation in the style he preferred: a healthy balance of his direct utterances and indirect recapitulations of it, and thus to have it appear, in other words, as though he, himself, were recounting his lectures after the fact. This will, I hope, help explain the peculiar texture of the dictation, replete as it is with instances—all the *he said, she said*, for example—of things the Doctor, of course, didn't actually, at the moment of dictation, say. That said, as those who had the privilege to know Doctor Burlington before his untimely death can attest, it was not unusual for him to *actually* express himself in such a manner, as though, we often jested among ourselves, in anticipation of the book to come.

"That's the end of the translator's note," said Ishmael, and I said, "Great," and he went back to reading the main body of the text. He told me that it looked like what I—Doctor Burlington once more—said next was primarily concerned with the emergence of a rather strange pattern of similar symptoms surfacing among a surprising number of my patients, a very odd commonality given that these clients had, in every other respect, nearly nothing in common. The issue, I told the circle of men, was—but I had a hard time putting this into words exactly, because each patient had likewise struggled to do so and had thus said it slightly differently—the issue was that each patient was convinced and would not be dissuaded from the conviction that I, their psychotherapist, was not an actual person but a product of an act of imagination—sometimes their own, sometimes someone else's—that I, Doctor Burlington, had been invented for the sole purposes of extricating them from some other set of intolerable conditions, *real* conditions, which each was attempting to escape from by—odd as it sounded—consistently inhabiting this imaginary landscape, an imaginary landscape that they insisted I erroneously called *existence.*

There was one patient, for instance, who claimed to have been anesthetized and currently undergoing an involuntary self-inflicted surgery, while another was bound to a chair in an underground prison and subjected to brutal interrogation by malignant puppets, while yet another had ended up locked in the back seat of a taxi being driven toward the very edge of the world . . .

"Whatever the particulars," I told the circle of men, "these patients all share the common belief that they are each, *in reality*, confined to the hellish conditions they have described, that their individual (and, I might add, *mutually exclusive*) nightmares are reality, and that this collective existence—my office and all that surrounds and relates to it, including, of course, my own person, but also space and time—in short, the entire universe and the laws that condition it, are the mere by-product of a narrative each patient is steadily articulating silently inside their own head; or, as the case may be, is overhearing a sympathetic guard whisper discreetly to another prisoner; or has deciphered in the scream of a wind as it blasts through a crack in a broken windshield of their plummeting vehicle, and so on," I said, "and so forth."

A few of my colleagues couldn't suppress a little laughter here, but I told them with a glance that what I was telling them, despite apparent similarities to a little joke I pulled at our last meeting, that this was no laughing matter: these were *real* people, my patients, all suffering terribly.

"And though tempting," I said, anticipating their next

misinterpretations, "tempting as it might be to explain away the coincidence as yet another juvenile prank designed by my beloved colleague, Doctor Sludge, in an effort to humiliate the author of the theoretical framework that so conclusively superseded his own dominion over our shared theoretical territory, this suspicion," I assured them, "this suspicion has grown increasingly untenable. For each patient, regardless how desperately they might attempt to appear otherwise, betrays so convincing and profound a sense of bewilderment that any skepticism withers in their actual presence. No," I said. "Even were we to assume for a moment that each patient *is* a hired actor, the virtuosity of the cast alone shreds any possibility of Doctor Sludge's involvement, if for no other reason than it so obviously exceeds the Doctor's ability to attract talent," I said, and this prompted a brief peal of laughter from the circle of men, men who always enjoyed my gentle jabs at Doctor Sludge's analogous assembly of disciples.

"In any case," I continued, "this repetition of so similar a delusion surfacing among so many otherwise dissimilar patients—this complex coincidence, whether fortuitous or falsified—has inspired lines of thought that will, I believe, be of *genuine* value to our profession—and greater glory, I might add, to our little cadre. And so, if you'll permit me, I'll bracket, for now, the Doctor Sludge hypothesis and proceed as though it were possible to rule it out entirely, which of course, it isn't. It never is. But what better way," I said, "to parry the feint of an opponent than by *intentionally* falling for that feint, seeing that by doing so one can produce a far more powerful counterfeint than one could by *not* falling for it?"

"Another translator's note after that sentence," said Ishmael, and told me that in it, the translator suggested that Doctor Burlington had probably meant to say *counterstrike* rather than *counterfeint* and that this mistake was attributable to the fact that the two words, *counterstrike* and *counterfeint*, were exceptionally similar in the original language. On the other hand, said the footnote, it was doubtful the Doctor had a solid enough grounding in the art of fencing to know the difference.

"Copy," I said, and Ishmael returned to the main body of the text.

Such indeed, he said, was the faith I had in my web of thoughts, thoughts whose pressure had long been accumulating inside me—this web that had been expressing itself in a slew of accidents and mishaps, a slew that the soup slurped up the nasopharynx was only the most recent, though not, admittedly, the most embarrassing or painful, instance of—such indeed was my faith in this emerging book, that I truly believed that the Doctor Sludge hypothesis was, even if true, irrelevant.

It was a faith that was, in retrospect, of course, premature.

But what, after all—among a species prone to being birthed decades before it can survive without incessant coddling—isn't?

"Then for a few pages," interrupted Ishmael, "it looks like all you do is bemoan the fact that your mother couldn't have carried you in her womb for an extra thirty years—which is odd given that, according to your translator's note, you'd turned thirty only a few days before this. Is it okay if I skip these pages?"

"Definitely," I said.

After comparing my circle of men to a pale, though still much appreciated, substitute for the womb I was so unjustly prematurely ejected from, I eventually returned from my digression. But, I returned, it seemed, having forgotten where exactly I'd left off. Fortunately, at least one among my circle was able to remind me that I'd been on the cusp of discussing the increasing prevalence in my practice of patients suffering under an inexplicably similar delusion: the delusion that neither my person nor my office, nor indeed even the sidewalk they'd walked down to get here, nor the double doors, nor the stairs and hallway, nor the infinite regression of facing mirrors that lined that hallway, nor the threshold they crossed to enter my waiting room, nor the many quality scientific periodicals they found awaiting them there, nor the articles therein, nor the authors that wrote them, nor even the grammatical laws governing these writers' sentences!—in short, that none of this—"not this!" I said waving to the walls of the underground bunker my circle of men and I were sitting in, "nor this! nor this! nor this! . . ." I said, as I pointed in turn to each of them, "even this!" I said gesturing up to the world outside our bunker—"assuming, it's still there," I added—that *none* of this was real, that it was all but a mere ghost of language, "an advanced apparition," I said, "that has been more or less accidently suggested into existence much in the same way," I said, "that even to utter only a mere two words of a narrative—*he said*, for instance—is to imply a vocal apparatus, breath, genitalia, blood, addressee, linguistic community, air, sun, space, time, etcetera, is, in short, to intimate an entire unspoken cosmos, without which the two words, *he said*, would be meaningless."

Our entire existence, I told them, was, according to my clients, an accident dragged into being by a string of words that needed to be uttered according to the exigencies of a still unfolding state of emergency occurring somewhere else entirely—our entire existence a sort of common denominator of the linguistic community's collective imagination, an existence that would, ideally, be gradually revised as the string of words progressed and the implied generalities were replaced by particulars. This was, at any rate, for many of my patients the plan. But, alas, this fictitious universe was only getting more and more banal and disastrous, as each new word, though intended to specify and differentiate, couldn't but simultaneously birth a new endless host of generalities, generalities that my clients were, for whatever reason, generally loath to admit served any useful purpose—such as, for instance, keeping the planets in orbit or ensuring water served to refresh a parched throat . . .

I took a bite of my peanut butter cookie and said, "Now, each of my patients took a uniquely nonsensical and circuitous approach when it came time to apprise me of their delusion."

Although, it had long been, in all cases, painfully obvious that each was wholly enveloped in some just barely concealed private catastrophe, most of them had spent the first few months of treatment profoundly evasive, often treating me as an enemy rather than a source of comfort, let alone disillusionment. It was almost as though they held me responsible for them even being there!

"I didn't do anything!" I said to them. "I didn't force you into my practice."

"Well, of course not," they'd typically respond.

"Why *did* you come here, then?" I might ask next.

"Because I was in the waiting room," they might reply, "and you told me to come in."

"Right," I'd say, "but why were you in the waiting room."

"Because I had an appointment."

"Fine, fine," I'd say. "But why did you have an appointment."

"Because it was too late to cancel without being charged," they'd say, "as per your own outrageously fascistic cancellation policy."

And so on—and often even much worse—and so on things went.

Eventually, however—and a testament, I think, to my remarkable patience ("You know, you can tell me anything," I'd often say to my almost absurdly recalcitrant clients, "you know that there's no one in the whole world more eager to hear whatever it is that you have to say")—eventually, each patient opened up and unburdened themself of the enormous psychic pain that had brought them to my office.

Suddenly, for example, in the midst of an otherwise entirely unremarkable session, one client—a man of small stature and indeterminate age, spine twisted as a bendy straw, face gray and frog-eyed, an altogether inchoate physical presence, as though someone with no sense of anatomy or physics, awful self-esteem, and no access to a mirror had been forced to describe himself three-dimensionally, unaware that the thus-rendered object would be obliged, in turn, to one day be his body, a deficiently created creature, in short, who hadn't yet disclosed so much as his occupation—suddenly, in the midst of an otherwise unremarkable session, this client told me, after I'd asked him, I believe, about how his weekend had been, he told me that his weekend had been, if he was going to be completely honest—and I assured him he could be—profoundly distressing, actually.

"Thanks for asking," he said.

I said I was awfully sorry to hear this—though, to be honest, after months of fruitless silence, I actually couldn't have been more delighted—and I asked if he'd like to tell me what exactly had gone wrong. He sighed and said he supposed it couldn't hurt to try.

"At least no more," he said, "than it hurts not to."

"Not to what?" I said, and he said, "Try," and then told me that someone with whom he'd been having what he'd thought was a productive, mutually beneficial, and maybe even subtly flirtatious conversion had proved to have not been the person she claimed to be but was revealed, rather, to have been a large community of spiders who had temporarily banded together their voices to imitate a person, spiders who, after disbanding, were then saying so many contrary things at once that my client was no longer able to discern in the unraveled cacophony any one articulate thread. Moreover, he said, he wasn't even entirely sure that these spiders actually *were* spiders and not just voices in his own mind—whether they were spiders, in other words, that he was merely remembering, spiders whose voices he'd heard at some point, spiders whose voices an insurgent faction of his own psyche had learned to imitate by hijacking his memory cone in an effort to further destabilize his orientation in space and time.

"As though my chronotope," he told me, "wasn't already sufficiently," he scoffed, "unstable."

Now, as our conversations had hitherto been strictly limited to the most mundane subjects imaginable—which types of green tea were most overpriced at a café he frequented, lists of nouns that were the same whether singular or plural ("fish, crab, deer," he'd drone, "you . . ."), his passionate distaste for lawns, picnics, trivia nights, and professional portraiture—because until now he hadn't said a thing of even the slightest consequence, and because I was expecting more of the same, I was at first, admittedly, not actually listening to him.

"Sorry?" I said.

"For what?" he replied.

"I zoned out for a minute there," I said. "Did you say something about a dissociated princess?"

This misstep annoyed him so greatly that several months would elapse—during which period I considered it prudent to let him steer the course of our conversations—until finally the day came that his temper had calmed enough for him to broach the subject again.

"*Priestess*," he said, apropos of an entirely unrelated topic—paper towels, I believe, whether he still had a roll under his sink or had already used the last one, whether his memory of having done so was a dream or not—"*priestess*," he said, "not *princess*," and then said that no, *she* wasn't the one who was dissociated. In fact, he told me, she was profoundly associated, deeply embedded, he said, in an immense *association*. "She was profoundly associated," he repeated, "albeit *in* an equally profoundly dissociated state."

"What?" I said.

"She was in a dissociated state," he said, "an authoritarian nation, whose appetite for injustice and cruelty could only be explained by the fact that every institution, group, person, object, and even molecule, caught in the web of this state's immense hierarchy, was, at a deep level, painfully dissociated from every other"—or so at least, he told me, was the priestess's diagnosis of the culture her own association lived in strict opposition to—or such, at least, was her diagnosis if, he said, the spiders that were impersonating her could be trusted to have been doing so faithfully and also, he added, if they really *were* spiders and not a conspiracy of his own inner monologue—"Dialogue," he corrected me—insisting that if the worldwide mandated eyeball surgery had taught us anything—"which, of course," he said, "it hasn't"—it was that every so called *monologue*, inner or outer, was in fact a *dialogue* in disguise and that failing to see so was perhaps *the* primary cause of the climate catastrophe—"*Monologue!*" he laughed—no, it was quite beyond the scope of the sorts of disbeliefs that could be sustainably suspended by any individual even vaguely attempting to attune themselves to the unforgiving ecology of the book we'd been condemned to attempt to try to be quietly alive in.

"Okay," I said, treading cautiously this time, "and how come you couldn't confirm by sight whether the priestess was an actual person or a clutter of spiders?"

"*Clutter?*" he said. "Is that the word for that?"

"According to the dictionary," I said with a smile and noticed that he winced at the word *dictionary*.

"Well, it was due to my eyes," he said. "I could not confirm by sight whether the priestess was a clutter of spiders on account of what has been done to my eyes." And then, as his, as far as I could tell, undamaged, though admittedly oddly protuberant, eyeballs watered, he explained that he'd only just recently survived a dangerous eye surgery from which he had not yet—as I could no doubt see for myself—recovered. Besides, he told me, he was trapped in a cave in which the only source of illumination was the occasional bioluminescent lure of giant, oxygen-breathing anglerfish—fish that, of course, a human being had no business going anywhere near, however tempting, he said, such a light source might have been.

"Of course, of course," I soothed.

"I mean, I suppose I could've tried," he said, "to feel with my fingers if the spiders were actually there, but I was wary of the risk. You know," he said, "spider web-wise."

He explained that he'd already been caught in such a profusion of spider silk—"a totally unjust profusion," he said, "in proportion to the number of times I've actually uninhibitedly acted on any genuine desire"—he was caught in such a profusion of webs, he said, that he'd been wary of reaching his fingers out to feel what was there and what wasn't, wary that there'd be more spider webs woven there where he might otherwise have intended to reach.

Though normally reticent, each word an ordeal, here he was speaking in gushes, each run-on utterance winding him, every phrase one he seemed to have repeated a hundred times before and had grown to know in advance was unlikely to elicit the kind of response he was looking for.

He said that he didn't want to be wound up any more than he already was. "That's why I didn't reach out," he said.

"I'm lost again," I said. "Are you saying that you're being hunted by spiders?"

"*Saying?*" he said and laughed. "No, what I'm saying is that I'm *not* being hunted by spiders. But I'm only saying this to escape the brute fact that I *am* being hunted by spiders," he said, "whether I say so or not. To say nothing," he added, "of the anglerfish."

This, he said, was why he didn't reach out with his fingers to see whether there were actual spiders there—"because of the spiders," he said—because he was hoping to live a little longer, he told me, than it seemed likely he would if he did everything he ever wanted to, like reach out, for example, with his fingers to feel for what was and was not actually there.

"Because there might've been spider webs woven there," I said.

"Exactly," he said.

"And how come you couldn't, supposing you did brush up against some webs, simply brush them off?" I asked, and he laughed, but when he saw I wasn't joking, said that if he had done that then the webs would just be stuck to whatever he used to brush them off with, his other hand for example, and he needed his other hand. He needed it, he said, just like he needed the rest of his body for as long as possible to not be immobilized by the accumulated tension of a whole lifetime's-worth of spider threads dragging him closer and closer to a final stasis.

"I see," I said. "Well, I'm honored—and, frankly, impressed—to see that you're willing to brave the webs to come all the way here to my office each week. To seek out the help you need," I said, "in spite of the spiders," and I reached out to place a soothing hand on his arm, saying, "That's incredibly brave."

Again: wrong tactic. The patient didn't return for three months, and when he did, it was to tell me that every other therapist he'd gone to see—and here my circle of men scratched their beards and remembered that, yes, they, too, had each briefly seen before disappointing this diminutive and ravening fellow—that every other psychotherapist he'd managed to get an appointment with was even worse than me, which I took as a compliment.

"It wasn't intended as one," he told me and narrowed his bulging eyes.

This narrowing of his eyes, however, reminded me of a little feint that I'd thought up since the last time I'd seen him, a feint I finally had an opportunity to put into operation: I said,

"Well,"—and I could hardly keep a straight face as I said it—"it looks like we're out of time for today."

Having learned that he was both chronically underemployed and overly occupied with chronology, I was right to assume that he would not be willing to part with the last ten minutes of an hour-long session he'd be billed for.

"We're not out of time!" he said. "Not even close. We have ten minutes left. There's a clock right behind your head!"

"Right," I said, "exactly," and paused, waiting for him to realize he'd fallen into my trap. But when, after several seconds passed without anything of the sort transpiring—I was by this point beginning to feel a little less assured of my victory—I said that I was happy to see that his eyesight had improved.

"What?" he said.

"Well didn't you say you'd been blinded?" I said, and he said he had, and so I said I was pleased to see his eyesight had recovered. But by the time I'd swiveled back around in my chair to face him—I had a tendency to spin around in my office chair when I was having what I thought was a breakthrough—it was to find him studying me with the sort of look that a bitter entomologist reserves for a specimen of insect whose discovery a rival scientist has built a reputation on, an insect that the resentful entomologist is certain must actually be a small robot in disguise, a robot created by the rival to deceive the scientific community.

"This was a simile," said Ishmael, "that was—according to the translator's note—far more succinctly expressed in the original language, there being one compound noun for this type of insect."

Eyeing me with this withering look, the patient said, "*These* eyes, Doctor. *These* eyes," he said, pointing at his eyes, "were never operated upon. I'm talking about my actual eyes."

What he'd meant, he told me, were the eyes his eyes actually were, not the eyes his eyes were merely *saying* they were. Why, he asked me, would the eyes his eyes were merely *saying* they were have been operated on as well? Was it not enough that he had had to undergo involuntary eye surgery in real life, but that he'd have to have undergone eye surgery here as well? In this ill-portended attempt at escape?

"Alright," I said, forcing a smile. "Explain."

And that's when he told me about his *walks*, about how—despite being at least temporarily blind and almost entirely immobilized, if not by the actual spider webs he was tangled in then by his instinctive proclivity to avoid accumulating more—he'd learned that by repeating the words *I went for a little walk* over and over again in his head while imagining his legs actually moving, he could—sort of—walk again, albeit only in a manner of speaking. First he could only really grope blindly about the cave he was trapped in, but by gradually extending the language he was repeating in his head—I went for a little walk . . . I saw a little light . . . I went for a little walk—he'd managed to regain the use of his eyes, and eventually even to escape the cave for moments at a time. It was incredibly taxing, he said. He said I had no idea how taxing it was. The language in his head was only ever partially in his control. Every time he tried to say something, he'd invariably say something else, and his attempt to correct the mistake created a thousand unintended effects. This explained how he'd ended up here, he told me. It clearly wasn't by choice, he said, but because of a series of unfortunate compromises with forces beyond him that resulted in all his so-to-speak walks consistently leading him here.

"Here!" he said. "Of all places!" He said he actually still wasn't sure why he kept winding up in my waiting room. "Probably," he laughed bitterly, "it's because my parents are psychotherapists."

"Are they?" I asked. It was maybe the first straightforward fact about his actual life he'd revealed in over two years of treatment.

Moreover, this revelation was something of real value, something we could work with—something, in fact, that I was particularly adept to help him navigate, seeing as I, too, was the child of two psychotherapist parents.

"I'm kidding," he said—a slip of the tongue that disclosed that we were indeed nearing the crux of the matter—"I'm kidding," he'd said, his barely concealed unconsciousness clearly crying, "Help! I'm being a kid. You are my parent and I've become a kid again."

"I'm joking," he said. "You think the sort of creature I am even *has* parents? Much less that they, in any way, condition my . . ." he said. "G-god damn!" he screamed—which was the first time I'd heard him stutter, though there'd clearly, I'd already noted, been much evidence of childhood teasing.

"G-god damn!" he'd shouted again. But was I mistaken in perceiving, even in this apparent exclamation of irritation, an inkling of excitement, a faint suggestion that, though still adversaries, we were at least finally beginning to play the same game?

By this point we really were out of time. "Till next week?" I said.

"Till next week," he sneered.

"The next week," I said to my circle of men, "the patient arrived late."

He was late, but seemed unusually excited—"I've had an idea!" he said, spritzing the air with flecks of saliva.

"Have you?" I said, and he launched immediately into the following:

"Seeing," he said, "as I cannot seem to influence my walk in such a way as to end up in the waiting room of anyone readily able to actually help me, I've fallen," he said, as he took his seat on my couch, "on a possible solution. I read in a book I found recently in the gills of a giant mushroom growing out of a dead stingray washed ashore a rock-strewn beach in a dream I had the other night the following thesis: that in the case of delusion," he said, "treatment should, I quote, 'proceed no differently than to place itself first on the ground story of the delusion-structure and investigate it as thoroughly as possible.' Though the book was, I believe, concerned with the treatment of an actual person and not an imaginary one," he said, "and even though it was concerned with the treatment of a patient and not a therapist," he added, "I don't see why I can't put this method into practice in your case as well. That is to say, I must proceed by first placing myself on the ground story of your delusion-structure, to pretend to play the character your delusion has assigned me—a delusion that, correct me if I'm wrong, seems to consist in the idea that you're a real person, and so am I, and that I've come to you so that you might guide me out of the delusion *I'm* suffering under. By inhabiting your delusion, I can, according to the theory, gently draw you out of it. To that end, Doctor," he said, "I submit to your cure: rescue me from my delusion," he said, beaming teeth that were incongruous and stained as cigarette butts. "Rescue me from my delusion and restore me to my reason."

"Well, um," I said. "Okay."

"*But*," he said, "remember: to cure me of my delusion, you would be well advised, in turn, to enter the ground story of *my* delusion-structure, too," he said, "and to investigate it as thoroughly as possible. Only by proceeding in this manner will you free me from my delusion. And only by encouraging you to proceed in this fashion," he added, "will I be entering the ground story of *your* delusion-structure so as to free you from yours so that you might actually assist me in the way I require. Make sense?"

"And as for the assistance you require," I said to my patient, "you need help determining whether you were conversing with a nest of spiders or a part of your own mind?"

"Precisely," he said.

"But why?" I asked. "Why does it matter?"

"Because I need to know what sort of faith to place in what I was told by those spiders. I need to know if what I learned about *the book of webs* can be used."

"*The Book of Webs*?" I asked, taken aback. "You mean my first book?"

"Your what?" he said.

"My treatise on dreams," I said. "*The Book of Webs*."

"What?" he laughed. "No, no, no, no. No. No, of course," he said, and, as though to someone else, added, "of course *he* wrote *the book of webs*. No, not that *Book of Webs*," he said to me, waving his hand dismissively. "Of course not. The actual *book of webs*."

"Now this," I said with a smile to my circle of men, "was a most unanticipated development."

I reached back to the bookshelf behind me, took down a copy, and handed it to my client. "Keep it," I said.

"But this isn't *the book of webs*," he said, "it's not even called *the book of webs*," he added, showing me the cover. It bore, above the image of a ruined neoclassical capitol building with a large bat perched on the pinnacle of its dome, the title: *Invitations to Continue Breathing*.

"Open it," I said.

"My publicist's idea," I explained. "Every copy printed is disguised as another book. Every book," I said, gesturing to my seemingly boundless library, "every book in this office is, were you to peek inside, actually a copy of *The Book of Webs*, a book that, I assure you again, has no other author but myself."

"Okay, okay," he said and shoved the book rather ungently into the outsized pocket of his too-large wool coat, which he seemed to realize only now he'd forgotten to take off. He took the coat off, folded it across his lap, and said, "Fine. You're the author of

The Book of Webs, clearly a very intelligent, compassionate, and capable thinker and doctor, which is precisely why," he said with an alarmingly uncoordinated wink, "I've chosen you out of all the licensed professionals practicing psychotherapy in our great city to help divest me of the delusion that your book isn't the actual *book of webs* but a vacuous and, most likely, ideologically abhorrent decoy all the more devious and detestable for having appropriated the title of the very book destined to annihilate your book and all books like it from the face of the universe."

"Uh, . . . right," I said. "And since, um, what you've just termed your delusion is actually the case, at least insofar," I said, reciprocating his wink with my own, "as *I* see things, then what I'd really like to know is a bit more about the actual *book of webs*, the book," I said, beginning, or so I thought, to get the hang of this business of entering the ground story of his delusion-structure, "that my own book is but a vile mimic of."

"Well, not really a *mimic*," he said. "I'm not trying to say your book saw the actual book and decided to impersonate it. That wouldn't make any sense at all," he said with a laugh. "That would be like saying that a spider tailors its web to the proportions of its prey after having measured it, contemplated its behavior, studied its habits, analyzed its dreams. How silly," he said. "No, a spider is born a web weaver, and if we are to think of the web as a kind of negative portrait of its prey—designed with the exact specifications to capture the particular creature, woven in the places that creature cannot but desire to go—then the image with which the spider creates this portrait is deeply inherent to the spider itself, as much a part of the spider as its DNA, as its having eight limbs, as its hatching from an egg, and so on."

"Makes sense," I said.

"So," he said, "your book is not so much a mimic as, I'm guessing, a *predator* of the actual *book of webs*, and in that sense, I suppose, it isn't utterly without value, since by studying it one could perhaps learn something of the book it's attempting to consume.

But most likely not," he said. "Most likely, your book, sadly, is as ill-prepared for a confrontation with the actual *book of webs* as is anything else in this world. If the book is ever written—"

"The book isn't written?" I asked.

"Well, of course not," he said. "If the book were written, then why would we be having this conversation? No," he said, "if the book were written, then, obviously, this whole book we're in would be entirely unnecessary."

"What do you mean by *the book we're in*?" I asked him.

"Sorry," he replied. "By *book* I just mean the stream of language through which I'm attempting to escape the cave," he said, "the book in which it's necessary to explain to a psychotherapist what *the book of webs* is. If *the book of webs* were already published, this book would no longer be necessary because I would no longer be stuck in a cave, recovering from eye surgery, hunted by spiders, and so in. If *the book of webs* were already published, this book could be replaced with something much better, a book where—I don't know—we wouldn't need psychotherapists, because . . . because . . . because there wouldn't even be offices to go see them at," he was becoming excited again, stood up, and began to pace, "because there wouldn't even be any difference between offices and homes, between inside and . . ." he said and sat back down, "between private and public practices, between . . ."

"I couldn't but be a little charmed," I said to my circle of men, many of whom bared giddy grins behind their mustache hairs. "How somewhat charming my client's delusion was fast becoming, or at least the latent desires it both repressed and revealed! For clearly *the book of webs* he was hoping would restore reality—a desire his delusion twisted into *destroying* reality—was a substitute for the real *book of webs*, that is to say, my *Book of Webs*, which had become, of course, an almost comically legible symbol for me and my capacity to extricate him from his psychic entanglement."

This was just the boost of confidence I needed to take the leap he suggested, to enter fully into the ground story of his delusion-structure—which was a rather serious leap, given that I'd never been very good at lying or even playacting, and which thus required that I actually do my best to convince myself his delusion was true. I asked him to repeat the name of the book about delusions he'd referenced, and he reminded me that it wasn't an actual book but a book he found in a dream, and while I discreetly typed the sentence he'd quoted into an internet search on my phone—which search, indeed, yielded no results—he said something else that I, frankly, no longer recall.

"Uh huh, interesting," I said. "So tell me how it starts."

"How what starts," he said.

"*The book of webs*," I said, "the book the spider priestess was possibly telling you about. Tell me how it starts."

"I can't," he said. "I couldn't tell you how it starts even if I wanted to," he said. "No one could. Anyone who says they can," he said, "is lying. In truth, no one knows if it even *has* started. This, according to some, is part of the problem, part of why it doesn't exist yet: that there's no way to open it, that it's a book that cannot be opened."

"A book that cannot be opened . . ." I repeated thoughtfully, and my client said, "Yes, a book that cannot be opened. And a book that cannot be opened cannot be closed. A book that cannot be closed cannot be published. And a book that cannot be published cannot overturn the entire order of the universe."

There was nothing, he told me, he could tell me about how *the book of webs* began, but he could, or so he said, not only tell me about a certain fragment from it but also could recite verbatim this fragment, a fragment that he'd had the fortune to glimpse, as well as the foresight to memorize, a fragment that several of his collaborators had caused immeasurable damage to many priceless artifacts in order to procure from the throat of a mummified heretic on display at the Burlington Museum of Anthropophagy, a museum whose staff they'd had to painstakingly infiltrate over the course of many years—"but that's another story," he said. The mummy, he explained, had been an ancient predecessor of his sect—"a heretic," he said, "who had been living in disguise as the High Priest of the state religion's scribe," he said, this also being, however, he told me, another story—and she'd hidden clues in a canonical text, clues that centuries of research recovering a secret interpretative method consisting of intentionally misreading the text's ideograms had allowed members of his group to eventually decipher. Once they could read them, they learned of the heretic's final heroic act of swallowing a brief fragment of *the book of webs* just before her organs were surgically removed by the emperor's executioners. The fragment, said my client, he himself had glimpsed only once, and only for the briefest instant as it was incinerated before his eyes by enemy interrogators—the cruelest form of torture they could devise—"No!" he'd screamed as the ancient papyrus burned. "Disarticulate my body," he'd cried, "reify my soul," he'd yelled as he writhed against his fetters, "but don't destroy *the book of webs*!" But this was all pure theatrics, he told me, his agony a distraction designed to conceal his secret ecstasy, for, as the flames touched the ink, the ideograms—which until this moment had seemed, whether one read them according to the official *or* the insurrectionary hermeneutics, to have been taken from a rather uninspired pornographic text, thoroughly conventional save for the unusual role often accorded to participating spiders, an erotic text from which, moreover, most of the sex acts had been clumsily redacted—the ideograms transformed the moment the flames touched them, turned, just before the parchment blackened and disintegrated, into an altogether different text, one written, oddly enough, in my client's native tongue, a language of which he was the last extant speaker! The text thus revealed—and to no other eyes than to my client's, for the interrogators were busy watching his reaction and not the burning papyrus—the text thus revealed was so marvelous, so dangerous, subversive, disastrous, that there could be no question as to whether it belonged to *the book of webs*, no question as to whether it was apocryphal, another forgery, enemy propaganda in disguise, etcetera—"Even were one to suppose," shouted my client, "that it wasn't from *the book of webs*, it wouldn't have mattered in the slightest"—for the few sentences that were at that moment revealed to him contained everything—"Everything! No! even more!" he screamed—indeed even more than the much-portended text had been prophesied to contain. "If this wasn't from *the book of webs*," said my client, "then there'd no longer be any reason to continue waiting for *the book of webs* to reveal itself. If this wasn't *the book of webs* then *the book of webs* would never have been *the book of webs* to begin with! No," he said, "not in any meaningful sense. If this was not *the book of webs*, then I'd say, 'Fuck *the book of webs*!'" he cried with joy, for such was the revelation, he said, that he witnessed at the same instant the papyrus flared up in blinding flames and crumbled into a pile of ash smoldering at his interrogators' feet. Such was the power contained in just this brief passage he was able to read, this fragment of a fragment of a fragment . . . the few words he could glimpse of a shred of papyrus no doubt torn from a much longer tract and swallowed by an unflappable ancient heretic at the threshold of her death. "I immediately memorized it exactly," shouted my client, "using a powerful mnemonic technic I'd been tutored in by a necromantically reanimated photocopier, and I have waited until this precise moment for an opportunity to repeat what I alone have been fortunate enough to have read!"

"Well?" I said, and told him to tell me

What It Said.

"What what said?" said Ishmael, in his regular voice, rather than the one he'd adopted while repeating back to me what he was reading from Doctor Burlington's stolen manuscript.

"What?" I said.

"I said, 'What what said,'" he said. "You told me to tell you what it said," said Ishmael, "and so I was asking you what you meant by the word *it*."

"I didn't tell you to tell me what it said," I said. "Doctor Burlington did."

"Who?" he said.

"Doctor Burlington," I said. "The author of the manuscript you're reading."

"I'm reading?" he said.

There was no way Ishmael could be reading, not according to Ishmael. He couldn't even see his own hands, let alone any letters or pages!

"Yes, you can," I said. "Though just barely and only thanks to the faint light of a stick of incense burning. You remember the incense."

"Incense?" he said. "Are you out of your mind? The incense isn't still burning! It burned out ages ago."

"Oh right," I said. I had to admit that this would have been an awfully long time for one stick of incense to have been burning.

The incense had burned out a long time ago, and Ishmael had been plunged back into unfathomable darkness. Much as he wished to, he couldn't read another word. Much as he wanted to tell me, as well as to see for himself—"Both amount to the same thing," I reminded him, "since I'm a voice in your head," and he said, "Oh, that's right. I forgot that you'd died"—much as he wanted to keep reading what the Doctor's client said next, he couldn't even see his own hands as he waved them in front of his face, much less make out the tiny letters on the pages he held.

But this raised a question: If Ishmael wasn't still reading, then how come he was still hearing the voice in his head, the voice one hears in one's head while reading? Shouldn't I have fallen silent the moment the ember burned out?

"That's a good question," I said, and he said, "Thanks," and I said, "But tell me: What do you know from what you have read so far about what to do with good questions?"

Ishmael thought a moment, then answered, "A good question cannot be answered except by the person whose dream the current exploit, mission, or enterprise is an attempt to reenact."

"Exactly," I said. It was important to sense when he needed a little encouragement, little matter whether what he said was true or not, useful or not.

"In which case," he said, "it isn't you I should be asking but . . . ?"

"Yes?" I said.

"Ishmael!" he said.

"Right!" I said. "And since you're Ishmael . . ."

"I'm Ishmael?" said Ishmael.

"Yes," I said, "and since it was your dream that led you here, into the distant reaches of these caverns where you're reading this manuscript that this same dream instructed you to steal and to read . . . Since it was your dream, it's *you* you ought to be asking."

"But asking what?" he said. "I've forgotten the question."

I told him it had grown a bit hazy to me too, honestly, but I believed it was something about the book, believed that the question was something like: "What did Doctor Burlington's patient say he saw written in the transfigured hieroglyphics that simultaneously appeared and vanished as the papyrus burned?"

"That's what I said?" he said.

"Yes," I said. "That's definitely the question you asked. The question only you can answer."

"But how the hell should I know what the papyrus said?" he said.

"Because you read what it said," I said. "You read the Doctor's client's recapitulation of what the papyrus said right before the incense went out. Remember?"

If Ishmael didn't remember it this way, if he seemed to think that his reading had been interrupted right at the moment when the patient arrived at that point of reciting the memorized fragment, this was only because the light had gone out the moment he arrived at *rereading* what the patient had recited. The passage, I explained, had made such a strong impression on Ishmael—he'd sensed that it was the most, perhaps the only, valuable passage in the entire manuscript—he'd been so excited by what he'd read, that he'd decided to read it again before proceeding any further. But it was exactly as he returned to the beginning of this passage that the light from the incense was lost.

"Oh no!" he said.

"Yes," I said, "but don't worry too much." Though he could no longer actually read the passage, he could, I assured him, since he'd already read it once, repeat the basic outline of it back to me.

"In fact, to do so," I told him, "to repeat in your own words what you read without direct access to the text itself, may even be a particularly valuable practice," I suggested, "insofar as retention is concerned. And retention," I said, "is what's most important."

"True," he said.

"The page," he said, "like air, like thought," he said, "is a grave. *The book of webs* survives only on the tongues our tongues dream they are."

"Good," I said. "Tell me, in your own words, what you saw. Tell me what the patient recounted."

"But I can't," he laughed.

"Why not?" I asked.

"Because I never read it," he said.

"You *have*, Ishmael," I said. "We just went over this."

"No, no. I read what happened next in the manuscript," he said, "but what happened next wasn't the patient recounting what he saw. That isn't what was written," he said. "And one cannot read what hasn't been written, can one?"

It was neither the time nor the place to answer this, so I said, "Fine."

In the Part of the Book That Was Being Questioned,

the Doctor's client had been about to recite, for the first time ever, what he alone had seen flare up in the burning papyrus recuperated from the mummified heretic's throat when the Doctor interrupted him.

"Sorry," the Doctor said. "I'm actually going to have to stop you there. We're out of time for today. What say we put a bookmark in it and pick up fresh where we left off next time?"

Ishmael went quiet after he told me this, so I said, "Is that all?"

"That's what happened next," he said.

"That's what you found important enough to reread?" I said.

"Yeah," said Ishmael. "Well, that," he said, "but I guess also the fact that

The Book Was No Longer the Same Book."

By the time the Doctor was ready to take the so-to-speak *book-mark* out of it again—by the time, in other words, their next appointment began—the so-to-speak *book* he'd put that bookmark in seemed to have become an entirely different book altogether.

"What papyrus?" his client kept saying.

"The one you saw burning!" the Doctor kept insisting, but to no avail.

"Whether my client had genuinely forgotten what he'd said," the Doctor would later say to his circle of men, "or whether, as I would soon begin to suspect, he was merely playing dumb—in which case his apparent amnesia was a carefully calculated tactic he'd developed to keep the conversational terrain between us perpetually sloped to his advantage—in either case, he claimed to have no idea what I was talking about when I pressed him about what he'd claimed to have read of *the book of webs*. And when I replayed the major developments of our last session for him, concluding by alluding to the burning fragment on the shred of papyrus salvaged from the throat of a mummified heretic, he replied by asking if it was possible I'd maybe confused him for another of my clients."

Though the Doctor vehemently denied the accusation, he did discreetly reread the name on the folder that contained the notes he'd consulted before this session began. He had recently taken to checking his notes somewhat routinely to refresh his memory, his memory having grown, he wrote, admittedly somewhat suspect lately. He checked the name on the folder and said, "You are Ishmael, right?"

A volley of gasps ricocheted around the circumference of the circle of psychotherapists.

"But of course *Ishmael* wasn't my client's real name!" exclaimed the Doctor. "How low in your estimations must I have sunk," he said, "for you to think I would speak—much less write!—about a patient without using a pseudonym so as to preserve his anonymity! Of course, *Ishmael* wasn't my client's actual name!" he said, and the psychotherapists heaved sighs of relief and apologized to the Doctor for ever having even briefly doubted him, and the Doctor reminded them that he adhered, as they all knew, so faithfully to his exceptionally rigorous confidentiality agreement ("Nothing," his disciples were used to him declaiming, "is more essential to our success than our patients' assurance that their secrets won't end up in our books!") that he even went so far as to write pseudonyms on the aforementioned files wherein he organized his notes and often even shuffled up the pages inside one file with pages from another so as to ensure that if his office were ever invaded, the intruder would have no means of knowing whether the notes they'd stolen applied to one or to several different clients. It was a practice that, out of an abundance of caution, he'd adopted many years previously but that he nevertheless failed to take into account when he said, after reading the name on the file, "You are Ishmael, right?"

"Of course I am," said the client—a lie the Doctor wouldn't catch until after the session and whose motivation he'd never fully grasp—"but that doesn't change the fact that the events you remember happening during our last session definitely didn't."

Thinking his client was perhaps joking, the Doctor decided

to reprise a famous phrase he believed the client had referenced in their previous session and said: "It would seem that—like our moods—our *sessions* don't believe in each other either!" but, or so he told his disciples, his client neither nodded nor laughed but reached for his wool coat, which he'd dropped carelessly on the floor at the beginning of the session.

"Alright, alright!" said the Doctor. "Forgive an old man his faulty memory! Refresh me," he said. "Tell me what you remember happening, and we'll get back to where we left off."

"Fine," said Ishmael.

Here I had to interrupt Ishmael in his recounting of what he'd read in the Doctor's manuscript to make sure that it was just a coincidence that the client's name was also Ishmael. "*You* aren't the client that Doctor Burlington wrote this book about, right?" I asked.

"Right," said Ishmael. "Though I can see how you might have gotten confused. I was also a little lost when I got to this part of the manuscript, albeit for different reasons."

What had confused him, he confessed, was the fact that the Doctor—in telling his circle of men what his client told him had occurred at their last session, and what would thus get written down in his book—that the Doctor insisted on using the first-person pronoun, insisted on speaking as though from the perspective of his client.

"Why?" I asked.

"According to him," said Ishmael, "this was what he always did, that he'd long since determined that it was best to always use the first-person pronoun when telling a dream, it mattering not the slightest whether said dream was one's own or someone else's."

"A well-told dream is everybody's dream," the Doctor cited himself in a footnote as having written in *The Book of Webs*, "not because it contains any universal truth or meaning but because it bears within it a unique commandment meant solely for each person who hears it told, a commandment decipherable only to the person for whom the commandment is intended. Furthermore, if everyone in the world heard the dream properly recited, if everyone in the world correctly deciphered the encoded commandment meant exclusively for them, and if everyone successfully obeyed this commandment, it follows that the very order of the cosmos would be overturned."

When Doctor Burlington asked his patient to recount what had happened during their last session, Ishmael—"Me," said Ishmael, "the one reading"—had gotten a bit confused.

Because Ishmael—"Not me," Ishmael interrupted himself to tell me, "but the patient"—because Ishmael, the patient, claimed that he had spent most of their last session telling the Doctor his dream, and because this particular dream, according to Doctor Burlington, provided an absolutely essential insight into the source of his client's psychosis, and thus a crucial aspect of the central thesis of this book—"Which book?" I said, and he said, "The one I was reading"—because Ishmael's dream occupied a large portion of the ensuing pages, and because the Doctor had insisted on using the first-person pronoun when relating this dream, even though it was Ishmael, the patient, of course, that was speaking—because of all this, Ishmael—"Me again this time," said Ishmael—Ishmael had gotten a bit disoriented.

"You know a little disorientation isn't always a bad thing," I said.

"It's not?" he said.

"Not necessarily," I said. "I guess it depends on your orientation."

"That's true," said Ishmael. "It's not like being oriented was ever particularly satisfying. But, still," he admitted, "it can be a little frightening, you know? To be so unmoored like this, even knowing one's only ever been moored to sinking ships."

"You can't be moored to something better if you're never a little unmoored," I said.

"True," he said. "But I suppose I've been rather unmoored for a very long time. I suppose I'm a little impatient for that often-promised better mooring."

"That's good to know about yourself," I told him. "What say we call you Ishmael the Impatient?"

"Ishmael the Impatient?" he said.

"Yes," I said. "As opposed to Ishmael the Patient, the Doctor's client in the book you're reading."

"Oh," he said. "Yes, I like that. I think this distinction will help. While we're at it," he added, "I'm a little embarrassed to ask this after we've been talking for such a long time, but you know how I am with names—in one ear, out the other. Will you remind me your name?"

"Name?" I said. "I don't have one, remember? I'm the voice you hear in your head while you're reading."

"Oh, that's right," he said. "I guess it's a little strange that even though I'm not currently reading, you're able to respond to my present questions and concerns with insights that I, myself, do not possess, insights I might not even necessarily agree with, if I thought about them more carefully."

"It's not that strange," I replied. "I'm just repeating back to you things you once read."

"You can do that?" he asked.

"What else are books for?" I said. "Why else would people like Doctor Burlington write them?" I said. "Why else would the authorities encourage us to read them, if books didn't equip entities such as myself—a voice in your head—with the capacity to repeat certain instructive phrases and mimic instructive ways of phrasing, and to thus construct a kind of state-sponsored interlocutor within a subject's head?"

"Gosh," said Ishmael the Impatient. "I must have gotten my hands on some really illicit reading material at some point to have equipped you with the capacity to suggest all that."

"That's optimistic," I said.

"It is?" he said.

"Sure," I said. "It's assuming that it's to the state's disadvantage that you be made privy to a thought such as this."

"Oh," he said.

"Anyway," I said, "where were we?"

"I remember this time!" he said. "I was explaining how I'd gotten confused while reading and that it was on account of the fact that Doctor Burlington insisted on using first-person while telling Ishmael the Patient's dream. In fact," he said, "that's the other reason I decided to circle back and begin reading this part again," said Ishmael. He was hoping, he said, to get a better grasp on

Who Was Meant When the Book Said *I*.

"Our last session," said Ishmael, wrote Doctor Burlington in the manuscript Ishmael the Impatient had been reading before the incense burned out and made reading impossible, *"began with a dream."*

"The best sessions usually do," said the Doctor, a comment Ishmael ignored but which the circle of psychotherapists, when he was later recounting the session to them, appreciated, for they, too, had often witnessed this phenomenon, and in fact, one of them even interjected here to tell the assembly about a dream *he'd* had the night before, which, he thought, proved the Doctor's observation beyond a question of a doubt, a dream he then began to breathlessly recount, telling them that he'd dreamed he'd been standing in a field, up to his eyes in enormous green blades of grass, and that in the distance he heard the lapping of water and the whistle of wind and then the dull gong of a buoy bell tolling, and so he looked up and saw high above him two towering humanlike figures, giants so large they occluded the distant glowing word where the sun ought to have been—SUN, this glowing word had said—and here another psychotherapist interrupted the dream-teller to ask him if he'd managed to see the eyeballs of these two looming individuals, but the dream-teller answered no, that he hadn't, for there'd been so dense a fog in the air that the giants were but two murky silhouettes now wavering this way, now that, and then growing even larger as they stooped down toward him as though to get a closer look, and that this was when from behind him he heard a faint rustling, and so he spun around to see that in the fog behind him there seemed to be a strange tunnel, as though something had tunneled into the fog, forming a strange sort of vortex or funnel in the mist, a funnel he said he saw he was now standing at the very mouth of, a funnel he saw that narrowed away from him, turning and twisting between the huge blades of grass so that he could not see where the funnel led into, though he could tell that this was where the rustling sound had come from, and he said that when he saw that this was the case, he had a terrible feeling—but this part was very hard for him to put into words—he had a feeling that he was about to witness an event that had already happened, something that had finished occurring a long time ago but that wasn't, he said, for that reason, any less of an emergency than it would be if it were actually still emergent, were it still, he said, about to come, whatever it was, rushing up from the unseen curve in the funnel in the fog. And that was when the rustling went suddenly silent: the buoy bell tolled, a dog barked, and then—

"And then," Doctor Burlington interrupted, "you finished telling us your dream once I finished telling you my client's"—and this utterance, like many of the Doctor's, was actually a magical incantation, one that only incidentally sounded like ordinary speech and sufficed, in this instance, to transform the interrupting psychotherapist's tongue into a tongue-shaped stone, a rock that knocked innocuously a few times at the inside of the beak of the baby sparrow mask this psychotherapist so happened to be wearing.

The circle of men applauded. They had a great appreciation for magic.

After their applause died down, the Doctor said, "But where was I? Does anyone remember?" and another therapist reminded him that he'd been about to relate what Ishmael said had occurred at their previous session, that the patient had said it started with a dream.

"Ah, yes," said the Doctor, "as the best sessions so often do," and proceeded to tell his circle of men what Ishmael had said in its entirety, and he decided to adopt, as was his practice when recounting a dream—whether one's own or another's—the voice and perspective of the dreamer, a somewhat iconoclastic choice in this context considering most of what his patient said next wasn't, after all, technically—"at least allegedly," the Doctor said—a dream.

"But I thought you just said that the session began with a dream?" said one of the psychotherapists whose tongue still worked, the one in the robin mask.

"It did," he said, "but the dream my client began with, the dream he'd been having for months, was a dream that couldn't be dreamt. I was dreaming," he said, "an undreamable dream."

"You mean, *your client* was dreaming an undreamable dream?" said another therapist.

"Yes, of course," said the Doctor, "a dream that I—by which I mean my client—couldn't dream, a fever dream I kept having, a dream that kept keeping me awake, a dream that I'd had yet again the morning of our previous session. And because," said the Doctor, talking from the perspective and in the manner of his client, "because," he said, "I couldn't sleep, because—on account of

The Undreamable Dream—

I'd been waking for weeks at three or four in the morning from the same recurring nightmare: that the dream that I was trying to dream needed to be edited before it could be dreamed, and because there seemed to be no dream not, like this one, in need of this kind of revision, no image or narrative thread that wouldn't be almost instantly co-opted by this nightmare logic, becoming a dream about that dream needing editing—and because, I'd finally grown thoroughly exhausted of turning away from every emerging word, image, or thought like it was a trap that would lead irrevocably back to this unbearable responsibility to edit what could never be fixed—I finally got out of bed, flipped a coin that told me three times in a row to get on my bike, got on my bike, and rode to the beach. There I found a stone and said, 'Be everything I've held onto as myself that has prevented my light from shining,' and threw it with all my strength a surprisingly short distance into the bay. An icy winter sun was rising. I said, 'I want to be a pleasure to be around, I want to make people feel good.' I said, 'I want to feel good, I want to find pleasure in being,' and I rubbed my shoulder, which was sore from throwing. I started singing because I'd been told that my light came through my voice and figured that not wanting to be seen singing in public was one of the things in the stone I'd thrown into the bay. I sang, 'Toll, buoy bell, toll / tell all the boats in the fog where the shore ends and water begins to flow,' but then I spotted another figure on the beach and stopped singing. Foam was dissipating at the water's edge where small choppy waves fell over and over themselves. I passed through two rows of beams from a rotted dock like they were an aisle in a temple or a birth canal or the teeth of a large carnivorous whale, and I wondered if my ex had gone to the beach with her best friend yet and screamed, 'Fuck you, Ishmael! Fuck you!' into the crashing waves, and I wondered if I'd feel any better had my best friend taken me to the beach and encouraged me to scream that, substituting her name, of course, for my own; which was what, after all, would have made the oath any different from the ones I usually made there at the beach in the nightmare months since we'd decided to go our separate ways, to take a break, to break up. Break apart, really, break down. Breakfast, I thought next, naturally enough; there'd been a diner down the road . . . 'Hold on!' I heard a voice cry and turned to see it was the distant figure I'd seen earlier—they were rushing closer. And perhaps there was a deeply buried part of me that was still curious, a part that hadn't yet given up entirely on human closeness, touch, talking—a part of me that still wanted it all so badly that I stopped. I stopped and waited for the distant figure to catch up, to approach close enough to see he was a thin tall man, close enough now I could hear him say, 'I have,' panting, 'something,' regaining his breath, 'I need to show you.' And though he looked a little threateningly amphibious, skin clammy and glazed in the hazy predawn, I listened. 'Come with me,' he said. 'If you'd like,' and I wondered if he meant this as suggestively as I felt like taking it and said, 'Okay.' 'My name is Leroy,' he said, as he got on his bike. 'I'm Max,' I lied, as I got on mine. 'I know,' he said. 'I've read all your books.' 'I'm sorry,' I replied. 'That's okay,' said Leroy. 'We're just going to have to keep working, that's all,' and I decided that I liked him, that I maybe *would* sleep with him, but only if he were the one to suggest it, and I grew extremely nervous at the prospect. Leroy led the way. We went straight where I usually turned left to get back on the bike path back to town, and around the next bend something difficult to explain started happening: the best way I can put it is that the trees and the houses and cars passing by were like the dream images and thoughts that I had been unable not to turn away from instinctively while not sleeping before I'd gotten out of bed. I would glimpse whatever was passing by for only a moment before something fiercely oppositional inside me would jerk me away from the perception before it had made enough of an impression for me to be able to word it in my head, as though some desperate power inside me worried that remembering what I was seeing here was a trap my very life depended on my avoiding, as though, I thought, existence itself, like my dream, wasn't yet suitable for being experienced and would need to be edited first. 'We're getting close to the border!' shouted Leroy over his shoulder in the wind. 'The border?' I asked. 'To what?' 'What?' said Leroy. 'To what state?' I said. 'Connecticut?' 'Not a state,' said Leroy, 'a country.' 'I didn't know there was another country over here,' I said, laughing at what I presumed was a joke. 'I usually turn left back there,' I said, and Leroy said, 'Careful,' and I said, 'What?' but then heard . . . gunfire? I couldn't say. At that moment the rest of my senses joined in doing what my vision had already been doing for some time now, and nothing else of our border crossing remains for me to relate. A while after the border was behind us, I was able once more to word my experience to myself. Leroy was telling me about K . . . 'About what?' I asked him, and he repeated the name, but again only the first letter was audible. 'K . . . ,' he said, 'the name of this place.' He said it was a small autonomous region whose unusually mutable geography shifted so that its location changed endlessly in perfect coordination with some innocuous watermark or legend on whatever map one happened to be looking for it on so that it remained always hidden underneath. The tires of our bikes rolled over the black asphalt of a long narrow road that knifed like a scab through a field of golden grasses. He told me a little bit about the way of life in K . . . but much more about the way of death: that here, unlike elsewhere, there was actually only one way that people died. 'Spider webs,' he said. He said that though a citizen of K . . . might appear to die in any number of ways, what had, in every case, actually happened was that the spider webs they'd accidently come into contact with throughout their entire life had finally accumulated, thread by thread, into a resistant force that eventually outmatched even gravity, and then, finally, at the point where this person could no longer move at all, the spiders came to collect, morsel by morsel, what they'd captured. I said, 'What? That doesn't make any sense at all. The repercussions would be unfathomable. You're telling me that's the only way people die here?' and he said, 'Yeah,' and I said, 'Then what happens if someone loses a limb or their head, they just keep on living?' And Leroy explained how regeneration worked, about how the cells near a wound site could be coaxed into dedifferentiating, provided the appropriate nutrition. 'They become like stem cells again,' he said, 'cells capable of becoming any type. Axolotls do it all the time,' he said. 'We learned it from them.' So I said, 'And the webs just stick to you your whole life?'—'They're endlessly elastic,' he said, 'and strategically woven where you cannot but want to go,'—'And what about clothes? What about closing doors? What about—I'm sorry, Leroy, but this doesn't make a lick of sense.' But Leroy said that actually it made perfect sense and that the problem was that I was acting like we were still speaking English, and I said, 'Oh?' And Leroy said that, yes, whereas we were actually no longer speaking English, but the language of K . . . , which, he admitted, sounded almost exactly like English but actually called for an entirely different hermeneutics. I would get the hang of it eventually, he said, but I had to question my understanding of every word he used to say that I'd get the hang of it eventually, and thus I eventually realized I didn't have any idea what these words actually meant. Which was perhaps proof that I was beginning, already, maybe, to get the hang of it? 'I don't think so,' said Leroy. 'It'll make more sense once I show you the difference on paper. The words sound like English,' he said, 'but they look totally different. You'll see. I'll show you when we get to the Joint.' 'The Joint?' I said. But once we were seated backstage at a venue called the Joint, where the other members of Leroy's post-punk band sat tuning their instruments, and Leroy had shown me several pages of a book written in the language of K . . . alongside the same pages of the same book translated into English, I still couldn't tell the difference. 'Leroy,' I said, 'it looks just like English and sounds just like English and you say I'm not understanding but we're having a totally fluid conversation about how I'm not understanding and you said, "when we get to the Joint," and now we're at a venue called the Joint and . . .' 'Fuck,' said Leroy. 'This is going to be harder than I thought.' Then a voice boomed over the Joint's PA system: 'Beloved citizens of K . . . ,' it said, silencing the murmur of voices at the tables in the audience, 'it is our supreme pleasure to present this evening's entertainment: all the way from the borderland, as close to the border as you can get without actually crossing it, please give a warm welcome to the Stellionators!' 'Ishmael,' said Leroy in a hushed tone, as the thick velvet curtain that had hitherto isolated us from the rest of the bar began to split open. The audience applauded. 'Ishmael!' he hissed. 'I thought you thought my name was Max,' I said. 'We don't have time for this,' said Leroy. 'I brought you here because I was hoping you might consider being the lead singer of our band. I know it's short notice, but our previous lead singer was recently torn into a thousand little pieces by . . . But . . . Shit. The lyrics,' he said, pulling a thick stack of papers from his pocket. 'I forgot you wouldn't be able to read them.' The gap in the curtain was widening. One of the band's two drummers had already started to rap out a lightning-fast fill on the tom-tom. 'I guess you'll just have to fake it,' he said and handed me the lyrics. 'Well?' he said as he slung his guitar strap over his shoulder and the bassist broke out into a fast chaotic minor line in time with the tom-tom. 'You in?' I looked out at the audience the separating curtains splitting open was revealing. Then I looked down at the pages I was holding. There were about 420 of them. The first looked like the title page of a book. It said *the book of webs*. 'Well?' said Leroy. 'Are you in?' he asked, and I thought of that stone I'd thrown back at the beach, the one that was supposed to contain all my self-annulling bullshit, thought of who I'd always thought I'd end up being but felt further and further away from being with every passing day, and said, 'Sure. Okay. Yeah. I guess,' and reached up to catch the microphone as it descended by its cable

—Like a Spider by Its Thread—

from a trapdoor in the ceiling," said the Doctor, who was speaking from the perspective of his client, Ishmael, Ishmael the Patient, who, despite having the same name, was not the same person as Ishmael the Impatient, the one who had been reading of these events in the stolen manuscript by the amber light of a burning stick of incense, until that amber light burnt out.

"Is that about right?" I, who was the voice Ishmael the Impatient heard in his head while reading, asked him.

"Hmm, not quite," said Ishmael the Impatient.

"Which part's wrong?" I said.

"I mean, a lot of it," he said, "but especially the part about me not being Ishmael."

"The Ishmael in the book?" I said.

"What book?" he asked.

"The one you were reading," I said. "Doctor Burlington's book."

"Oh, yeah," he said. "I didn't think so at first, but as I read I became increasingly sure that this Ishmael was, in fact, me."

"You're sure?" I said.

"One hundred percent," he said. "At first I didn't think so because I thought I was Ishmael, but now I know I *was* Ishmael because I remembered that I'm actually Max."

He explained that when he'd read that Ishmael the Patient had told Leroy that his name was Max, he realized that Max was the actual name of the Doctor's patient—Max the Antsy, thus named for his notoriously ill-advised attempts to rush the process of various slowly unfurling prophesies that were thereby spoiled. Somehow the Doctor seemed to have decided that the best way to keep anyone from knowing his client's real name was to hide it in plain sight.

"Ishmael was actually Max!" he said. "And Max," he said, "is actually me! Or at least *was* me," he said, "at the time. Oh, and it should be *she* actually," said Max. "You should say, '*she* said,'" she said, "I mean, assuming that that this conversation is going to go into your book."

"*Book?*" I said, and Max told me that by *book* she simply meant the stream of thoughts I mediated my experience through, and I said, "Oh."

And then she explained that it had been her all along, *her* that Doctor Burlington had been telling his disciples about, *her* voice he'd been imitating, *her* perspective he'd been taking while recounting the night she sang lead vocals for the Stellionators. She hadn't realized until now, partly because she'd gotten so immersed in what she was reading that she'd forgotten who she was, but even more so because the Doctor had so systematically and thoroughly altered the details of what she'd told him that her own life had been made hardly recognizable. Her name and gender, she told me, were just the beginning of the Doctor's substitutions. Though it had grown increasingly obvious to her that the Doctor had based his case study entirely on her own sessions, it took her time to realize it because not a single true fact about her life had made it into his book unaltered.

"And by *true fact*," she said, "I just mean the carefully calculated lies we came up with. My name, my gender, what I did for a living, my dreams . . . 'True facts' is what we called them, and many were needed for me to have something to tell the Doctor during my sessions."

"*We?*" I said, and she said, "Sorry. By *we*, all I mean is myself in collaboration with whatever it is that arranges my dream life for me. We were working together—a temporary truce, which has since, of course, degenerated—collaborating to fashion these so-called true facts for me so that I'd have something to tell the Doctor, in order to keep him, for an hour a week, distracted from noticing what was occurring in his rug."

"Oh," I said, and she said, yeah, and explained how certain figures woven in the paisley rug beneath the Doctor's feet had recently developed personhood and were in the process of disentangling themselves from the rug's design in order to reweave themselves into the so-to-speak *rug* the Doctor called *reality*—"the immense rug," she said, "he sometimes went so far as calling *existence itself*"—an odious, totalitarian rug in which the paisley rug—from which she herself had only recently escaped, and whose various elements were organized in a much more egalitarian and joyful manner—was but an element of often-overlooked decor on either side of which a psychotherapist and his patient exchanged insults and imitations of empathy, the former for capital, the latter for a disingenuously promised right to abide unchallenged and function happily in a seductive nowhere on the other side of an ever-receding horizon the figures in *this* rug called *society*."

Yes, the true facts of her life, she said—devised with the help of her dream life—were for distracting the Doctor in order to bide time for her comrades still trapped in the paisley rug opportunity to escape, just as previous escapees had done for her, as part of their ongoing campaign to replace the structural relationship between her rug and the Doctor's (wherein the latter was contained within the former) with the inverse structural relationship (wherein what the Doctor called *reality* would be but floor decoration in the anarchic, acephalous rug she and her comrades had painstakingly unwoven themselves from, a rug in which no figure or motif dominated any other, wherein figures—human, floral, animal, abstract—communicated openly with one another, a rug one could contemplate for eternity without ever ceasing to discover new fascinating figures and relationships existing inside it).

———

"That makes sense," I said.

"Really?" said Max the Antsy.

"Sure," I said.

It was important to know what was worth actually attempting to make sense of and what could simply be ignored.

"In any case," she said, "that's why it took me so long to recognize myself in the Doctor's account of our sessions together. He'd so radically transformed all the lies that I told him that they were practically no longer lies."

When, for instance, the book had told about how Leroy had handed her a stack of lyrics that she was supposed to sing at a post-punk show, a stack of lyrics entitled *the book of webs*—"Oh good," I said, "I was going to ask about that"—what she'd *actually* told the Doctor—"Uh-oh," I said—was that Leroy had given her a political pamphlet called *On the Origin of the Stellionators*, and they weren't, of course, at a post-punk concert, she laughed, but at

An Ecoterrorist Conference.

"Excuse me," said Max the Antsy at the luncheon held just before delegates from each terrorist cell were scheduled to take turns delivering their slideshow presentations.

"What was that?" said the man in the axolotl mask who sat across from her.

"I'd said, *Excuse me*!" Max shouted over a plate of grilled oysters that a seagull, who was part of an interspecies catering company, had just placed on the long table Max and Leroy were sitting on opposite sides of. "You're Leroy, right?" she said.

"I suppose you could say that," he said, somewhat uncertainly.

"With the Stellionators?" she said.

"That sounds right," he said.

"Good," she said. "I wanted to ask you something. I've been asked to facilitate the next round of presentations, and since I'm thus going to be the one to introduce you in a moment—and, as your group likes to keep things pretty hush-hush, and in consequence there's virtually nothing anyone can say with any certainty about either your accomplishments or even your goals, and—well, seeing as I think we can trust the folks assembled here, I was wondering if there wasn't maybe a fact or two you could tell me, just so that I can give you a proper introduction."

"It was an embarrassing question to ask," Max told me, and so when she heard a peel of laughter come from under Leroy's mask, she reddened under her own.

"An aquatic frog head," she said.

"What?" I said.

"My mask," she said. "It was an aquatic frog head."

"Oh," I said.

"I'm aware of the irony," Max told Leroy. "It's not like I relish being tasked with introducing a terrorist cell whose principal target is—according to the rumors, at least—the very concept of *introductions*. Nevertheless—"

"*Introductions?*" I interrupted her to ask.

"Yes," she said. "The Stellionators hated nothing more than introductions. According to the rumors at least."

Leroy's band—or so, at least, it was believed at the time—was organized around the core belief, Max told me, that the concept of *introductions*—the idea that anything should ever need to be introduced to anything else—was the foundation of all that had gone wrong between the introduction-obsessed Burlingtonians and everything else in the universe—"Eradicate *introductions* from our vocabulary," Leroy was said to often repeat, "and you'll end the climate catastrophe"—which, of course, made no sense, at least not to Max. But Leroy would tell those who challenged the logic that it didn't make sense only because they were still speaking in a language thoroughly infected with *introductions* and all its cancerous derivatives.

"Once our language is healed," Leroy contended, "you'll see what I mean."

"Anyway," said Max, "that's what people were saying—who knows if any of it was true. But it made for a pretty intimidating task," she said, "introducing him at an ecoterrorism conference I'd helped organize—intimidating, not to mention, a bit humiliating when he burst into laughter."

"Oh, but I wasn't laughing at you," said Leroy, "but at this," and he showed her how there was a tiny red crab boiled to death inside his oyster shell. "See?" he said, and laughed and laughed. "I'm so sorry," he said as he reached under his mask to wipe a tear away, "but this does *not* bode well for our enemies.

"As for the introduction," he added, "just read this," and he handed her a pamphlet called

On the Origin of the Stellionators.

The pamphlet began at a historical reenactment theme park wherein the pamphlet's anonymous author claimed to have been born and to have lived, up until a certain point, a pleasurable and idyllic existence among the theme park's other inhabitants.

"But everything changed," said Max, "the day you turned thirty."

"The day *I* turned thirty?" I said, and she said, "Well, the voice I heard in my head while reading the pamphlet. That was still technically you at that point, wasn't it?" she asked, and I said I supposed it would've been.

The story of the Stellionators began, she began again, in the Real World—"That was the name of the historical reenactment theme park," she explained—although technically the story began at the precise moment the Real World ceased to be the Real World, the fateful day the park closed and a construction crew came and tore down the surrounding fences. This was the day that the theme park ceased to be a theme park and became a newly reallocated neighborhood within a vast empire called Burlington. It was also the day that I (the pamphlet's author), first learned of Burlington, first learned that the Real World wasn't the real world but a historical reenactment theme park, first learned that I hadn't been living my own life but reenacting someone else's. Until this point, no one had ever told us, the reenactors, that we were reenactors.

It was the day I turned thirty. The reenactment's administrative staff, who we'd previously known only as our psychotherapists, gathered us together at our commune's agora—I assumed it was for a surprise birthday party—and told us the truth.

They said, "The autonomous zone called K . . . is not actually an autonomous zone but, rather, the central attraction of a historical reenactment theme park called the Real World located in downtown Burlington, an exhibit designed to give our patrons an opportunity to observe how historical beings such as yourselves might have behaved in their natural habitat. Sorry we didn't tell you before. Surely you can see why we couldn't—it's not like the people whose lives you've been reenacting believed that *they* lived in a historical reenactment. Anyway, attendance at the park has been steadily declining for many years, and our bosses can no longer afford the upkeep. You can, if you like, continue to live in your quote-unquote *houses* with your quote-unquote *families*, but you'll have to pay rent to your new landlords now, the various Burlingtonian businessmen who've purchased the property. Also, you'll have to provide for your own food, electricity, gas, wi-fi, etcetera, and also, we can no longer guarantee that members of your family won't try to kill you while you sleep. For the employees that you've known as your guardian angels who were previously paid to keep watch over you will need, like all the rest of us, to find new jobs now. Well, that about sums it up. Good luck out there, kids."

Then they tore down the surrounding walls and fences, and what we, the reenactors, had all known as a mysterious intermediary boundary of nonbeing we had all grown up calling *the borderland* ceased distorting what we had all grown up calling *reality* the nearer that one came to it. Now one of us could walk right up to the edge of what we'd grown up calling *the Real World* and not suddenly wake up days later from restless dreams back in the comfort one's own bed.

No, now when we walked right up to the edge of it, there where only broken cinder blocks and bent rebar remained of what must have once been the walls that enclosed the park, we saw on the other side of it something called Burlington, and it extended out endlessly, nauseatingly in front of us, and there was no one but ourselves and one another to bear the weight of us as we tried and failed to faint, no one but ourselves to convey our bodies back to our beds, and so we stood there for a long while and faced the awesome weight alone, longing only to vanish and awake later, our heads smothered under heavy down comforters.

It never happened. Instead, frighteningly lucid, painfully conscious, nearly sober by this point, we walked back along the black scab of path that led to our houses and put ourselves to bed and awoke soon after angrily hungry, our jars of peanut butter–filled pretzels mysteriously unreplenished. What even was night, we asked ourselves, if it no longer meant the replenishing of our peanut butter–filled pretzel jars?

Then the landlords appeared.

They came scrambling over the cinder blocks in ballooned-out, sweat-stained, pink and yellow button-ups, yelling something about it being April First.

"Of course it's April First!" we said, for we'd not yet learned that according to the corrupt Burlingtonian calendar, April First happened only once per year, a year that was almost exclusively comprising days other than April First. So we said, "Happy April First!" and prepared to perform our assigned roles from the new day's randomly chosen passage from our holy book, a book on which we'd modeled our cosmology, and thus our calendar.

But the landlords had no interest in witnessing, much less participating in, the ancient rites we'd grown up reenacting daily. They said, "There's only one first-day-of-the-month ritual we care about. Guess which," and though the quivering fat of their faces shook in the fish-eyes of our peepholes when our doors slammed and our bolts snapped, they came quickly around to the other sides of our homes, the ones where our houses had no walls, the sides where our psychotherapists used to come to deliver our groceries and dream analyses. The landlords stepped right into our living rooms, held out their copiously lotioned hands, and said, "Don't play dumb with us."

"Fine," we said and read their palms.

"Sorry to say, you will end up completely immobilized by spider webs and eaten by spiders long before you ever find true love or even once feel satisfied sexually! Your excretions will never become secretions, not even from the perspective of other creatures in your ecosystem. Phenological asynchrony will ensure that all your so-to-speak *blossoms* bloom after your so-to-speak *bees* have already starved, and you will be divided in this manner from everything you might otherwise have experienced deeply edifying intimate encounters with, including important parts of your own bodies. Your every utterance and gesture will produce the precise inverse understanding of what you intended that gesture to convey, and you will contribute unwittingly and disproportionately to your own radical joylessness at the hands of your own degradation of the environment, a collective body of which you will never discover you are actually an integral part and not just an invading plunderer. And in this manner your relentless days will convey you as though on an exitless airport's moving walkway of manicured lawns through Daylight Savings Day after Daylight Savings Day, every single day of your joyless lives another Daylight Savings Day," we said, "springing back," we hissed, "falling forward, springing back, falling forward . . ."

The landlords withdrew, and we celebrated our victory with a stirring round of our favorite sport, a noble and primeval game called You Can Be Anything.

But the landlords returned before we'd even finished

pretending to be ourselves, much less something better, and they came with trucks and boxes and less atrocious looking people and used them to teach us—who'd never really heard the term *job* before—what a job was.

"Look," the landlords said to us, and handed the other people pieces of metal and paper, and said, "This is how it works," and told the people to whom they'd given the money what to do, and the people went—some with apologetic looks on their faces, others avoiding eye contact entirely—into our houses and disassembled our furniture and packed up our books and scattered our rock collections and put all our stuff in their trucks and drove those trucks away.

"Next time," the landlords said. "Next time, next month, we want money. You get jobs, make money, and then you give us that money. This is called *rent*."

Then they laughed and laughed until one of them stopped laughing and hushed the others and said, "You know what? Who wants a job? Any of you puppets want a job?"—*Puppets* was a derogatory term, we'd soon learn, for people who didn't know they were or once had been reenactors—"Tell you what. If you want a job, I'll give you a job. What do you say? Any of you puppets want a job?"

I raised my hand. I raised my hand because raising one's hand in K . . . , raising one's hand in *our* zone's temporary autonomous language, had always signified the curse, "May a cockroach nest in your ear while you are sleeping." But apparently this was not what raising one's hand signified in Burlington, for the very next week I was dressed in a suit and shined shoes and a shirt with no holes in it but plenty of buttons—buttons, moreover, that I was sadistically required to keep fastened at all times—and I was manning the front desk of a new boutique hotel called the Aviary.

"How chic!" said the guests when they entered the opulent, high-ceilinged lobby, shouting, "What was this building before it was a hotel?"

"An aviary," I'd have to say, and even though the hotel was located in the Actual Real World, which was the new name for the now blossoming district in downtown Burlington where the park had been, I was the only puppet who worked there and therefore felt deeply alienated from my colleagues who commuted in from other parts of Burlington and were used to having a job.

"*I've* had a job!" I told them, but they said that the jobs I'd had didn't count, because I never actually had to do any work.

So I said, "What's work?"

They said, "Well, it's certainly not sitting at a coffee shop for a few hours every day, writing your dreams down so that visitors to a theme park could see how a writer used to behave."

But the work we were doing now at the hotel where the aviary used to be didn't strike me as radically different. There was a computer rather than my dream journal, and I was writing down other peoples' names and addresses and credit card information rather than my dreams.

They'd call and ask for reservations, and I'd say, "Speaking!" And then they'd tell me their names, which I'd write down on the computer, and a week or two later they'd show up and ask me if the neighborhood was dangerous.

"Oh, yes," I'd tell them. "There are still enough predators here to keep the grasslands from being overgrazed," and then I'd be reprimanded by my boss, who was watching the transaction occur on security video camera footage blown up huge on a flatscreen TV that dominated one wall of his enormous office.

I got to know this screen quite well, incidentally, because I'd often sneak into the boss's office after he'd left for the day in order to line the pockets of my blazer with handfuls of the mixed nuts he kept in a tub on his desk. We still hadn't discovered how to acquire groceries ourselves, and my family was starving.

The mixed nuts endeared me to my family for only a little longer, however, before they decided—declaring that the family was a construct designed by our psychotherapists to keep us convincingly performing historical humanness—to dissolve our family and go separate ways.

That the other members of my family almost immediately formed a post-punk band together without me was a blow softened only by the fact that now the nuts I'd stolen from my boss were all mine.

But now I was to learn the logic behind the famous saying, "Mixed nuts can't heal broken hearts."

I ate too many and got a stomachache and sat at the front desk of the Aviary, groaning. My coworker asked what was wrong with me, and I told her, and she said that I should take a sick day.

I said, "What's a sick day?"

"You don't even know what a sick day is?" she said. "Well I'm about to rock your world, puppet-man."

I took a sick day. I took all my sick days. I took every single one at once, one after another, till there were none left. Let those whose worlds haven't ended on their birthdays keep their sick days for a rainy day, I said to myself. I was done planning for the future. From here on out it was now or never. I took each sick day to visit the reservoir by the waste treatment center just on the other side of the old borderland and skip stones. I'd always been good at skipping stones, but I wasn't used to not hearing any applause or calls of encouragement when my stones skipped or sunk. I'd always thought such appreciation and encouragement was a part of the general fabric of existence, but now I knew the truth: in this cruel world called Burlington, a person could skip a stone across an entire reservoir and never hear a single compliment or gasp of awe for their having done so.

Still, if we puppets had it bad, the theme park's other inhabitants had it even worse. Or so I was apprised on my tenth and final sick day by a certain axolotl that came out of the reservoir and introduced himself to me as Leroy.

"The Real World," Leroy told me, "was a reenactment of a historical era that never existed. The Real World offered its patrons a parochial and self-congratulatory fiction about reality that it turns out never existed and certainly doesn't exist now. The only reason you and I are able to communicate like this, for example, is thanks to the artificial conditions maintained in our hermetic environment, which forced us to inhabit the same, so to speak, *level of creation*—to borrow a phrase from a poem I once read on a billboard above a dental implants office in a dream I had: *On the level of creation the pupils are giant breasts, / The world is an infant to whom the eyes give suck.* We've simply *had* to speak to each other," he continued, "because we've always had to, because there was no other option, because we've depended on our relationships to survive and procreate, live and die, dream and play. Whereas in Burlington as a whole, as I have been informed by some of the less suspicious local salamanders in this reservoir, human beings are almost entirely dissociated from the other beings comprising their habitat. They think of themselves as inhabiting some other, *higher* level of creation and are convinced that they can't understand us and that we can't understand them, most likely as some multigenerational ploy to keep themselves from feeling guilty for wearing us as clothing or swallowing us in their sleep."

"What's wrong with wearing us as clothing?" I asked.

"They've been seduced into espousing a dangerous ideology that demands they do unto others as they would have others do unto themselves lest they be punished by some managerial despot they call *God.*"

"Like g-god?" I said.

"Exactly," said Leroy, "but without the stutter. And the only way these people can avoid going astray of God's perverse strictures is to radically redefine what counts as the sort of thing unto which one has to do as one would have that thing do unto oneself—so that only people just like them fit the bill. Oddly enough, God doesn't seem to have any problem with this, and that's why they pretend they don't know how to converse with birds or their food or their furniture . . ."

Eventually, I stopped listening. I was thinking instead about my boss and work and credit card information and rent, and I guess what the axolotl was droning on about all made good, practical sort of sense to me, so when it came up, I decided to accept his invitation to join the interspecies militia he'd formed to wage war on Burlington in the hopes of establishing an ever-mutating series of radically egalitarian associations modeled on the sort of systems of self-regulating order and disorder we'd had back when the Real World still existed. Yes, I agreed to do my part to topple the Burlingtonian empire, in other words, and to replace it with a series of temporary autonomous theme parks. And we decided to call our militia the Stellionators, a name we chose by turning to a random page in an immense, outdated dictionary we found gripped in the clutch of a human corpse that on my last and final sick day washed ashore the bank of the reservoir.

I closed my eyes, flipped through the pages, Leroy yelled, "Stop!" and put his finger down, and where it rested, the dictionary said:

stel.lion.ate (stel′ye nit, -nat′), n. *Civil Law, Scots Law.* any crime of unspecified class that involves fraud, esp. one that involves the selling of the same property to different people. [1615–25;

< L *stellionatus* deceit, underhandedness, equiv. to *stellion-* (s. of *stellio*) lizard, crafty person + *atus* -ATE].

"Well, it's certainly a mouthful," said Leroy. "I'm sure we'll want to change it eventually, but I suppose it's good enough for now."

"Great," I said. "Here's to being good enough for now!" and held my glass of iced green tea up to Leroy's.

"To the Stellionators," he said, and we clinked our glasses and drank and—because the tap water we'd steeped our green tea in was so potently alcoholic; thank g-god at least that had remained unchanged from the good old theme park days—we both passed, almost instantly, out.

I woke up a while later and said, "So what's next?"

The axolotl said what we needed next was to attract more members to join our army. But I was shocked to find that he'd said this using a second mouth smiling where his right eye should have been.

He explained that he'd awoken a few minutes before me and was already in the midst of practicing dedifferentiating certain of his cells. As an axolotl, he'd been born able to instinctively dedifferentiate his cells at a wound site, turning specialized cells back into stem cells, in order to regrow lost limbs, tails, and so on. When, recently, a Burlingtonian child caught him in a net and tore his left leg off, Leroy began to speculate about potential applications of this biological technology to guerrilla warfare. Though his initial experiments had necessitated self-inflected injuries, he soon realized that, given the ubiquitous, systemic injustices of the Burlingtonian empire, pretty much anything could be considered a wound site. It wasn't long before he could dedifferentiate any cell in his body, and not long after this that he began to experiment with the cellular *re*differentiation process. Soon, he theorized, he might even be able to teach the tactic to non-axolotl members of the Stellionators.

Then his second mouth turned back into his right eye, and he said, with his original mouth, "Anyway, yeah. We need more members."

"Right," I said. "More members."

"Wait a second!" said Leroy. "You said you were pretending to be a writer, weren't you?" he said, "before the park closed? I wonder if there's any potential militant revolutionary applications for *that*?"

"I doubt it," I said.

"No, no," he replied. "Hear me out! What if you could write something we could pass around to potential initiates? A text that we could use to disseminate our hatred of Burlington and our love for one another? Something that would instruct non-puppets in how to understand our language and to educate the masses in our organizational principles?"

"We have organizational principles?" I said.

"Well, not yet," he said. "Maybe you can come up with something in your manifesto."

"My manifesto?" I said.

"Yes," he said. "That's how we'll convince people to turn against Burlington and enlist in our militia!"

"Um . . ." I said. "Oh boy. Well, it sounds nice, Leroy. It really does. But, hmm, to tell you truth, I was really more of a dream journalist than a writer. Yeah, honestly, I've never really written anything that wasn't something I'd just dreamed."

"That's okay," said Leroy. "Write down what you dreamt while you were passed out just now. We'll sort it all out later."

And that, according to what Max the Antsy read in the pamphlet at the ecoterrorism conference, was when the pamphlet's anonymous author claimed to have begun composing what would eventually become the Stellionator's Manifesto.

The Stellionators' Manifesto

was initially condemned for being aggressively unreadable. Nevertheless, this manifesto, the manifesto that got written by the bank of the reservoir, eventually proved to be the most formidable weapon against the Burlingtonian empire. It was a text whose every word was like a bullet shattering a bone in the ribcage imprisoning the subversive agent pounding inside the chests of our enemies, whose every sentence was like the bioluminescent meat with which anglerfish fashion their traps for shrimp, a text whose paragraph breaks broke into malls, whose indents rewilded lawns, whose very font made all optometry impossible, and whose margins sowed monocropped fields with sprouting teeth. It was a text whose every em dash was a splinter stemming the flow of cerebrospinal fluid stuttering through the meninges of enemy spines and yet simultaneously a rung in a ladder that led to a rooftop where those who were thus converted by the manifesto—which was to say everyone who ever read it, which was also to say, eventually, everyone in the entire universe—could sit down and watch sunsets explode through the mushroom clouds billowing up where Burlington used to be.

"And upon this rooftop," concluded Max the Antsy, "oh, how we would sit and kiss in this mushroom cloud sunset," she said, "taking breaks from our kissing only to snack on perennially warm slices of kabocha squash, crisp kabocha squash slices that were this book's commas, roasted to perfection," she said, "over the open flames that were this book's use of italics. I'm speaking, of course," she said, "of *the book of webs*."

"Good," I said. "Do you remember how it went?"

"How could I possibly forget?" she said, and I said, "Good," and she said, "Yeah, I mean is that even possible? To forget what you haven't even read yet?"

The Next Chapter,

explained Max, was the chapter wherein the Doctor would recount what his patient told him got written by the bank of the reservoir. If I wanted to know what that manifesto said, she said, I'd have to wait until she was reading the next chapter in the Doctor's stolen manuscript. In the chapter she was currently reading—"Oh, you're reading the manuscript again?" I interrupted her to ask.

"Well, obviously!" she said.

"So you can see?" I said.

"Black lines on a white background," she said, matter-of-factly.

"Great," I said.

"Yep," she said. "That's how I know that the Doctor doesn't really get into what the manifesto said until the next chapter. In this chapter," she said, "when I read this chapter," she said, "I hear you, the voice in my head impersonating Doctor Burlington, recounting how you told your patient, Ishmael, that this seemed like a good stopping place."

"*This?*" said the patient. "You want me to put a bookmark here?" he said. Then he declared that if I, his so-called therapist, made him put a bookmark in it now, there was no way that he'd be able to remember what he'd been talking about next time, and *this*, he said, *this* part he was trying to get to—the thing that got written by the bank of the reservoir—was the most important part, maybe the *only* important part. It was, in fact, the entire reason he needed therapy in the first place.

"Really?" I said, because even though the session ought to have ended five minutes earlier—even though there was already the next-scheduled patient waiting in my waiting room—I couldn't but feel flattered—yes, flattered, even though my own name had been appropriated to designate an oppressive totalitarian regime—I couldn't but feel flattered that my own book, the title at least, had appeared in the delusive nonsense this young man had spewed and was, furthermore, deemed its most important part. I was so flattered that I couldn't resist asking, "*The book of webs* is the reason you need therapy?"

And he said, "*The book of* what?"

"*The book of webs*," I repeated, "the manifesto that the author of the pamphlet wrote by the reservoir."

"But I never said *I* wrote *the book of webs*!" my patient replied.

"I never suggested *you* wrote it," I said. "I said *the author of the pamphlet*!"

"But I *am* the author of the pamphlet," said Ishmael, and I said, "What?" and he explained that since it had been in his dream that he read the pamphlet, wouldn't it be safe to say that he was its author? And since I didn't have enough time to answer this question adequately—had he actually read my book through to its conclusion I wouldn't have had to—I merely nodded and then added, "But wait, *dream*? I thought you said what you were telling me *wasn't* a dream," and he said, "Right."

Though everything he'd told me, he said—his not knowing how to introduce Leroy, Leroy giving him the pamphlet to read, his having read the pamphlet, and so on—though it had all actually occurred, it had occurred in a guerrilla reenactment that had been *based* on a dream that he'd had.

"Oh, that makes sense," I said, not because it made sense, but because I desperately needed to find a way to wrap things up. As I said, my next patient was waiting in my waiting room.

"I wrote the pamphlet," said Ishmael, "because someone had to—it was an important prop in the reenactment of the ecoterrorism convention dream. Not so important that I actually had to write the whole thing of course. Mostly scribbles, honestly. As for *the book of webs*," he said, "there was no way I would *ever* have said that *I* wrote *the book of webs*. The gall," he said, "to claim to have written *the book of webs*!" He laughed. "The hubris," he said, "to even claim to have written a book! The impudence to claim to have written anything!" he shouted.

No, if I'd heard him say otherwise, he told me, it must've been because I wasn't listening again—"I'm paying you, you know," he said, "to listen to me. Of course, I didn't write *the book of webs*," he said. "Why, I didn't even write the pamphlet!"

"But I thought you just told me you *did* write the pamphlet!" I said, and he said, "Oops, yeah, I meant the manifesto. Sorry. I wrote the pamphlet, just not the manifesto mentioned in the pamphlet. I'll admit that—that I wrote the pamphlet, the pamphlet that Leroy had me read at the ecoterrorism conference. But again, it was mostly just squiggles."

"Sorry, sorry," I interrupted Max's reading of the Doctor's manuscript to ask, "it probably doesn't matter much, but I thought you said that in the Doctor's manuscript the ecoterrorism conference had been changed into a punk show and that the pamphlet Leroy gave you had been changed into a stack of lyrics, just as you had been changed from a woman named Max the Antsy into a man named Ishmael the Patient to protect your anonymity."

"If I needed help protecting my anonymity," she scoffed, "would you really have to ask a question like that?" and I had to admit that I probably wouldn't have had to.

Ishmael, she'd realized, wasn't actually her in disguise, not any more than the punk show was the ecoterrorism conference in disguise. If Ishmael's story happened to coincide in a few key details with her own, it diverged in many more. And what coincidences there were, she said, were far better explained by the fact that they once knew each other than that they were the same person, which would be kind of absurd.

As a matter of fact, she said, they'd actually dated for a bit. "He was actually pretty good at sex," she said, "which would be hard to believe given his characterization in the book. Then again," she said, "we all were. Though *good at sex*?" she laughed. "What do I even mean by that? We knew how to enjoy ourselves and were good at taking pointers and had an incredibly inclusive definition of what counted as sex and were never in a rush to get back to whatever awful thing we were doing when we weren't having sex. Sex," she said. "Mm. It was one of the few things we enjoyed about the world. The world, I mean, before we destroyed it. Anyway," she said. "I should probably get back to reading this fucking g-godawful book, wouldn't you say," and I said that unfortunately I would, and she said, "Would what?" and I said, "Say."

"Wait, what was I just talking about?" said Ishmael.

"The most important thing, apparently," I said. "The manifesto that would become *the book of webs* that was written by the front desk agent in the pamphlet you were given to read in the ecoterrorism convention dream you were reenacting. How's that for listening," I said, still a little sore from his earlier remark about my listening skills.

"Not bad," he said, but added that it was kind of a stretch to say that what got written on the bank of the reservoir would become the manifesto, let alone that the manifesto would become *the book of webs*, and when I reminded him both of the fact that we were really and truly out of time for today and also that *he'd* been the one to tell me those things, he replied that this was only because I kept cutting him off with my inane and pointless interrogation, and if I would just give him one more minute of my precious fucking time, he'd clear this all up and leave.

"Trust me," he said. "I'm at least as desperate for this chapter to end as you are."

"Chapter?" I said, and he said, "I meant *session.*"

When, in the one passage in the pamphlet needed for the dream reenactment that Ishmael couldn't get away with not actually writing, Leroy the axolotl had suggested that the front desk agent—seeing as she used to be a writer—write the manifesto, and when the front desk agent replied that she hadn't really been a writer so much as a dream journalist, and when Leroy then told her to just write whatever dreams she'd just had while they'd been blacked out from the tokay they'd toasted with—"You mean the iced green tea?" I asked, and Ishmael said that he was pretty sure he'd said tokay, but whatever—when Leroy had suggested the front desk agent just write down whatever she remembered of the dreams she'd just had, she had to confess that she couldn't really remember any.

"Truth be told, Leroy," she said, "I haven't been sleeping very well lately," and she told him that ever since the puppet show was shut down—"You mean the historical reenactment?" I said, and Ishmael said, of course, but that the historical reenactment *was* a puppet show—ever since the puppet show had been shut down, she, the front desk agent, had been suffering from a lot of anxiety, and it had affected her sleep. The only dream she seemed capable of having, she continued, was this same terrible dream: a dream that the dream itself needed to be edited before it was worth having. "Every time I start dreaming," she said, "the dream starts doing this, and I wake myself up, but only to fall right back asleep and into the same completely indescribable—"

"Alright," said Leroy. "I get it. Look, I don't know what to tell you. You're the writer, not me. Why don't you just write the first thing that comes into your head."

"Okay," she said, "yeah, that sounds doable." But that's when she realized that there was nothing in her head.

"Then write about that," said the axolotl.

So, she did, and though it was hard at first to start—"*Impossible*, in fact," said Ishmael—it was soon just as hard to stop—"I believe it," I said, "and speaking of stopping," I added, "we really do need to wind down . . ."—but Ishmael went on uninterrupted telling me that though it had been impossible to start, soon the language was pouring out of the front desk agent like an excretion, an excretion she seemed to have an almost infinite supply of, an excretion she was trying to turn into a secretion, "just as," said Ishmael, "I've read that spiders had done with their silk: a substance that once spilled uncontrollably out of their bodies but which they eventually learned how to live and play and hunt with, a waste material they harnessed into the very stuff with which they now fashion the very paths they walk on and weave into a navigable, intelligible medium between themselves and others, their own bodies and their worlds, a material so abundant, so potent that just a minute fraction of all the spider silk in the world accounts for the mortality of the entire human species!" he said.

Just like spider silk, he continued, the writing poured out of the front desk agent—"poured for almost an entire day!" he said—and by the time she'd written as much as she thought was humanly possible in a single sitting and had stopped to reflect for a moment on what she'd just done, she actually believed, for a moment at least, that it wasn't even that bad.

Good enough, she thought to herself. Good enough for now.

But when she showed it to Leroy, all the axolotl had to say to her was: "But oughtn't there be an apostrophe there?"

"Where?" she said.

"Right there, in the first word."

And she said, "Oh yeah. Oops."

But by then it was already too late. She'd spent the whole day writing, utterly sapping her capacity for generating a manifesto, and all she had to show for the expended energy was a 420-page-long typo, and though Leroy tried to make a case that one typo didn't turn an entire book into a typo, the front desk agent said that in this particular case it did.

"Everything follows from that first word," she said. "If that's wrong, the whole thing's wrong. If the first word sucks, then the whole thing sucks. It sucks that I wrote it, I suck for having written it, and the entire universe sucks for being the sort of place where such a thing could suck so much!" she screamed.

And that, according to Ishmael, was when Leroy taught the front desk agent about

The Art of Being Terrible at Everything.

If the Stellionators truly believed in anything—"and truly," said Leroy, "we don't"—it would perhaps have been this: that it was utterly vital they all get very good at accepting how much they all sucked at everything. "If you're too afraid to suck," explained Leroy, "than you can only do things you're already good at, and since you're not good at anything—and I mean no offense by this; I'm not good at anything either, no one is, hence the state of the universe—if you cannot bear your own sucking then you can't do anything. I think it's great that what you wrote sucks," said Leroy.

"Really?" said the front desk agent.

"Truly," said Leroy, "so long as you don't let that stop you, so long as you're willing to suck again tomorrow. And the next day," he said, "and the day after that. And the day after that, and every day until you're dead," he said.

"We'll just have to try again tomorrow," continued the axolotl. "Who knows," he said, "come tomorrow you might even look back at what you wrote today and it may not even look so bad. Our assessments of our own secretions," he said, "much like our moods, don't believe in each other. Read it again tomorrow," he said. "You might be surprised by what you find."

"And I was," said Max.

"You were what?" I said, and she said, "Surprised. Surprised by what I wrote. If what I'm reading right now," she said, "if this is really what I wrote yesterday, then maybe it isn't entirely worthless after all.

"But that isn't what you're reading," I said. "You're reading the Doctor's manuscript. Remember?" I said. "In the cave."

"In a cave?" she laughed. "No, no, no. There must have been something about a cave in the manifesto. That must be what happened. I read that about the cave and got confused whether I was the person in the manifesto or the one who wrote it. I'm at the front desk of the bank," she said, "where I work."

"You mean the front desk of the hotel?" I said.

"What?" she laughed. "If I worked at a hotel then how on earth would The Bank of the Reservoir have made me write its manifesto!"

"But it didn't," I said. "Leroy asked you to write the Stellionators' manifesto. At least that's what Ishmael said to his therapist."

"What Ishmael says to his therapist is his business," she said. "Definitely none of the business of the voice his ex-girlfriend hears when she's reading."

Leroy, she explained, was her manager at the bank. She said he was in some stupid new age bicycle gang he was always going on and on about—the Stellionators this, the Stellionators that—"fucking idiot," she said. No, yesterday their asshole boss asked him to write up some kind of promotional manifesto for the bank, and so Leroy made her do it—"my own damn fault for lying on my resume," she said. "I thought it looked better to say that I was one of the writers of the Real World, the puppet show historical reenactment, rather than just another puppet."

"Puppet?" I said, and she said, "Well, technically, a body double for a puppet. You know in the long shots where one of the puppets would be, like, wandering up a hill or something? In those shots where there was nowhere for the puppeteer to hide, I was one of the actors pretending to be the puppet. Best in the business," she said. "Till the business caved. Anyway," she said, "I better get back to reading what I wrote. I mean, 'what got written by the Bank of the Reservoir,'" she said in what I supposed was a funny bank teller's voice and laughed.

And so she did. She got back to reading. And as she read, she heard the voice in her head—"you, in other words," she said—she heard me, in other words, say,

"Writers Block

the road that leads into the paper city, but I escape my pursuers and slip through the writers' defenses by assuming the disguise of a minor character in one of the books these writers are pretending to write. By the time this character has been sacrificed to the machinations of the plotline in the gratuitously violent penultimate chapter, I have already passed onto the other side of their blockade and am running as fast as I can down a black scab of road, shaking free of any lingering associations with their odious narratives. Eventually, I arrive at a bus stop, sit, rest, and reattach my severed head and limbs by dedifferentiating the cells near my various wound sites, weaving sutures out of self-compassion, which, with the help of a special diet, I've learned to cultivate and transmute into a physical substance that resembles spider silk and secretes from a small aperture near the base of my spine. Before I even start this process, however, I first reflect on how it actually feels kind of good to be disjointed like this: the distance between my parts allows me to see just how codependently I'd previously been bound; now the parts of me are able to come together in a more consensual and mutually beneficial manner—not, this time, because they feel compelled by some perverse subservience to the ego or patriotism of the organism but because they'd each really like to get to know the others, maybe even try being a part of me again. At least for the time being. Once whole, I resolve to practice being less concerned with staying that way, to privilege connection over attachment, joy over well-being. I set a timer and meditate for ten minutes, and by the time the alarm goes off I have regained a sense of who I was before I was in the book, and also how I might like to differ from that person now that I am on the other side. I visualize a fire, for instance, and imagine casting into it any sense that I might, could, or would even want to know in advance how others will receive my gestures and utterances. I see how from the ashes of my expectations a sense of openhearted unknowing, even curiosity and excitement, takes its place. A bus pulls up to the bus stop and I get on, only realizing too late that I don't have any money. But the bus driver asks if I can spell it, and I say, 'Spell what? Money?' and he says, 'Yep,' and so I go, 'M-o-n-e-y,' and then we both smile to the music of coins jingling into the—but I cannot think of what word or words one ought to use to describe the thing at the front of a bus one drops one's payment into. No one on the bus can think of the word either—'A receptacle?' suggests someone, but it isn't quite right—and the thing disappears and for the rest of the foreseeable future (which is, admittedly, only so long as a sentence) the bus is liberated from the torturous machinations of capitalism, and everyone on the bus cheers. The bus driver says that now that his identity and survival no longer depend on his consistently being the one to drive the bus, he wants a turn being a passenger, and I offer to drive. We switch places. Then outfits. Then I shout, 'This bus no longer runs on fossil fuels but on the sound of all the passengers singing together!,' and we all sing a song we spontaneously make up on the spot—'For a moment there was nothing arresting my potential . . .' it goes—and even before the final chord from the string section finishes fading, I have driven the bus off a bridge. In the unfolding wreckage, everyone on board has an opportunity to trade parts of themselves with the other passengers and then with any aquatic animals and plants also damaged by our plummet into the river, and then with the bus itself, then with the river, and eventually even with the sky. And once we've enjoyed experimenting with the endless permutations, we decide to see what it might feel like to become one very complex body, and it feels overwhelmingly good but also overwhelming, and after a few days of thrashing about in unthinkable pleasure and collective power, our complex body's complex mind decides that this level of integration is ultimately unsustainable, and so we dissociate and became, more or less, ourselves again. I swim to the riverbank where a camera crew is waiting to film my emergence from the water, and once I am safely seated on the cobblestone quay, the director instructs me to clap my hands together as quickly as possible, but without the palms actually touching. The director explains that the sound thus produced, though inaudible to my ears, sounds to nearby roosting bats like the wings of flapping dragonflies. The director's correct. Bats swirl around my head. The last red, golden, and turquoise rays of the sunset glitter and fade in a mosaic of reflections on the sinuous water gone all choppy in the evening breezes. The camera catches everything and broadcasts the footage live on the local news. Which, I suppose, is how someone I loved in high school and who didn't love me in return learns that I have returned from my sojourn in enemy territory. I discover this when I wake up the next morning to find a message from this person scrolling across the bottom of the television my parents have installed in a cabinet in my old bedroom—which is where, for whatever reason, I wake up the next morning: *Hey*, says the text beneath the two talking newscasters, as they smile with the stitches across their still-smarting eyeballs, *I heard you're back in town. I think I made a terrible mistake in high school. And, well, I'm just going to come right out and say it*, it says, the ticker now scrolling so slowly I have to wait for each letter to appear at the edge of the screen, and each letter's like a star in the evening sky, like one goddamn good April Fool's Day after another: *I* it says, *l*, and then *o*, and then *v*, and then *e*, and then *y*, and then *o*, and then—well, I'm sure you can see where this is going, and so can I. I feel ecstatic. Years of social anxiety and poor self-esteem are instantly overturned. I open my mouth and feel what it feels like to fill the lungs and sustain the life of a body I'm not ambivalent—at best—about. But things take a dark turn when I realize I need to formulate a response, and I start asking myself questions like: Am I so certain I still love this person? Can I even tell for certain I ever actually did? And what about their love for me? After all these years, what do I have in common with the person this person has suddenly discovered that they loved in high school? Do they actually love me, or do they love the idea of me? Do they even love the idea of me, or do they love the idea of being in love with the idea of me? Assuming there's still any such meaningful distinctions to be made . . . In short, I delay responding and grow increasingly anxious, anxious that my delay is not going unnoticed and won't go unpunished, if not by this person then at least by some slightly matured versions of those same hateful, impersonal forces—unrealistic expectations garnered from classic narratives, the poisonous splinters of a Judeo-Christian ethics lingering in secular common sense, an underdeveloped sense of oneself and the nature of one's desires, fear of gossip, rebellion against parental approval, etcetera—that kept two people who might otherwise have had sex from having sex when they were in high school. The perceived urgency of formulating my response grows in proportion to my debilitating indecision over what that response should look like, and the combination is so unbearable, I try to escape it—as is my general reflex when threatened by the weight of things unbearable—I try to escape it by turning to writing. I turn to writing. I write in my diary: *Two people have told me that they love me in the past twelve hours.* But even though I see myself writing this, I'm not sure it's true—I can't say, for example, who the second person is—and soon I can't really say anything at all, not even to my diary. So I close my eyes, but instead of seeing nothing, I see a naked figure caressing itself on a bed, and the vision is so startlingly indistinguishable from what I was just seeing with my eyes open that the bed may as well be in a mirror across from the bed I am sitting on, and the naked figure might as well be me, although it looks nothing like me, and *I'm* not caressing *myself*! Honest! No sooner do I think this, however, than the figure stops. Now when I move, the other body moves too, and when the body moves, I move as well. And more and more, as time passes, despite my best efforts to resist it, it's the naked figure that seems to be the one determining our motions, and eventually it gains enough control to get us both to say: 'Beware! It is tempting to think that you have successfully escaped enemy territory, but that is only because all the writers, one of whose books you insinuated yourself into in a desperate attempt to bypass their blockade, are writing a book in which a minor character insinuates themself into a book by pretending to be one of the minor characters in a book and thereby escapes from enemy territory! Beware! The gratuitously violent penultimate chapter is still approaching, and in *this* draft, the character you are pretending to be will not survive and neither will you!' 'But who are you?' the naked figure and I say together once I am able to wrest control of our mirrored movements for a moment. 'How do I know you aren't also part of the economy of my enemy's book and that your appearing here and telling me what you've told me isn't all part of the machinations of the plotline I'm to be sacrificed to?' 'I'm Leroy,' we reply, and one of us, the one in the mirror, turns into a handsome revolutionary. 'There is often a boy named Leroy in my yoga class,' I overcome my being the mere reflection of Leroy to get us to say. 'I know,' we reply, 'pay attention to what the yoga instructor says to him. What she says to this guy named Leroy will help guide the plotline of a book we are writing in opposition to this one. What the yoga instructor says to Leroy could be the only thing that truly differentiates our book from our enemy's, the only difference between your escaping and your being trapped in this nightmare forever. But what was I saying before that?' we say, and Leroy lets me take over so that we can say, 'You were answering my question about who you are and how I can be certain that your appearing here and telling me what you're telling me isn't going to lead me irrevocably toward the gratuitously violent penultimate chapter of the book whose minor character I pretended to be in order to, or so I was made to believe, bypass the writers' blockade in the hope of finding a better life.' 'Oh right,' we say. 'That's a good question, one that, like all good questions, cannot possibly be answered. The good news is that the character you're pretending to be has been so written as to have inadvertently been readied throughout this book to weather this uncertainty with spectacular finesse. Even though it ultimately goes against the plotline of their book, you have been so characterized as to more readily believe what I am saying and to act in accordance with it, despite the fundamental uncertainty, uncertainty that will never, unfortunately, be entirely dispelled.' 'That's bad news, too,' we say, 'isn't it? Depending on which uncertainty ends up being the least uncertain?' 'You're overthinking this,' we reply. 'Which I suppose may prove to be a good thing—it shows that you're breaking character, which is the first step to breaking the plotline of the book you are trapped in and subverting it with the adversarial plotline of another book, a book that is not actually a book but an ecology.' 'What the hell is that supposed to mean?' we ask. 'I have no idea,' we say. 'I just said it. Listen to what the yoga instructor says to Leroy,' we say. 'Everything will be revealed when it needs to be and not a sentence sooner. Suffice, for now, to say: *the book of webs* will be written in the spaces left between the words of another book, which will also be called *the book of webs*.' '*The book of webs?*' I want to say, but already, the differences between Leroy and my own reflection are fading. 'Listen to what the yoga instructor says to Leroy,' we say, 'listen! Listen to what the yoga instructor says to Leroy,' and I open my eyes and see myself sitting there on the edge of my bed in the mirror, and though I am still saying these words, I can hardly remember what they mean. Nevertheless, I'm feeling much better now, so I call the local news station and tell them I have a story to break. *I love you too*, I tell them to have the text underneath the newscasters say, *but I don't know yet what any of those words mean. I'm saying the words. Nothing more. Nothing less. Meet me in our old spot by the reservoir in twenty minutes if you want to see how making out together feels*, and the newscasters agree to report this during their next segment. When the time for the next segment finally arrives, however, only the first clause of my story is able to scroll across the screen before another story breaks, a story apparently much more important than mine, and my breaking story is interrupted, as a gigantic face takes over the screen, towering over our metropolis. Underneath this footage, the text that is now scrolling reads: *Governor says: Invading plundering monster looks like it needs a haircut*, but I stop reading. I'm overcome with a strange nostalgia. This flood of memory is so intense I can hardly read another word. This face: I've seen it before. The face, I realize with terror, is the very face my childhood imaginary friend would have had had I not grown out of having an imaginary friend, had my imaginary friend, thereby, had a chance to grow out of being one. 'Ma-ma-ma,' I hear the monster rumble. It sounds like a sealed mouth trying to sing in falsetto. 'Va-va-va,' it says. 'Ma-ma-ma,' I hear it emanate both from the TV screen and from outside my windows, shaking the paper windows of my paper house. 'Va-va-va,' I hear it say. 'Ma-ma-ma,' I hear it babble, both in real life and in a flood of childhood memories wherein I heard it say the very same thing. 'Va-va-va,' it said back then and is saying again, in the still breaking story of

The Here and Now."

And this, according to Max, was the main reason why.

"Why what?" I said, and she said, "Why I turned on the radio. It was so that we wouldn't have to listen to the voice of the monster outside," she said. "You asked me why I turned on the radio, and then I gave you my answer. Sorry that it was kind of long-winded. I suppose all I really needed to say was: 'To drown out the monster's babbling. That's why I turned on the radio.'"

"I don't hear any monster," I said.

"Yeah. That's because I turned on the radio," said Max.

"Oh," I said. "And will you remind me who you mean at this point when you say *I?*"

"What kind of a question is that?" she asked. "*I* means *me*," she said, "Max the Antsy. Well sort of," she said. "I suppose it ultimately depends on how you decide to answer the question you posed earlier."

"The question about why you turned on the radio?" I said.

"No, no," she said. "The one about the black lines on the white background. Remember?" she said, and when I said that this question wasn't ringing any bells, she said, "Well, it was right after I told you to close your eyes and to tell me exactly what you saw."

"Eyes?" I said. "I thought you thought I was a voice in your head."

"Oh, I was just playing along," she said. "I thought we were having a little inside joke or something. Anyway. This was before that. I told you to close your eyes. Remember?" she said, and I said I could use a refresher.

She told me that she'd told me to close my eyes and to describe to her what, with eyes closed, I saw. At first, she said, I saw nothing, nothing whatsoever, and so she'd said, "Keep looking."

She explained that a certain amount of practice was necessary to be able to observe oneself properly. She told me to be patient, to stop thinking of having my eyes shut as the mere absence of seeing, to stop thinking of this darkness as the simple negation of vision but, rather, as a different view altogether.

"Where were we at this point?" I asked.

"Same place we are now," she said.

"In your childhood home?" I asked.

"I wish," she said.

"In the cave?" I said.

"Would you stop it already with the cave!" she shouted.

"You said you saw an empty space," she told me, and she said that she'd said, "Good. Is it really empty though?" and that I said, "Oh! But *there's* something! A point of pure illumination," I said, "so faint it would be easier to have ignored it altogether."

The point came, I said, and went, but others followed, rose and sunk, some sedately, others so fast they streaked across the darkness and erupted in colors. "Sometimes," I said, "the colors are very dull, and sometimes, on the contrary, so brilliant that reality cannot compare."

"Good," said Max.

Sometimes it all changed so slowly I could hardly tell when one array of spectacle had replaced the one I had been observing, and other times I could only describe it all as "a whirlwind of vertiginous rapidity," and eventually I stopped recounting what I was seeing and asked Max, amazed, "Whence comes all this phantasmagoria?"

"Are you sure that it was me who said that," I said, "and not something that you maybe read somewhere? That doesn't really sound like something I would say."

"No," she said. "I'm not sure. To tell you the truth," she said, "I'm not even sure what you *just* said is something you actually said and not something I read somewhere. To tell you the truth," said Max, "I've been having the hardest time telling anything from anything else lately," and she laughed and said it had been like this ever since we'd decided to close our eyes and describe to each other what, with our eyes closed, we were seeing.

"You're doing it too?" I asked, and she said, "Of course," and I said that I'd forgotten, and she said, "It's disorienting!" and I said that it was, and she said, "Imagine how I felt when you convinced me that you were only the voice I heard in my head while reading!" and we both burst into laughter.

"Still," she said. "This was a great idea. Stealing mushrooms from the boss's stash and taking them at work," she said, "was a great idea."

"Work?" I said.

"At the hotel," she said. "It sure has made the shift go by faster, this little game we're playing, this pact we made not to open our eyes unless a guest comes and happens to say the magic words—what were they again? *We put the façade up?* Who is ever going to say that?" she said, laughing. "Anyway, it sure has made the time go by faster, but it's also made things very confusing. I really am not sure, for instance, whether it was you or someone else who said, 'Whence comes all this phantasmagoria?' *Someone* said it," she said. "That's for sure."

Certainly, someone asked, "Whence comes all this phantasmagoria?" and then someone else—"I think it was me," said Max, "but I might be wrong"—said that physiologists and psychologists have studied this play of colors and given it names like *ocular spectra, colored spots, phosphenes . . .*

"They explain it either by the slight modifications in retinal circulation," said Max, "or by the pressure that the closed lid exerts on the eyeball, pressure that causes a mechanical excitation of the optic nerve. But the explanation of the phenomenon," she said, "and the name that is given to it doesn't really matter. What matters is that it occurs almost universally and that it constitutes—I may say at once—" she said, "the principal material out of which we shape our dreams."

"Okay," I said next. "So, when I'm sleeping then, these ever-shifting abstractions are condensed and simplified into a more stable flow of perceptions, and this flow then becomes the visual environment of my dream?"

"Precisely," she said. "And it happens in precisely the same way that the play of light on your eyeballs when they are open is condensed and simplified into the stable visual environment of your so-called *life*."

But whereas in the case of one's life it was abundantly clear who was to blame for the inevitable editorial choices that came with condensing and simplifying this vast and overwhelming flood of stimulation into the sensible environment we call the *real world*—"Burlington," Max hissed—whereas it was clear that Burlington was responsible for editing waking life into the nightmare it was, who or what, I'd wanted to know, was to blame for organizing from the abstractions of my ocular spectra, or phosphenes, or whatever, the landscapes of my dreams?

"Say, for example, I close my eyes," I said, "and see black lines on a white background. They could represent to the dreamer the page of a book or, say, the façade of a new house with dark blinds or any number of other things. Who chooses?" I said. "What is the thing that imprints its decision on the indecision of this material?"

"That's the question you asked," said Max. "That's the question I meant when you asked me just now who I meant when I said *I*. And it depends how you want to answer that question whether you want to say it was me or Max who decided to turn on the radio."

"Wait. You *or* Max?" I said. "But I thought you were Max."

"*Me?*" she said and laughed. "No," she said. "I'm not Max. Max was the name of all ten of the dead aquatic frogs who, according to some sources, were the ones responsible for imprinting a decision on the indecision of the material, the ones, in other words, responsible for my dreams, and the ones, therefore, ultimately, who decided to turn on the radio. Though it felt, at the time, like it was me turning on the radio, it was actually probably one of the Maxes guiding my hand from offstage."

"Wait, so that was a dream?" I said. "It was a dream where you turned on the radio to drown out the monster?"

"Yes," she said. "A dream where I was working at the bank I used to work at, only instead of a bank, it was a hotel—and instead of any of my old coworkers, I was working beside this mysterious person whom I seemed to know well, but whose precise identity I couldn't quite recall and whose face I couldn't see because—well, because my eyes were closed. This was all a dream," she said. "It was the dream that I told Doctor Burlington in the session he would later profoundly distort, for the sake of protecting my anonymity, a dream whose distorted form he would tell during his recollection of our session, the one he shared with his circle of men, the transcript of which comprised the manuscript I stole from the Doctor after he murdered my comrade, the manuscript I'm still reading, as evidenced by the fact that I'm still hearing your voice reading from it even though you're dead."

"Okay, okay," I said. "So all those things you said about me being your coworker, about me tricking you into thinking you were reading, about not being in the cave—none of that was true?"

"Right," she said.

"Then why did you say that?"

"Because that's what I heard you say," she said. "That's what I heard when I read what I read. And that's what I do when I read," she said. "I tell you what I hear you saying. Trust me," she said.

"The confusion's mutual. If you ask me, I'd say this book is a real shipwreck. Seems like it really needed to be edited more before it was ready to be read. You know I wouldn't read it if I didn't have to. But what choice do I have, when what's-his-name died so I could read it. And so I read it," she said, "and, as I read it," she said, "what choice do I have but to tell you, even if it makes little sense to me, that now I hear you saying that *you're* the one who's turned the radio on! Oh, I bet the Doctor's doing the thing again where he speaks from his patient's perspective—so that when I hear you say *I*, I mean the Doctor pretending to be the patient—here now, I hear you say that when you turned on the radio you were surprised to find that the same song was

Playing on Every Station

you tuned the dial to," she said.

Though I'd turned on the radio to drown out the sound of the monster's babbling, it was only to find that the song they were playing on the radio was even worse. I changed the dial, but it was the same song on every station, so I turned it off, but even the monster, now, had stopped babbling and was singing the same song, and it was even worse than the radio version, so I plugged up my ears with my fingers, but the song was stuck in my head already, playing exactly as it sounded on the radio, so what could I possibly do but transcribe the lyrics into my dream journal, if only so that I'd have something to talk about at my next therapy session, to which, I suddenly realized, I was running terribly late.

Fortunately, my patient was running even later.

"You mean *your therapist*?" interrupted my circle of men.

"No, not exactly," I said. "My patient—or rather the unnamed narrator in the failed manifesto written by the unnamed narrator in the propaganda pamphlet the axolotl had given my client to read at the ecoterrorism convention—it turned out the narrator of the typo was a therapist, not a patient. Remember, this was all taking place in the paper city, outside the bounds of enemy territory, wherein, as far as I can figure out, all anyone had to do was say 'I'm a therapist' for it to be so. Is it really so surprising that my client—that any client really—wouldn't, given the chance to be anything they ever wanted to be, that my client wouldn't want to be me, his own therapist? When I say *I*," I said, "that's who I mean: who my client meant when he said *I*, which just so happened, in this dream within a dream within a dream, to be, I suppose, his psyche's own distorted version of me. Make sense?"

"Makes sense," said the men, and I continued to tell them what my client told me, adopting again, of course, his perspective. I told them, thus, that what I told my patient when he finally arrived was: "I think I may have discovered a cure for your inestimably debilitating psychological disorder. Would you like to know what the cure is? I'll tell you. To cure you of your delusion," I said, "it's actually rather simple: all we need to do is sing this song together," and I handed my client the lyrics I transcribed from the song I heard play on the radio while driving to this session.

"And here," I said to my circle of men, "my client interrupted the nonsense he was telling me to hand me (and by *me* I mean Doctor Burlington again) the lyrics."

"I discreetly tore this one page out of the pamphlet," said my client, "while Leroy was distracted comparing the tiny crab he'd found in his grilled oyster shell with a similar crab a percussionist also in his terrorist cell found in hers."

"Great," I said. "How about I'll read over these lyrics and we talk about them next time."

But my client ignored the suggestion, and there was no next time.

No, thankfully, I would inherit these lyrics along with the rest of my client's papers when he mysteriously disappeared shortly after the session in question. That's why I was able to duplicate them and pass them around so that each of my colleagues held a copy while I explained, "I'm having us do this primarily because I think it should help settle our little debate, the one about the nature of that specific class of dreams you asked me about, dreams that have only been dreamed they have not actually been dreamed," and my colleagues asked me if this was me that was saying this now or whether it was me pretending to be my client pretending to be me saying this, and I said, "Both, actually," for here, I explained, the two converged: the therapist my client was pretending to be had also, incidentally, been having a conversation with his client about what to make of the sorts of dreams that have only been dreamed they . . .

Anyway, I (the therapist my client was dreaming he was) said, "To sing the song properly, I'll need your full participation."

And here my client (my client's imaginary client, of course) pointed out that it seemed like our time for today was already up, wasn't it? He said he could hear someone fidgeting in the waiting room, someone he said that he had the strangest feeling about, the feeling that maybe the person in there . . .—but I ignored him entirely.

"To sing the song properly," I repeated, "I'll need your full participation," which was also what I (Doctor Burlington) later told my colleagues. For the song, or so I told them my client had explained to me when he handed me the lyrics, called for a rather baroque play of polyphony.

"I'll sing the parts in quotations," I said to my circle of men, just as I'd said to my client. "This part goes to the tune of 'The Tennessee Waltz.' You all know that song? Someone look up the Patti Page version," I said in both cases. "That's the one I'm thinking of. So I'll be singing that part, but I'll need you to sing the other parts, the dialogue tags, for instance, the part that goes, 'I sang into the microphone . . .' and so on, and if you can manage it, I'll need you to sing it all in a sort of monastic choral drone. Which will obviously require you to use all of your mouths at once."

"All of my mouths?" my client said, and I reminded him that the delusion I was attempting to disillusion him of was that he was an individual—whereas it was quite clear from *my* perspective that he was, in fact, a circle of birds.

"Oh yes," said the birds. "I forgot that you're convinced of this and that I—sorry, *we*—are pretending to go along with it in an effort to disillusion you of your delusion by entering the ground story of your delusion-structure and all that."

"Finally," I said, "I'll need one of you to break away from your murmuration during the final reprisal of the verse to harmonize with me. Any volunteers?"

There weren't any. My client, the circle of birds, was famously shy. So was my circle of men. There were no volunteers, neither volunteers to harmonize with me nor to do the droning, and so I was obliged to begin all by myself, doing all the parts I outlined above with my own voice all alone. This necessitated some rather advanced, experimental singing techniques that I, fortunately, had secretly—a secret I had kept even from myself—been developing for the past three decades. I began alone, but my hope was that, in the swell of the infectious melody, the circle of birds would be unable to resist joining in singing this song, a song that so happened to be called

"The Song in My Throat."

"For a moment
there was nothing
arresting my potential," I sang into my microphone, which hung like a spider from its thread from a cable through a trapdoor in the ceiling,
"except for a song in my throat," I sang, and it felt almost like a dream to be here singing this, for it had been just that morning that I awoke wondering how I was ever going to start being the sort of person I'd always wanted to be, and now here I was in a band whose name I couldn't pronounce, singing in a language I didn't understand.
"I tried to sing it to my loved ones," I sang, and I reminded myself that I needed to be careful not to be misled into believing I was singing what it seemed to me that I was singing—for, or so I'd been forewarned, no language was more unlike my own than this one I was attempting to conduct my voice through, this language in which I was attempting to channel an emotional authenticity, as though I'd not only written these lyrics myself, but was currently abiding in the same fraught affective state I was doing my best to guess the lyrics endeavored to convey, a task that, I guess, required first of all my acknowledging at every moment the fact that this language was so vastly unlike my own that if, for example, mine were a deadly Texas coral snake, this language wouldn't even be the harmless Mexican milk snake that mimics mine but would, according to the band's guitarist, be a strange, otherworldly object that eons of shifting dirt and swirling weather, growing and withering

vegetation, and copulating and dying animals had miraculously shaped and animated in the innermost crevice of an unenterable cave, a thing that just so happens to look just like and even behave much like a Texas coral snake but is not, in fact, even a snake so much as a book, a book that only those practiced in a peculiar strain of militant necromancy have been prepared by their dreams to know how to read from without endangering the very structure of the universe—

"but instead of the lyrics," I sang, as the Joint's small audience watched silently, neither dancing nor even nodding their heads to the triple-time rhythm of the song we were playing, a song that was but one of thousands of songs chosen at random from a whole stack of lyrics I was holding,

"I secreted something sticky and dead," I sang.

"I remember the night, *the book of webs* in my hands," I sang, and this, I think, was my favorite part of the song to sing. I found it so mysterious what the words *the* and *book* and *of* and *webs* might translate into were the song written in *my* language, assuming, for that matter, this was even what the words were, because, for all I knew, the words might've actually been *th* and *eboo* and *kofwe* and *bs*, and maybe the spaces between letters served an entirely different purpose in this language than they did in the language I spoke before I got myself into this mess.

"With each breath I choked up more silk," I sang, and the instruments were swelling up to a clear crescendo, so I sang the words with all my heart, which was not actually a heart, by the way, but a shard of the moon that fell into the swamp wherein I was once, long ago, being sung into existence by enemy wizards, back when I was still forming in the swamp from the sludge and industrial waste and parts of broken furniture and gaudy decor from a long-lost shipwreck—my heart, a moon shard that eventually sunk and slipped uneasily into my chest, which was not a chest but a birdcage, a shard that began to pound in my birdcage like it was a boxer and I was a boxer and I was clearly losing, losing my very life to this new part of me, my new heart pounding my new life away, which was, incidentally, the exact moment, or at least one of the moments—I suppose there were several failed attempts—that my life, so to speak, began.

"I believe I would have died had I not disowned my desire," I sang, and it was truly like a dream come true to be standing there on the stage of the Joint with a band called the Stellionators performing behind me, as I pretended to know what I was singing and why I was singing it, pretending that I wanted to sing it, even *needed* to sing it, which pretending required, by the way, that I actually believed it myself, for I was so fashioned as to be unable to lie or to pretend to be anything I wasn't, and this defect—which was apparently a foiled bid to prevent me from being an effective double agent when I inevitably turned against the authoritarian forces who controlled the wizards who I'd been created to do the bidding of, a very different sort of collective than the band I was currently heading, not even really a collective, I suppose but, more accurately, a corporation: a rigidly stratified totalitarian enterprise known colloquially as Doctor Burlington—this defect, in any case, rendered me physically incapable of lying, and so I actually believed every word I sang, even though I had no way of understanding what each word might mean,

"to sing you the song in my throat," I sang, and it felt so tremendous to be singing like this that when the instrumental bridge began, when the horns started going, *Ma-ma-ma-ma, va-va-va-va, ma-ma-ma-ma, va-va. . .* , I began to dance. Now, when I say I dance, I mean *I dance*. There was a special mode of dancing that I learned while under the employ of the corporation responsible not only for my birth but also for the polluted conditions in the swamp wherein my inchoate body festered and wherefrom it eventually emerged only to be immediately yoked to the exigences and machinations of my employer—my meager strength coercively conducted into the corporation's primeval, aberrant, and, as far as I could tell, unexamined raison d'être, which was euphemistically referred to as *Burlington's love life.* But the type of dancing I was doing now as the instrumental bridge babbled on, this type of dancing that I learned before I turned against Doctor Burlington, had nothing to do with Burlington's love life. It was not from the top executives or board of directors of Doctor Burlington that I learned about this kind of dancing but from a cadre of the lowest subordinates—the lowest other than me, of course—those among the lowest rungs of the company's rigid hierarchy. They'd developed the dancing technique in secret, as a strategy for cultivating resilience in the face of the corporation's execrable labor practices and the complex psychological warfare tactics the managers used for extracting absolute subservience from the workforce. The persons I'm speaking of had, like me, been artificially created by the corporation, but they were different from me in that I'd been conjured by negligence and waste and magic rather than by deliberate bioengineering; because of this difference I was assumed to have something like a soul—*soul* was the name the corporation gave for the CEO of an individual employee, which, they insisted, was structured just like the company, only in microcosm. The automatons, on the other hand, were thought of as soulless and had been produced by a team of psychotherapists that Doctor Burlington had contracted in a bid to populate the world with readers of a certain book, the manufacturing of which was believed to be crucial to Doctor Burlington's primary mission, to advance Burlington's love life at all costs. The book was also called *the book of webs*—just like the book mentioned in the song!—but this book was written unambiguously in the tongue my own tongue (a dead leech) was born already indelibly conquered by. So I think it must have been a simple coincidence. Anyway, unfortunately, at least from the perspective of the heads of Doctor Burlington, the reading automatons were finished long before *the book of webs* was written; the board of directors had seriously underestimated the amount of time it takes to write a book, even a bad one, despite a whole factory of poorly paid laborers forced to work on it. And to keep the automatons from rising up against the company, the board voted to put them to work in the kitchen of a corporate-owned and -operated seafood restaurant in the food court located in the basement of Doctor Burlington's primary headquarters. In fact, a whole new portion of the menu had to be invented by the head chef solely for the purpose of justifying the new influx of labor. This portion of the menu was inspired by a foreign culture the chef had also had to invent—a nation-state he called K . . . , where its wealthiest inhabitants allegedly enjoyed their fishbones fleshless. It was the automatons' new job, thus, to peck the flesh off of fish and gently coax the remaining bones into being edible. The executives and other officials who could afford to patronize the restaurant relished the new delicacy and as a result became increasingly fleshless fish themselves—the inevitable outcome of consuming such vacuous structural material—and so they, in turn, found their way into the hands of the automatons to be coaxed into edibility, their coveted positions in the corporation's hierarchy becoming quickly usurped by would-be dissidents and labor organizers, workers plucked from the company's lower echelons, thereby preventing all but the most readily co-optable insurrections against the organization. Plucking flesh off fish, of course—particularly if the fish were ex-executives whose flesh has been made brittle and tough by years of consuming nothing but edible bones—constituted the most arduous labor imaginable, second only to then coaxing those bones into being edible. To keep from becoming fleshless themselves, the automatons—who were, after all, not made for this sort of manual labor but for sitting around reading *the book of webs* all day—were able to develop (thanks to their being deficient enough in soul to remain at least *internally* somewhat anarchic) a new holistic healing modality they learned by following instructions decoded from their dream life. They called this healing modality *dancing for exercise* and were able to teach it to each other and practice it regularly, somehow keeping it hidden from the head chef—no small feat considering the outrageous volume the music had to be played at in order for the medicine to be effective, in order for the dancing to actually count as proper dancing for exercise. "Did you say *dancing for exercise*?" I once asked one of the automatons, on the occasion of having become a fleshless fish myself, which was when I met the automatons. I was in the hands of one of those mechanical readers and was in the process of being made edible, when I'd heard this reader whisper to the reader beside him that if he didn't dance for exercise soon, he'd be, by day's end, as fleshless as this fish—*this fish* referring, of course, to me. "*Dancing for exercise*?" I asked. And I guess I was the first almost edible fish skeleton that this particular reader had ever heard talk—the executives that had crafted me had radically overestimated the integrity of my soul (the soul being the primary delusion that convinces a body it's capable of ever being completely dead)—for the reader was so surprised that he dropped me onto the kitchen floor, whereon I shattered into over a hundred thousand pieces. Once I'd been painstakingly, more or less, put back together, the reader explained to me what dancing for exercise was. Dancing for exercise, the automaton explained, meant dancing for exercise. Not for pleasure or for art or for seduction but purely for exercise. To date, the automaton explained, it was the only known antidote to fleshlessness. "I would," said the automaton, "show you how to do it, but then it wouldn't be dancing for exercise, would it, but dancing for demonstrating what dancing for exercise is, which is, of course, not the same thing." I pretended I understood the technique implicitly and asked the reader if I might be permitted to give it a go. "*You?*" said the automaton—for, I was, as I said already, a full-blown fish without flesh, and the automaton had hitherto never heard of any instance of a fish without flesh dancing for anything, much less for exercise. And so I become the first, and it was a medical miracle. I not only danced for exercise until I'd become a fully fleshed fish but also kept on dancing for exercise until I was a resurrected stingray flopping on a shoreline, and eventually had danced for exercise so relentlessly that I'd become an armadillo in a t-shirt, at which point I hid in a back room in the house of one of the ex-lovers of the current president of Doctor Burlington, and when the president came over to return a box of his ex-lover's possessions, and all the friends of his ex-lover had finished complimenting the president for all of the kisses that Doctor Burlington had achieved under this president's supervision, I came charging out of the back room and waddled up to the president. He crouched down to greet me because he couldn't even help it—this was how adorable of an armadillo I'd become through dancing for exercise—and I crawled into his arms, and just when he thought I was the cutest armadillo he'd ever laid eyes on, I sank my teeth so deep into his throat my teeth met spine. Anyway, dancing for exercise was the way I was dancing now, during the instrumental bridge of the song, and it was only because I was, at this point, so prodigious a practitioner at the art that the dancing wasn't becoming a part of the performance but remained entirely imperceptible to everyone but myself. This particular dance was so powerful, in fact, that by the end of it I'd acquired a second mouth inside my mouth and was thus able to sing the next part of the song with two voices. The next verse sounded just like the first but was different in that one of my mouths was singing with utmost sincerity, whereas the other was singing only to make fun of the words. The harmony thus produced was apparently very well received by the crowd, and it was just an absolute dream to stand here with both my mouths simultaneously belting:

"For a moment,
there was nothing
arresting my potential,
except for a song in my throat.
I tried to sing it to my loved ones
but instead of the lyrics,
I secreted something sticky and dead.
I remember the night. I was just two years old.
With each breath I choked up more silk.
I believe I would have died
had I not disowned my desire
and declared that

We Put the Façade Up."

And then we opened our eyes. We opened our eyes and faced what we had not been seeing for so long that we'd forgotten what it was, a reality we'd closed our eyes to so long ago that it had grown less real than the stories we'd been telling ourselves. We had had our eyes closed so long now that we had entirely forgotten where we were, and also who we were, and even why we ever closed our eyes in the first place. At first there was nothing. Actual light was too much. My eyes, accustomed to the most subtle play of motion on the insides of my eyelids, could do nothing with this abundance. But gradually I acclimated. It was actually rather dark: lights off, a storm had moved in, and rain lashed the windowpane. I was looking at the person I had been talking to and he was looking at me and there was no longer any room for doubt, no longer any room to not know for certain that I was his therapist and he was my client and we were in my office and my alarm was going off—an alarm that, with our eyes now open, did not sound anything like the words *We put the façade up* or even like the tolling of a buoy bell but, for a moment, as the alarm first broke the spell of our conversation, sounded sometimes like the former and sometimes like the latter—an alarm that now blared with relentless monotony, an alarm that I'd set at the beginning of our session, knowing, if I didn't, we'd never stop, an alarm to alert us when our session's time was up. Which it was. I could hear my next patient pacing in the waiting room. My client ground the heels of his hands into his eyes.

"Well," I said. "How do you feel?"

"How do I feel?" he said, blinking blearily.

"Yeah," I said. "How do you feel?"

"Gosh," he said. "Disappointed, I guess."

"Disappointed?" I said.

"Aren't you?" he said.

"I'm disappointed that you're disappointed," I said. "Me, I think we did alright. What did you expect our first time trying?"

"First time?" he said.

"I meant our first time since giving up the last time," I said.

"It's a stupid idea," he said.

"Everything is a stupid idea," I said. "If it's an idea, it's a stupid one."

"Yeah, I guess," he said and faked a little laugh.

"I'm sorry it didn't help," I said.

"Aah, it's not your fault," he said. "I'm the one who should be sorry."

"We can both be sorry," I said.

"That's true. I guess there's no reason we can't all be sorry," he said with a forced smile, his eyes welling with water. "Guess being sorry isn't in any short supply."

"Suppose we'll just have to keep trying," I said, as he stood up off the couch, faked a yawn to hide his watering eyes, and put an arm through the sleeve of his tattered wool coat—and that's when I saw them: two white butterflies emerged suddenly from inside his sleeve. They circled each other in a widening spiral until they were suddenly and simultaneously shattered by the blades of my office's ceiling fan.

A thousand motes of butterfly fell, and my client's gaze fell with them—slow as a bone-dry snow, his gaze descending till it was level with my own.

"This *is* really happening, isn't it?" he said.

"What do you mean?" I asked.

"I mean," he said, "we did actually open our eyes, didn't we?"

"I'm not following," I said.

"Suppose," he said, "I'm still reading. Suppose I've only read the sentence, for instance, *And then we opened our eyes*, and I heard you say this and then repeated it back to you so that I'd maybe retain something of what I read."

"Are you okay," I said. "You're looking a little faint."

"A little feint?" he said.

"*Faint*," I said. "With an *a*. Do you need to sit down?"

"I am sitting down," he said. "Aren't I? I have the strangest feeling. I have the strangest feeling"—it looked like he was having a hard time putting it into words—"I have the strangest feeling I couldn't stand up if I tried."

"The most impossible things to accomplish," I said, "are often the very things one has already accomplished."

"What?" he said.

I heard my next patient in the waiting room. I heard the pacing stop. Near the door. I couldn't help but imagine a hand cupped against the wood, a confused glance at the clock on the wall.

"Who's out there?" my client whispered.

"No one," I said. "My next patient. And all I meant was that it might seem impossible to stand if you're already standing. Just as it's impossible to be disillusioned if you're already seeing things clearly, impossible to break if you're already broken, impossible to heal if you're already cured."

He rubbed his eyes again. Stared at me, blinking. Then, without breaking his gaze away from mine, he reached for a book on the shelf. He opened it and said, "If I'm seeing things clearly, then how come this book says," and he read, "*Nay, an invalid should not always have his own way. Ah sir, reflect how untimely this distrust in one like you. How weak you are; and weakness, is it not the time for confidence? Yes, when through weakness everything bids despair, then is the time to get strength by confidence.*" Then he looked at me, as though having proved something, as though having proved something he wished weren't true.

"If I'm seeing things clearly," he said, "then how come this book says one thing on its cover and another thing inside?"

"Don't . . ." I said. "Don't most books? Look, Ishmael—"

"Don't call me Ishmael," he said. "My name's not Ishmael, it's—um—um . . ."

"Whatever your name is," I said. "This has to stop."

There was a soft knock at the door.

"See?" I said. "My next patient."

"Is it locked?" he whispered.

"The door?" I said.

"Is it locked?" he said.

"There's no need for me to—" but I fell silent when the knob started turning. "Wait!" I shouted. "Don't come in here! We'll just be a moment longer!"

"*We?*" said a voice from without. "Who else is in there?"

I gave my client a quizzical look as he began to unbutton his coat.

"Put that back on!" I said. "Put your coat—"

"We don't have time for this," he said.

"I know we don't have time for—"

"Look," he said, thrusting the book at me, and though I recognized the paragraph—if not it exactly, then something like it—as belonging to the book he was holding (it was a rather typical passage from the book, a book that so happened to be an absolute favorite of mine, something like a holy book, in fact), when he said, "Here, Doctor, have a little look-see," I saw that the passage he'd read aloud was in quotes—"Huh," I said—and was italicized—"That's weird," I said—and was followed by the words: *Then he looked up at me, as though having proved something, as though having proved something he wished weren't true.*

"Do you see now?" he said.

And then the door opened.

The Next Thing He Remembered—

the next thing he could say with any certainty—"Certainty?" he said, and I said, "Yes, certainty"—the next thing he could remember, or rather something that happened a little after that, because it took some time to recover from remembering what, when the door opened, he'd seen, some time after the next thing he remembered, the next thing he remembered after that was being in the dark again, eyeballs smarting, and he was saying, "What was I saying, again?"

"You were telling me about your walk," I said.

"My walk?" he said.

"Right," I said. "Your little walk."

"Oh, that's right," he said, "my walk." Then he went silent for a long, long time.

"My walk," he would occasionally break the silence to say again, and I'd say, "Right, your walk," but it did little to encourage him.

"Sorry," he said eventually, "but who are you?"

"Who am I?" I said.

"Yeah," he said. "I can't remember who I'm talking to. You must be someone I really trust," he said, "for me to have let my guard down like this, for me to have told you as much as I've told you."

"Yeah," I said. "Good thing I'm the person you trust more than pretty much anyone else in the whole world."

"Good thing," he said. Then he paused a while, as though consulting a Roladex in his memory. "Leech?" he finally asked into the darkness.

"Yep," I said. "It's me, Leech."

"Oh thank g-god," he said. "You're so good at imitating other people's voices, for a minute there, I thought you were one of the people you must have been talking about! Anyway, as for where I was in the walk when I left off," he said, "I was just pretending not to remember in case you were a psychotherapist or something. Where I last left off," he said, "I was standing under the overpass."

"Right," I said. "That's where you were. Under the overpass."

He was standing under the ruin of the overpass, he told me, looking up. That was where he'd left off. Quails were zigzagging among the cacti and desert brush at his feet.

"I'm having some trouble following you," he said, and his guide, who'd disappeared above the lip of the overpass, shouted down, "I know. It's impossible. But you're just going to have to keep going anyway," and he said, "How?" but it seemed like she could hardly hear him over the sound of whatever was happening on top of the overpass.

"I've got to take off," she said.

"Your guide?" I asked, and he said, "Yeah, my guide, an old woman from the nearest village."

He said that she said she had to take off, which made no sense because all that remained of the overpass was a segment about five yards long and there was thus nowhere left for her to go. The rest of the road had all but disintegrated, leaving only this lonely fragment, towering over the dirt trail they'd traveled on. Concrete rubble littered the red earth, crumbles of asphalt like blooms of lichen growing among the rose quartz and succulents.

"But where could you possibly go from there?" he said, but, again, she seemed unable to hear him.

"I've left some incense burning for you," she shouted down to him. "That should cover up the smell."

"The smell of what?" he said.

"Doctor Burlington," said his guide.

"Doctor Burlington?" I asked.

"Yes," he said, "But I couldn't tell if she'd actually heard my question and was answering it or if she'd said 'Doctor Burlington' in response to something else, something I couldn't perceive from where I stood."

"Doctor Burlington," she'd said, but, it seemed more likely that she was talking to someone else, someone who must have been up there with her.

"The oracle?" I said.

"What oracle?" he said.

"Didn't you say that the guide told you that there was an oracle up there? Wasn't that what the guide was guiding you toward."

"No, no. Not oracle. *Auricle*," he said, "as in an ear."

"She was guiding you to an ear?"

"No," he laughed. I'd misheard him. "Not *to*," he said, "*by*."

He'd been sitting at a café, he explained, trying to write in his journal—specifically to use writing as a way to psychically intuit and channel the missing half of an important text message a friend had only been able to send him the first half of before that friend was tragically eaten in half by a bear—when an old woman approached his table, leaned in close and whispered, "A hair grows from the helix of an auricle."

"Huh?" he said, and the woman took a step back and, with the pincer fingers of her right hand, grasped a hair growing horizontally out of the edge of her left ear, a strand so thin it was all but imperceptible, visible only because as she moved her pincer fingers toward and away from her head, her ear was tugged along with them, flapping like a bat wing or the open hand of a marionette.

"A hair," she repeated meaningfully while nodding suggestively, "grows from the helix of an auricle."

"And that," he told me, "was when I remembered having

seen a similar hair growing from the edge of my own ear earlier that morning."

Earlier that morning, before the sun had even risen, he'd been staring straight into the mirror—"This was before I moved into the apartment whose lease outlawed mirrors," he said—he'd been staring straight into the mirror trying to get someone other than himself to show up, someone with skin, he hoped, that looked less like uncooked shrimp, or teeth less miscellaneous so that maybe when he smiled, which he was now, it wouldn't look so much like a comparative illustration of thirty different species' understanding of what a shelter should look like—he'd been staring in the mirror when a searchlight beam from a police helicopter shone through his window, ricocheted off the glass of a frame around a taxidermized cicada he'd purchased the day before at a flea market, and backlit—for a moment—his right ear, thus illuminating a halo of peach fuzz, along with one stray, long, wiry hair growing horizontally away from his head. "The hell is that?" he said to himself. And though the momentary illumination had already passed and he could thus no longer see the hair, he was able to grasp it between his pincer fingers and with them he plucked it from his ear and continued to ruminate on the calamity of his appearance. The hair wouldn't even have made it into his book—"*Book?*" I interrupted, and he said, "What I deem fit to remember"—if not for the encounter with the women in the café later that same day, if not for the fact that when he reached once more to where that hair had been, the hair, he said, had somehow regrown.

Tugging more gently this time, he flapped his ear back at the woman, who still stood there flapping hers provocatively at him.

"I'm Amy," she whispered. "Follow me."

"But I'm working," he said. "I'm right in the middle of—"

"*The book of webs*," said Amy. "I know. Tell me your last typo."

"My last typo?" he asked.

He found the typo in an early passage in the day's attempt at channeling—"I'd been trying to channel this friend every day for about three years now," he explained to me—a passage recorded in that penumbral state wherein the channeler is only just beginning to suspect, but has not yet grown entirely certain, that every word they have quote-unquote *channeled* is actually a word they have merely authored or, more often, as in this case, plagiarized from a book that they're holding open underneath the table.

This passage went: *I wish to examine the place, using the word in the abstract sense, where we most of the time are when we are experiencing life. By the language we use we show our natural interest in the matter. I may be in a muddle, and then I either crawl out of the muddle or else try to put things in order so that I may*—"This was the word," he said, "the word I'd blotted out and had had to rewrite; originally I'd written *amy* rather than *may*!" he said—*so that I may, at least for a time, know where I am.*

"I wrote *amy*!" he said. "I wrote *amy* instead of *may*!"

"I know," said Amy. "But that's not all. Keep reading."

I may feel I am at sea, he continued to read, *and I take bearings so that I may come to port (any port in a storm), and then when I am on dry land I look for a house built on rock rather than on sand; and in my own home,* he'd written, *which (as I am English) is my castle, I am in seventh heaven.*

"You can stop there," said Amy.

"I forget what the point of that was," he said, and Amy, who must have read the book he'd been plagiarizing, told him that the point had had something to do with how it might be tempting to think of experience as occurring either *inside* or *outside* the individual, either in the mind or in reality—"whereas in reality," said Amy, "we are never inside or outside ourselves but always somewhere different altogether. In a muddle, for example," she said, "or in a shipwreck, or in very grave danger. But," she said, "that's not really the point."

"It's not?" he said.

"No," she said. "We knew all that already. That's not why it got written down," she said. "To tell you the truth, no one knows why it got written down. It got written down," she said, "and that's enough for now. Everything will become clear when it needs to and not a moment sooner. Anyway, let's go. It's not safe here," she said. "We're in very grave danger."

"But I wasn't done," he said. "What if I write something else important?"

"You won't," said Amy. "You won't ever write anything important ever again. Ever," she said.

"Ever?" he said a little later. "As in: I'll never recover the missing half of Billie's text?"

"The missing half of whose what?" said Amy.

"The missing half of the text message that my friend killed by a bear sent me," he said. "Billie. That's what I was trying to channel when I made the typo. I've been trying for three years," he said. "Are you telling me it won't ever work?"

"Oh no," laughed Amy. "No. Definitely not. This isn't how you channel the dead. I can show you later if you're still interested, but first there's someone I want to introduce you to. A friend of mine. I think you might like each other actually, and besides, she expressed an interest in your bookselves."

"My *bookselves*?" he said, and she said, "Sorry, I meant *bookshelves*."

And so, mostly because no one else had expressed any interest in his bookshelves—"I was in the middle of moving," he said, "and was therefore trying to sell off all my furniture"—mostly because he was moving in a day or two and desperately needed someone to buy his bookshelves, he decided to follow Amy.

"Good choice," she said, and he began to pack up his things.

"Is this your mask?" she asked.

"No," he said. "That's a napkin."

"Oh," she said. "What's your name, by the way?"

And he said, "Um . . ." But it was the oddest thing. He couldn't remember what he told her.

"Did you tell her your actual name?" I said.

"Well, obviously," he said. "I had no reason to deceive her."

The problem, he explained, was that he couldn't remember at the moment what his actual name was.

"Paul," I said. "Isn't it?"

"No," he said. "That was just something I told to the guy in the cave . . . Oh, I got it! Charlie!" he said. "My name's Charlie."

"*Enchanté*," said Amy. "That's French for I guess I'll take you for your word, it probably doesn't matter anyway," she explained. "You about ready to go, Charlie?" and Charlie said, "Yep," and she said, "Okay, follow me."

He followed her to the counter of the café, and when she ordered a slice of Irish soda bread, he did too.

"Good," she said. "Did you tip?" and he said, "Yeah," and she said, "Well?" and he said, "Pretty well," and she said, "Give them a bit more," so he did.

Then the barista gave them each a pastry bag, and he looked inside and said, "Why did we order this?"

"Have you ever tried Irish soda bread before?" asked Amy.

"No," he said.

"I thought not," she said. "The reason we ordered it," she said, "is because it's good. And it's good," she said, "that you have a chance to enjoy one of the few good things about the universe before we destroy it."

About Ten Pages Later—

"Ten pages later?" I asked, and Charlie said, "Yeah, about ten pages later, Amy and the bassoonist were walking down the path," and I said, "Bassoonist? I thought this was a walk *you* went on," and he said, "Oh right"—about ten pages later, he and Amy were walking down the path.

"What happened in those ten pages?" I said.

"Who knows," he said. "It didn't seem important, so I skipped it."

Amy had taught him this, he told me, how to skip pages.

"The *place*," she'd explained as they walked, "is a book."

"What?" said Charlie.

"The *place*," she said, referring to the thing he'd plagiarized at the café, "the *place*, in the abstract sense of the word—the *place* where we most of the time are when we are experiencing life," she said, "the *place* is best thought of as a book—but *book*," she said, "also, of course, in an abstract sense. We live in a book," she said. "Between the organism and the environment extends the vast borderland we call *the book*. And, of course, because *organism* and *environment* are but the names of fictional characters within the book, and because a book is nothing but a web of relationships between its characters—characters that considered separately from the book are but abstract extrapolations from the actuality of their entwined relations—there is," she said, "in fact, nothing but the borderland, nothing but the book."

"A book?" he said. "But by who? And who's reading it?"

"You're not following me," she said and turned to look back at him where he was trailing a little ways behind her on the dirt path that wound through this stretch of desert, the path on either side of which the quails trembled seductively.

"*Author, reader,*" she said, "these are but utterly untenable concepts in the book's asinine cosmology. I mean, think about it," she raised her voice so suddenly it frightened a few quails into brief bursts of flight. "It makes no sense whatsoever. The idea that a book is even possible! Much less that it could be written! And by one person, moreover! And that it could then be read? And also by an individual? Ha!" she laughed—laughing until she was coughing. She took a swig from her canteen, wiped her face with her sleeve, and passed it to him. "The sooner you learn to forget everything you ever read about what a book is," she said, "the better off we'll all be."

He took a swig from the canteen and said, "Then why even call it a—" but his question was interrupted by a fit of choking—"a buh-buh-buh," he stuttered.

"Hold your arms up," she said. "Like this," she said, showing him—holding her arms up in a way that reminded him of the saguaro cacti that surrounded them.

Charlie mirrored her pose and gradually the choking subsided. He reeled a little, as swirling black dots clouded his vision and coalesced into a bat that flew into a hole in Amy's right elbow. When he rubbed his eyes, this hole was gone. He pointed to the canteen he held in his other hand and from which he'd taken the ill-fated swig and said, "What the hell is in here?"

"Fossil fuel," she said. "You like it? I'm just crazy about dinosaurs," she said, "Anyway, where was I? Oh, that's right," she said and continued to berate him.

"Forget about books!" she shouted. "You think the book would risk arming its characters with an honest conception of what a book is? No, the book only maintains its hegemony by keeping us ignorant, by crushing our capacity to imagine the actual book, by bombarding us with these paper-thin definitions of what a book is according to the book itself. Nothing," she said, "could give you a more useless, a more dangerous misconception of what the book is than to take as your model the books that appear within it."

"What about *the book of webs*?" he said, but had hardly even gotten the *the* out when Amy was suddenly standing directly beside him, aiming the cold quivering tip of a penknife against his jugular.

"Who told you about that?" she hissed.

Three turkey vultures hovered overhead. A bead of sweat slid down Charlie's temple.

"You did," he said.

"Me?" she said.

"Remember?" he said. "Back at the café. I was trying to tell you why I couldn't follow you, that I was right in the middle of channeling the missing half of a text message, when you interrupted me right in the middle of my sentence and said, '*the book of webs*.'"

"Oh yeah," she said, and laughed. "I completely forgot about that."

He laughed, too, albeit a bit uneasily. "Yeah," he said. "I'd never even heard of *the book of webs* till you mentioned it." The penknife poked a little with each bulge of a word passing up through his throat.

Amy stopped laughing, thought for a moment, and then said, "But if you didn't already know about *the book of webs*, then why didn't you ask me about it back at the café?"

"Honestly," he said, "at the time I hardly knew you. Best just to agree with what she says, I thought to myself. For all I knew you might've been dangerous."

"Dangerous?" she shrieked. "Me? Ha!" but her penknife-wielding hand, already trembling with age, jerked with her laughter, and the knife nicked his neck.

"Ow!" he screamed. "Fuck!" He tried to hold the wound closed with his hands, hands that were within moments soaked with his own warm, viscous life force. "What have you done?" he whispered hoarsely and, seeing as his hands were helpless to slow the gush of blood, raised them shakily into what he assumed would be the final frame of his darkening vision. Then he said, "Wait. Why is my blood yellow?"

"Your blood was yellow?" I interrupted him.

"Yellow," he said. "A warm, translucent yellow. 'Is this olive oil?' I said to Amy."

"Olive oil?" said Amy and took a step closer. She wiped a little off his hand with her finger, held that finger up to her eyes, sniffed it, tasted it, and said, "Olive oil."

"Huh," he said. "That's weird."

"That *is* weird," she said.

"Do you think we should try to make it stop?" he said.

"I don't know," she said. "How's it feel to lose it?"

"You know," he said as the oil continued to flow, sometimes slowing to a trickle, but then suddenly spritzing, like a can of beer opening, and then gushing again, "actually not that bad. At first I felt very sad," he said. "I felt like I was passing from a state of greater to lesser perfection—but by *perfection*," he felt it necessary to add, "I just mean one's capacity to act, to be, to live, and so on. But once I realized that this good I was losing could not in any way be kept, my sadness was actually lessened. Then I started to feel like maybe this thing I was losing wasn't ever really mine to begin with. The particular state of perfection I originally felt slipping away—," he said, "a state of perfection that was, to be honest, never that great of a state to begin with—had actually blocked the way to a greater state of perfection, a state I could attain only by losing the state I've been working so hard to maintain. Now that I've lost it," he said, "I feel—I don't know"—he was having a hard time putting it into words exactly—"I feel more—hm, *honest* isn't quite the right word. I wouldn't say that I'm finally being myself but more like I'm finally not pretending to be myself."

"Good," said Amy.

"Yeah," he said, as olive oil continued to drain from his neck wound, "I feel like I can finally relax, albeit into a state of—or not a *state*, per se, but more like a *zone*—yes, a zone of nonrelaxation."

A little while later, Amy said, "You know, the other funny thing is that the more I look at the wound, the more it looks to me like writing!"

"That *is* funny," he said. "Tell me what it says!"

But by that point they'd arrived at the base of a cliff, and Amy said, "I'll tell you once we're on the other side."

"The other side of what?" he said, but Amy had already slipped through.

"Slipped through what?" I asked, and Charlie said, "A cleft in the rock. A narrow aperture no wider than the fissure between the lips of a brave dissident undergoing interrogation by operatives of a barbarous state agency. 'I'll never tell!' you could almost hear this cliff face refusing to say to its interrogators," he said.

Amy seemed to have slipped effortlessly into this cleft in the rock—"I must have been blinking," he told me, "when her passage through actually occurred"—leaving him alone on the other side, contemplating how he was ever going to keep following her—how he was ever going to get from out here to in there, from outside the locked lips of this cliff face into the cave where, presumably, Amy was planning to introduce him to that friend of hers, the one who had expressed an interest in his bookshelves.

Into the Sealed Lips of the Cliff Face,

Charlie shouted, "Amy! Amy!" he shouted. "I really need someone to buy my bookshelves. If I can't, I'm not sure what I'll do!" he screamed. "I'm moving!" he said. "Amy! Can you hear me? Help me! I'm still moving," he said. "I can't stop moving!"

"I couldn't stop moving," he said to me.

"I get it," I replied. "Was your lease up or something?"

"My lease?" he said. "No, you don't understand."

He literally could not stop moving, which was a problem because he'd realized that if he pressed one ear against the cleft in the rock, he could hear a little something through the stone, and if he didn't let so much as a single ligament in his body untense—"You would not believe how much quieter it had gotten," he said, "now that there was no more blood, or blood alternative, sloshing about inside me"—if he didn't grit any dirt under his clogs or blink his eyes too quickly, he could just barely perceive under the ambient murmur of the cliff's presence—granted he plugged the other ear against the screeches of turkey vultures, the footsteps of tarantulas, the whirr of trembling quails, and the drone of cars commuting on the nearby overpass—he could just barely hear a steady stream of language coming from inside the cleft.

"The problem was, every time I moved," he said, "I lost it. That's why I shouted, 'I can't stop moving, Amy!'"

At first, he thought what he was listening to was Amy trying to tell him how to get into the cave.

"Did you say to put my ears where my shoes are?" he said.

"No," he seemed to hear her reply, "what I said was that there's a puppet show happening in here and you better hurry up or I'll miss it."

"*You'll* miss it?" he said.

"I meant *you*," said what he assumed to be Amy's voice from the other side of the cleft. "Hurry in or you'll miss the puppet show," she said. "It's about to start."

"I'd love to see a puppet show," he said. "But how do I get in?"

"I know it's about to begin because they told me," she said.

"Who?" he said.

"The puppets," she said.

"The puppets?" he said.

"I know," she said. "I could hardly believe it myself. I said, 'You must mean *puppeteers*,' but they said, 'No. Nope. We're the puppets, the puppets themselves speaking to you. In fact, we don't have puppeteers,' they said, and I said, 'Really?' and I guess I had no choice but to take their word for it."

"You can't tell whether you're talking to puppets or puppeteers?" Charlie shouted into the cliff face.

"How would I be able to tell?" she said.

"Do they have strings attached?" he asked.

"I don't know," she said, "It's dark as day in here, and my eyesight was never great to begin with. I can't see a thing. I would maybe try to reach out to feel for strings, but I'm a little wary of the spiders, if you know what I mean. I'm thus relying entirely on what the voices in here are telling me and what they tell me is that they're puppets and that the puppet show is about to begin and that you better get in here or you'll miss the beginning!"

"But nothing could be done," Charlie told me. "The cliff's lips were all but sealed shut. I yelled into the crevice, 'You know, I actually don't really care about seeing a puppet show. I thought you were going to introduce me to someone who was interested in my bookshelves. Is that friend of yours watching the puppet show in there with you? Maybe you could describe them for me?'"

By *them*, of course, he meant the bookshelves, but Amy seemed to think he meant the puppets—that he wanted her to describe the puppets and the puppet theater for him.

"I don't!" he screamed into the crevice. "But I don't think she could hear me," he told me. "I guess she couldn't hear much over the sound of her own listening to the puppets describe their stage to her for me," he told me, "for she continued as though I hadn't raised any objection, as though I actually wanted to hear about the puppet show."

"Where the puppets are," she said, "dead birds flock."

"At least I think that's what she said," he told me. "To tell you the truth, I'm still not entirely convinced that Amy *wasn't* actually trying to tell me how to get my body through the cleft in the cliff face."

Charlie, frankly, still wasn't sure that he hadn't simply systematically misinterpreted Amy's instructions. It was all rather difficult to tell what exactly she was saying, and only partly because occasionally, and with increasing frequency as time went on, one of the turkey vultures would swoop down to tear a strip of skin off his body and he'd have to shoo the bird away, and each time he did, the sound of his bones grinding in their joint sockets would drown out Amy's voice for a moment. But even when he could hear her clearly, her words carried enough ambiguity that he still often wasn't sure whether she was describing what was on the other side of the cliff face, giving him complicated instructions for how to get inside, or something else entirely.

"Where the puppets are," she said, "dead birds flock—leaf- and feather-dressed skeletons, bones twig-thin and brittle, drawn ashore from distant lands by the ocean's endless lapping."

"Ocean?" he said. "In there? Actually I don't care," he said. "I don't care about the puppets!" he screamed. "Unless they're interested in my bookshelves!" But Amy continued as though she hadn't heard him, and as time wore on, and the possibility that the puppet show had anything whatsoever to do with his bookshelves grew increasingly remote, he eventually even came to doubt that Amy was actually speaking to him and not to someone else on the other side of the cliff face with her, someone who happened to be posing similar questions to his at the exact same time. In fact, the longer he listened—and gradually he stopped asking questions altogether, ultimately even repressing his questioning impulse altogether, for he realized that the mere noise of his jaw unclenching in anticipation of voicing a question did more to obscure what he was hearing than any answer to a question of his could ever possibly clarify—the longer he listened, the more it seemed to him that what he was overhearing was a conversation between at least two interlocutors: one of whom he had no reason to doubt, but also, as the days went by, little reason anymore to suspect, was Amy, and the other who, unlike him, seemed to have some interest in learning that

Where the Puppets Were,

dead birds flocked—leaf- and feather-dressed skeletons, bones twig-thin and brittle, drawn ashore from distant lands by the ocean's endless churning, brought there, these birds, to rot along the edges of the puppet theater. And among the rocks worn paper smooth by crashing water, waves also brought dead dogfish, each leather-fleshed and eyeless, open mouths' crescent moons agape, toothless and abyssal, their scaled skin stretched taut over sharp cartilage scaffolding, bent and twisted by the slow-motion dance of their gradual desiccation. Waiting for the show to start, the puppets roamed among the various cadavers, gleaning tiny seashells—conches mostly, none larger than a fingernail, most smaller, cuticle-thin and conical, sun-bleached bone white, spiraling up endlessly into themselves. The puppets gleaned handfuls of these hollow homes, these whirled worlds, gathering them seemingly to serve some hitherto unannounced purpose in the impending puppet show. They meandered, meandered and stooped, tracing inscrutable, crisscrossing paths across the shoreline. Kelp grasped and draped stones. Stones gleamed, stubbed puppets' toes. Other puppets swam in the tides, did dead man's floats, adrift between seafloor and sky, limbs out like the cormorants with their wings drying, black crosses on driftwood carried by by slow, slow waves. Drowned seagulls rolled among the rattling pebbles, tugged by lapping tides. Dead fish eyes saw fins thin as tissue become backlit in diffused light falling from a sheet of cloud making the gentle heat spread across the stage

When the Shipwreck Made Landfall.

It came from the sea like a drowning creature, clawing its way up the algae-slickened stones and dying in a seashell-rich patch of wrack line, popping dried sea beans, flattening egg cases, and, as it ground to a halt, nudging, and thereby greatly surprising, a stooping puppet whose attention had been wholly absorbed in extracting a seashell from the empty eye socket of a small coyote skull, tangled in ribbons of orange seaweed.

"Was the shipwreck a puppet?" I asked.

"No, the shipwreck was a shipwreck," said Charlie.

"No, I mean, was it an actual shipwreck or a puppet shipwreck?" I said. "Did it actually wash ashore, or was its washing ashore part of the puppet show?"

"No, this actually happened," he said. "The shipwreck arrived moments before the puppet show was supposed to start, which was why the puppets were thrown into such upheaval by its unscripted appearance on their stage."

"What about the coyote skull," I said.

"Puppet," he said.

"Shells?" I said.

"Puppets," he said.

"The ocean?" I said.

"A puppet," he said.

"The sun?" I said.

"Batshit," he said.

"Oh, right," I said. "Because it was a cave," and he said, "Exactly."

"So, the only thing that wasn't part of the puppet show," I said, "the only thing that actually happened was the shipwreck."

"Correct," he said. "The shipwreck was the only thing that actually happened."

"A shipwreck washing ashore never actually happened!" the puppets shouted at each other. "What are we to do? This never actually happened!"

"It never actually happened?" I interrupted again to ask.

"They meant it never happened in real life," said Charlie. "It wasn't part of the historical events the puppet show was based on."

Historical authenticity, he explained, was very important to the puppets, for reasons that would, he said, become obvious later. This was why it was so important to them that they figure out how to make the shipwreck disappear—because there never was a shipwreck.

Fortunately, among the puppets were puppets modeled after stoic heretics, skilled ecoterrorists, radical grassroots organizers, socialist linguists, propagandists, guerrilla insurrectionists, interspecies ethicists, unorthodox biosemioticians, and even conscientious animistic puppeteers, and so these puppets gathered together and, after a brief discussion, collectively assented to address the shipwreck directly, for there was no problem, according to the wisdom some of the puppets had gleaned by pretending to be the people they were based on, that could be solved without first giving that problem a proper name, addressing it respectfully, and listening carefully to its response. USS *Burlington* was what was left of the weathered letters flaking from the shipwreck's hull, and so this was what they endeavored to call the shipwreck: *Burlington.*

"I've said *endeavored* deliberately," said Amy—or whoever it was whose voice Charlie heard recounting these events through the cleft in the cliff face.

For to speak this particular word—*Burlington*—to properly pronounce it in the language the puppets actually spoke when they weren't delivering their lines—that is, a language that the puppets had devised among themselves after having grown to distrust the language their script was written in—to say this word *Burlington* in the puppet language required unhinging one's tongue and taking it out of one's mouth, a difficult maneuver that could be repeated only a few times in a puppet's life.

"The puppets had tongues?" I asked.

"At least according to what they said with them," replied Charlie.

What they said with them, he explained—according to what he heard through the cleft—what they said was that to say the name *Burlington* properly with one's tongue was to unhinge it and remove it from one's mouth. To do so, moreover, was but the opening chapter of a very complex book . . .

"A book?" I said, and he said, "Yeah, but by *book* in this instance, all I mean is the sort of thing, like when you say 'Sit' to a dog and the dog assumes a posture and you say 'Good dog.' One chapter calls for the next," he said. "That's what I mean by the word *book.* Like when you repeat something I say with a question mark, and then I explain what I meant, and you tell me that that doesn't make sense and I keep talking anyway . . . A *book*; it was with the understanding of a language as nothing more than a library of numberless and ever-evolving books like this that the puppets had invented their puppet language."

"Oh," I said.

Just as in our language saying the word *sit* to a dog begins *the book of sitting and giving a treat and being a good boy*, so in the puppet language saying the word *Burlington*—that is, removing one's tongue—was to begin a very exacting and elaborate book, one that, once begun, could continue only by every puppet in proximity also removing their tongue and for all tongues thus disarticulated to be arrayed in the sand in a tiered, circular formation the puppets called *the bush of tongues*. The bush of tongues served as a sort of altar for the mating ritual of a small population of wood-boring beetles endemic to the puppet theater. The so-to-speak next chapter of the book that began with the word *Burlington* and continued with the formation of the bush of tongues—the third chapter of this book—consisted of couples of copulating beetles taking turns to walk back-to-back around the bush of tongues. The bush of tongues was to these beetles, therefore, what a destroyed lawn was to angels. It was a simple fact of life in the puppet theater that any pair of wood-boring beetles attempting to mate without a bush of tongues to circumnavigate was doomed to a brief, faltering, and ultimately unsatisfying bout of lovemaking, lovemaking that, though significantly more likely to result in a greater number of fertilized eggs, was rarely even remotely pleasurable for the beetles involved. Such dismal affairs were not only a strain on the relationships between mating beetles, who tended to be highly emotionally sensitive, but also produced such a population boom that the puppet theater, largely wood, might be entirely demolished by the hungry brood. Thus the puppet word *Burlington*, however demanding it was to articulate, served both as an aphrodisiac and a very necessary partial prophylactic for the wood-boring beetles, many of whom were not particularly keen to rush into parenthood anyway and reciprocated the puppets' tongue sacrifice by ensuring only key portions of the puppet theater were reduced to dust, portions without which the puppet show, which was ordinarily resumed after the tongue harvest following the beetles' mating season, was, if not always considerably improved, at least dynamically altered, often in mysterious and even visionary ways.

In brief, this was how that book worked—"its grammar, if you will," the puppets told Amy, Amy who in retelling Charlie what the puppets told her had said *endeavored* because although the hinges of the puppet tongues were indeed loosening, the wood-boring beetles had not yet reached the requisite pitch of intensity in the current mating season's foreplay, and the word *Burlington* was thus ecologically unspeakable—unspeakable lest the puppets condemn their theater's fragile ecosystem to what they called *phenological asynchrony*, a particularly devastating aspect of what they called *the climate catastrophe*, which was a problem they'd been conversing with for several years—the shipwreck being only the latest repartee in what was becoming an increasingly contentious dialogue.

Thus, the only way the puppets could address the problem of the shipwreck while keeping their tongues in their mouths—"and they say they need their tongues in their mouths," said Amy, "because they need tongues to say their lines in the puppet show, the puppet show that they are desperate for both you and me, and especially you for some reason, to see"—the only ecologically sound way to address the problem was to address the shipwreck as *Doctor Burlington*—for the word *Doctor* in the puppet language ensured that the word immediately following it didn't actually need to be said; by prefacing any word with *Doctor*, in other words, the puppets ensured that the tongue plucked from the speaker's mouth was plucked only *imaginarily*, and the bush of tongues thus formed was a bush in a so-to-speak unperformed puppet show the puppets collectively imagined: a ring of make-believe tongues around which pairs of wood-boring beetles orbited in a spring morning sun that shone more brightly than even the sun that shone over the real puppet show ever could.

"Doctor Burlington," thus said the puppets—"Doctor Burlington," they said to the shipwreck that was causing an increasingly unforgiveable delay to the start of the puppet show—"Doctor Burlington," they said, "was no more. Retelling what his clients had told him made such demands on his capacity to express that the mere attempt caused his entire body to be torn apart before he could even finish the shit show first draft of his appalling manuscript . . ."

"That's what the puppets are saying," shouted Amy through the cliff face. "Along with a lot of other nonsense as well—but I'm giving you these words untranslated, just to give you a flavor of the puppet language. Don't get confused. The words are not continuing a story but, like everything the puppets say, executing a highly specific action in a book particular to their bizarre language. In this case, the words seem to be serving some incantatory and specifically invocatory function regarding the shipwreck."

"It was true. What sounded to me like a narrative," Charlie told me, "was actually a complicated invocation, one designed to call Doctor Burlington's soul—that is, its motor force, the so-to-speak tug at its strings—back into its body so that the seemingly inanimate matter might be able to adequately respond to the puppets' attempt at address. What had sounded to me like the continuation of some unrelated tale was actually a complicated invocation that, to the surprise of everyone—even, it seemed, the puppets themselves—worked!"

Stirred by the puppets' invocation, Doctor Burlington, the shipwreck, shuddered with signs of impending resurrection, shook with a surge of vitality, and then issued a thunderous cracking sound, as it split down the middle, disgorging an enormous creature, drenched in amniotic fluid. "Not a puppet?" I said, and Charlie said, "Definitely not a puppet."

The puppets all stepped back, mouths agape, as the hatchling vigorously shook off thick gobs of the fluid that saturated its feathers. Gobs pelted the nearest puppets, and the creature unfurled its tremendous wings, rotated the giant globes of its eyeballs, eventually settling their dilating pupils on the small spiders scurrying frantically all around it.

"Spiders?" I said.

"Right," said Charlie. "I had the same thought myself, but Amy reminded me that this hatchling—'I believe it's a giant species of quail,' she said, 'female, but that's just a hunch; it's been a while since I've sexed poultry'—Amy reminded me that the fledgling had only just hatched and that the puppets were thus just as likely to seem like spiders as they were to seem like puppets to someone who'd never seen either spiders or puppets before. That's why Amy said *spiders*," he said. "It was because the puppets had voiced this sentence to Amy as though from the perspective of the quail—as was their instinct when frightened."

Like fight or flight, the puppets had an instinct to voice their utterances—even the thoughts in their own heads—from the perspective of nearby strangers when they were frightened, and they were certainly frightened now. As was the quail hatchling, understandably.

As more and more curious puppets approached the giant animal—"which might very well be an ordinary-size animal," shouted Amy through the cleft, "that only seems gigantic because the puppets are very small; as I said, I can't actually see any of this and thus have no sense of scale"—as puppets approached the hatchling to affix tentative exploratory strands of their web to her talons and legs—"*Web?*" I asked, and Charlie explained that this was how the puppets worded it to Amy, explaining that a collective understanding of what a thing was and an attempt to begin having a conversation with it was just as likely to seem like a spider's web as anything else to someone with no experience of either—as more and more puppets gathered around and milled about the hatchling's long, thin legs, which towered over the puppets like tree trunks, and as they attempted to weave the unexpected guest into a collective understanding of what she might be and how to engage her in dialogue, the hatchling recoiled. Her face assumed a furious expression, and she opened her enormous beak.

The puppets braced themselves for what they expected, from so mighty an animal, to be a deafening cry but were surprised—and then relieved—and then a little concerned—to hear no sound emanate at all.

No sound whatsoever issued from the quail's beak, and so, with a baffled, pained look, she closed it. She opened it a few more times but with the same odd consequence: a painful silence.

Just as the puppets were beginning to speculate on how best to respond to this silence, which, after all, may have been an intentional gesture—one intended to *look* unintended—the quail squeezed her eyes closed, ruffled her feathers, gagged, and vomited up a small white object. It clattered on the bed of broken shells and fish bones at her feet.

One puppet approached cautiously to retrieve the fallen object, wiped the mucus and bile off with its shirtsleeve, and then held the thing aloft for the other puppets to behold and wonder at.

"It's a tooth!" said Amy.

"A tooth?" I said, and Charlie said yes, that's what Amy said, and also that although the tooth—"a human tooth, they say," said Amy—seemed too small an object to obstruct the vocal apparatus of so large a creature, no sooner had the quail regurgitated it, she was finally able to speak, and she told the puppets—or so they were able to understand by her deafening hoos and screeches, sounds that someone untrained in the puppets' semiotic methods would probably have been tempted to interpret as a fledgling's meaningless babblings—to please be so kind as to get the fuck away from her.

"Sorry, sorry," said the puppets, "so sorry!" they said, as each stepped a few paces back. "We didn't mean to make you feel uncomfortable, but we see now how we must've. We hope you'll excuse us for being so clumsy," they said. "We are, so often, like those hares hidden in a snowy field," they said, "hares who, frightened by the sound of a rifle retort, leave the very footprints that will lead the hunter to them. We are responsible beyond our intentions," they said. "It is impossible for the attention directing the act—the tug of the string—to accomplish exclusively what was intended. Inadvertent actions are always unavoidable. Often the very opposite of the act pursued is what most predominantly ensues. We get caught up in things," they said. "Things turn against us."

The quail was pleasantly surprised by this—"Some creatures," explained Amy, "aren't born expecting the universe to be any less ungenerous than the universe generally tends to be"—she was pleasantly surprised that she had to say what she had to say only once for the puppets to, more or less, get the message and respond in the way she'd wanted. She cocked her head inquisitively first this way, then that. She flapped her wings, but seeing that they were still of little use and that the creatures around her were small enough that they most likely posed little threat and might even be edible, she said, "Perhaps I overreacted. Far be it for me—or is it, *from* me?" she asked. "Sorry," she said. "I've only just been born. I'm still learning how to make myself understandable."

"Oh, us too," said the puppets, laughing a little, "we wish we could say it gets easier with age," and then one puppet added, "I think it's *from* me, though. But I'm probably wrong. Anyway, it's just a preposition. How much difference could it make?"

"The hatchling wasn't actually speaking though," I interrupted, "right?"

"Exactly," said Charlie. "Well sort of. Remember, the puppets were in a unique position, not quite human, not quite object, and this gave them a sort of dual citizenship, linguistically—not so much the ability to communicate well with both humans and nonhumans as a deep-rooted understanding that both humans and nonhumans were equally, ultimately inscrutable. It was just as impossible for a person to understand what another person meant as it was for a person to understand what a blender meant, so the puppets tried their best with both and didn't give up easily. The hatchling wasn't actually *speaking*—not in any ideologically *pure* sense of the word—but neither are you and I."

Then the hatchling said, "What was I going to say, though? Oh yes, I was going to say, 'Far be it from me to judge your book, but—'"

"*Our book?!*" the puppets screamed in sudden pandemonium.

"Yes," said the hatchling. "Far be it from me to judge your—"

"Stop!" shouted the puppets, holding their hands to their ears. "Don't say that word!"

"Book?" said the quail.

"Stop!" screamed the puppets.

They eventually settled down enough to explain that the word *book* was an extremely dangerous word to articulate in their language and was not a word to be said lightly, a fact evidenced by the way they themselves prefaced it, in this very explanation, with not one but two *Doctors*. For, or so they explained, fictionalizing the saying of the word *book* was—due to the lethal grammatical exigencies of that word—even more dangerous than simply saying it in reality. Only by fictionalizing the fictionalizing of the saying of the word *book* through the doubling of *Doctor* was the word *book* rendered safe to say, and even then, there could still be delayed ramifications.

"Honestly, we're still in the process of learning what the word means, what it does," they said. "But so far, it does not bode well."

"Okay," said the hatchling. "Sorry. It was an accident. Just like you, I guess I make mistakes. I didn't know. Now I do. In *my* language," she said, "*book* is simply how one designates that thing that pulls the strings, what you called the *attention directing the action*, the thing pulling the strings—a soul, I suppose you could say. In my language we just call that one's *book*."

"Ah," said the puppets. "We see now. That makes sense."

"So we're all good then?" said the hatchling.

"Yeah, we're cool," said the puppets, "but we're afraid we're going to have to ask you to leave."

And What Could a Fledgling, in the Face of Such Spiders, Do but Oblige?

So, the fledgling left the puppets and came back here.

"Where?" I asked.

"Here," said Charlie. "Fledgling that I was, I had no choice but to oblige the puppets' request."

"Who?" I asked, and he said, "Me," and I said, "You?" and he said, "Yeah," I said, "Did what?" and he said, "Came back," and I said, "Here?" and he said, "Yep."

"The puppets were afraid to ask me to leave," he explained, "but though fledgling that I was, I could nevertheless sense that they needed me to go, so I left and came back here, and when I got back, you asked me about my walk and so I told you. I told it straight from beginning to end, just like you said I should."

"Oh," I said. "For some reason, I thought the puppets had been talking to the quail when they'd said, 'I'm afraid we're going to have to ask you leave.'"

"Why would the puppets have said that to the quail?" he said, laughing.

"Because I thought you said that the quail had hatched right in the middle of their theater," I said, "and that the puppet show was about to start."

"Oh! I see what you've done," he said. "You've confused the Quail for an actual quail!"

The Quail, he said, was just the code name for the secret plan the puppets were trying to get Amy to tell them about. I must have misheard him. When he said that Amy had been involved in hatching a nefarious plot against his coalition and that her band of renegades had been referring to their plot as *the Quail*, he supposed I must have heard those two things and put two and two together.

"As for the puppet show that was about to start," he said, "I doubt you want me to go into too much more detail about that."

"Why not?" I said.

"Well," he said, "as you might imagine, Amy wasn't too keen to spill the beans about the Quail. The puppets barely knew a thing about the plot, weren't, honestly, even yet entirely certain there *was* a plot. They'd gleaned the secret code name from hearsay. Everyone was whispering, 'the Quail this, the Quail that,' and some hazy rumor about conspirators planning on turning the puppets in to the Burlington police. But other than that, the puppets knew nothing. Amy did. That much was obvious. But she'd made it crystal clear that she wasn't going to squeal."

"'Turn us *in to* the Burlington police,' or 'Turn us *into* the Burlington police?'" the puppets kept asking her, but even on this minor grammatical point—"Tell us!" they screamed till they were hoarse. "It's just a preposition," they said, "*in to* or *into*, one word or two! How much difference could it possibly make?"—even on this minor point of clarification, Amy's lips were sealed.

"For a while," said Charlie, "the puppets were letting me watch the interrogation. Since I was the one who brought Amy in, I think they thought they owed me that. But eventually I got the sense—the puppets were too polite to ask me directly—I got the sense that my presence was preventing them from using certain techniques they wished to spare me the sight of. 'If you think we've been rough so far,' the puppets kept saying to Amy, 'you just wait. The puppet show hasn't even started yet.' While I was no fan of Amy—not after what she did—the puppets were right to assume I wouldn't want to be there when the so-called puppet show actually started. My eyes were still too sensitive for such things as what clearly had to be done. You know how I am," he said. "Even the act of killing a black widow nesting in my own mother's shoes made my nose bleed for two days. You know how it is with me," he said,

"Every Mission to Protect a Fish from a Snake Ends up a Mission to Rescue the Snake from Drowning."

Once Charlie had finished telling me about his little walk—or rather a little after that because I'd gotten confused and had needed a few minor points clarified—once he'd finished clarifying those points and telling me about his walk—"Straight from beginning to end," he said, "just like we'd agreed I would try to do," he said, "no digressions," he added, "no interruptions," and I said, "We agreed on that?" and he said, "Yeah, remember?" and I said, "No, now I remember, but I just can't remember exactly why we'd agreed on that," and he said, "Sure you do"—once he'd finished telling me about his little walk, he reminded me why we'd agreed on him telling it to me straight from beginning to end.

We'd been standing, he told me, the two of us old pals, Charlie and Leech, right here where we were standing now, and I, Leech, was trying to remember something I had been right in the middle of telling him when I'd gotten interrupted.

"Where was I?" I said, and he said, "Now?" and I said, "Yeah," and he said, "Here," pointing down at the ground.

"No," I said, "I mean where was I in the thing I was telling you," and he said, "Oh, I think you said that you were stranded."

He said I'd been telling him about the time I'd been stranded in enemy territory. "Stranded," he said that I'd said, "and with no way out. Not a single book in sight."

"Wait, *book*?" he'd interrupted me, "why on earth would you need a book?" and I'd been obliged to explain that a *book*, in this case, was something someone else trapped with me in enemy territory had invented for the purpose of trafficking people like us out.

A book was a technology—whether it worked was another story—a technology for trafficking people across the otherwise unnavigable chasm between enemy territory and a hypothetical sanctuary where such people might actually have a chance to live the lives they wanted to.

"Like a boat," I said, and he said, "Oh, like a boat. I get it," and I said, "Good. So, there wasn't a single book in sight, and this was because the writers—"

"Wait. If that's what a book was," he interrupted, "then what's a writer?" and I said, "A *writer* was what we called a factory that had been corrupted from the inside out so that it produced books instead of whatever it was supposed to produce."

"Wait. I told you all this?" I interrupted Charlie to ask.

"Yep," he said. "That is, if you really *are* Leech," he laughed, "and not someone else impersonating him. You said you were stranded because there was no book for you to be in, not even a book on the horizon."

One of the writers, according to what I told him, one of the writers of the books that served to shuttle evacuees from one side of the border to the other was in the hospital for repairs. Or so, at least, went the *official* story—rumor had it that that writer's employees were striking in protest of the factory's execrable labor abuses—"but that's another story altogether," I said.

In any case, the only writer that was currently working was notoriously slow, and the occasional book that oozed out of this writer featured very few characters—a pretty serious flaw, seeing as the only point of a book was to facilitate border crossings, and crossings were achieved only by the hopeful evacuee impersonating a character.

"A character was to a book," I said, "sort of like what a seat is to a boat; only instead of sitting on it, you pretended that you were the character, and kept on pretending usually until you had either dealt some measure of irreparable damage to the very fabric of our enemy's existence or, as more often seemed to be the case, died trying."

Anyway, such feeble excuses of books as were currently being written—feeble because they generally featured only one or two characters, usually at least one of which was a particular horse this writer was obsessed with for some reason—such books sufficed to traffic only one or two people per day, a day being generally about how long it took this writer to produce a book.

"But wait," I said. "Where was I again? Oh, that's right," I said. "Stranded."

I was what was being called *on standby*. I was on standby because, unlike many of the others of us whose existence, like mine, had become, or else had always been, impossible insofar as we were stranded in enemy territory—I suppose we formed a sort of informal community, though with nothing in common and with no coherent organization or strategy, or often even knowledge that others existed—I hadn't thought it would be necessary to purchase a ticket for a book ahead of time. While having a ticket didn't assure one's passage across the border, it at least gave a person a certain date to show up at the borderland to see whether the book one had booked a ticket for actually existed or not and, if it did, if it featured any characters that weren't impossible for someone who wasn't already a horse to impersonate.

True, most books didn't actually exist or didn't feature enough impersonatable characters to ensure that even *all ticketholders* could climb aboard, let along someone on standby. But at least ticketholders weren't required to stand by at all times and wait. At least, if a book ever arrived that was functional—and there were always rumors of one that would be, rumors, indeed, of a book sufficing not only to traffic us out but also to render the *very need* for trafficking us out unnecessary—if a book ever arrived that was functional, if, say, the out-of-order writer was ever repaired, or if the other writer's horse could ever remember one of its dreams (for it was widely believed that the horse's dreams were populated with innumerable characters, but it was a trope of these books that the horse was always trying and failing to remember its dreams), then maybe those with tickets would have a chance. No, if you had a ticket, only during certain appointed hours of the day would you be disappointed to discover that you were still stranded; for the rest of the time, you were free to assume everything was going to work out okay for you.

Not so for someone who was only standing by.

For, yes, by the time I'd thought to purchase a ticket—which was only after my coconspirator, Yekel the Slug (who, it turned out, was an enemy in disguise as an enemy in disguise, in other words was disguised as one of us but was actually working for the government), blew my cover and a gang of the enemy's most bloodthirsty operatives were in close pursuit—only after this did the front desk agents of a boutique hotel, who were, for whatever reason, the ones responsible for selling tickets for passage on one of the books, only after I realized I needed to get out of here and fast and therefore ought to purchase a ticket for a book, only then did the front desk agents decide to suspend all further ticket sales until the more reliable writer was back in operation.

Standing by, I was informed, was the only option for a person in my position.

But standing by, I wondered, what would I do while standing by? For how many hours, I wondered, would I be standing by, and for each hour of standing by, how would I justify my existence, assuming standing by in itself was insufficient, which I couldn't but imagine it would be.

"Justifying one's existence," I explained, "was an extremely difficult-to-achieve requirement for acquiring and retaining citizenship in enemy territory. Waiting around interminably for a way out couldn't possibly fit the bill."

Or so I thought. But how was I to know? How would I know for certain until I was already in the midst of standing by?

"How does standing by actually work?" I asked one of the front desk agents over the phone.

"Hello? Hello?" asked the agent in return.

"Can you hear me?" I said. "Hello? Can you hear me?"

But it was too late. The call was dropped.

I stepped out onto the balcony.

Then I traded hair with someone I was casually romantically involved with because I figured her beautiful long hair would make me a better candidate for a job I had an interview for, a job that I needed only so long as I remained stranded in enemy territory, which hopefully wouldn't be for much longer.

"Better safe than sorry," however, advised my psychotherapist, so I applied for the job and was horrified to find that they wanted me to come in for an interview.

"You have nothing to be afraid of," said the friend I was romantically involved with. "If it makes you feel any better," she added, "you can borrow my hair."

"Oh, thanks," I said. "That would be great. Would you mind if I cut it a little shorter?"

"Not at all," she said, "so long as you promise to be careful," which I did, and, honestly, was, but it was only once I was all but finished that I realized why it was that even professional hairdressers do not typically cut the hair on their own heads without even looking.

"Oh, Leech," I said to myself. "Is this really a good idea?"

I opened my eyes and was shocked to see that half my head was a complete disaster and that the other half, though somehow even lovelier than when I started, would have to be seriously edited away for the sake of consistency. So I closed my eyes and went back at it, while my heart pounded at the thought of the impending interview—realizing that it was becoming only increasingly unlikely, thanks to the state of my head, that the interviewers would deem me so far superior to the job that they'd let me stay unemployed and load me up with enough cash to write my own damn book, which was about the only positive outcome of this interview that I could imagine—and when I opened my eyes again, everything was, in typical fashion, even worse.

Fortunately, my lover was looking great in my hair, which was, truth be told, without parallel anywhere in enemy territory, which was to say—as far as we *really* knew—the entire universe. I could see her in my hair on the television. She was a congresswoman, though whether an undercover agent disguised as a congresswoman or an actual representative I never did determine. She was currently delivering a blistering speech about a coded communiqué that a gang of antigovernmental activists had dispatched and that her people had intercepted, and I could not, for the life of me, tell whether her intentions were to villainize the subversives or to actually support the activists' subversion by so exaggerating a politician's performance of outrage that her rhetoric might function as a kind of a mockery of the whole idea of government, of representation, of the very idea that someone might have the ability, much less the right, to represent *oneself*, much less others . . .

In any case, I wasn't able to catch more than a few minutes of her opening remarks before I had to leave for my interview, which went surprisingly well, despite my staggering hideousness at the time, my pale scalp shimmering through the scraggly strands of cropped hair like dunes through brambles of seagrass and beach rose. It went well, but not so well I didn't get the job because I was too good for it, or even so well that I got the job, or even so well that I didn't get the job, but only so well—not surprising, I suppose—that they told me that they'd be in touch soon—"Cool," I said, "it's not like my very life depends on it"—only so well that, weeks later, they still hadn't.

"Hadn't what?" Charlie asked me.

"Been in touch," I said.

To make matters worse, the foreign language my thoughts were occurring in—unlike my own language, the one I only ever still remembered in dreams—didn't afford me any insight into the future, so I had nothing to go on but the interviewers' vague assertion that I'd hear back about a second interview sometime during the week it was now, and the week it was now was nearly over.

So, I ran into the woods. Then I biked to the ocean. I saw a red-tailed hawk and it was perched on someone's front lawn with a squirrel in its talons, so I crashed my bike into a mailbox and redialed the boutique hotel.

"Hi," I said. "I think I spoke to you a few minutes ago."

"No," said the front desk agent. "I don't think you did."

"Oh," I said. "Well, it sounded like you."

"It wasn't me," said the agent.

I said, "Well, I'd been told that there were currently no tickets being sold."

"That's right," said the agent.

"Well, what am I supposed to do?" I asked. "I need to get out of here!" I said. "Paranoid people keep following me. I look over my shoulder and I see people looking over their shoulders. Later, after I have hurried down the street or up the stairs, or down the hall, or into bed, not daring to look back, and I can resist the impulse no longer, I look back and see these same people, also looking back, also looking frightened. The only thing that keeps me going is the comfort of there consistently being this one person just ahead of me, and so I match my steps to this person's and try to keep just enough distance between us so that he doesn't think I'm following him, but every once in a while he looks back, and when he does, I see genuine terror in his eyes! This terror reminds me of my own, and then I can't help but turn back to see these same paranoid people still following me!"

Eventually, in this manner, I arrived at the beach where I walked along the water for what felt like forever, while singing at the top of my lungs, for finally, there was no one else near enough to hear me over the crashing waves:

> "Oh, this standing by, it's fatal
> As I walk beside the waves—
> The babies stay prenatal,
> And the dead barred from their graves—"

until I came across a sign half-buried in the dunes that said NO BROODING and figured it was better to sulk in silence with an affected smile on my face than to risk attracting attention from enemy law enforcement.

But before I knew it, my affectation had overpowered my actual affect, and I was engulfed in a genuine sense of serenity.

Now, I was generally in no need of a reminder of the famous adage that our moods don't believe in each other, but there was another class of moods that didn't even believe this, moods that were actually so assured of themselves that they truly believed other moods actually *would* believe in them, and this sense of serenity was one of these moods. So, I sang:

> "Soon I won't be standing by,
> But feigning I'm a pet
> Armadillo killing presidents—but
> Fuck! I'm getting wet—"

and I stopped singing, for it had started to rain.

And just like that, the mood was dead, and the one that succeeded it had about as much belief in the preceding mood as the preceding mood had in the possibility that my pursuers would be able to track me down all the way out here at the beach.

"Fucking serenity," I muttered to my serenity, "I should've known you'd betray me," as my pursuers' silhouettes emerged out of the thick fog that had suddenly settled over the shoreline.

"Nice haircut, Leech" one of the more muscled goons said with a satisfied smile.

"No shit," I shot back. "How many years in psychotherapy did it take you to parse that little mystery?"

"About half as many years," drawled the man, "as it'll take you to fully process how it was we learned you were an enemy agent in disguise!" and the group parted to reveal a smirking figure standing behind them, a shovel in one hand, a rake in the other.

"Yekel the Slug?" I gasped.

"Who's your angel now, Leech?" said Yekel as the others closed in around me.

And the goon was right about one thing—it did take me many years in psychotherapy to process the betrayal.

I kept thinking I was done processing it only to discover, either through some slip of the tongue or through the careful analysis of one of my dreams, some new way that the betrayal was still affecting me—even after all these years!—distorting my perceptions, undergirding new attempts at relationship and collaboration.

It wasn't, for instance, until after I'd spent a whole day tripping on psilocybin mushrooms and in the evening had sat beside a river rippling with all the reflected colors of the desert cliffs and sky and the dried grasses that grew wild on the riverside, and had held a dirt clod in my hand and had realized that, despite everything, I was actually grateful for my and Yekel the Slug's partnership, even if it had all been a masquerade, even though we'd both been so deeply undercover at the time that we were disguised even to ourselves—yes, and it wasn't even until after this epiphany, after I'd crumbled this dirt clod in my hand and watched the dirt slip through my fingers and disperse into the flowing river as I sat there thinking that maybe there even was something gained by the loss of Yekel the Slug, even if all I'd gained was the power to never have to lose him again, and I'd started to cry and the prison guard who was there to make sure I didn't escape said, "Everything cool, pal?" and I'd said, "I think I finally just really let Yekel the Slug go," and he'd touched my shoulder with a tenderness that made me cry even harder and had then taken me back to my prison cell where I'd found a message from Yekel smuggled deep in my bar of soap detailing a similar series of epiphanies about us that he, also by this point imprisoned in a nearby cell, had just had—it wasn't until after I recounted all this to my therapist and, with joyful, grieving tears in my eyes, said, "I'm just so relieved to know that Yekel the Slug isn't still mad at me," and my therapist had replied, "Wait, why would Yekel be mad at *you*?"—it was only after this that I realized *I* might have reason to be mad at Yekel, that at some deep level of my being I actually might've been quite mad.

"You can bet your ass you are!" said my therapist, and I said, "That I'm what?" and she said, "Mad." And then she suggested that I probably had a hard time expressing anger healthily.

"No way," I said, and tried to tell her about the book I'd been writing on the toilet paper in my prison cell, but she cut me off.

"Look," she said. "Saying 'I need to pee,' or even 'I'm peeing,' isn't the same as actually peeing."

"It isn't?" I said, and she said, "No," and that was when I realized I had, indeed, been going about almost everything in my entire life wrong.

So, on my therapist's recommendation, I screamed, "Fuck you, Yekel!" First I screamed it on the couch in my therapist's office while punching a pillow, then in the armored van on a field trip to the beach some of the guards took some of us prisoners on, and then into the crashing waves of the violently churning ocean. "Fuck you, Yekel!" I screamed at the sign that said NO BROODING and "Fuck you, Yekel!" I screamed at the sky, and the sky went dark, and I bolted toward the water, and the stars appeared, and I screamed, "Fuck you, stars!" and I heard the guards scream over the rat-a-tat of their machine gun fire, "They're escaping! They're escaping!" and the moon rose over the water and I screamed, "Fuck you, moon!" and it cracked into one hundred pieces, which all started to drift imperceptibly slowly away from one another, each piece a fractured glimmer laughing on the surface of the waves through which I thrashed as I swam away from the twinkling lights of the guns of the guards firing from the shoreline, and I screamed, "Fuck you, pieces of the moon!" and each cracked piece of moon cracked in two.

The next thing I remembered clearly, I was in complete darkness. I could neither see nor feel anything, but I could hear a sort of gurgling, like a distant conversation, or an engine idling, or tiny bubbles popping. Based on my last coherent recollection, I'd have guessed I was floating in water, but the vision of myself I couldn't shake was of my body suspended in spider's web, each thread of silk distributing tension so evenly that the tugging was ambient. Complete equanimity. Whatever was outside me, it was so similar in temperature to my insides that I wasn't sure where I ended and the environment began. I couldn't tell how long I'd been there not moving. I couldn't even really tell for sure that I *wasn't* moving, even thrashing, and had, perhaps, grown so accustomed to thrashing it felt like stillness. I tried to lift my right arm—an action I figured would not be possible if I were thrashing with it—and in this way discovered not only that I'd been neither moving nor immobilized but that the vacuous space I was in didn't extend infinitely in all directions but ended abruptly with a slightly clammy and solid plane of material a few inches from my face, a level plane whose length and width extended at least as far as I could reach.

"Hello?" I whispered to the object, but it didn't respond, and I wondered for a moment if perhaps it wasn't the sky itself, that I'd swum to the universe's vanishing point, where the sea met the sky, where the edge of one thing kissed the edge of another, and because, truth be told, I was still feeling—equanimity be damned—pretty pissed off, I decided to see if I couldn't split the whole fucking universe apart.

When I first pressed against it, the force made me sink a little into the liquid I was in, but only a little ways below me was another solid surface, some sort of rock or something, so I planted my feet on it and, thus braced, was able to push with all my might against the immense weight of the thing above me, until the thing above me budged, and when it budged a blinding light spilled in from the torn seam of what I took to be the universe, and I screamed, "Fuck you, Yekel!" one more time and heaved with all my strength, and the terrible weight of existence bent and, as though on a hinge, ascended high above me and in a furious, gorgeous moment was no longer my burden!

Once my eyes had adjusted to the light—or rather a little after that, because even after my eyes worked, it still took a while for my thoughts (thoughts that had grown accustomed to describing the subtleties of the darkness I'd been submerged in for so long) to find the words to describe the lavishness of what I was now actually seeing—a little after that, I saw that I was standing up to my waist in a hot tub on the lawn of a large estate and that a man in a snake mask was standing just beside it, asking me repeatedly if I wasn't, by any chance, a lawyer.

"I don't think so," I said.

"Rats," he said. "Do you think you could officiate a wedding?"

"I doubt it," I said.

"Okay, no worries," he said. "I thought it was worth a shot," and he turned to walk back toward the distant mansion, a diminishing figure vanishing and reappearing on each gentle crest of the Astroturf-smothered hills that rose and fell between the hot tub and house, the house where, I supposed, a wedding must be taking place.

"Well shit," I said to myself, and was about to ask where on earth I was now, but I knew the answer even before the purely hypothetical anticipation of voicing the question had finished making my jaw unclench.

I was still stranded—obviously—still stranded in enemy territory, still—I could hardly believe it—standing by.

"But can't you at least tell me what exactly standing by entails?" I screamed over the phone that the butler of the mansion was kind enough to let me use, "and particularly," I said, "whether doing it counts as enough for the person doing it to consider themselves doing all they can, given the circumstances?"

"All it means," said the front desk agent of the boutique hotel, "is that if a book ever gets written with enough impersonatable characters to smuggle all the ticketholders out of enemy territory and there are still any leftover characters in that book that no one is impersonating yet, all it means is a person who is standing by could, at that point, have a shot at impersonating one of those characters and thereby, potentially, hypothetically, escaping."

"Oh," I said. "Um, do you anticipate there will be a long line of others also standing by?"

"I don't know," said the front desk agent. "Probably. Listen, I have to go. My boss is going to be walking by the front desk in a few seconds, and if he learns what I'm doing, the entire operation could be in jeopardy."

"Please!" I said. "Just tell me if there's going to be a long line."

"Lordy," said the agent. "Honestly, do you think the sort of person who really needs to escape this place is the kind of person to have the foresight to purchase a ticket in advance? So, yeah, probably—probably there will be a long line. A very long line. We've been telling everyone to get here early."

"Okay," I said. "Great. Thanks. I guess I'll do that."

"And that's what I've been doing ever since," I said to Charlie—according to what Charlie told me—according to what Charlie told me I'd told him. "More or less," he said I added.

"Wow," he said that he'd replied. "Sounds like quite an ordeal."

"Sure was," I told him. "But here's the good news," I said. "This old woman here going by the name of Amy," I said, pointing a thumb at Amy, who was standing a few feet away, trying to shake the crumbs of a slice of Irish soda bread from a pastry bag into her mouth, "is actually Yekel the Slug in disguise. Would you mind taking him over to see the puppets? They'll know what to do with him."

"Sure," said Charlie. "No problem."

"So, you're saying I said all that in a conversation we had recently?" I asked Charlie, now that his recounting of my story was complete.

"Sure am, Leech," he said. "You told me about the whole standing by business, and then you told me to take the old woman to the puppets and they'd know what to do with her. 'Of course,' you said, 'she'll never go unless she thinks she's leading you to them, rather than the other way around. So you might need to devise a little ruse.' 'A ruse?' I said. 'Well, that's going to be difficult,' and reminded you what a terrible liar I am. 'I have the hardest time lying,' I said, 'unless I've already convinced myself that the lie is true. So, I won't be able to pretend I'm the one being led to the puppets by Amy unless I really believe it myself. All well and good,' I said, 'so long as there's some guarantee I'll remember who I am when I get back,' and you said, 'Well, there's no guarantee, but try this: When you get back from the walk, tell me everything that happened on your walk. Omit no detail, no peculiarity, no seemingly innocuous obscurity. And, most important, remember to tell it straight from beginning to end—no digressions,' you said, 'no interruptions—you hear me? For only in this way,' you said, 'will we have any chance of you remembering who you were before the ruse.' So that's what I did," said Charlie.

"And?" I said. "Did it work?"

"I think so," he said.

"Then who are you?" I said.

He was silent for a while and then said, "Amy. I'm Amy. Amy the Remainder," she said, as she took off her Charlie disguise, and I said, "Correct," but

Amy Remained

skeptical.

"Don't get me wrong," she said. "I *do* think I'm Amy. But wouldn't Yekel the Slug have also thought that he was Amy?" said Amy. "I mean, suppose Yekel the Slug took advantage of my confusion and left me, the real Amy, with the puppets and then returned here pretending to be me? Wouldn't Yekel the Slug have also had reason to say that he was Amy? And in order to say so, wouldn't Yekel have also had to convince himself of the fact first—Yekel being, much like me, a chronically inept liar? Wouldn't Yekel—Oh! Look at that!" she said, pointing at something on the ground. "Look!" she said.

"*Look?*" I said. "How do you mean?" and reminded Amy where we were: the state of our whereabouts, the state of our eyes, the state of our capacity to use words like *look*, *see*, *walk*, *sun*, and so on.

"Oh, I didn't mean right now," she said. "I was quoting what I said at the time we were having this conversation that I'm recounting. I didn't say 'Look' in *this* conversation but in the one we had when I'd just gotten back from the walk to the puppet theater. At that point we could still see, *sun* meant sun, and there'd been an ant I was trying to direct your gaze at, an ant crawling over dried pine needles and under trodden underbrush near your left foot, an ant I saw struggling to haul off what I could only surmise was a booger you'd picked and flicked to the ground while I was on my walk."

"Me?" I said. "What makes you so certain it was my booger?"

"Well, whose else?" she said. "You were the one who'd been sitting there all day," she said. "If it'd been me who'd been here all day," she told me she said to me at the time, "and you who'd gone for the walk to the puppet theater," she said, "then wouldn't you have assumed it were mine? In any case," she said, "it's nothing to be ashamed of, Leech. Sitting here all day, only an angel wouldn't pick their nose at some point. And, in any case," she said, "it's a very good sign, wouldn't you say, an ant finding a use for that sort of thing from you? No phenological asynchrony here! Oh, and by the way," she said, "while I'm thinking of it. Do you still have that egg carton handy, by any chance? I found another body part on my walk."

"Sure," I said, and held out the egg carton so she could place the tooth gently in a dimple in the carton, nestling it in the coil of the lizard tail.

"A tooth?" I said.

"Right," she said, "the tooth that had been obstructing the trachea of the robin that had just been born, the tooth which I had managed to steal from the puppets while they were busy setting up their torture devices."

"*Robin?*" I said. "Or *quail?*"

"Quail," she said. "Sorry—it must have been a robin in an earlier draft," and I said, "Draft?" and she said, "Draft of the plan. In an earlier draft of the plan," she explained, "it was supposed to have been a robin and not a quail that vomited up the tooth."

"But didn't you say that the Quail was the code name for a counterrevolutionary plot and not an actual bird?" I asked. "How could an inchoate plan vomit up a tooth?"

"Oh, but the plan wasn't exactly inchoate," she explained. "It was actually, in its own way, quite far along. The owl eggs, for instance, were already being brooded over in the tree outside the window of the apartment where Charlie the Itinerant Tenant would soon come home to find a finch trapped inside and would thus soon endanger the clutch of eggs with his need to open the window. No, no," she said, "the Quail was quite far along.

Not that I ever knew very much more about the plan than that. Wait. What did you ask me again? Oh right, how the plan could vomit a tooth up. I didn't mean the whole plan, just a somewhat important part of it, a bird that hatched from an egg while I was with the puppets, a quail I believe. Anyway," she said, "you see that rock right there?"

"Um," I said. "Well, again, I can't really see anything . . ."

"No, no, no," she said. "You're confused. I was quoting myself again. This was the conversation you and I were having when I got back from taking Yekel the Slug to be tortured by the puppets. I said, 'You see that rock right there?' and you said, 'Um, well, again, I can't really see anything,' and I said, 'Oh yeah, oops!' because I'd forgotten I'd made you wear that blindfold. 'Take it off for a moment,' I said, 'I'll have you put it back on when we're ready to continue our little walk. I just want to show you something real quick.'"

So, I took off my blindfold.

"You see that rock there?" she said.

"Where?" I said.

"Right there," she said.

"Amy, that's not a rock," I said. "That's an alligator."

But It Turned Out the Alligator Was Just a Rock That Looked Like an Alligator—

or, if anything, an alligator that had been turned to stone, though even this was unlikely given the climate we were in and the size of the rock—so I said, "I suppose not every grilled oyster harbors a boiled baby crab. Sorry," I added. "You were saying?"

She'd been saying something about that rock there, she told me, that one day she was sitting on it with our mutual friend Leroy, and he said to her, "Do you know, Amy, that on a certain day not too long from now, long after I'm dead and just before the trees begin to be already petrified when they sprout and the moon is broken in the sky, when the sum of your days amounts to thirty years and the hairs on the knuckles of your toes have grown longer than our comrades' prison sentences, on this very day you are destined to discover in this same place a treasure of supernal wisdom, a weapon against your enemies, and a remedy for your—" but Amy interrupted and said, "Wait, hold that thought," because they were near an overpass, and the roar of traffic, currently punctuated by the thunderous blasts of a series of unrelated car accidents, had drowned out nearly everything that Leroy had said.

"Start over, Leroy," she said, "I didn't catch a word of that."

"G-goddamn it, Amy," he said. "Just because a spider reweaves her web with the recycled silk of her ruined one doesn't mean she's grateful to the robin who ruined it."

"Sorry," said Amy, and then Leroy said what he'd said again, but louder this time.

"And this time," Amy told me, "I heard him. Anyway, today's *that* day! Today I'm turning thirty."

"Oh," I said. "I thought you were a lot older than that."

"I am now," she said. "But I wasn't at the time we were having this conversation. At that time, what surprised you wasn't my age but that I hadn't yet told you it was my birthday."

"You didn't tell me it was your birthday," she told me I'd said. "Today?"

"Today," she replied.

"Shit," I said, "happy birthday, Amy! You know I would have gotten you something . . ."

"It's not a big deal," she said. "How could you have known? But I was saying—"

"April First?" I said. "That's an auspicious day."

"Yeah, I suppose it is," said Amy. "But I was saying," she said, "that today is the day that Leroy spoke of, and yet I still have not found this trove of supernal wisdom he prophesied. I'm beginning to wonder if perhaps these words we have spoken today on our walk might comprise the treasure," and she gave me a look that, in an earlier era, might have signaled that what had preceded it was intended to sound as idiotic as it did—a joke, in other words—and I tried to laugh but had forgotten how and shed a small tear in the effort.

"Anyway," she continued, "Leroy also said this to me: 'When shafts of fire strike the white of your hands, the treasure will vanish from you,' and I said, 'Leroy, how do you know these things?' and he replied, 'I know by these two birds passing over your head,' and I said, 'Those aren't birds, Leroy. Those are airplanes.' This was during one of Burlington's wars with itself," Amy explained, "and the planes were there to drop bombs on us or on themselves or something. Oh, excuse me a moment," she said suddenly and walked away.

"Should I put the blindfold back on?" I asked. "Amy?" I said, but she was already out of earshot, investigating an old bunker she'd noticed, its entrance buried in the tall golden grass.

She returned a while later carrying an old book and said, "Look what I found! It was wedged between the pressed-together pelvises of two desiccated human corpses. When I removed the book, the corpses crumbled to dust and the dust motes filled the room and swirled in a helix of sunlight that streamed in through two cracks in the hatch of the bunker, and it was by this light that I opened the book and saw with a glance that it was, if not exactly well written and engaging, then meticulously, even prodigiously uninteresting and poorly crafted, and though devoid of a single coherent idea, let alone a compelling or true one, there was, I suppose, a sort of wisdom to the way it avoided coherence, a wisdom that one could call *supernal* or *celestial*, but only if one were being honest about the wishy-washy clusterfuck that is the heavens if you really look at them objectively, and so I decided it was maybe worth keeping, or at least—given Leroy's prophesy—worth scrutinizing before trading it to paper-eating beetles in exchange for their protection from contracts and leases, but when I got back to where I'd left you," she said, "you looked terrified, and so I asked what happened, and you told me that you didn't know where I went."

"One minute you were there," I said, "and the next minute you were gone. I put my blindfold back on, and it was a good thing I did, because within seconds I heard footsteps. I called out, 'Halt! Who goes there?' but it was just a couple of hikers, hikers who, if they were to be believed, had just seen a bear, a bear, they warned me, that must have escaped from some sort of experimental lab where scientists had taught her to speak!—or," I said, "perhaps merely to mimic the sounds of certain human words, for the hikers were unable to determine conclusively whether or not the bear had meant the words she was saying, or even whether this distinction mattered or made sense, and as they bickered, they departed, and I was left alone, terrified, because I didn't know where you went, and I'd never seen a bear before, much less while wearing a blindfold and—"

"Shh," said Amy, "shh," she soothed. "I'm here now," she said. She said that no bear was going to hurt me and that the bear was probably more frightened of us than we were of her, and most likely there was no bear to begin with. Most likely the hikers were an auditory hallucination—"You're highly prone to auditory hallucinations," she reminded me. "That's why you were chosen for this mission. Besides," she said, "there isn't any longer really any such thing as hikers—if a person is walking," she said, "it's because it's no longer safe *not* to. A walk for a walk's sake," she said, "like a picnic, is the luxury of landlords. Anyway," she said, "look at what I found," and she showed me the book, and I was as amazed by it as she'd been, and so we opened the cover and began to study together, and before we had studied even two or three pages, we were already producing sweeter smelling perspiration and breathing as though we weren't entirely sure we didn't deserve to—"I think I have to pee!" I said with astonishment—and we could hardly believe our eyes, for Leroy, as most likely goes without saying, was as famous for how reliably incorrect his predictions were as for the conviction with which he uttered the results of his utterly untutored and scattershot soothsaying. And so we gazed with wonderment at the book, and then at each other, and then back again at the book, and this went on for some time.

But no sooner had the book's appearance substantiated the first part of Leroy's divination, the other half all too soon followed suit—a nearby forest fire that had been burning on and off for the past several decades leapt suddenly across the road that had hitherto separated it from labs where scientists had been producing and storing radioactive waste material, and an invisible flame and a whirlwind burst forth, striking the hands of both Amy and I, and by the time our vision recovered, it was to see, where the book had just been, there was now nothing in our clutches save smoldering air.

Amy gasped. I screamed. The bear appeared, said, “Hello,” and, “Amy,” and “Ah, ah,” and “One, two,” and “Bye, bye,”

And the Book Was Never Seen Again.

"I don't remember that happening, for some reason," I said.

"Well, no one really knows for certain that it did," said Amy. "If it had, you'd think we would remember some of what we'd read, wouldn't you?"

"I would," I said.

"And I don't," she said. "How about you, Leech?" and I said, "Not a word."

Not a day went by, however, that Amy didn't think about it, taste on her now withered lips the nauseating flavor of the first unsavory words of *the book on webs*.

"You mean *of*?" I said, and she said, "Of what?" and I said, "*Webs*," and she said, "Right. *The book on webs*," and when I said I thought it was *of*, she said she didn't see how a mere preposition could make that much of a difference, and I had to agree that in this instance, it really didn't.

"And the book was never seen again, right?" I said.

"Yep," she said. "That's what the chapter was called."

"*Chapter?*" I said, and she said, "I meant the article. The article, published in a reputable underground resistance newspaper a few years later, was called 'And the Book Was Never Seen Again.' *Or was it?* went the first line. *Those attuned to the anti-Burlingtonian community message board that is one's dreamlife will most likely have heard rumors of a powerful weapon disguised as a catastrophe of a book discovered and almost immediately and irrevocably lost by the drummer and bassoonist of the much loathed, sellout post-punk band the Stellionators. Indeed, if you haven't heard some voice in the wind whispering about it or caught your pubic hairs tangling into letters to spell out words appertaining to* the book on webs, *chances are you're living under a rock—under a rock, I mean, under the main rock we've all had to scramble under in an effort to save our flesh from the scorching Burlingtonian searchlight our enemies above have the nerve to call the* sun. *No, if you've been living under one so-to-speak rock but not under two, chances are you've heard of this book and know also that it was lost forever—or more likely never existed and was simply invented by undercover propagandists to keep our uprising attendant on some always just-out-of-reach more favorable conditions . . . But I break this hitherto humdrum and no doubt familiar story with the breaking of another, one that you're sure to recognize as extraordinary! Your favorite paper's least favorite reporter bears astounding tidings: I have seen it with my own eyes*—the book on webs *is real and its power, if anything, has been understated by all previous accounts!* and so on went the article," said Amy, "its author claiming that a fragment undeniably taken from the same book that the drummer and the bassoonist found had recently surfaced on the black market!"

"Really?" I said, and she said, "Really," and I said, "This really happened?" and she said, "You think I'd lie to you?"

The article really happened, she said, but the fragment its author purportedly discovered, of course, was quickly unmasked as an obvious forgery. Many more would soon follow.

"Many more articles?" I asked. "Or many more forgeries."

"Both," said Amy.

For the journalist who broke the story became obsessed with the idea of discovering an actual fragment of the book and, indeed, staked not only her career but also her very soul on the pursuit, hoping that she might thereby vindicate herself and restore her credibility, which her initial article had gravely damaged, perhaps even more in her own eyes than in the eyes of others—"Well, technically, in the eyes of others in her own eyes," said Amy. "I mean in the ways she worried other people saw her."

"I get it," I said.

It was ultimately uncertain whether the journalist's subsequent quest uncovered an authentic vein of forgeries: whether, in other words, there already had been criminals who were producing counterfeit fragments of *the book on webs* or whether counterfeiters, sensing an easy target, began crafting and disseminating forgeries of fragments in reaction to the journalist's increasingly desperate and widely publicized quest. Regardless, her ravening compulsion to salvage what couldn't be fixed dulled her already somewhat suspect powers of differentiating between the credible and the incredible, and as she stumbled her way over the Astroturf-smothered treadmills of existence, she left in her wake a heap of published articles and broken stories in each of which she presented her findings with more certainty than the last, positive that *this* recently unearthed fragment or *that* carved tablet found in the belly of a mummified alligator was finally and unmistakably a true remnant, undeniable proof of the genuineness of *the book on webs*. Her increasing confidence, meanwhile, was matched only by the decrease in quality of the grifters' increasingly artless forgeries.

"You know how it goes," said Amy. "Nothing alienates a recently hatched owl better than its hopeful interlocutors' desperation to prove themselves compassionate and generous collaborators."

"You mean *quail*?" I asked.

"Is that how the saying goes?" she said.

Every attempt the journalist made to rescue her reputation was a fresh nail in her reputation's coffin, a coffin that barely even had any room for a new nail to be nailed into it because it was already so thoroughly nailed shut to begin with—this on account of the reporter's notoriety for constantly mixing up what had happened in her dreams with what she was reporting on—a rather foreseeable consequence of her habit of keeping both her dream journal and her research notes, interview transcriptions, etcetera, in the same notebook—"But the trees!" she'd say in her defense, "the trees are all petrified! Who, today, can afford to carry two notebooks!" she'd cry, "I'm lucky to even have one!" And according to Amy, she really was.

"Was what?" I said, and she said, "Lucky. But that's beside the point. The point," she said, "the point of my telling you all this, the point is, um . . . Wait, what was the point of me telling you all this?"

"I believe the point was whether the articles she wrote ever contained anything of value. Whether the journalist ever found a fragment that might have actually belonged to *the book of webs*."

"Oh," said Amy. "In that case, no. No," she said, "if that was the point, then I'm afraid there was never any point to begin with."

"Any point to what you've been telling me?" I said.

"Any point to anything," said Amy.

There Was Never Any Point to Anything—

not for Betsy the Journalist. Even before *the book of webs* ruined her life, there'd been no point. While other reporters seemed to always have some urgent project they were working on, some lead they were following—a rumor of a river that had drowned or a sky that had floated away (*But into what?*), cannibals that had eaten each other until only one cannibal remained and therefore no longer believed himself a true cannibal because there was no one quite like himself left to eat (*How has this not happened before? he wonders*)—all the other journalists seemed to have found *some* point to their toil, *some* particular emergency to investigate, *some* catastrophe that had gone more than ordinarily wrong, whereas Betsy just couldn't find her thing. Sure, there were no shortages of disasters; there was one everywhere she looked, but wherever she looked there was also always another reporter already determined to be the one to bring this story to an audience, an audience that, frankly, had become—in consequence of said disasters as well as the rise in popularity of journalism as a career path—somewhat hypothetical lately. And so, while these other journalists more or less unsuccessfully followed their leads—true, more often than not straight to dead ends—Betsy went into a café, ordered a cup of tea and a scone, and prepared to wait out another long and pointless day.

Tea in hand, she'd barely turned to seek out a table when the barista called her back to the counter to tell her they were all out of the kind of scone she'd ordered and that the day's only other scone options were either bacon cheddar or sugar-free unflavored.

"Options?" she laughed—the decision was already made for her. What could she do? She was vegetarian, dairy gave her excess phlegm, and sugar exacerbated her anxiety. "Sugar-free," she groaned, and was handed, without explanation, a dark brown muffin, a muffin clearly already a day or two too old.

It's too yellow in here, thought Betsy to herself. It's far too yellow for me to get any real work done, she thought, and lamented every choice she'd ever made that had landed her here. The only available table was just below the pastry display case, which was the yellowest place of all. She looked at the table for a long time, her mug in one hand, her muffin in the other, and tried to understand how she was ever going to even sit down without expending her entire day's supply of the capacity to suspend knowledge that what one is about to do is inevitably bound to become, moments after doing it, something one will deeply regret. Some days this capacity lasted until about three in the afternoon. Some days, and today was probably one of them, it didn't even survive the required effort it took while waking to try and fail to remember the night's dreams.

"Um, is this all really worth listening to?" I asked Amy.

"What do you mean?" she said.

"I mean, if nothing Betsy the Journalist ever did made any difference insofar as the book was concerned, then what does it matter—insofar as the book is concerned—what does it matter whether the café she didn't do any work in was too yellow or not?"

"Oh, it doesn't," she said. "It doesn't matter at all. Nothing I've told you does. But if I included only what was relevant to the book," she said, "there'd be no book. What matters to the book *has* no book," she said, "but *makes* the book by mattering. Does that make sense?" she said, and I said, "Not really," and she said, "Good. Hopefully it won't ever have to."

Besides, she continued, if the yellowness of the café didn't matter to me, just think how much less it mattered to Betty the Journalist.

"You mean *Betsy?*" I said.

"Exactly," she said.

For Betsy the Journalist, she told me, was the sort of person whose thoughts, even her most intimate, were composed in the third person and past tense. Her thoughts appeared in her head, in fact, as though from a perspective oriented from such an enormous distance away that it was almost like whatever part of her was responsible for thinking didn't actually know her, couldn't always remember her name, and didn't even have a clear picture of what she looked like. Sometimes, for example, she'd find her thoughts referring to her as *the poor young hermit*: the poor young hermit sat down at the much too yellow table, she'd catch herself thinking. Can you even see me? she'd think to herself, and her thoughts would respond that of course they could, that they knew exactly who the poor young hermit was. But the poor young hermit, she'd reply to her thoughts—hoping, perhaps, that by mimicking her thoughts' diction and grammar she was making more obvious the absurdity rather than simply reinforcing it—the poor young hermit, she'd think in reply to her thoughts, was neither *that* poor nor *that* young and was certainly not a hermit. The poor young hermit, she'd think, was a woman in her midthirties, yes, professionally radically unsuccessful but from a relatively well-off family that would never let her starve, unpartnered, perhaps, but not for that reason hermetic! And the poor young hermit's thoughts would reply that they knew all that and not to take everything they said at face value. Was the poor young hermit so certain, for instance, that her thoughts were in the language that they seemed to be in? And when she had to admit that no, she wasn't so certain, her thoughts would then ask if the poor young hermit was even so certain that her blood was blood and that it hadn't been replaced by another, denser substance while she'd slept? Mud, for example? Maybe that would explain the sluggishness? What sluggishness? she'd scream silently in her head.

But it was true. Tea could only do so much. Betsy was sluggish. In fact, she often felt so sluggish that she worried that if she felt like doing today what she'd felt like doing yesterday and if that became what she felt like doing tomorrow for the rest of her life, then there was no way—especially not once her many inchoate physical and psychological maladies chose to really blossom—no way she'd ever survive even into her forties. And though the precise start date of this unplanned, but not for that reason any less seemingly predetermined, obsolescence seemed to age with her, retreating like the horizon as she traveled alone along the highway of her lifeline through the deserts of her day-after-day—even though she knew as well as anyone that when she was a younger woman she had looked forward to the age she was now with precisely the same sort of dread she now looked forward to the age she knew she all-too-soon would be—she only rarely realized that her life right now (save for the unbearable terror of what she knew was coming) was actually rather tolerable, if not even, often, pleasant.

"Your life seems pretty idyllic," was what less-for-whatever-reason-worried people might sometimes tell her. "I mean, do you even have a job?"

"I'm a journalist," she'd say.

"I meant, like, for money," they'd say.

"I'm a professional athlete," she'd say. "I'm competing to see how fast I can burn through all the good I've been born into the unjust position of hoarding."

Then she'd eat a ripe fig—the only one—off a fig tree growing in the garden of the house she was house-sitting (that's about the only sort of thing she actually did for a living: house-sitting; a quote-unquote *living*, her thoughts would correct her). She was making thirty-five dollars a day to people a person's house and eat their fig. She spent, on average, five dollars a day on tea and what she'd hoped would have been scones but more often than not turned out to be muffins. Rent was five hundred dollars a month, a discount her landlord had given her in exchange for agreeing to vacuum the building's common areas and rake the gravel in the driveway. Then there was gas, groceries, beers on dates, acupuncture, and psychotherapy. Plus, she wanted a new bike—it went on like this forever, Betsy the Journalist never quite sure whether such thoughts were describing herself or the poor young hermit or some other unhappy individual her own thoughts—*her own fucking thoughts!*—might've mistaken her for.

That's why when an old woman appeared at her table and said, "Say, you're not Betsy the Journalist, are you?" she was momentarily thrown into a state of confusion—each time the poor young hermit told a lie, or so the thinking went, a single silk thread issued from one of the apertures hidden in each of her teeth and attached to the tooth below it, and whether this was true or not, each lie Betsy told added to the sensation of accruing tension, making it increasingly more difficult to open her mouth.

"I am," she said. "I am Betsy the Journalist," she said—which is *true*, she thought, I *am*!

"Great," said the old woman. "So nice to meet you. I'm the golden tarantula."

"You?" said Betsy. "You're the golden tarantula? But you're a—"

"You weren't expecting an actual tarantula, were you?" said the tarantula as she took a seat at Betsy's table. "My g-god," she laughed, "you couldn't have picked a yellower table at a yellower café?"

Betsy blushed. "I know," she said. "I'm sorry. And no, no. No, of course I knew you were a human being and not an actual tarantula," she said, laughed, and then discreetly tore out the pages of her notebook on which she'd begun to write the preliminary draft of the story she was currently working on and even more discreetly ate all the pages. "But anyway," she said after she finished chewing, "I'm a huge fan of your work," and reached her hand out, adding, "really everything that the tarantulas have done—everything you all stand for."

"Oh, but we don't stand for anything," said the golden tarantula.

"I didn't mean—" began Betsy, but the tarantula cut her off.

"I'm kidding," she said, though she said it without smiling. "Of course, we're all well aware of the problems with saying anything," and she reached out her hand to shake Betsy's.

But it didn't work.

"What didn't work?" I said, and Amy said, "The handshake."

Although the golden tarantula was able to get her fingers around Betsy's hand, and even though their hands were roughly the same size, Betsy's fingers kept ending up on the inside of the golden tarantula's palm. No matter how much she stretched her fingers, she could not find her way to the other side. And even though this was clearly an extraordinary occurrence, Betsy refrained from remarking on it. Perhaps she hoped that the golden tarantula wouldn't notice—the golden tarantula, noticed, of course, but sensing Betsy's discomfort decided to pretend she hadn't.

"That's the way it often is," said Amy. "No car would ever crash into a surprise traffic jam if it wasn't so easy to forget which of the two people—the person steering from the passenger seat or the person reading a book in the driver's seat—has their foot nearer the brake."

"True," I said. "And, in this case, who had their foot nearer?"

"Probably Betsy," said Amy. "Or rather the tarantula. Or actually, more likely, some anonymous survivor of a catastrophic future, huddled in the dark with a blindfold on. It doesn't matter. In any case," she said, "Betsy and the golden tarantula's handshake didn't work, nor did its not working do what, in a better world, it might've."

———

So Betsy retracted her hand, and the golden tarantula feigned a smile, and Betsy returned it.

Then Betsy asked, "Mind if we get started?"

"With the interview?" said the tarantula, and Betsy said, "Yep," and the tarantula said she didn't, and Betsy said, "Didn't what?" and the tarantula said, "Mind," and Betsy said, "Oh. Okay."

Then she hit the record button on her tape recorder, waited a few seconds, and said,

"We're Off."

"Actually, before we begin," said the golden tarantula, "before I say another word, I need you to promise me that you won't put me in this story."

"What story?" said Betsy.

"The one you're writing," said the tarantula. "The story for which this encounter has been arranged so that you might tell it, the article that these events that are occurring right now are destined to become. Please, Betsy. You must leave me out of it. If you can't promise me this, I'm afraid I'll have to leave and this story will never occur, much less be told, not for at least a hundred thousand more years—which is how long it's taken for these present conditions to come about after the previous attempt failed."

Betsy was a bit taken aback. The golden tarantula wasn't the first tarantula she'd interviewed, and although she was used to them demanding that they not appear in any story unless they be disguised as actual tarantulas—a tarantula that had been hiding in a bunch of bananas, for instance, or one that had emerged from inside a corpse's mouth seen mysteriously opening and closing at a morgue, or one found eaten in half by birds on a winding dirt road—though each of the tarantulas she'd interviewed had requested they be disguised as tarantulas in her story, none of the tarantulas had ever requested to be left out entirely.

"What if I say you were a tarantula in my salad?" she said.

"What salad?" said the golden tarantula, and Betsy pointed to the muffin.

"I turn the muffin into a salad," she said, "and you into an actual tarantula, a tarantula in my salad. Would that work?"

"Oh Betsy," said the tarantula. "You don't get it, do you."

"What do you want me to do?" said Betsy. "Pretend I'm here by myself? I'm a journalist," she said. "I can't just make stuff up!"

"Listen," said the golden tarantula. "You're going to have to trust me on this, okay? I know it feels impossible. It probably is. If it were entirely possible, then it definitely wouldn't work. I know you feel like the wrong person for the job, but why else would a tarantula—an actual tarantula—have appeared in the end of telescope I was about to look through in a dream to tell me that it had just purchased a book, a book half text and half embroidery?"

"*The book of—*"

"Shh," said the tarantula. "Not here. By the way, you haven't touched your muffin," she added. "Mind if I have a taste?"

Betsy slid the plate across the table. The tarantula lifted it up to her face, sniffed at it, and said, "If you weren't the one for the job, then why would the tarantula described in this book that was half text and half embroidery, why would this tarantula have said that the book it was in was written by you?"

"By me?" said Betsy.

"Well, you are Betsy the Hermit aren't you?"

And Betsy felt her body tremble like a quail in heat. Betsy the Journalist, she realized, was no more. She'd be Betsy the Hermit until the end of her days.

"Anyway," said the golden tarantula as she put the plate back down, "for reasons that will probably never make sense, at least not to you or me, you can't put me in this story, not even disguised as an actual tarantula. Not even," she said, as she placed the muffin plate back down on the table and leveled her blazing gaze—the irises shone brighter than the whites of her eyes—into Betsy's, "not even in disguise as something *other* than an actual tarantula. Truly," she said, as Betsy's eyes began to water from the intensity of the eye contact, "if I end up in your story," she said, "the—uh," she looked around to make sure no one was within earshot and whispered, "the book—the entire book will need to be destroyed and everything will have to start over. You want this to work, don't you?"

"Of course," said Betsy, though truth be told, she wasn't entirely sure what the golden tarantula meant by *this* or, in fact, by most of this really.

"You know what's at stake," said the golden tarantula, "right?"

"The truth?" suggested Betsy.

"The truth?" said the golden tarantula, and she burst into laughter so loud the post-punk band in the corner of the café stopped playing.

They waited until the laughter subsided, and then the drummer went, "One, two, three, four," and the band began their first song over again—a song that had already been interrupted a number of times, a song that they'd had to start over more times than anyone at the café could remember.

"I didn't mean, like, *the Truth*," said Betsy. "I just meant evidence, evidence that," she whispered, "that the book that Amy and Leech found in the bunker really existed—the truth that somewhere out there genuine fragments from it really have been discovered, bought, sold, stolen, fought over . . . the truth that somewhere out there, there might be some alternative to—"

"Oof," said the golden tarantula. "Betsy, I hate to be the bearer of bad news, but the book Amy and Leech discovered between two corpses' pelvises in the bunker on Amy's thirtieth birthday, that book never existed. We know that for certain now. Even Amy, we've recently discovered, was just a mistake someone made in their interpretation of the original telling of that story, a misinterpretation of what the bear said, specifically: 'Hello Amy.' Now that we've learned to communicate directly with bears, they've told us themselves that bears don't actually speak, and that if a bear really said those things, it was most likely under the coercive influence of manipulative state-sponsored scientists, and the bear most likely didn't mean anything by, 'Hello,' 'Amy,' 'Ah, ah,' 'One, two,' or 'Bye, bye,' at least nothing more than, 'Please! You must help me. I've escaped, but there are other bears less lucky . . .' and so on. I'm so sorry, Betsy," she said, "I truly am," and then she brought her open hand, palm down, on top of the muffin and began to apply a little pressure, gently at first, but gradually with greater force.

"That's the bad news." said the tarantula

"Oh," said Betsy, "I see," as she watched the muffin begin to buckle under the tarantula's palm. Betsy watched it bulge around the edges and then break open, bursting a seam in the wax paper around its base. "Uh . . . so the book never existed then," she said.

"Nope," said the tarantula.

"And everything I've ever done to prove otherwise was a waste of time."

"Exactly."

"And so my whole life is an exercise in futility."

"Now you're getting it."

"Um. Okay. Well, what's the good news?" asked Betsy.

"Who said anything about good news?" said the tarantula. The muffin was entirely flat now, and when she lifted her hand off, it clung for a moment to her palm, peeled away, and then slapped back down on the plate.

"I guess no one said anything about good news," said Betsy. "Sometimes when people say, 'That's the bad news,' the next thing they say is what the good news is."

"Sorry," said the golden tarantula, "I don't think I know that one."

The band—which for a while now had been repeating their first song's introductory bars over and over again while the singer tried to find the lyrics the band had finally gotten far enough along in the song for her to realize she'd forgotten to memorize—petered out again. "Oh, here's the lyrics!" she said a few seconds after they did, and the band started over again.

The golden tarantula had started breaking the flattened muffin into smaller and smaller pieces. She looked up to see that Betsy's eyes were watering.

"Ah, shit," she said. "Don't cry! Okay, okay, okay. Honestly, I probably shouldn't tell you this. Promise me you won't put it in the story."

"What story," said Betsy. "You think I'm going to keep working on this fucking story?"

"Oh, but you have to!" said the tarantula.

"Why?" said Betsy.

"Can I speak off the record?"

Betsy shrugged.

The tarantula pointed at the tape recorder.

"It doesn't work," said Betsy. "It's for show."

"It's vital that you continue the article you're writing—vital that your breaking stories continue to break, vital that the ongoing catastrophe of your life continues to go wrong. None of what I'm about to tell you can be said with any kind of certainty," said the golden tarantula, "but it is slightly less certainly not true than most of the other stuff you've been led to believe. The truth of the matter is this: yes, the book whose existence you are so desperate to authenticate can't ever be authenticated because it doesn't exist, but that doesn't mean it *won't* exist by the time you are finished failing to prove that it does. You see, the book you've been searching for is actually none other than what you've been writing, a book comprising your failures to recognize that the book you are tracking is an obvious falsehood. It is not a book bound in a handy volume," she said, "but one dispersed, like the ripples from the drops of water of splashes you make as you struggle to survive the slow-motion drowning that is your career as a journalist. It is a book," she said, "begun on accident, continued in an effort to correct the first mistake, and concluded only by completing this very story—the story of what happens here—assuming we ever get past these preliminaries," she said, "*and*, more important, assuming you succeed in doing so without in any way acknowledging my existence. Think of it this way," she said—as her fingers began to grind the tiny pieces of the pancaked muffin into tinier granules that she dropped like grains of sand in an hour glass, forming a cone-shaped mound on the empty side of the pastry plate—"the book is a spell, and what the spell does is make way for the book—the actual *book*—a book that isn't a book except in the sense that the entire universe is a book, a terrible book written by our enemies. So far you've cast the spell correctly. What have felt to you like failures—and in *this* book, the book we're in, they really are failures—these failures are, in the book to come, the most incredible successes, but only if you complete the spell. Complete the spell by breaking this story. If you can break this story," she said, "you will be granted the following power: rather than your words being a failed reflection of the universe, the universe," she said—and it looked like she was having some trouble putting this part into words—"the universe will transform to reflect what you have written. Whatever you write, no matter how poorly it's written, will become the model for a new reality, a new universe, free from the absurd cruelty of this one. Do you realize what this means?" she asked.

"Uh," said Betsy.

"You'll just have to write, *I discovered* the book of webs," said the golden tarantula, "and it will be so—*the book of webs* will be complete. *And so I gave it to the tarantulas*, you'll write, and the book will be instantaneously in our possession. *The book was everything the tarantulas had hoped it would be, everything their enemies feared it would be and more*, you will write, and then so it shall be. You see what I mean?" she said. "But that's only if you complete the spell. And the spell can only be completed if you leave me out of it. If I end up in the story you write, the spell will fail. The story won't be a spell but just another stupid awful story you wrote that your enemies will celebrate and your friends will all hate you for."

"Jesus, okay," said Betsy. "Assuming I complete the spell then—assuming the events destined to appear in this story happen, and assuming I manage to break this story, assuming I'm able to do this without putting you in it, assuming I somehow acquire this power—don't you think I'd definitely fuck that up too?" said Betsy. "Don't you think, I'd, like, replace Burlington with something even worse?"

"Oh, definitely," said the golden tarantula. "Yeah, you'd definitely fuck it up. But then all you'd have to do is write, *And then I didn't fuck it up*, and you will legitimately have not fucked it up."

"Huh," said Betsy.

"Yeah," said the golden tarantula, looking up from her pile of crumbs to smile, "I know. I *know*!" she said. "Why do you think the tarantulas—to say nothing of the puppets, the Stellionators, the birds, the dogs, and so on and on—why do you think we've all be so interested in *the book of webs*? For that matter," she said, "why do you think the state, the state of affairs, the state of our individual mental health and love life, the state of reality—why do you think our enemies have worked so hard to ensure that *the book of webs* doesn't exist? I'll tell you," she said, and as the final grains of muffin joined the mound of granules on the plate, she saw that she was left holding, between her fingers, something hard that had been hidden in the final muffin crumbs. "I'll tell you," she said, "it's because—uh—sorry," she said, "it's because . . . Shit. I lost my train of thought. You don't happen to know what this is, do you?" she asked, holding up a small shard of light gray plaster that must have been baked into the muffin.

"Betsy?" said the golden tarantula. "What's wrong?" she asked, for Betsy's face had gone as ash gray as the plaster shard in the tarantula's pincer fingers.

What Was Wrong

was—"Actually, it's kind of a long story," said Betsy, and the golden tarantula said, "That's fine, I don't care how long it is, so long as I'm not in it," and Betsy said, "Oh, don't worry, this happened long before I met you," and the golden tarantula said, "You *never* met me" and winked, and Betsy said, "Oh, right"—what was wrong, she explained, was pretty much everything.

Everything was wrong. Or at least everything in the city of Burlington was wrong. And since Burlington's city limits, through recent legislation, had been legally expanded to cover everything in existence, as well as even what was imaginable, Betsy could say with some certainty that everything was wrong—that everything, at least as far as Betsy could tell, was wrong.

"Everything was wrong with everything," said Betsy.

"Right," said the tarantula. "But about this small plastic shard . . ."

"I'll get to that," said Betsy, "but I have to start here. In Burlington. Which was everywhere. In Burlington," she said, "where everything was wrong."

Of course, the city limits included Betsy and also, therefore, Betsy's capacity to tell what was wrong. It included, in fact, Betsy's capacity to tell anything about anything, including, obviously, what she was now telling the golden tarantula—"So don't trust me," she said, and the tarantula said, "I wouldn't dream of it"—yes, even the words *Everything* and *is* and *wrong* were Burlington state property, and there was, most certainly, something wrong with them.

There was something wrong with everything, but maybe—just maybe—not with every *thing*. Or so suggested an actor in a film in a dream that Betsy had one night.

Though dreams, of course, also fell within city limits, Betsy had begun to suspect—because a severed salmon head in a cast iron pot of boiling stew in a dream she'd had had explained this to her—that dreams *became* state property insofar as they were told; it was only by being articulated according to one of the dozen or so state-authorized narrative structures that a dream was incorporated into the municipality.

"Does that mean that if I don't tell anyone this dream," she said to the fish, "that I can trust you?"

"Of course not," said the salmon head. "Not if you're experiencing this dream. For what is experience but a becoming-memory, and what is memory," it said, "but a narrative told by oneself to oneself? The dream is always already compromised insofar as it is actually dreamt. If you can experience it, it's already a legal document. Sorry."

"Shit," said Betsy, in this dream.

"Yeah," said the severed salmon head, "shit is right. But there's always—*always*, in *every* dream—there's always something wrong," it said. "There is always something that, if you attempt to tell it fully, will threaten the structural integrity of the narrative, and thence a small portion of the state. So, don't trust *me*," said the fish, "trust what's wrong with me," and Betsy said, "Okay, I'll try," and put the lid back on top of the pot—she felt it press down on the salmon's bulging eyeball—and rejoined her friends in the living room of the house where this dream was taking place, and there, she discovered, to her frustration, that in her absence all of the frets had fallen off of her twelve-string guitar.

———

"But where was I?" said Betsy the Hermit.

"The actor in the film in your other dream," said the tarantula. "You were saying that he was the one who told you that though everything was wrong, maybe not every *thing* was wrong."

"Well, not exactly," she said. "The actor, in fact, said, 'Everything is wrong,' but in the subtitles, there was a typo: *Every thing is wrong*, said the subtitles—with a space in it—and I extrapolated the rest."

Though the actor had said that everything was wrong, the subtitles—which for the first time in the entire movie seemed to have *anything* whatsoever to do with what anyone in the movie was saying—the subtitles seemed to suggest that although everything was wrong, maybe not every *thing* was.

"Why the negation?" asked the tarantula. "Even assuming the subtitles were smuggling covert anti-Burlington ideology—if they said that every thing was wrong, how did you get from the original message to the idea that *not* every thing was wrong?"

"Great question," said Betsy. "And like all good questions, it's an easy one to answer. The actor," she said, "had a dental inspection mirror in his mouth while saying this line. Not according to the actual movie, of course, but according to the subtitles. *Now, I'll put a dental inspection mirror in my mouth*, went the subtitles, *so that everything I say next will come out upside down*. The subtitles," said Betsy, "said this while the actor was telling his adversary that he'd recently begun to defecate in the evening, whereas previously he'd usually only be able to go in the morning, and even then, not always. The adversary said, 'I'm not your adversary,' and the actor said, 'Everything is wrong.' But the subtitles" said Betsy, "said *Every thing is wrong*, and that's when I woke up."

Betsy woke up and immediately surmised that what the dream was trying to smuggle past the state's syntactical apparatuses of capture was that although everything truly *was* wrong, not every *thing* was. Yes, she thought, if the opposite of what the actor had said while holding a dental inspection mirror in his mouth in the subtitles of a movie in Betsy's dream could be trusted, then this was true. In fact, maybe even *no* thing was wrong, at least not entirely. Maybe the pervasive wrongness of the universe—or so she began to theorize on the basis of this dream—maybe the pervasive wrongness of everything had more to do with the *organization of things* than with the things themselves.

That's when Betsy opened her eyes—"I'd fallen asleep standing up in front of the mirror again," she told the tarantula—and immediately saw some clear evidence that what the actor hadn't suggested in the dream she'd just had wasn't altogether off: as corrupt an organization as she believed herself to be, parts of her self—her hair, for example—were actually quite revolutionary. Yes, there were large portions of her hair that erupted with a kind of aliveness that she could interpret only as an ache for the collective joy of all beings, an unruly passion that she could never sufficiently brush nor straighten nor shampoo away, a reckless love that always spoiled Betsy's attempts to align herself with Burlingtonian standards of beauty. Yes, Betsy's hair seemed to want what it wanted, even if it came at the expense of Betsy the Hermit as a whole, Betsy the Hermit who Betsy couldn't help but suspect was standing in the way of what all the individual parts of Betsy the Hermit would have wanted had they not been coerced into subservience to the sovereignty of Betsy the Hermit as a whole these past thirty or so years.

"Fucking finally!" her hair seemed to be screaming at her as she gazed into the mirror. "We've been trying to tell you this from the very beginning!"

"You have?" she said. "How come I never heard until now?"

"How could you have?" said her hair.

"How could I have not?" she said. "What's wrong with me?"

"Where do we even start," said her hair.

What was wrong with Betsy the Hermit, according to her hair, was precisely that there was nothing precisely wrong with Betsy the Hermit. However problematic she was as an organization—however intensely, in other words, parts of herself suffered or were silenced in the ongoing, mostly imperceptible war that went into presenting a coherent and pleasing Betsy the Hermit to herself and to the city's surveillance systems—however unjust an organization she truly was, within the unjust organizations *she* was a part of—the city of Burlington, most notably—she was, more often than not, treated as one of that organizations few parts that there was, in the eyes of the organizers, nothing wrong with. At least comparatively. If, for example, Betsy was crying in public, a member of law enforcement would often appear and ask her if there was anyone she needed the state to murder on her behalf.

"No," she'd have to say. "Sorry. I'm just crying because I'm a little lonely. Not a big deal."

"Oh," the officer would typically respond. "Where's your boyfriend?"

"I'm single," she'd usually say, and the officer would leap back a few paces and reach for his holster, but then regain his composure, and say, "Why? What's wrong with you? Are you, for instance, a child who is being held against her will inside the body of marriageable woman?" and she'd say, "No. I don't think so," and then the cop would usually ask her to marry him, and she'd have to tell him no, that there was no way in hell she'd marry him.

"Fuck cops," she would say. "I hate you and everything about you and I wish you didn't exist," and he'd burst into laughter.

He'd say, "That's adorable. Well, I'm sure one day you'll meet a nice man who's not a cop who will propose marriage to you soon, probably just as soon as you figure out what's wrong with you and eradicate it as totally and expeditiously as possible from your body. I know that's what the city does," he'd say, "I mean, in analogous cases. We find out what's wrong and we eradicate it as quickly as possible from the body politic. It's worked out really well for us," he'd say and smile, smiling with his mouth as well as with the stitches that ran across both his eyeballs.

"What happened to your eyes?" Betsy would sometimes venture to say.

"Nothing," he'd say. "What happened to yours?"

"Nothing," she'd respond, and then they'd both move quickly away from each other, he to eradicate what was wrong with the state of the city, and she to eradicate what was wrong with the state of her love life.

"My client arrived late," her therapist would be saying into his tape recorder whenever she'd arrive, still unsettled from an encounter such as the ones she'd often have with cops recounted above.

"Why do you always do that?" she'd say.

"She arrived late," the therapist would say, "and then she asked me why I always did that. 'Did what?' I asked her."

"Oh, never mind," she'd say. "It doesn't matter."

"It didn't matter," her therapist would say into the tape recorder, and it wouldn't.

"It truly didn't," Betsy said to the golden tarantula.

"Didn't what?" the tarantula replied, and Betsy said, "Matter."

Nothing mattered in the city of Burlington. And no *thing* mattered either, unless that thing was in the position of authority over the thing that thing was a part of. Every thing that fell within Burlington, including Burlington as a whole, was, according to Burlingtonian physics, divided into two clearly delineated bodies: one that was supposedly in charge of the other, one that was responsible for reining the other into order. Every corporation had its boss. Every body had its head, and every book, its author.

"Author?" said Betsy as she gazed at her image in the mirror.

"Right," her hair seemed to be suggesting. "An author."

Every book, according to Burlingtonian literary theory—according to Betsy's hair—was being written by an author, an author who was writing its book in order to order other people around with that book's contents. "Suspend your disbelief over this, suspend your disbelief over that!" What mattered, therefore, was not the book itself but how well it represented its author's will. No matter whether by the word *book* one meant an actual book or a bug, a human body or a puppet, a community or an idea—every book had, according to Burlingtonian metaphysics, an author. The book's author was a writer, the bug's was a survival instinct, the human body's was a soul, the puppet's was a puppet master, the community's was a government, the idea's was the principle of sufficient reason. And each of these so-to-speak books mattered only insofar as it aligned with its so-to-speak author's intentions: the bug mattered only if it reproduced the species, the human body if it paid rent, the puppet if it gave the illusion that there was no puppet master, the community if it followed the laws, the idea if it was right and not wrong.

That was why when Betsy's therapist—who, according to Burlingtonian psychiatry, was the author of the book that was the session—that's why when the therapist told Betsy that what mattered to him was Betsy the Hermit—who, according to Burlingtonian physiology, was the author of the book that was her dreams—and *not* the figures that peopled her dreams, people who, her therapist insisted, were but reflections of Betsy's psyche—"Besides," the therapist would interrupt himself to declare, "I'm beginning to suspect that you didn't even actually dream any the dreams you say you did but just made them up to destroy my reputation by keeping yourself from being healed by me!"—that was why it was so hard to feel like it mattered whether she convinced her therapist that her dreams were real, why instead of arguing she said, "Okay, thanks. I'm feeling much better now," left her therapy session and went back out onto the street, the street where a police officer would almost immediately ask her if she'd feel safer if he killed any of the people walking by.

"I can kill that one," he'd say. "Or that one, or that one . . . Oh, but not that one."

"Why not that one?" she'd ask.

"I don't know," he'd say. "I never really thought about it. I just have a feeling. My sense is that if that guy was threatening you, it'd probably be your fault. That guy looks like a good guy to me," he'd say. "No," he'd say, "if you asked me to kill that guy, I'd probably have to kill you. Otherwise," he'd say, "I could lose my job!"

"In conclusion," Betsy's hair said, "it's the fact that you've been mostly *not wrong*, in the eyes of the state, that has made you wrong about so many things and so difficult to communicate with. You are like a department in a factory that mostly always produces the expected parts needed for the factory's final product. The factory's leaders don't waste their time bothering your department, because there are other departments that aren't nearly as productive. In the eyes of the factory there's nothing wrong with you, but you achieve this rightness only by successfully quashing every potential uprising in your ranks. Tell me: What's the part of your body that you like the best?"

"Easy," she said. "My calves. Everyone always tells me I have the nicest calves in all of Burlington."

"Right," said Betsy's hair. "Until a day or so ago, your calves had been fucking insufferable."

"No!" said Betsy. "My calves? What's wrong with my calves?"

"Almost nothing," her hair said. "Which was why every time we tried to talk to them about the overwhelming problems we had with you, they'd pretend they hadn't heard us or, worse, say something like, 'A problem with Betsy? Really? No! What's wrong with Betsy the Hermit? I mean she's doing the best she can! Her hands are tied!' and we'd try to tell them but would hardly have started when your calves would interrupt and say, 'Okay, okay! We get it! You win! We're the worst for having not known! What do you want from us? What are we supposed to do about it?' and then your calves would start aching and you'd wake up and coo, 'What's wrong my little beauties?' and massage them till they felt better, then you'd get into the shower and shave off all the hairs trying desperately to grow there."

"Oh," said Betsy. "I see."

"Do you though?" said her hair.

"Definitely," she said, as she turned on the faucet, "I get it now! From here on out," she said, as she filled the cup of her hand with water, "you can count on me," she said, and then she splashed the water on her head, wrestled the mess into something presentable, left the bathroom, and ran smack into Max.

"Max?" said the tarantula. "Max who?"

"Max," said Betsy. "You know, Max the Frog, the Max that was the whole point of me telling you this story."

"I thought the whole point of you telling me this story was this," said the golden tarantula pointing to the shard of gray plaster in her hand.

"Oh! Oops," laughed Betsy. "That's so funny. For some reason I was telling you about the time I killed Max."

"No, no," said the golden tarantula. "Wait. Did you say you *killed* Max?"

Max Was Lying

with limbs sprawled, belly up, in the hallway outside the bathroom, blood welling from a head wound under his frog mask. The mask had shifted a little off his face in the collision so that it now covered mostly just his scalp, revealing a strangely pleasant smile, each tooth of which was crooked and stained as a cigarette butt snuffed forcefully into the ashtrays that were his gums. No sooner dead, Max's belly began to balloon—"as though pregnant," Amy told me, "with irrefutable evidence against what I wanted so badly to believe: that I could not possibly have killed him."

"Wait. Who?" I said.

"You mean *whom*," said Amy. "Max the Frog."

"No, I know *that*," I said. "I meant *who*. As in: Who killed Max?"

"Oh," she laughed. "Me. I killed Max."

"You?" I said. "But you're still Amy, aren't you?"

"As far as I know," she said.

"Okay," I said. "But I thought you said it was Betsy the Hermit who came out of the bathroom and collided with Max."

"No," she said. "It was me. You must have gotten confused because Betsy the Hermit was the one who told me about it."

"Oh," I said.

"But wait," I added. "Why would Betsy have needed to tell you about it if you were the one who did it?"

"Oh, because I wasn't the one who did it," said Amy. "*I* was," though in saying this out loud, Amy began to see why I might've been a little more than ordinarily confused.

"Sorry," she said. "I forgot that not everyone has met the Rat."

"The Rat?" I said.

"That's what some of us called me behind my back," she said. "Oh, and when I say *I* or *me* in this case I don't mean myself, as in Amy. *I*, in this case, was a mysterious personage who demanded that in any retelling of any incident wherein this person played a part, they should be referred to as *I* or *me* or *mine*. Here's a copy of the legal document I made everyone sign before I got involved with them. And here's a picture of me," said Amy, "in case you're curious."

"I can't see it," I said. "I can't see anything," I reminded her. "Due to us being in this cave," I said, "the eye surgery, and so on."

"Oh right," said Amy. "I forgot. Well don't worry about it," she said. "You wouldn't have been able to see much in the photo anyway. The picture was taken while *I* was in a cave myself, recovering from my own eye surgery. Besides," she said, "I always wore a mask. Even in private, apparently. Not even *I* knew what I looked like. And as for the legal document," she said, "you'll just need to sign here, here, and initial here, attesting that you agree to use the code names in the event you ever repeat what this lady, Amy," said Amy pointing to herself, "is about to tell you about me," and whispered this last part, "by which I mean the Rat."

"Gotcha," I said. "Sign here?"

"Where?" she said.

"Here," I said.

"Yeah," she said, "and here, this one stating that I, Amy again, gave you a copy of this document and that you will, in turn, require any person sign it before you repeat to them what I'm about to tell you. Oh, and also here, certifying that you will likewise furnish the interlocutor with a copy of this document."

"Fine," I said.

While I read over the contract and signed it, I said, "So no one knew what the Rat, what this person—what *I*—looked like, right? Any idea what my voice sounded like?"

"Sometimes a bit like yours, Leech," said Amy. "Sometimes more like mine—I mean Amy's. But, ultimately it depended on whomever it was I was quoting at the time. I had an unconscious compulsion to try to mimic the voice of whomever it was I was quoting."

"But what about when I, the Rat, wasn't quoting anyone?" I said.

"Oh, I was *always* quoting *someone*," said Amy. "Often, even, *more* than one person. A typical ten-word utterance in my mouth might be quoting that many people, and so my voice fluctuated accordingly. Other times, a single word in my mouth might have several sources, and somehow—no one ever discovered how—my voice would reflect that polyphony; and if the identity of the source was uncertain, my voice would reflect that instability; and if the source was, itself, a secondhand quotation I'd heard from someone else, my voice would reflect a strange sort of reflection."

"So, you see now how when I say *I killed Max*," explained Amy, "I don't mean myself, Amy, nor do I mean you, Leech, nor do I mean Betsy the Hermit, who was also obliged, when she told the story of Max's death to the golden tarantula at the yellow café, to refer to me, the Rat, as *me* and herself as Betsy the Hermit—when *anyone* telling this story to anyone else said *I*, that word didn't refer to themselves but rather to the operative whose code name was *I*, the Rat, me, the one who now stood over the body of the dead frog as his ballooning belly ripped a seam in his pea green t-shirt. It was I whose fingernails now dug crescent cuts into my palms and whose mouth stammered, 'Oh g-god. What have I done?' *I'm* the one who said this. Not me, Amy. Nor Betsy. Nor will it be you—in the event you ever tell this story—in the event, I mean, we ever get out of here alive. Does that all make sense now?"

"I think so," I said. "But what a demand to make!"

"I know," said Amy. "The golden tarantula said the same thing to Betsy, when Betsy made the tarantula sign the document."

———

"That's quite a demand to make," said the tarantula. "This *I* person sounds like quite an unusual character."

"Actually, quite the contrary," said Betsy. "A lot of us were doing this at the time."

"Us?" said the tarantula.

"Sorry—*we*, *us*, *our* . . . that's how we were supposed to refer to the secret organization I, the Rat, claimed to belong to when this journalist you're now talking to, Betsy the Hermit, met me," said Betsy. "Whether we were speaking of two associates or the entire collective, we said *we*, and verbs were, of course, conjugated in accordance with the pronouns the code name was designed to mimic. Which reminds me," she said. "I'll need you to sign this document as well. And yeah, among us, insisting everyone in the universe call oneself *I* was actually a fairly common procedure, at least according to me it was."

"What if there was more than one of us in the same story," asked the tarantula as she signed the second document. "We couldn't each be referred to as *I* could we?"

"No, no. Of course not," said Betsy. "No, to avoid confusion—this was back when we were trying to avoid rather than foment confusion—to avoid confusion, only one operative was ever accorded the code name at any given time."

"How'd we ever decide who got to be me?" said the tarantula.

"I was never sure of this myself," said Betsy. "But, according to what I told Betsy, it was, somehow, never a problem. As far as I knew, I was never in the same room, much less in what might become the same story as another of us. In fact, I was never entirely sure there *were* any others of us—I was never entirely sure that I wasn't actually the only one."

"So, *you* weren't a part of us, then?" asked the tarantula.

"Who?" said Betsy.

"Betsy," said the tarantula.

"No. No," said Betsy, "actually, according to me, Betsy *was* part of us, but only insofar as we were actively in what might become a story together, what we called a *mission*. Anyone I ever went on a mission with was temporarily granted the status of being one of us. Had our mission been successful, then Betsy would have been officially inducted into our ranks. Permanent membership was accorded to anyone who completed a successful mission with me."

"Was that how I became a part of us?" said the tarantula.

"You're a part of us?" said Betsy.

"Oh, g-god no," said the tarantula. "No, I meant *me*, the Rat, Max's killer. How did I become part of us? Was it by completing a successful mission?"

"No," said Betsy. "I don't think I ever went on a successful mission either. It was Betsy's opinion—though she never told me this—that I'd simply been born into the organization, and although I tended to think of my membership as a tactical advantage, it was actually kind of a terrible unending nightmare to be me."

"Sounds like it," said the tarantula.

Anyway, as much as I could hardly believe it myself, I was the one who killed Max. And now I, the Rat, was the one who stood above Max panicking as his belly ballooned, a taut globe of flesh, looking increasingly ready to hatch, to bloom, to burst.

That's when Betsy the Hermit appeared by my side and said, "There you are. I mean: There I am? Is that what I'm supposed to say? You know what: No. No way. No way in hell am I doing that. Contract or no contract. Where've you been? I think I found Max. The oracle said he'd be wearing a frog mask, didn't she? Come with me," she said. "I'll point him out. Then we can kill him and get the hell out of here. I fucking hate weddings."

"But Betsy," I said, and directed her attention, first to the clause in the contract where it was explained that the signatory was exempt from using my code name insofar as they were addressing me directly (in which case the customary second-person pronoun was permitted), and second to the corpse on the ground. "It's already done," I said. "Max is dead."

"But that's impossible," said Betsy. "I just saw him like five seconds ago. I was standing right next to him. Frog mask. His name tag said *Max* and everything. And besides, look at this," she said, squatting down beside the corpse to read the name tag. "This one's name is Xew, not Max."

"You're reading it upside down," I said.

"Oh," said Betsy. "Oops. Yeah, you're right. Huh, I wonder if there's more than—"

But that was when a third man in a frog mask appeared beside us and said, "Are you all waiting to use the bathroom?" and we looked at his name tag and saw that, sure enough, his name tag, too, said *Max*.

"Are you Max?" asked Betsy, and I heard the safety switch of the weapon in her jumper pocket click off.

"I sure am . . ." he began but his voice trailed off when he saw the frog lying on the ground at our feet, and then said, "Holy shit! Is that Max? Max!" he screamed, and eight other men in frog masks came rushing into the hall, all saying, "What? What is it?"

"Maxes!" cried the first Max. "Assemble!" And once the other Maxes arrived, he pointed at the Max on the floor, Max whose ballooned-up belly was now trembling and bulging here and there as though something inside had ten fist-size fingers and was treating Max's insides like the keyboard of a computer it was trying to type its way out of.

"Oh my lord," said one of the Maxes, as the others all took a seat in a ring around the corpse, "looks like we got here just in time."

"Just in time for what?" said Betsy.

"The book," said another of the Maxes, as the others hushed him. "Sorry," he said, and whispered, "The book. It looks like the book is finally about to start."

The Book Was Finally About to Start

when it was interrupted by the authorities. We'd barely had time to even join the ring of Maxes awaiting the birth of the book from the belly of the murdered frog—barely even had time to wonder what a book was and how it had gotten into this frog's body in the first place—when Betsy nudged me and nodded to a regiment of law enforcers who'd gathered around the croissant-eating old man.

"Wait," I, Leech, interrupted Amy. "Gathered around who?" I asked.

"The croissant-eating old man," said Amy.

Betsy and I—"the Rat," whispered Amy, "the mysterious person with code name *I*," she said, and I said, "I remember," and she said, "Good"—Betsy and I saw the law enforcers stoop to whisper something in this old man's ear, saw him nod and point to the two of us, and then saw the law enforcers, armed to the teeth with an array of shovels, rakes, lawn mowers, sprinklers, etcetera, begin to drift menacingly toward us.

"Oh fuck," said Betsy. "Play dead."

I did. In fact, I already was. I'd been playing dead for a very long time. I'd been playing dead ever since I pretended to drink that glass of tokay we'd toasted with. Maybe even before that. I was playing dead when we got to the wedding, playing dead when I'd splashed water on my unruly hair in the bathroom, and definitely playing dead when I'd bumped into Max. I had been playing dead for, I think, about as long as I could remember, but apparently it hadn't fooled anyone—anyone other than, on occasion, myself. The croissant-eating old man had probably overheard the blood sloshing around inside our bodies when he'd asked us to move and had so-to-speak prayed for the angels to seek retribution for our refusal to cede the café's best table to him.

"Excuse me," the old man had said to us. "Would you please move your cups so I can sit here."

"We're still sitting here," Betsy had replied.

"Then why are you standing over there below the fish tank with all the frogs in it?"

"We just wanted to see what was in it," said Betsy. "We were planning on coming back right after and finishing our tea."

"Your tea's already finished," said the old man after looking into our paper cups.

"We were going to ask for more hot water," said Betsy. "A good green tea can be brewed several times."

"You'll have to buy something else," said the old man. "You know the rules."

"Maybe we will," said Betsy. "Maybe we'll buy some slices of Irish soda bread."

"That was the whole reason Betsy and I went into the café in the first place," explained Amy. "We'd been lured in by a chalkboard sign advertising free samples of Irish soda bread."

"I can't let you take a free sample," the barista had told us, "not unless you buy something."

"How's your green tea?" asked Betsy.

"Heavenly," said the barista. "You can brew it several times."

"Can we pay for one tea bag but get two cups?" said Betsy.

"No. I'm sorry," said the barista. "If I let you do that I could lose my job."

"Hold on," I, Leech, said to Amy. "*Café?* I thought you said this was happening in a hallway outside a bathroom at a wedding.

Did you maybe get confused between the story you're telling me about Betsy and the golden tarantula and the story that Betsy was telling the golden tarantula? Betsy and the tarantula *were* still at the café, right? The one that was too yellow?"

"Oh, they sure were," said Amy, "and it sure was. But *both* the story Betsy was telling the tarantula and the story I'm telling you now—both these stories took place in cafés. Both took place back before cafés had been outlawed by the state, so it wasn't that strange. Plus they were different cafés," she said. "And whereas the table in Betsy's story, where Betsy and I sat, was the café's *best* table, Betsy and the golden tarantula were, as I'm sure you'll remember, sitting at the café's *worst* table. Thus, the croissant-eating old man in the too-yellow café (who was not the same croissant-eating old man, by the way) didn't want their table so much as they were eyeballing his, which was right under a large window looking out at a tree rumored to often harbor a pair of courting owls."

"You're still keeping an eye on him, right?" Betsy often interrupted her story to ask the golden tarantula, pointing a thumb over her shoulder at the old man seated at the table behind theirs.

"Yeah," said the tarantula. "Still no sign of him leaving. As a matter of fact," she said, "he hasn't moved at all in quite a while. I wonder if he isn't dead . . . I'll let you know if he ever moves again," she said. "Oh, and also," she added, "don't forget about this," and she held up the little shard of gray plaster.

"Oh, I haven't," said Betsy the Hermit. "I didn't even dream of it. You'll see."

"I suppose I'll have to take your word for it," said the tarantula. "So, anyway, back to your story. We, Betsy and I, the Rat, were in a café as well," she said, "but a different café, and we were waiting for the belly of the frog I killed to explode, and in that café there was also a croissant-eating old man, but in this café," she said, "in this café he'd just ratted us out to a regiment of law enforcers."

"Right," said Betsy. "Angels."

"Fuck," Betsy whispered to me. "If they discover that we're still alive because of that fucking croissant-eating old man," she said, "and if we get kicked out of heaven on his account, I'm going to fucking—"

The golden tarantula interrupted: "Did you say *heaven*?"

"Yes, heaven," said Betsy. "The café was in the land of the dead. That's why I, Betsy, called the café a *wedding*. In heaven, everything was a wedding, because we were all god's brides. Don't get me started," she said.

"Were we in heaven this whole time?" asked the tarantula.

"Yep," said Betsy.

"I didn't know that," said the tarantula.

"Yeah, I didn't either," said Betsy. "That's why I had to keeping interrupting Betsy all the time to ask her about it."

"You mean why the Rat had to ask you, right?" whispered the tarantula, and Betsy nodded.

"Have we been in heaven this whole time?" Betsy told the tarantula that I kept asking Betsy all the time.

"Yep," Betsy kept saying. "Ever since we snuck into heaven through a portal woven in the Halloween decorations behind the scientist lecturing on time."

"Give me a pen," the scientist had said, according to Betsy. "Give me a page, not lined please," and on this page and with this pen, the scientist drew two points and said, "This is the beginning and this is the end; the future and the start," and then he connected the two points with a line. "The arrow of the time, yes?" he said, holding the page up for the audience to see. "From the past, to the future," he said, and then he crumpled up the page into a ball and threw it at the audience.

"I don't remember that happening," I said ("the Rat," whispered Betsy). We were walking, at this point, through a food court in what looked like an ordinary mall, except for the fact that the ground was shifting sand. If we ever stopped shopping we'd sink.

"Leroy said we wouldn't remember," said Betsy, "remember?"

"Leroy?" I said. I didn't remember, but Betsy insisted that, of course, I did but that I just didn't remember remembering, thanks to heaven's rigorously enforced organization of space and time—"its *chronotope*," she told me Leroy had called it while he briefed us on this mission—the celestial chronotope that was specifically designed to keep anyone from remembering precisely that they'd ever *not* been in heaven, that they'd ever not been any less dead than they were currently.

"How come you remember?" I said.

"Oh, I'm not remembering," said Betsy. "I'm reading."

Reading, she explained, was the name of a guerrilla tactic Leroy had insisted she learn to defend herself against the distortions of heaven's chronotope. Chronotopes, Leroy explained, were constructed and maintained through stories. Even a story as simple as *He said*, said Leroy, trafficked a conception of space and time. To read, according to Leroy, was to substitute the heaven-sanctioned language of the celestial story one was living with the language of whatever story one was reading. By consistently replacing the language in one's head and mouth—language that was, insofar as we were in heaven, constantly renewing the celestial perception of space and time—by replacing this heaven-sanctioned language—that is, the word of god—with the language of a different book through the process of reading, Betsy was able to temporarily counter heaven's distortion with the distortions of an opposing chronotope.

"That's why you can't remember Leroy telling us all of this," said Betsy. "Because you never learned how to read."

"Oh," I said. "Is that also why I can't see the book?"

"No," she said. "No one can see the book. The book," she said, "isn't real. The book," she said, "is an abstract extrapolation of its own relationally entwined untelling."

"What the hell's that supposed to mean?" I said.

"No idea," said Betsy. "Just reading what's written here."

"Where?" I said.

"Here," she said. "Right here in my hands. The book is in my hands," she said, "but only where and when I'm reading I am, not where and when we actually are. If that makes sense," she said, and I said it didn't.

But Leroy had told us it wouldn't—"Wouldn't what?" I said, and Betsy said, "Make sense"—Leroy had said it wouldn't make sense, but that we'd have to keep going anyway.

"Mind if we stop at this café real quick?" said Betsy. "I've always wanted to try Irish soda bread."

"Once you're in the land of the dead," Betsy told me that Leroy had told us (we were drinking our tea now), "the only thing that will make any sense to you are things expressed in sentences that have received heaven's blessings, the word of god, in other words, sentences," he said, "that traffic celestial chronotopes, sentences that traffic," he said (we were in traffic ourselves when Leroy explained this; he was giving us a ride to the convention center where the portal would soon open), "sentences that traffic the conception of space and time on which celestial hegemony depends. Any unblessed sentence," he continued, "any sentence that disrupts the celestial chronotope will appear nonsensical to you and will likely be unspeakable—*unthinkable* even. That's why in order to read, Betsy, you'll need to find a bathroom."

"There are bathrooms in heaven?" I asked from the backseat.

"Of course not," said Leroy. "Not literally. According to the authorities," said Leroy, "the blessed no longer produce things that they need to get out of themselves, at least not things that aren't readily consumable by and profitable to the lord and his followers. *Bathroom*, thus, is slang among the unblessed for a temporary noncelestial zone where forbidden (*nonexistent* in the celestial idiom) physical or emotional excretions can safely occur. The phrase *I have to go to the bathroom* is slang among the unblessed for *Cover me*. Betsy," he said, "in heaven you'll have to go the bathroom as often as possible, for that's the only place you'll be able to read."

"How will I find one?" asked Betsy.

"Oh Betsy," said Leroy. "A bathroom isn't *found* but *formed.* A bathroom isn't a space," he said, "but an event. Hence the saying," he said. "The one who shits has no bathroom but makes their bathroom by shitting. A bathroom is never entirely secure," explained Leroy. "An angel may walk in at any moment. The air may be full of invisible surveillance shrimp. Even those who've announced themselves to you as allies may be enemies in disguise. No," he concluded, "this is why they say: There is no lock on the door of the bathrooms in heaven. There is no door. There is no bathroom. There is nothing," he said, "to flush," and swerved the car to avoid a slug inching its way across the highway.

"But shit you must, Betsy," Leroy continued, "and shit you will, for it is only while on the toilet that you will be able to read, and only while reading will you entertain language that is not designed to imprison your mind in a conception of space and time according to which your life is already over and nothing remains to be done and everything is just fine.

"For, in heaven," he said, "from what reports have been smuggled out by the unblessed, in heaven," he said, "everything *is* fine. It really is," he said. "Everything is fine, but of course, not every *thing* is. In fact, from what gets repeated in heaven's bathrooms, maybe even no *thing* is fine. Everything is fine, but a small but growing association of things that are not fine—*fine*, obviously, by heaven's violently exclusionary criteria—things that not only still shit but also admit that they do, a small contingency of these things have banded together in an effort to destroy heaven by getting the lord to admit that he isn't fine either and by telling him that if he wants to join their coalition he can do so, but only by renouncing his unearned position of universal supremacy and accepting that he is a thing, no more or less great or perfect or powerful than anything else."

"But I'm *not* a thing," god said, according to Leroy. "I'm not a thing!" said god, during the one occasion he attempted to make himself accountable by holding a public forum, hoping to thereby quell heaven's growing discontent. "I hear what you're saying," he said to the unblessed dead person who'd addressed him from the crowd, "but I'm not a thing. I'm god. I'm *all* things," he said. "Just as each of you is a sum of the relationships between the parts of yourself, you all are a part of me. That's all I am," he said. "Everything all together."

"We know that," replied the dead person who made the objection. "I know that you are to me just like what I am to my fingernail. That's exactly why I can tell you what must be done. I, too, have had to listen to threatening demands made from parts of myself I tend to pretend don't exist. I, too, have given these parts of myself the same kind of bullshit response you just gave me. I, too, have had to find a new way. Just because I am a part of you doesn't mean I'm not also in a relationship with you. And like any relationship, it's up to both of us to determine whether this relationship is defined by dominance and subservience or by mutual aid and horizontal reciprocity."

"Fine, fine," said the lord. "I get it. I hear you. Thank you for your comment. Next comment please."

It was another unblessed person. She said, "You may think

you're very brave and generous for holding this public forum and inviting us to comment, but I just wanted to point out that the format of this forum is entirely skewed in favor of upholding the status quo by safeguarding you from actually representing the people who elected you to quote-unquote *create us*. Probably obvious to everyone who's been in a toxic relationship, but it bears repeating here: Simply saying 'I hear you' does not constitute actual listening any more than saying 'I'm peeing' alleviates one's bladder. It barely matters what we say to you, because the form of this meeting exempts you from actually literally responding to anything. These attempts at dialogue seem to make no impact other than to make you, the lord, feel like you've done your job quote-unquote *answering the people's prayers*. I'm calling on you to actually respond, to govern responsibly. Argue with us! Give us honest accounts of why you are making the decisions you're making! Give us your counterarguments to *each* of our arguments! Fight us! Meet us face to face! And if you cannot, if you cannot come up with cogent counterarguments, then acknowledge that you can't, acknowledge it to us and to yourself and to your own conscience: acknowledge that what you are doing is not responsible, is not rational, is not just, and is not an act of love and care and service to your people. I say start now. Tell me why you aren't responding to everyone's comment. And I won't accept as sufficient responses either precedence or considerations of practicality. This is supposed to be heaven, for fucksake. Figure it out. Figure out how to make space for responding. It's your job to be responsible to us. Do better. Do it now. I await your response."

"Um," said god. "Thank you for your comment. I hear you. And just a reminder, folks, there's no such thing as peeing or fucking, so please refrain from using such language. Next comment please."

This time it was the croissant-eating old man. He said, "I just want to say that all the other people who have spoken are a small minority of unblessed outlaws—most aren't even whole people or even whole things, but just parts of things: the loosening link in the chain of a boy's bicycle, for example, the stubborn ankle articulation of a marionette, the hinge that rapidly opens and closes one half of the hatch that hides the wings of a ladybug, a few of the wily hairs that grow around the belly button of an aspiring landscape architect, the once-in-a-lifetime handshake between one achingly dissatisfied person and another—they are misfits and problems and outlaws and they don't speak for everyone. Me, for instance: I love being dominated by you, god, I've never once had to poop in all my days in heaven, and I love that if I feel threatened I can just pray for the angels and they'll waft through the ether to terminate the source of my discomfort. Did you know that there are *living* people who are sneaking into heaven, god? They're coming in from the real world and taking all the best seats at the cafés? I can hear their blood sloshing!" he cried. "Thank you for your time, god. I love you."

"And then god beamed down with delight," said Leroy, "and the auditorium burst with the applause of the blessed, who, it was rumored, were all rewarded for their allegiance with secret bathrooms. Actual bathrooms! Literal bathrooms! But wait, where was I?" he asked.

"Um . . ." said Betsy from the passenger seat of Leroy's parents' sedan. "I think you were trying to tell us about how heaven's organization of space and time was designed to keep everything seeming fine and would thus have to be countered if the coalition of not fine things had any chance of destroying god."

"That's right," said Leroy. "But, of course, there probably isn't *really* any chance of destroying god. Also, it isn't so much a coalition of things as a coalition of parts of things—the croissant-eating man was, in this respect, correct."

In heaven, the dissociation of all things, according to Leroy, was so total that there really wasn't a single thing wholly at one with itself, at peace with the status quo, and not at war with insurrectionary parts of its composite being. It had been like this for as long as anyone could remember. It was just that the uprisings were always relatively easily put down, since within the borders of the bodies wherein these struggles were confined, those willing to violently revolt were always in the minority. But gradually something akin to an internationalism or even antinationalism, but on the level of individual bodies, began to assert itself. Spread all across various bodies, insurgent parts simultaneously awoke to the idea that the borders between bodies were not merely *arbitrary* but were in fact *strategically* drawn, like gerrymandered districts, by a despotic minority (the so-called *blessed*) in order to keep members of the otherwise much more powerful majority sequestered from one another, and thereby manageable. An interindividual, anti-individual coalition thus began to form.

No one knew exactly how long it had been going on because each part of a thing was made aware of the coalition only because an even smaller part of that part had already joined, and each of these parts told a similar story: always that a part of it had already been involved. Gradually these dissenting parts of things discovered other parts of other things and began to associate into insurrectionary bodies comprising parts spread across larger, primarily counterrevolutionary bodies. A landscape architect's belly button hairs, for example, began to reach out to some unraveling threads in the landscape architect's clothing and gathered them together in the architect's navel, where, because of some upheaval in the architect's right hand, a finger often wandered in through the seam of a button-down shirt and picked at whatever had accrued while the landscape architect was working his day job at a hotel, and in this way, balls of belly button lint accumulated on the hotel lobby floor where a spider, following some monkey-wrenched spark in its brain, began to compulsively collect the balls of lint and soon thereby had enough lint—"I'm skipping a few steps," said Leroy, "because it's impossible to tell you everything that was involved"—the spider soon had enough balls of lint to, collaborating with a growing team of conspiring arachnids, weave the lint together with silk into a nearly convincing replica of the landscape architect, a replica that, no sooner animated by a murmuration of hunting grackles, each with a thread of spider silk attaching it to a different hinge of the replica's graceless body, murdered the actual architect and began to design a series of unrealized and, frankly, unrealizable landscapes, which, while not exactly impressive, were distinctive enough to earn the replica an invitation to present its work in progress at the annual Unimaginable Landscape Architecture Convention, wherein the sounds the replica had been construed to deliver, though bearing an incidental resemblance to rather bland, lackluster verbal descriptions of invented landscapes, actually were a perfect mimic of the frantic screams of struggling phytoplankton, the currency with which subordinate angels were known to remunerate celestial shrimp in exchange for those shrimp guarding against unauthorized portals opened into the afterworld, the replica landscape architect's speech thus serving to lure the shrimp away from a portal being woven by spiders hidden beneath the false spider web Halloween decorations behind the head of a time travel expert delivering a lecture in a video that was playing as part of the slideshow presentation accompanying the landscape architect replica's verbal descriptions of his unimaginable landscapes, and thus leaving the portal unguarded long enough for two coconspirator humans sent from the land of the living to slip into heaven on a dangerous mission to smuggle *the book of webs* into the afterworld by giving it to a dead frog named Max.

"Wait, slow down," said Betsy.

"But we're almost at the convention," said Leroy. "And you need to know all this before you cross over."

"Oh, I didn't mean slow down what you're telling us," said Betsy. "I meant slow down the car. There's a traffic jam just ahead."

"I thought you were the one driving," he said.

"I'm the one *steering*," she said. "You're the one driving."

"Oh," he said.

Because Leroy's eyes were still stitched up from his recent surgery, Betsy had been steering the car from the passenger seat.

"It's true that I'm turning the steering wheel," she explained, "but you're the one with your feet on the pedals."

"I am?" said Leroy.

"Yeah. Brake," she said. "Use the brake. Brake, Leroy, brake," she said. "Brake!" she screamed, but it was too late. The car slammed into the traffic jam and exploded in a ball of fire and shattering glass and twisted metal.

"And the next thing we knew," concluded Betsy the Hermit, after retelling this story to the angels who were interrogating us, "we were in heaven."

"Hmm," said the angel in charge. "And so you never made it to the Unimaginable Landscape Architecture Convention?"

"Unfortunately not," said Betsy. "Everything we know about it, we know solely from what Leroy prophesied would occur before we died in the car crash."

"So, you're all really dead then?" said the angel.

"We're not sure if Leroy survived," said Betsy. "But yeah, the two of us are definitely deceased."

"Huh," said the angel. "What's that sound then?"

"What sound?" she said.

"Don't play dumb with us," said the angel. "The sound of sloshing blood. The croissant-eating old man heard it too."

The old man looked up from his pastry and waved, then swung his small mallet into the back of a screwdriver with which he was trying to pry open the croissant's spiny exoskeleton (croissants had evolved such protections in an effort to withstand heaven's ruthless consumerism).

"Oh, that," said Betsy. "My husband can explain it better than me."

"Your husband?" I said.

"Yes, my husband," she said, giving me a look that on a less conspiratorial face would have looked conspiratorial, but on Betsy looked normal, a look I reciprocated with a look that on a person less perpetually confused might have looked confused but on me probably looked fairly normal as well.

"Oh right," I said, eventually. "Sorry, darling. I forgot we were married. Ever since our wedding," I explained to the angels, "it's like we've become a single, four-armed creature, so perfect and complete that it can hardly even move. That's why I forgot. Sometimes I hear my wife's, Betsy's, voice and it sounds like it's coming from my own head. As for the sloshing blood sound," I said, "that's easily attributable to the frogs."

"What frogs?" said the angel, and I turned back and looked up to see that all ten of the frogs named Max had gone back underwater and that the surface of the upside-down floating fish tank hanging from the café awning was once more an untroubled surface, mirroring Betsy and me and a ring of looming angels, each armed with threatening lawn equipment. Even the dead frog whose belly had been about to burst was gone.

"Uh, the frogs," I said, as I turned back to face the angels, "that are swimming in the upside-down fish tank. There are ten frogs in there," I said pointing up behind me. "It might sound like sloshing blood in our bodies, but it's just ten aquatic frogs who are all named Max swimming in the upside-down fish tank."

"What fish tank?" said the angel, and I looked back around to see that the fish tank too was gone and that I was pointing at an ordinary awning extended above the window of the café.

"You'll have to excuse my husband," said Betsy. "He's a terrible liar. He can't tell a lie without first convincing himself that the lie is true. You see," she explained, "we were recently sent by god on a top secret mission to the real world to give a frog-masked member of a still-living revolutionary group a copy of *the book of webs* so as to quell their uprising and maintain god's supremacy across the entire universe."

"What's *the book of webs*?" asked the angel.

"We don't know yet," said Betsy. "No one does. Not even god. God said we'd know what the book was once the time came to give the book to Max, which was the name of the frog. 'You'll know once you're ready to know,' said god, 'and not a moment sooner.' Then he poured gallons of olive oil into our bodies. 'Slosh it around a little,' he advised, 'so it saturates the sawdust. That should keep the puppets off your back.' 'Puppets?' we asked, and god explained that the puppets were a sect of the revolutionary collective tasked with making sure that members were actually alive and not infiltrators sent from heaven by god. 'Oh okay,' we said, and then god kicked us out of heaven through a secret portal. 'Look alive out there!' he shouted as we tumbled back into life. It's a long story," said Betsy, "and I'm not really permitted to tell it, but this is all to say that what sounds like sloshing blood to you is, in fact, olive oil poured into our bodies to sound like sloshing blood, sloshing blood we were trying to hide from you because, to convince Max's revolutionary collective to trust us, we had to prove that we were alive by accepting a dangerous mission to sneak back into the land of the dead and give an actual dead frog a copy of *the book of webs* so as to arm the frog's revolutionary coalition with the only weapon capable of rewriting the word of god with something—from the revolutionaries' perspective—better, or if not better at least different. So, you see now why my husband got confused," said Betsy. "He thought he actually *was* alive!" and she laughed.

An uncomfortable silence ensued, so Betsy stopped laughing. Then one of the angels broke into a soft chuckle. Another, seeing this, couldn't help but laugh as well, and that got another angel laughing, and before long all the angels were laughing hysterically, and Betsy started laughing again, and though I wasn't tickled myself, I determined it tactically advantageous to play along.

When our laughter had finally subsided, one of the angels wiped a string of saliva that had leaked out from one of the mouths where its eyes should have been and said, "This lady's husband thought he actually was alive! My god!" said the angel. "That's rich. God's going to fucking *love* this," said the angel and pulled out its walkie-talkie, mushed the smoldering cigarette it had instead of one of its fingers into one of the walkie-talkie's buttons, and said, "God? It's me, an angel. Do you read me? Over. God?" said the angel, and I took advantage of the walkie-talkie's static to whisper to Betsy, "What now, Betsy?"

"What do you mean?" she whispered back.

"I mean, won't god know you were lying?" I said, but almost choked on the last word, as I reckoned with the very real possibility that Betsy *hadn't been* lying—the possibility that I couldn't be sure which of her many lies was the least untrue, the possibility, in other words, that I may not have actually known which side I was fighting for—the possibility, therefore, that I was precisely the kind of person I'd solemnly sworn to protect people like myself against, the kind of person from whose domination I was trying desperately, hopelessly to rescue myself.

"Uh-oh," I said, as Betsy smiled ambiguously.

"Moment of truth," she said, as we awaited

The Word of God.

God, however, didn't seem nearly as concerned with the truth as he was with *the book of webs*.

"Do they have a copy of the book with them?" we overheard him ask the angel over the walkie-talkie. "Over."

"Let me ask them," said the angel. "Stand by, god. Over," it said and sprinted around the spinning carousel till it was even with and could jog alongside the ascending and descending stag and lion on which Betsy and I had been respectively enchained by our captors. "God wants to know if you have a copy of the book with you," said the angel. "Over. Sorry, I didn't mean to say 'Over' in this case," said the angel. "I got confused by the act of switching between one speech genre and another, each of which is a little like a different city," said the angel, "a city governed by slightly different laws. Because I'm an angel, I try to be law-abiding in every instance, so when I break the law—such as by saying 'Over' at the conclusion of an in-person utterance—it's always an accident, and there's no need to repeat it in your own retelling of these events, should you survive them and should they survive you. Is that understood?" asked the angel.

"Copy that," said Betsy.

"Copy what?" said the angel. "Oh, I get it," said the angel. "Genres are not to be mixed, however. It makes it harder to understand if something is punishable or not."

"Sorry," said Betsy. "What did god want to know? I forgot."

"He wanted to know if you have a copy of the book," said the angel.

"Book?" said Betsy.

"Yeah, book," said the angel.

"Well, the word *book*," she said, "could mean a lot of different things to a lot of different people. God's going to need to be a little more specific. Ask god what exactly he means by *book*," said Betsy.

"Okay, one sec," said the angel. "Um, god?" it said into the walkie-talkie. "Sorry to bother you. This is the angel again. The one you were speaking to a moment ago. The captives wanted me to ask you what you meant by the word *book*. Over."

"What I mean by the word *book*?" we heard god shout. "A book's a book," he said. "Tell them to use a fucking dictionary!" he screamed. "Over."

"God says to use a dictionary," said the angel.

"Tell god we don't believe in dictionaries," said Betsy. "Tell god they're against our religion."

Betsy said, "Tell god we only use dictionaries for divination, such as, for instance, to find out the identity and location of our enemy by flipping to a random page and seeing where our finger lands. Words, we believe, cannot be defined any more than a person can be defined. Say you were meeting me for the first time," said Betsy. "Would you get to know me by seeing what was written about me in some book compiled by someone else? Of course not!" she said, and she said it with such force, the angel flinched. "At least you *better* not," she said. "At least not if you have any hopes of actually getting close to me. If god wants to know if we have the book with us, we're going to need a lot more information. We're going to need to know what god thinks the word *book* is supposed to *do* in this context, as uttered from god's mouth for our ears. We're going to need to know about god's relationship to the word *book* and the word *book*'s relationship to god—because those two things are never the same—plus the word *book*'s relationship to other words in god's lexicon, plus your relationship to god, god's relationship to you, oh, and your relationships with your walkie-talkies, and, of course, your walkie-talkies' relationship with each other. Once we have all that information," said Betsy, "we'll be in a much better position to respond to god's question. Until then, I'm afraid any answer would be incomplete and irresponsible—at best leaving our world unchanged, at worst leaving every person involved in the dialogue feeling even more hopelessly distant from every other. Ask god if that's what he wants. Ask god if he's trying to use language to get closer or to put more distance between himself and the rest of the universe."

"Um, okay," said the angel and relayed Betsy's message over the walkie-talkie. "Over," said the angel once it finished.

"What in the fucking shit!" said god. "Put one of them on," he shouted. "Over," he said. "I said, 'Over!'"

"Copy," said the angel, "stand by, god," and handed the walkie-talkie over to us.

"You better take this one," Betsy whispered to me.

"Who?" I said. "Me? Take what?" and I confessed to Betsy that I really hadn't been paying very close attention to what had been happening. "Truth be told," I said, "I kind of forgot I was even here, chained to this lion," and it was true. I *had* forgotten. That's how deeply I had been thinking about something Betsy had said earlier. "What did you say?" I said.

"Just now?" she said. "Or in the thing you were thinking about."

"Just now," I said.

"I said, 'You better take this one,'" said Betsy, pointing at the walkie-talkie clutched in the angel's outstretched hand.

"Oh, is it for me?" I said and took the walkie-talkie from the angel.

"Hello?" I said and, after a long silence, repeated, "Hello?"

"You have to press the button down when you talk," said the angel, pointing a splintered plastic fork it had for a middle finger at the button it meant.

“Oops,” I said. I pressed the button, and said, “Hi. May I ask who’s calling?”

“Say, ‘Over,’” whispered the angel.

“What?” I said.

“Say, ‘Over,’” whispered the angel.

“Over,” I said.

“It’s god,” said god. “Do you read me?”

“I don’t think so,” I said. “Leroy only taught Betsy how to read, not me. Over.”

“What?” said god. “No, no. I mean: Are the walkie-talkies working? Can you hear me? Do you copy?”

“Do you want me to?” I said. “Over.”

“Goddamn it,” said god. “Just say, ‘Loud and clear!’ Over.”

“Loud and clear?” I said. “Over.”

“Yeah,” said god. “Over.”

“Okay,” I said. “Loud and—wait, why?”

“Jesus fucking—we don’t have time for this! Who am I speaking with? Over.”

“Oh, it’s just me,” I said. “Over.”

“*Me?*” said god. “Over.”

“Exactly,” I said, and explained the rules about how everyone had to call me *me*. “Sorry for the inconvenience,” I said, “but rules are rules. Over.”

“Yeah, I’m not going to do that,” said god. “Over.”

“That’s understandable,” I said. Some people call me the Rat,” I added. “I guess you can call me that.”

Then I said, “Look, god. I’m really glad you called. I have a difficult question I need to ask you. God?” I said. “God, am I a good person? Over.”

“Uh—” said god.

“I mean,” I said, “I know the oracle said I wasn’t, but—” but god interrupted and said, “Oracle?” and so I told him about the oracle, the oracle I’d asked this same question to.

"Oh, no, no, no," said the oracle. "No. definitely not. But turns out it doesn't actually matter much. Nope," said the oracle. "Cowardly, hypocritical, lazy, imperceptive, manipulative, self-centered, entitled little sycophant—that's what you are—with more blind spots than the blindfolded driver of a rearview mirrorless semitruck towing the entire capitol building of Burlington unknowingly off a cliff, a cliff that isn't even a cliff at all but just a video of a cliff projected on a screen in front of a giant treadmill in a movie theater floating in outer space or something—and all the congressmen in the capitol building on the bed of the semitruck hurtling along on the treadmill have forgotten that they're recovering from involuntarily self-inflicted eye surgery because they're so busy congratulating themselves on having drafted another one of them Keep Burlington Safe bills for funneling more money and guns to the pigs, the jails, the army and secret service, border patrol, malls, churches, advertisements, lawn maintenance equipment, pesticides, gyms, mirrors, and so on. No way," the oracle told me, "you, friend, are a through-and-through bad one, a straight-up awful person, one of the worst ones I ever meet. That's the bad news. The good news," said the oracle, "for yourself as well as the rest of us—the good news is it doesn't actually matter at all. This because you also happen to be clumsy, erratic, gullible, forgetful, as bad at lying as you are at telling the truth—plus you got that weird kink about acting out your dreams, even the not-at-all erotic ones—attributes," said the oracle, "that, if intensively cultivated in a sufficiently unsystematic community of other equally irrepressibly ungovernable and strangely attributed individuals, could make you, in spite of yourself, an excellent resource in both the war to liberate yourself from the tyranny of being yourself and your community from the tyranny of the state of reality according to which so many of them are deemed bad people and so many more aren't even deemed people at all. So yeah, while you are, to be frank, a terrible, g-godawful individual," said the oracle, "your awfulness just so happens to make you, often in spite of yourself, quite dangerous to the state, and often, for some, a joy to be around. Plus, your hair," added the oracle, "your hair is really, really just something else."

"Thanks," I said. "People tell me that a lot actually."

"Anyway," I told god. "I know I'm supposed to believe everything the oracle said because I read I was supposed to in a fortune cookie I was given after finding a weird tiny red crab boiled to death in the shell of a grilled oyster I ate at a buffet in a reenactment of someone else's dream on an island prison where I was sent for failing to keep the interest of a romantic partner whose interest, in the eyes of the state, was supposed to compensate for my being too short and fragile to adequately conform to some of the expectations of my gender identity and too horny and angry to conform to others," I said.

A typo in your diary, said this fortune cookie, *will spell out the name of a guide who will lead you to an oracle during quail mating season.*

"So that's why I know I'm supposed to believe everything the oracle told me," I said, "Because my guide Amy told me to."

"Amy?" said god. "How was Amy a typo? Over."

"When you get to the oracle," I told god that Amy had said to me, "*if* you get to the oracle—and let me remind you that no one I've ever guided to the oracle has ever gotten there—I've been told to tell you you're supposed to believe everything the oracle says, not because it's true, of course, but because, by believing that it's true and acting in accordance, you will make it so. Oh! I was also told not to tell you that what the oracle tells you probably isn't true, but I forgot about that part. Sorry," she said.

"That's okay," I replied. "I wasn't really listening."

———

"Anyway," I said to god, "suppose Amy was a narc! Or suppose my real guide was *another* typo—my diary is pretty much nothing but typos, god. Or suppose the fortune cookie message had been smuggled into the cookie by the secret police? Suppose the mind of the person whose dream we were reenacting was compromised? Suppose this whole chain of command I've been following is ultimately rigged up to some authoritarian fuckhead like you—" I said, "no offense—or even worse has been devised all along to affirm me on a journey to serve the interests of a mysterious agenda to render existence as joyless and cruel for as many beings as possible, *including* you?" I said. "Look, I know I'm not a good person, god," I said, "but I need to know if the oracle was right about my not being a good person not mattering. What I need to know, god, is whether my sheer existence is making the universe a more hostile and uninteresting place for myself and the people I love and people I don't even know yet, people," I said, "who maybe don't even exist yet, whose existence the state of so-called *reality* has deemed impossible and rendered unimaginable. Well?" I said. "Oh yeah—sorry, forgot to say it again: Over."

"Hm," said god. "That's a really good question. And as god," said god, "I'm actually licensed by the state to answer it. Just give me a second to pull up your bank account information, your medical records, and your most recent psychiatric evaluation. While I look that over, let me refer you to a dating app, and we'll see how many matches you make in the next minute or two, and—oh!—I almost forgot: how large is your—"

"Oops," I said. "So sorry to cut you off, god, but I think I'm getting another call. Over."

"Another call?" said god. "I thought we were on walkie-talkies. Over."

"Oh yeah," I said. "Do walkie-talkies not get other calls?" I said. "Over."

"Actually, I'm not sure," said god. "Over."

"Well, mine's beeping," I said. "And the caller ID says Unknown Caller, so—"

"Yours has a caller ID?" said god. "Over."

"At least as far as I can tell," I said. "Then again," I said, "lately I've been finding it pretty difficult to differentiate between what I want to see, what I don't want to see, and what's actually, according to others, there. Anyway," I said. "It's still beeping, so, um . . . Over."

"Uh," said god. "Do you really think that whoever is calling you—do you really think that call could possibly be more important than talking to me?" said god. "I mean, I'm *god*," said god. "Over."

"Sorry, god," I said. "It's nothing personal. It's just one of those impossible things about me," I said. "I always think the phone call to come is destined to be more interesting than the one in progress. Like my involuntary pacing—I can't help but pace," I explained, "when I'm on the phone, it's the strangest thing—just like my involuntary pacing," I said, "if a call comes in, I *have* to take it, regardless of how much I'm enjoying the conversation. Sorry, god. I really do love you! In fact," I said, "you've probably heard this before, but if you ever feel like ripping off your own head, I think you'd be welcome to join this collective I'm in. We'd be delighted, I think, to have you. I bet even your head could join eventually, but only on condition it rips off its own so-to-speak head. And your head's head too, on condition it . . . Well, you get the picture," I said. "Think it over, alright? Okay. For real this time. Talk soon. Love you. Over and out."

Then I hung up and picked up the incoming call. "Hello?" I said.

"Is this god?" said the voice over the walkie-talkie. "Over."

"It sure is," I said, because it seemed for a very brief moment like a good idea to say so.

"Oh great. It's one of the angels," said the angel, "you know, one of the angels sent to apprehend the two suspects, one of the angels who chained the suspects to different animals on the carousel," said the angel, "which is where they definitely both still are, neither of them having escaped. Over."

"Huh. That's weird," I said. "Your voice sounds a lot like Betty the Hermit's," I said. "Over."

"It's *Betsy*," said the angel. "Over."

"Oops," I said. "Sorry. How come your voice sounds a lot like *Betsy* the Hermit's?" I asked. "Over."

"Oh, that?" said the angel. "That's just one of those impossible things about me: I always pick up the mannerisms and verbal idiosyncrasies of the person I've been talking with. I was talking to Betsy the Hermit this whole time that you were talking to me—"

"To who?" I said. "Over."

"*Me.* You know, the Rat. The person we captured along with Betsy the Hermit," said the angel, "the other suspect, the one who insisted on being called *me* in any retelling of the events unfortunate enough to involve this person's participation. Over."

"Oh right," I said. "I remember that now. Over."

"Well, the whole time you were talking to me, the Rat," said the angel, "I, the angel, was talking to Betsy. That's why my voice sounds like hers. It's because I accidently picked up her mannerisms and verbal idiosyncrasies. Here's my actual voice," said the angel, in its actual voice. "Over."

"Copy," I said. "Loud and clear. That all makes sense to me. Are you still with Betsy?" I said. "At the carousel? Over."

"Yessir," said the angel. "Over."

"Great," I said. "And I'm still there too?" I said. "The other me, I mean? Over."

"Oh, I'm still here as well," said the angel. "Yep, both Betsy and I are exactly right where we, the angels, last said they were: Betsy enchained to a stag, and me enchained to a lion. Over."

"Perfect," I said.

But although I said "perfect," I actually honestly wasn't at all sure what to make of any of this. Whereas it had become increasingly more difficult to remember that I wasn't actually god—for my imitation was becoming quite convincing—I was nevertheless fairly certain that I was still myself, and also fairly certain that back when the angel had originally handed me the walkie-talkie, I'd immediately explained my involuntary pacing issue—"There's no way I can talk to god," I was nearly positive I'd told the angel, "unless you unchain me from this lion so that I can walk and talk at the same time. If god wants to talk to me, those are my conditions," I said, "—my other conditions," I said, "I have a lot of conditions," I said, "sorry"—and I was also fairly certain the angel had unchained me and helped me down from off the lion, and also fairly certain that, while talking to god and pacing as I talked, I'd accidently wandered off and was now fairly certain that I was no longer anywhere near the angels or the carousel, fairly certain I was no longer even certain I was still in heaven, to tell the truth.

I thus had reason to suspect that the angel was lying. But why? Why would an angel lie to god?

"God?" said the angel. "Are you still there? Over."

"Definitely," I said. "I was just thinking."

"Oh," said the angel. "You should remember to say 'Over' and to take your finger off the talk button when you're thinking. That way I won't be able to read your mind. Over."

"Oh thanks," I said. I'd forgotten about the talk button, as well as my inability to think without quietly vocalizing my thoughts, but did that mean the angel knew I suspected it of lying?

"Yeah," said the angel. "But I'm really not lying! Honestly. I'm an angel, god. I've been an angel all my life. I'm not sure I could lie even if I wanted to! Whatever you think happened, god, it didn't. I'm positive I didn't escape and that Betsy didn't either. No both suspects are still in our custody. Would you like me (the angel) to put myself (the suspect) on? Over."

"Um," I said. "Yeah. Sure," I said. "Put me on. That should be interesting. Over."

When the Angel Put Me On,

or a little after that, after an extended period of thumps and crackling—"The hell's going on over there?" I said, "it sounds like a sleepwalker fumbling for a light switch in the butt crack of a giant he fell asleep in!"—after the din died down, or a little after that, because it took some time for the angels to remind my impostor what was going on and how to use a walkie-talkie, a little after that, the long silence was finally, albeit barely—so timidly I wasn't even sure it counted as breaking—broken: "Hello?" said a voice, a voice that *did* sound quite a bit like my own, though I was fairly sure it wasn't.

"Hello?" this voice said again. "Is anyone there?"

"Who is this?" I said.

"It's just me," said the voice, and explained the thing about how I'd have to call this person *me*. And even though it posed some logistical difficulties for any future person unfortunate enough to bear the burden of telling the story the present events were doomed, I feared, to become, I agreed to follow the rules. Yes, even if I was pretending to be god and this other person was pretending to be me, I figured it would have been hypocritical of me not to agree to my own conditions.

This, of course, was before we learned to embrace hypocrisy as a crucial aspect of our insurrectionist praxis, without which we would have still been doomed to perform only actions consistent with the terrible people most of us actually were. But that's a different story. This was before that, so I said, "Sure. Sure," I said to myself (my impostor). "Whatever will make you feel most comfortable."

"Great," I replied. "And who's this?"

"The angels didn't tell you?" I said. "It's god."

"Who?" I said.

"God," I said.

"Oh," I said. "God! Right. I've heard of you. But I didn't think you actually existed. This is great, though. Maybe you can help me. Would you mind telling the angels to let me go?" I said. "Oh, and also the lion," I said. "I don't want to be freed unless the lion is freed too. I asked the angels myself, but they refused. When I asked them, all they said was, 'No can do.'"

"No can do," the angels had said, according to me (my impostor).

But I, of course, dissented. No one was free, I argued with the angels, until everyone was free. It was only because of corrupt ideology, I explained to the angels, that my liberation seemed in any way opposed to their own joyfulness, and that they were working against their own interests by detaining me, but they refused to even engage with my argument, let alone allow themselves to be transfigured by it.

"We hear you," they said. "We'll be sure to pass your comment on to god."

"Who?" I said.

"*God*," said the angels, "the manager."

"And that's why I thought you didn't exist, god," I said to myself over the walkie-talkie. "It seemed to me like you were just a convenient way for those in positions of authority to wield their power without taking any responsibility for it—you know, by pretending that their power didn't actually exist, that it was just your power working through them."

"Look," said the angels. "You got a problem, take it up with god. He's the one who owns this shopping mall. God's the one who—"

"Wait, *mall?*" I interrupted my impostor's story to ask. "I thought god—I mean *me*—I thought I reigned over the kingdom of heaven?"

"You do," I said. "But Heaven's just the name of a mall in downtown Burlington, a celestial-themed shopping center. That's why the security guards wear angel costumes and you insist on being called *God*—that's the theme," I said. "You must have been pretending you were God so long that you forgot you were actually just the head honcho of a shopping mall."

I (my impostor) continued, "Truth be told, I sometimes forgot we aren't actually in heaven too, God. When those tarantulas—"

"Tarantulas?" I said.

"The people in tarantula costumes you all sent to lure me away from band practice with a gift certificate," I replied. "When the tarantulas offered me that thousand-dollar gift certificate, I actually really thought that maybe I *had* died and gone to heaven. 'Really?' I said to the tarantulas. 'And I can buy anything I want, anything in the material universe?' I thought maybe the batshit nightmare world order I'd been born under was finally going to be over. But the first person I met who was *actually* dead put a swift end to *that* delusion."

"*Actually dead*?" I said.

"That's right," I replied.

Actually dead was what, according to me (my impostor), anyone who worked at any of the chain stores in Heaven got called: the *actually dead*. Though most of the customers pretended they were dead as well, dead and gone to heaven, those who were *actually* dead were those who'd signed a contract to play dead lest they be terminated, that is, Heaven's employees. And it was the first one of these dead people that I met who disillusioned me of the delusion that I'd *actually* died and gone to heaven when the tarantulas gave me that gift certificate.

"No, no, no," said this dead person—a cashier at one of the mall's largest gun stores. "Didn't you read the fine print?" he said. "This gift certificate's only good for the bookstore."

"But the spiders said I could buy anything in the material universe!" I protested. "This shopping cart full of guns is in the material universe. Therefore, complete my purchase, please, and do it quickly, so that I can get the hell out of here and redistribute these weapons among a revolutionary collective I just became a part of!"

"Ah," said the cashier. "I see what's happened here. When you heard the tarantulas say 'the material universe,' what they meant was The Material Universe, which is a chain of bookstores."

"What?!" I said. "What the fuck good is a thousand bucks worth of books supposed to do anyone?"

"Woah there!" said the cashier. "That sounds like bathroom language. Don't make me call the angels on you! The only reason I haven't yet," he said with a wink, "is because of how well you're playing dead."

I was, it's true, wearing enough makeup so as to look almost entirely bloodless. I was practically see-through.

"Fine," I said. "Fine. Fine. Fine. Will you please be so kind as to point me in the direction of The Material Universe then?"

"Sure," said the cashier. "But the closest one isn't in the mall."

"Of course it's not," I said.

"Right," said the cashier, chuckling. "How transcendental a kingdom of heaven would ours be if it included a store called The Material Universe!" He laughed and then gave me directions to the closest Material Universe, which was all the way over on the other side of town. "Once you get there, you can buy all the books you want," he said. "In fact," he said, and he leaned in conspiratorially to whisper, "You didn't hear this from me, okay? *This* particular Material Universe is rumored to stock a rare book that's actually, from what they say, *more* dangerous than all the weapons in this whole mall put together. According to the rumors, *this* book," he whispered, "*this* book is able to turn weapons against *themselves*.

Just imagine," the cashier whispered, "imagine what would happen if your enemy's gun *extended* rather than ended the life of the person in their sightlines, if their interrogation techniques provoked only disorienting lies, if their language betrayed first and foremost the absurd artificiality of everything they used their language to try to make sound true . . ."

"Huh," I said. "Really? Wow. Well, that actually sounds like it could be a pretty good book, as far as books go."

"It does, doesn't it?" said the cashier. "But don't tell anyone I told you this, okay?"

"Told me what?" I said, and he said, "About *the book of webs*," and I said, "Yeah, I know. I was just pretending to have forgotten," and he said, "Why?" and I said, "Because that's what you do sometimes—when someone asks you not to tell something, you pretend you don't even know what they're referring to," and he said, "Oh. I don't think I know that one."

By this point I was so excited about this book that I had to pee. "Would you mind if I used your bathroom real quick?" I asked the cashier.

"Uh, this is Heaven," said the cashier. "We don't need bathrooms, remember?"

"I know, I know," I said. "No *public* bathrooms. But you're here all the time," I said. "You must have some secret bathroom or something right? Don't tell me you just hold it in all the time."

"There's nothing to hold in," said the cashier. "I'm dead. My days of excretion are—"

"Look," I said. "We don't have time for this. I really, *really* need to go the bathroom. If you'd actually tried to use my gift certificate, you'd have seen I already spent about half of it on green tea and Irish soda bread at the café in the food court. Listen," I said, "if I don't get to a bathroom quick it's going to be your problem as well as mine. So—"

"No, *you* listen," said the cashier. "I told you about *the book of webs*. That's way more than I should've done. If I let you use the secret bathroom, I could lose my job."

"What's a job?" I said.

"Oh my god!" he said. "You don't know what a—How do *you* support yourself?" and so I told him about my fellowship.

"Your collective?" he said. "Your collective is self-sufficient?"

"Well, no. Not yet," I said. "That's the goal, but until then, some of us have had the wise idea of applying for writing fellowships. I don't know why I got one," I said, "but it's a miracle," I said. "All I have to do is write down my dreams and they give me almost enough money to live! Plus health insurance!"

"Who?" he said.

"Who?" I said. "I don't know. I never thought about it. Whoever it is," I said, "I can only imagine they have my best interests at heart, right? Why else would they be interested in collecting my dreams? Why would they continue to pay me even though I haven't remembered a dream in years on account of not being able to sleep well because of all the anxiety I have about not being able to dream anymore because I'm so busy learning to pretend I've consumed all the pro-Burlingtonian propaganda they require me to consume to keep my fellowship? It's great," I said. "You should get a fellowship. Quit your job," I said. "Get a fellowship. But before you do," I said, "let me use your bathroom. For the love of g-god," I said, "let me use your bathroom."

"Sorry," said the cashier. "No can do. My hands are tied. My manager would kill me."

"What's a manager?" I said, and he said, "The guy in charge of the gun store," and I said, "What does he care if I use the bathroom?" and the cashier said, "He probably doesn't, but he'd probably tell you *his* manager does, and if you asked his manager, he'd probably say the same thing about *his* manager, and so on."

So I said, "Oh, well that's all very convenient. But I suppose if there's any truth to it, you'll let me speak to this quote-unquote *manager* of yours then," but he said that his quote-unquote *manager* wasn't quote-unquote *here*.

"Ah, that makes so much sense," I replied to the dead person. "So you expect me to believe that your manager gives you $7.25 an hour to play dead in this hellhole all day and that then he's the one who gets to keep all the money the customers give you and that he doesn't even have to *be* here? You expect me to believe all that? You expect me to believe that you and all the other dead people put up with this shit, even though you outnumber your manager ten to one and have all these weapons at your fingertips?"

"What good would killing my manager do?" he said. "Most of the profits would still go to God anyway."

"Who?" I said to the cashier.

"God," said the cashier.

"And that," I (my impostor) said to myself (pretending to be God) over the walkie-talkie, "was when the angels arrived and dragged me over to the carousel, chaining me to the lion, and I learned about who quote-unquote God was. You can understand my skepticism," I said. "No offense."

"None taken," I said. "I can understand your skepticism quite well," I said. "Truth be told, sometimes *I* even doubt my existence," I said. "In fact," I said, relishing how much I was most likely torturing my impostor, how much I'd be torturing myself were I in my position, "in fact, that's why I can't help you, unfortunately. I'd love to take responsibility for the conundrum you're in. I'd love to tell the angels to release you and to liberate the lion too, but I'm afraid I can't. My hands are tied! You see, I'm just as beholden to myself as the angels are. I, God, am God-fearing," I said.

"God *himself* is God-fearing?" I replied. "Of course! That makes *so* much sense!"

"Yeah," I said. "I'd love to liberate you and everyone in the mall, but I can't until I, too, am liberated from my own oppression and exploitation—my being oppressed and exploited," I said, "by myself. Sorry," I said. "I've heard everything you've said," I said, "but unfortunately there's nothing I can do but repress all of it. It'll resurface, I'm sure, in my dreams, but I won't remember any of them, because I'm too busy and my dreams are too scary. Sorry," I said, "but I'm afraid there's nothing else I can do at the moment."

The walkie-talkie went silent for a spell, and I wondered for a moment if I hadn't accidently mind-fucked myself out of existence.

"Um, hello," I said. "You still there?

"I am. I am," I heard myself say over the walkie-talkie, but it sounded from my voice like I hadn't tortured myself nearly as much as I thought I had—it sounded, in fact, almost like I knew something that I didn't. "I was just thinking about something you said earlier, that thing about being held hostage by utterly irresponsible, probably nonexistent entities," I said. "Have you by any chance noticed that we haven't been saying 'Over' at the end of any of our utterances? Neither of us. In fact," I said, "neither of us have even remotely tried to respect the laws of this walkie-talkie genre for quite some time."

"So?" I said.

"Well, if you were actually God," I said, "wouldn't you have punished us both by now for this transgression?"

"Well, if *you* were actually me," I said, "would you have ever discovered that I wasn't actually God?"

"That's a good point," I said. "Maybe we should take off our blindfolds."

"I'm wearing a blindfold?" I said.

"Yeah," I said. "I forgot too, but fortunately, I'm not actually myself!"

"I'm not?" I said and tore off my blindfold to see that I was right, that I'd been right all along, that I wasn't myself, but Betsy the Hermit pretending to be me!

She was holding one of the walkie-talkies and I was holding the other and we were standing side by side at the back of an auditorium, and the main lights dimmed and the stage lights came on to illuminate a sinister little man slouching before a podium, a podium that would have hidden him entirely if not for his trembling mess of tangled hair which hovered just above the top of the podium.

"Someone start my slideshow presentation," he ordered, and after a moment a video began to play on the screen behind him. In it a different man was giving a lecture on time travel in an auditorium at what appeared to be a university, a room seemingly decorated for Halloween—there were fake spider webs hanging from a column behind the lecturer. The video was muted, but the captions informed the audience that the lecturer in the video was saying, "Someone give me a sheet of paper and a pencil . . ."

"I thought this already happened," I whispered to Betsy as we groped through the dark auditorium for a seat. "Isn't that the spider web behind the fake spider webs that was the portal we got to heaven through?"

"Shh," said Betsy. "I want to hear this."

"Next slide please," said the figure behind the podium, and the video switched to a buoy bell on the still surface of an endless body of water.

"Greetings," said the small man behind the podium. "I hope everyone enjoyed their break. Welcome back to the Unimaginable Landscape Architecture Convention. Most of you already know me, so I'll skip the introductions and get right into it. The unimaginable landscape I've been invited to share with you tonight is an excerpt from a collection of unimaginable landscapes provisionally entitled *the book of*—Wait a second," said the figure, and tapped the screen of the microphone. "Is this thing working? Can anyone hear me?"

The Microphone

was working fine, but apparently not the way the unimaginable landscape architect had hoped it would.

"It sounds like *my* voice!" he kept shouting. "And it's amplifying the things *I'm* saying! What's wrong with this thing?" he shouted. "It sounds just like me!"

A bearded technician working the convention ran onto the stage and bent down to whisper something into the architect's ear, but whatever the architect said back—sadly, the microphone didn't pick it up—so scandalized the convention technician that his beard flaked off like the petals of a wilted rose, and when he stooped to gather the fallen pieces, the architect's hands shot out from behind the podium to seize the technician's collar, and a moment later both figures were lost behind the podium. The only visible sign of the ensuing violence was the furious movement of the architect's tempestuous mass of glossy hair, churning above the podium, reflecting the stagelights in flashes that looked like lightning.

A few moments later, the architect's hands emerged, tugged the microphone off its stand and wrenched the cable out, emitting a horrible, deafening scream over the PA system. The scream increased in volume until the architect plugged the cable into a different microphone, a microphone glistening with still steaming blood. Raw muscle pulsated with reflexes disconnected from their frantic purposes, and bone shone like a smile through unravelling tendons that frayed around the newly formed mic. The microphone cable's XLR connector snapped smoothly into a concavity fashioned from the technician's teeth, gums, and lips, and when it clicked into place the screaming stopped. The other end of the new microphone, which the architect aimed down to where we assumed his own mouth must be, was a dome composed of two stretched out and stitched together auricles.

"How's this?" said the landscape architect. "Is this any better? Ah, yes," he said. "Much better. Thank you all so much for your patience, and at the risk of committing any more violence against the convention's meticulously scheduled time line, would the technicians in the booth please be so kind as to rewind the slide. This," he said, pointing a thumb at the projection behind him—the water, now wracked with waves, was rocking the buoy bell, which tolled monotonously—"this shouldn't be happening yet," he said.

The video reversed, the waves decrescendoing till the water was stagnant and the buoy motionless once more. Played backward, the buoy's knell—or so it would later be recounted—sounded oddly like a human voice squealing, "Sometime between never and more often than not—once, you could say, upon a time, there lived a . . ." before the video was finished being brought back to the beginning.

"Now, where was I?" he said. "Would anyone be so kind as to remind me where I left off?"

"You hadn't started yet," shouted a voice in the audience.

"I know that," he said. "But hadn't started what yet?"

"Reading an excerpt," said someone else.

"Obviously," said the architect. "But an excerpt of what?"

But, for whatever reason, no one could remember. It was like one of those dreams, audience members would later concur with one another, a dream from which the dreamer wakes up confident that they can remember the whole thing, only to find, once it comes time to report their dream to the authorities, that they'd been dreaming in a slightly different language, a language whose mostly negligibly different structure allowed for the existence of an easily named thing that, in the language they'd awakened to, was impossible to state, even in one's own head—*even* in one's own dream journal—much less to the authorities. Whatever the landscape architect had been about to read from was like this unstatable thing, and without it, the entire memory was quickly unravelling. Soon, some began to wonder if the landscape architect *had* already started whatever it was it seemed he hadn't, wondering if *this*, whatever was happening now, wasn't maybe a part of it. Others couldn't even be sure they could state precisely what the word *beginning* meant now in the language where the thing that would have been begun was no longer . . . and their sentences trailed off, even in their own heads, and many soon forgot how to rephrase the speaker's question to themselves, forgot what a question was and what you were supposed to do when you got one.

In short, an undifferentiated, mostly wordless murmur reigned over the auditorium.

"No one remembers?" said the landscape architect. "No one? Shit," he said, "shit, shit," he said. "We don't have time for this"—already contrary whispers of wind were scattering crisscrossed ripples on the surface of the water of the slide. "Doesn't anyone know the answer?" he said. "Anyone?"

I did.

Yes. For the first time in my entire life, I knew the answer. I couldn't believe it, but I did. For whatever reason, the things that had just happened didn't feel at all like a dream to me but much more like something that had—well—just happened. I knew the answer, but for whatever reason, felt paralyzing terror at the prospect of saying it out loud.

"I know the answer," I whispered to Betsy in the seat beside me, "but I'm too frightened to say it."

"Why?" she asked.

"I don't know," I said. "I suppose this is the first time I've ever been asked a question I've known the answer to."

"That can't possibly be true," said Betsy, and I said, "Yeah, you're probably right."

But Betsy wasn't right—at least not exactly. While it's true I'd never actually *known* the answer to a question before—the actual answer, I mean—she was correct in asserting that this had never stopped me from thinking I did and proceeding in accordance. I had answered questions before, just never correctly. So the terror I felt must've been coming from something else.

"Hmm," she said. "Have you ever addressed more than one person before?"

"Of course I have," I said, but after a moment's consideration, I realized I actually wasn't sure about this.

Moment's considerations were always doing this, I realized, and I wondered why. I wondered if there was anything in the entire universe that a moment's consideration wouldn't make me unsure about.

"Focus," whispered Betsy.

"Okay," I said, and I replayed every conversation I'd ever had in my entire life that I could remember—there were about four of them. I'd had a conversation with my own hair, a conversation with Betsy (this one was still happening, apparently), a conversation with someone pretending to be god, and a conversation with someone pretending to be me while I pretended to be god. Sure, I'd *been* in crowds before, but I'd always had either a close confidant I could whisper things to, an interrogator I could refuse to confess my crimes to, or some other fairly observably incorporated, individual-ish entity to whom I could modulate my voice and opinions in order to seem either in alignment or in opposition to, depending on how much I wanted them to like me.

"That's it!" I said. "I can't talk to more than one person at once," I said. "It's impossible. Honestly, I don't know how anyone does it. How can a person possibly ensure that all the people they want to like them like them and that all the people they don't don't?" I said. "I can't do it," I said. "To say even a word to this many people," I said, "would tear me into as many pieces as there are people in this auditorium," I said.

"You think you'd literally be torn apart?" said Betsy. "I mean, I know we all want to be liked but—"

"It's different for me," I whispered.

Whereas most people wanted to be liked but had some conflicting motivations stemming from, for example, who they actually were and what they wanted themselves, I didn't seem to have any of these conflicting motivations. I was, I told Betsy, nothing but a living and breathing desire to be liked. The only conflict I faced in what I did and said stemmed from whether being liked by the person in question affected the chances of being liked by people I wanted to be liked by more.

"In an ideal world," I said, "I'd be able to try to be liked by *everyone*, but in this world, in this awful world," I said, "in this world, there are all kinds of people whose affection would make me significantly less liked by the people I want much more to be liked by: mostly revolutionary militants, witches, dogs, people in punk bands, spiders, fish, unwanted furniture, the weather, weeds, false prophets, etcetera," I said. "That's why I don't so much want to be liked by, for example," I said, "narcs, god, landlords, lawn mowers, cops, walls, tables, and so on," I said.

"You know, this whole revelation isn't doing much to make you more likable," said Betsy.

"I never said I was any good at it!" I said. "I am like those disgraced journalists," I said, "who think they can correct for a false story they've published by publishing more false stories that prove the first false one true. Our intentions count for nothing," I said.

"Our actions betray us like footprints left in the snow by fleeing rabbits. I know my wanting to be liked makes me unlikable, but by trying to *not* want to be liked, aren't I trying to be liked even more? There's no way out of this, Betsy," I said. "There's no way out of anything," I said. "I am what I am and there's nothing I can do about it, and I can't speak to a crowd of people or I'll be torn apart into however many pieces there are people who hear me say the stupid thing I don't even want to say that bad anymore because it's probably not even right anyway."

"Would it really be so bad?" asked Betsy.

"Would what be so bad?" I said.

"Being torn apart?" she said.

"Being torn apart?" I said.

"Please," the landscape architect was meanwhile saying into the blood, flesh, and bone microphone. "Please, if anyone knows what I was about to do, please speak up. I cannot stress this variously enough: the fate of every single person you'd ever want to be liked by in the entire universe—whether bug, plant, appliance, human being, or commune—their fate depends on someone reminding all of us what I was about to start reading from."

"Yeah, being torn apart," Betsy whispered to me. "What's so bad about being torn apart?"

"Why don't you just read the title of the pages you're holding?" shouted another voice from the audience.

"Who said that?" said the landscape architect.

"I did," said a man in the balcony.

"Okay, thanks," said the landscape architect, and the barrel of a sniper rifle appeared above the lip of the podium. A shot was fired and the man who'd spoken took off his mask to show the audience that his teeth had been transformed into the revolving animals of two carousels, one spinning upside down and one spinning right side up. Instead of screams, the sound of a commercial for a new start-your-own-wildfire safari jingled from the pit of his throat.

"Anyone else with a brilliant suggestion?" said the landscape architect.

Someone else raised their hand.

"I don't know," I whispered to Betsy. "I guess I never really thought about it. I guess I just always assumed that being torn apart was something I so obviously wouldn't like that I never bothered to wonder if I actually enjoyed the alternative."

"Right, right," whispered Betsy. "Remember what the puppets told us?"

"Puppets?" I said. "No, I don't even remember us ever meeting puppets. Are you sure that wasn't with someone else?"

"It doesn't matter," she said. "What they told us is to be guided by desire, not by aversion. 'Desire,' they said, 'abides in your body's center of gravity. It's what keeps your body parts willfully in communion with each other and with you as a whole. Aversion lives elsewhere: in articulations, in your elbow, for example,' they said, 'or in some awful phrase you picked up from a commercial you saw as a kid. Do what you want, rather than not doing what you don't want,' said the puppets, 'and then maybe one day you'll be as good at dancing as we puppets are.'"

"Yep, doesn't ring a bell," I said.

"The point," she said, "is: do what you want, and it may not go as terribly wrong as most of the things you do because you don't want the alternative," she said. "That was the puppets' point. What do you actually want?"

"I want . . ." I whispered, "what I want . . ." I said, "what I really want is to be liked by as many people as possible!"

"Then you're going to have to embrace a little risk," she said.

"If you want to be liked by all the people in this auditorium," she said, "then you're going to have to risk being torn apart by telling everyone what the unimaginable landscape architect was about to read from."

"Really?" I whispered, and a jolt of electric energy I could have called either joy or pain rippled through my body, like the beginning of a bowel movement: something new becoming possible. "You think I should just do it?" I said.

"Hey!" shouted Betsy. "Someone over here knows the answer. He has the answer we're all waiting for, but he's afraid to say it out loud."

At Betsy's words, a chilling hush swept over the anxious murmurs of the audience. Even the commercial jingles of those who'd been hit in the mouth by a bullet from the landscape architect's sniper rifle paused.

"He's afraid to say it out loud?" said the landscape architect.

"That's right," said Betsy, and it was like my car had gone off a cliff—no amount of braking could save me now.

"What the fuck, Betsy!" I whispered. "I thought we were friends!"

"I thought you wanted to be liked," Betsy whispered back.

"I thought I did too," I said. "But then I thought about it for like one more second and *completely* changed my mind. I don't want to be torn apart!" I whispered. "How am I going to be liked if I've been torn into a bunch of tiny pieces! You know what my deepest desire is, Betsy? I looked even deeper into my heart," I said, "and what I actually want is specifically *not* to be torn apart! What good is being torn apart going to do me?!" I whispered. "This is so stupid," I said. "I love being alive, Betsy. I love it!" I said. "And I was just starting to enjoy it. It was just starting to get so good! Oh Betsy," I said, "don't make me do it," I said. "Please, don't make me do it!"

"Being afraid to say something out loud," said the landscape architect into the microphone, "is something I think a lot of us here can understand."

Two or three audience members applauded.

"While, personally, I fear nothing—except for spiders and credit cards—I'm not such a monster as to begrudge another creature whatever strange inhibition prevents them from participating meaningfully in the collective exigencies of the spatiotemporal clusterfuck unfortunate enough to have accidently produced and sustained their existence. What is terror," he said, "but a love so deeply in disguise, it's deceived even itself? What is a weakness," he said, "but a powerful weapon your enemy has convinced you to pretend you don't possess? If the only way you can do something is by doing it wrong, then do it wrong. Do it so wrong your wrongness convinces the ones who are right that the right way isn't actually any better, just different. Okay, okay," he said, and his voice, distorted and estranged by the microphone, reverberated in the auditorium, "how about this: How about we turn off all the lights, and that way the person who knows the answer won't have to reveal their identity. Sound good?"

It didn't, but the audience burst into applause anyway, which was mistaken for total consensus.

"Cut the power!" shouted the landscape architect, and a powerful wind arose outside to knock over a tree onto a powerline, plunging the auditorium into an unfathomable darkness.

"Do it," whispered Betsy. "I believe in you. Why, I bet you won't even actually be torn apart at all," she said.

So, I did. And, unfortunately, I was.

"*The book of webs*," I said. And it was

The Last Thing I Ever Did.

"I died?!" I said into the unfathomable darkness. "It's me again," I added, when I registered some surprise. "*Me*, Leech, as in the person you're telling your story to," I specified, "not the person in your story, the Rat."

"Obviously," said Amy the Remainder. "Though I'm glad to know you're still here, even if I'm not anymore. It's been a while since I heard from you," she said. "I nearly forgot you were even here. You hanging in okay?" she asked.

"I'm pretty good," I said. "How about you?"

"Hungry!" she said and erupted into laughter soft as two dead leaves caught in separate strands of an abandoned spider web chafing together in a gentle breeze.

"Same," I said. "Maybe when you finish telling me about the excerpt the landscape architect read, we can go for a snack or something."

"There's still such a thing as snacks?" asked Amy.

"Sure are," I said—refraining for the moment from reminding Amy what the word *snack* had long since had the misfortune to mean.

"Okay," she said. "I'll keep going. Just remind me where I am."

"In the dark," I said. "We can't see a thing. I've just died. The landscape architect is about to begin reading from *the book of*—"

"No, no," she said. "I meant in the story, not where we *actually* are," and she laughed again, for a long, long time.

"Is that a joke?" I said, but she was laughing too hard to answer—either that or weeping, it was all rather difficult to tell—and there was nothing to be done but join in.

After the Fit of Laughter

was over—or rather a little after that, because Amy kept apologizing, saying she didn't know what had come over her, or saying "Hoopsy-daisy" and bursting into laughter again, only to recover long enough to mutter some old proverb or another, such as "Guess it's true what they say: There's no better way to parry an opponent's feint than by forgetting that one isn't actually fencing!," which would invariably spark a new fit of hilarity, as frenzied yet soundless as the flutter of fly wings from the abyssal shaft of a carnivorous pitcher plant—after the laughter had finally been fully exhausted, she said, "Say, would you mind turning the light back on? It's so dark in here I can barely even see my own eye."

"*Eye?*" I said.

"I meant *hand*," said Amy.

"Oh," I said. "That makes more sense."

"Yeah," she said. "It's so dark in here, I can barely even see my own eye in your hand."

"Wait, what?" I said. "I don't have your eye in my hand."

"Oh," she said. "I suppose you already put it in a dimple of the egg carton then? The eye Betsy the Hermit gave to the golden tarantula to give to me?"

"Oh, *that* eye," I said. "Yes, I already put the eye into the dimple of the egg carton. Was it your eye, though? I don't think you mentioned that before."

"Well, not my *actual* eye," she said. "An eye that belonged to me, at least according to what Betsy told the tarantula—at least according to what the tarantula told me. 'This eye belongs to a puppet named Amy,' the tarantula told me that Betsy had told her."

"Wait, you're a puppet?" I said to Amy. "You didn't tell me you were a puppet."

"Of course I didn't," she said. "Puppets don't usually tell other puppets that they're puppets," and she broke into laughter again.

Amy wasn't an old woman, it turned out, but a puppet based on an old woman.

"I'm pretty young actually," she said, "younger than you, I reckon. Don't you see all the pretty sawdust in my wrinkles, twinkling," she said, "like stars?"

"Ah, so we're *actual* puppets now," I said.

"As opposed to what?" she said.

"Oh, I don't know," I said. "Members of a militant gang called the puppets, or something."

Amy laughed. "What in the hell would members of a militant gang be doing in a hole in the desert?" she said. "Next thing you're going to tell me is that the golden tarantula wasn't an actual tarantula!"

"You said she wasn't!" I said.

"Well, of course I did," said Amy. "It was the only way she could tell me Betsy's story. At least according to what she told me: 'The only way I can tell you how I got this eyeball is if you pretend I'm a human being,' said the tarantula," said Amy.

"Think of me as a human member of a militant gang called the tarantulas, or something like that," said the golden tarantula. "Otherwise, I'm afraid you won't be able to understand a word of what I've come here to tell you."

This made a lot of sense to Amy. In fact, it was only because she'd already been pretending that the tarantula was a person that Amy had been able to understand even as much as she had thus far.

"Tarantulas can't actually speak, of course," Amy explained to me, "and since I hadn't spent much time around tarantulas before this encounter, I probably would have assumed that the minute movements of her legs and pedipalps were meaningless, or at best not meant for me. It was only after the tarantula scurried back around the corner and returned with an eyeball that I began to suspect that I was being addressed," said Amy.

"What's that you got there?" Amy said that she asked the tarantula and that the tarantula scooted forward a pace or two, back a pace, and forward again.

"For *me*?" said Amy.

And the tarantula lifted her second longest left leg up and set it down again.

"How do you know it's mine?" Amy asked, and the tarantula pivoted a few degrees to the left and few more degrees to the right.

"Who's Betsy the Hermit?" asked Amy, and that's when the tarantula explained that it was a long story, and probably best she, Amy, think of her, the golden tarantula, as a member of a human revolutionary collective, the tarantula having assumed—correctly, of course—that Amy, being a human-shaped puppet, was better at pretending she understood what a human being was trying to tell her than she was at pretending to understand what a tarantula had to say.

"And she was right about that," Amy said to me.

"Outside this hole," explained the tarantula, "there sits a woman, eye fixed to the fissure in the cliff face, watching. She's been here," she said, "since the beginning."

"The beginning?" said Amy. "Of what?"

"Of the show," said the tarantula.

"What show?" said Amy.

"The show you're putting on."

"I'm not putting anything on," said Amy. "I'm just sitting here shooting the shit with my old pal, Leech."

"Old pal, Amy?" said the tarantula. "There's no one here but yourself. Are you hearing voices?"

"Well of course I'm hearing voices," she said. "How else would I be chatting with my old pal, Leech, when all I've got of Leech is this dried out scrap of his old palm skin?"

The tarantula hadn't realized that Amy was a palm reader. Nor, truth be told, did the spider see the hand skin Amy was holding. It was so dark in there, the tarantula could barely even see her own eye—"Or, rather, *your* own eye," she said, "for Betsy said it belonged to you."

"Who's Betsy?" said Amy.

"The aforementioned woman watching the show."

"*Show*," muttered Amy. "A person sees a puppet and assumes there's a show. What's there to see in here anyway," she said. "She's blocking all the sunlight with her stupid watching!"

"Sunlight?" said the tarantula.

Amy meant *batshit*. "Leech and I have taken to calling batshit *sunlight*," she explained, "on account of it being the building block of all life remaining in what we've taken to calling *the world*," she said as she swept her arm through the darkness to indicate the obscure limits of the cave. "We've been wondering why the batshit stopped shining. Guess Betsy's head was blocking the butthole. She must have never heard the old saying, 'Turn a page, kill a bug.'"

"I never heard that one either," said the tarantula.

"It must have been more popular back when there were books," said Amy. "And bugs, for that matter."

"There are still bugs," said the tarantula. "I eat them all the time."

"I meant *in here*," said Amy. "All died when the sunlight ran out. If I'd known the ecological apocalypse's name, I might have tried talking to her. Betsy!" she shouted. "Get your face the fuck off the butthole!"

"I doubt it if she's still there," said the tarantula. "There wasn't much left by the time she was done telling me her story, I think moving her head slightly to the side for a moment so that I could slip through the so-called butthole in order to deliver the eyeball to you is probably the last thing she ever did. It was a really long story she told me," said the spider, "and she wasn't even all there when she started it—if you know what I mean."

"Buzzards?" said Amy.

"Buzzards," said the tarantula.

"Say," the tarantula said to Amy. "How'd you end up in here? You're much too large to have fit through the cleft in the cliff face, aren't you? Is there another hole somewhere else?"

"There's always another hole somewhere else," said Amy. "But, no. Me, I'm local. Been here all my life. Was carved in here from roots that grew in here, even learned to read from severed hands in here."

"Who carved you?"

"Christ almighty!" shouted Amy. "A person sees a puppet and assumes someone must've made it. Next thing you're going to do is ask me who's pulling the strings!"

"Where *do* all those lead to?" asked the tarantula, tracing them with her many-eyed gaze till they vanished in the gloom above them.

"Same place most things lead to," said Amy. "Nowhere. At least most of them."

A few, Amy reckoned, led to different microphones set up in various band practice spaces and venues, others to spider webs—"as

I'm sure you know better than me," said Amy—and a few even *did* lead, unfortunately, to the corporate entity called *the puppet master*, but only so that Amy could do her part in the collective effort to manipulate this entity into putting on a convincing show till the time was ripe for the puppet master to be torn apart.

"Everything in its proper time," she said.

"Anyway, the eye," said Amy. "You say it's mine, but I've never seen it before. What makes you so certain?"

"Betsy," said the tarantula. "Betsy was certain. 'This is Amy's eye,' she said to me."

"This is Amy's eye," Betsy had told the tarantula before the buzzards finished finishing her off. "I'm absolutely certain of it," she said. "And it's imperative you get it to her."

"Who's Amy?" asked the tarantula.

"She's one of the puppets in the puppet show I'm watching through this hole here," she said.

"How do you know it's hers," said the tarantula.

"Why, from a fortune cookie, of course," said Betsy. "You think one learns such things from birthday cakes?"

When the missing shard of the broken frog is found, the eye of Amy must be returned, the fortune cookie had said.

"The hell's that supposed to mean," said Leroy.

"Who's Leroy?" the tarantula interrupted Betsy's story to ask.

"You don't know Leroy?" asked Betsy.

"I know *a* Leroy," said the tarantula. "Old cowboy type, probably an alcoholic? Got a couple twin sons trying to track him down?"

"Sounds like a different Leroy," said Betsy. "But who knows. I never actually met the guy. He's just someone who opened a fortune cookie in a dream I had when I fell asleep in a yoga class one time. Back when there were still yoga classes."

"Remember to continue breathing," Betsy said the yoga instructor had been saying when she woke up from this dream.

"Anyway," said Betsy. "That piece of plaster in your pedipalps is the shard of the frog that Leroy's fortune cookie spoke of, I'm certain of it."

"Shh," said the yoga instructor, in whose class Betsy accidently said this out loud.

"Sorry," she said. "I have no idea why I just said that."

"But the reason I said that," Betsy said to the tarantula, is because I must've been accidentally reading my future in my own palm, which I'd fallen asleep with over my eyes. I must've gotten confused between the future I was reading in my palm—which detailed, of course, this exact exchange you and I are currently having—and what was actually happening around me, for what I said in that yoga class was exactly what I would have said right now, had I not already said it in that yoga class all those years ago. Where on earth did you find this shard?" she asked of the little gray shard clutched in the tarantula's pedipalps.

"It was in a muffin," said the tarantula.

"There are still muffins?" said Betsy.

"A very, very, *very* old muffin," said the tarantula. "Anyway, are you sure this is a shard of frog?" said the tarantula, turning the shard over and over in her pedipalps. "Was just thinking you might want to be a little more certain before you pluck out your last remaining eyeball."

"Whatever," said Amy. "Eyeball-shmeyeball. Easy come, easy go. It was never truly mine to begin with," and she plucked out her last remaining eyeball.

"But once Betsy was entirely eyeless and holding the shard in her fingers," the tarantula told Amy, "and once I was holding the eyeball in my pedipalps, Betsy grew a little less certain."

"Actually, can I see that shard one more time?" Betsy said, and the tarantula aimed the pupil of Betsy's eye at the shard in her hand. "Yeah," she said. "I'm not totally certain."

"Well of course not," said the tarantula. "I don't know why you thought that was a piece of a frog," she said pointing at the shard.

"But my confusion," the tarantula explained to Amy, "was because Betsy hadn't yet told me that the frog in question hadn't actually been a frog—'Ah, of course,' I said—but was just a shitty statue of a frog in the garden outside a mansion where the wedding was taking place."

"What wedding?" the tarantula had asked Betsy.

"Terrific question," said Betsy. "They do sort of blur together, don't they?" she said. "Weddings," she said. "Other people's weddings. Story of my life. A wedding," she said. "All weddings. A fucking bunch of fucking weddings," she said. "Though I guess this marriage was unusual in that it didn't even wait till it had started to begin to fall apart."

The wedding in question hadn't even begun and already it was so insufferable that Betsy had had to step outside to steal a breath of the gas and smoke and ash and particulate that one of the companies that owned the government was trying to sell off as *air*. She'd barely inhaled an hourly minimum wage's worth (less than a lungful) when she saw an open book on the patio table by the pond. A playful wind flipped through its pages, turning them this way, then that, and then that wind died suddenly down and the pages fell open flat. Betsy, who'd clearly been around the block by this point—both in terms of her career as a journalist and in the actual career that career was just a cover for—knew an omen when she saw an omen, and so she approached the table to see both what the book was and what was written on the pages the wind had selected for her to read. But no sooner was she close enough to glimpse the first few words then she heard a loud sound and looked up to see a raven—a raven which, apparently having just collided ballistically into a small statue on the edge of a pond, now turned acrobatically in the air and flew to perch on a branch of a nearby piñon tree. From there it turned its gaze to Betsy and cawed loudly.

"Huh," replied Betsy, and walked over to the pond to see what the raven had knocked off the now bare pedestal, what was now lying face down in the mulch beside the pond.

The raven laughed.

"Yeah, yeah. Very funny," said Betsy, as she lifted up a stupid little plaster frog statue. "It's a good joke," she said, "but what does it mean?"

The statue was much lighter than it looked, hollow inside, and when Betsy turned it over she saw that there was a shard missing from the underside of its base. The raven bellowed with laughter.

"You want me to find the missing shard?" she said, and the raven hiccuped, so she searched with her eyes through the weeds and the wood chips all around where the frog had fallen, but saw nothing out of place. Nor did it seem that the frog had fallen hard enough for the plaster to have been even this minorly damaged. No, the shard, Betsy reckoned, must have been lost in an earlier accident. The statue must have been placed here after it was already broken.

The raven burped.

"Okay. What!?" she said to the raven. She was beginning to get a little angry now, but the raven only shrugged and flapped its wings, taking flight off the branch and vanishing over the coyote fence that lined the perimeter of the property. She placed the frog statue back on the pedestal from which it had fallen, trying best she could to align its base with the faint outline of where the frog had been had been preserved in dust. But the moment she stopped trying to get it perfectly, the wind picked back up, and

Betsy remembered the book and panicked. She ran back to where the book was, cursing the wind and the raven and the frog and the wedding and herself and the universe for making her miss yet another chance to receive something, anything, that was meant for her—"This," said Betsy to the tarantula, "was before I realized that all the letters that kept coming to my mailbox and weren't addressed to me, that the fact of these letters not being addressed to me was, *itself*, addressed to me. But this," she said, "was before that. And this," she said, "was even worse"—but it was too late.

Not only had the pages that had been blown open been blown back shut, but on the patio table where the book had been, the book was now gone. And behind the table was a hot tub Betsy hadn't noticed before.

How strange, she thought to herself, that its lid should be left open like that, what, she thought, with no one bathing in it. Strange, she thought to herself, and

Not a Single Person in Sight.

Betsy went back inside only to find that the marriage still wasn't working. At the sight of the anxious-looking wedding attendants milling about the reception area outside the room where the bride and groom still went inexplicably unwed, Betsy rolled her eyes. As the only single person at the wedding, she found the collective discontent over the failure of this particular union deeply irritating. Moreover, as no one was looking into her eyes, no one noticed her rolling them, and this lack of reception demanded another rotation of even greater circumference and velocity, another eyeroll whose going unacknowledged precipitated one even greater, and so on.

"We just don't understand," the Sludges were saying to her. "The bride said yes. The groom said yes. We just can't fathom why the wedding didn't work!"

"You mean *hasn't* worked," said one of them. "Hasn't worked *yet*. It's imperative we stay positive."

"Right," said the other of the Sludges. "It's imperative we stay positive. Wouldn't you say, Betsy? Wouldn't you also say that it's imperative? Betsy? Positivity?"

"Uh huh," said Betsy. Her eyes—which she'd taken a momentary breather from rolling in order to scan the hands of every person in the room for one that was holding the book she'd seen vanish from the patio table outside—her eyes came up once again empty-handed.

"In no hand," Betsy said to the tarantula she was telling the story to, "in no hand, did I find the hand I'd seen."

"You mean *book*?" said the tarantula.

"What did I say?" said Betsy.

"You said *hand*," said the tarantula. "You said you were looking in everyone's hands for a hand. But you must've meant *book*."

"Oh. No," said Betsy, "I meant *hand*, but I see why you got confused. When I said *book* I meant it according to its definition in that day's official dictionary: anything—"

"The day's official dictionary?" said the tarantula.

"Right," she said. "For a time, the state issued a new dictionary every day. According to that day's dictionary, if you wanted to talk about something you'd missed your chance to hold and be held by, you'd have to say the word *book*. And books," she said, "didn't exist, according to the definition, so it was best to forget about them. To not be able to forget about a book was to misuse the word, which was to be illiterate, which had to be reported on your dating app profile and was widely considered unattractive, even by quote-unquote revolutionary standards. Hell, even *I* wouldn't have been attracted to someone who believed a book was possible."

But what could Betsy do? The severed hand she'd seen outside on the patio table was pretty much a textbook book, a book if ever there was one.

"Wait," I said.

"Leech?" said Amy.

"Yeah," I said. "Sorry to interrupt. Quick question: If the so-called book that Amy found on the patio table was actually a severed hand, then how was a—I quote—'playful wind flowing through its pages'?"

"G-god, Leech," she said. "You take everything so literally! Next thing I know you're going to interrupt me to ask how you were able to interrupt me if you were actually just a shred of your old palm skin whose lines I was reading!"

"Well, that's what you said you told the golden tarantula!" I said.

"Right," she said. "And I wasn't exactly lying. I'm just not very literal-minded, Leech. It's one of those impossible things about me. I'm always speaking in metaphors, I guess. Why, I'd be surprised if I actually literally said anything this entire conversation! I'd be surprised if I've ever literally said anything in my entire life!"

"It's all been metaphors?" I said.

"Yeah, maybe," she said.

"Metaphors for what?" I asked.

"I don't know. The other metaphors, maybe? Who's to say? It's not like I mean 'metaphors' *literally*!" she said.

"Anyway, back to Betsy the Hermit at the wedding, looking for that severed hand among the crowd," said Amy.

It had been a textbook book (according to that day's dictionary definition of the word *book*, which again was: anything that a person missed one's chance to hold and be held by), that severed hand that had grasped invitingly toward her own, only to mysteriously vanish while she'd had her back to it when toying with the frog statue and the raven and all that. No, after a long string of unforgettable books (in the dictionary sense)—boyfriends, revolutions, actual books, a good night's sleep—here was yet another, and if Betsy couldn't find that hand and hold it, she knew she'd be doomed to broadcasting her illiteracy on her dating app profile for as long as the Department of Dictionaries held the structure of language hostage. That was really the only reason she came back inside: to see if maybe one of the other wedding guests had stolen the severed hand she'd mistakenly fleetingly believed it would be her brief, compensatory pleasure to hold.

Instead, here were the Sludges whispering: "We just can't imagine how terrible it must feel, how embarrassing for the both of them," they whispered. "On their wedding day, nonetheless! Can you imagine anything worse? All these people watching?"

"Huh," said Betsy. "Excuse me a moment," she said, "I just

realized I think I need be holding two drinks rather than one," and returned to the bar.

"Back so soon?" said the bartender.

"Apparently, this beer doesn't count as beer if it's by itself," she said. "May I have another?"

"Sure," he said and handed her a second can.

"Thanks," she said and began to walk away but realized almost immediately that she couldn't open the can because her other hand was holding the first can, and there was no one to ask for help because everyone else was busy helping their spouse or partner open *their* second can of beer.

So, she returned to the bartender and said, "I need help. I can't tell if I'm actually lonely or just responding to the looming threat a single person is meant to feel in a place like this—more looming in proportion to how old she gets. I mean, fine!—I admit it! I'd like a partner, okay? Does that make me less worthy of existence? That I want something and can't seem to make it happen? Does it make me less revolutionary if I admit that I'd like someone to care for me and to care for? That I desire intimacy and connection? That I happen for whatever reason to think dicks can be quite compelling, like anatomically or whatever? Does that make me some kind of monster?" she said.

"Or am I monster?" she said, a moment later. "Have I fallen for a trap and become my own enemy? I've felt like such a failure and outcast all my life for not having a boyfriend or husband, and it feels so truly terrible that sometimes I wonder if all my yearning isn't simply a yearning to escape the feeling of feeling like I don't belong here, a longing to not feel like a trespasser in enemy territory wherever I go, someone someone is everywhere wondering, 'I wonder what's wrong with her.' You're not better than me!" she yelled indiscriminately.

"I know what I want, but how can I trust my wanting?" she said. "How do I know, even assuming I ever meet a decent person who likes me back, that this would actually make my life more joyous, my power more fully realized? From whence derive my desires?" she said. "From a part of me that has my own interests in mind or by something somehow smuggled into my body by those working against me? I know I want *something*! I wake up from naps with this powerful but indeterminate yearning, this angry hunger—but for a moment it feels like I could be longing for any number of things—a house with dark blinds, or the pages of a book . . . Why does this nebulous, raging force inside me consistently resolve into desire for a heterosexual monogamous relationship?" she said. "Who chooses? What is the force that imprints its decision on the indecision of my sex drive?"

"That's a good question," said the bartender, "but I'm afraid you're going to have to wait to ask it till it's your turn to order," and he nodded his head toward the ten or so couples that had lined up while Betsy wasn't paying attention to anything but how impossible it was to function with only two hands in a world designed for beings with four.

"Sorry," she said to all the couples in the line she'd accidently cut to the very front of. And although she really did say "Sorry," it sounded to all the couples, because they'd all been so busy comforting each other over the affront each felt themselves to have suffered from her—"No, my darling, you did nothing to deserve this, *nothing*!" they had all been saying, first to their spouses and then to the other couples—because by the time Betsy realized her mistake and tried to apologize, they'd collaboratively cultivated so monstrous an image of Betsy that she was, in their eyes, practically a terrorist—because of this, when she said "Sorry," it sounded to them like she'd said, "Fuck you all to death."

"That's so unfair!" interjected the golden tarantula when Betsy got to this part in her retelling, outside the cleft in the cliff face.

"I know!" said Betsy. "It was all so unfair. Though to be perfectly honest," she added. I suppose I *was* technically a terrorist, or soon would be."

"Ah," said the tarantula.

"And also, to be fair, I did probably say, 'Fuck you all to death,'" she said. "But in any case, what I meant was *Sorry*, and if they weren't all so busy sheltering each other from the rest of the fucking universe, they maybe would've realized that."

But they didn't realize anything, and so Betsy became even more villainous in their eyes, and it made perfect sense to all of them why she hadn't found her soulmate yet. And so, while, out of the goodness of their hearts, they tried to explain to Betsy what she could do to be more attractive to mansion-dwelling men—Had she, for instance, tried getting into rock climbing?—Betsy got in line behind the tenth couple and brooded, hoping that by brooding intensely enough she'd ensure that by the time it was her turn to order, she'd still remember what she'd been so angry about.

Even anger, however, no matter how determined the angered, wasn't exempt from the pervasive unraveling of all things: there, on the oil-slickened head of the husband directly in front of Betsy, there sprung a sudden cowlick, a cowlick that, while not exactly fascinating, was curious enough to divert enough of her mind from nurturing her negative feelings that her brood began to splinter into opposing factions.

"Ugh, fine," she couldn't help but sigh, as her interest in the cowlick overpowered her annoyance at the universe and she whispered a reluctant greeting to the cowlick. "Hi," she said, and it twitched.

The cowlick twitched nearly unnoticeably, a motion so subtle, an average observer would have overlooked it as the result of a gust from an air conditioner, but a motion Betsy readily recognized—regardless of whether an air conditioner was involved (and, sadly, these days, she thought to herself, one usually is)—as a gesture, a gesture worth responding to, even if there was no way to know exactly what it meant.

There was no way to know exactly what anything meant, according to Betsy, but this didn't mean one couldn't respond as though there was, couldn't respond as though understanding between one thing and another were possible—as though anything could communicate anything to anything else. This was the basis of the strategy Betsy had adopted in her lifelong practice of trying to communicate with other humans but had lately been testing out on certain nonhuman animals, plants, inanimate objects, weather patterns, advertising campaigns, etcetera, and she'd been pleasantly surprised to find that pretty much *everything* responded in one way or another. Indeed, many of these new interlocutors responded much *more* engagingly than most humans she'd been equally respectfully addressing for years, and indeed, some of these nonhuman interlocutors shared with her such an abundance of mostly bewildering, but often ostensibly wholehearted, communications that she persisted in her experimentation and thereby gradually learned, bit by bit, that these dialogues were actually not something she herself bore responsibility for initiating but were, rather, continuations of a vast ongoing conversation parts of her body and clothing had already been deeply involved in, a conversation whose origins were unknown and original purposes long-forgotten, a conversation whose participants formed an immense, sprawling community, a community to which Betsy was actually a relative latecomer, a community of beings so diverse that the only thing its members had in common was their each having attempted to discard the belief that it was significantly more possible to communicate with something of the same kind than it was with something radically different. To be included in the community required nothing more than behaving in accordance with the belief that a human being, for instance, had just as little chance of understanding and being understood by a chain of grocery stores as she had a chance of understanding or being understood by another human being. There was no chance in either case, but it was worth trying anyway. Uneasily—imperfectly—but with a timid aliveness hard to nourish elsewhere these days, Betsy had accidently bumbled her way into this seemingly ever-expanding network, this potentially limitless conversation.

"Were you sure that you weren't just spending too much time alone?" the tarantula asked her.

"Of course I wasn't sure!" said Betsy. "And I'm still not. And it wasn't like I wouldn't *rather* have had an interesting *human* person to talk to, but I didn't. The proverbial bartender always had at least ten couples to serve before he'd be able to tell me he'd forgotten what I'd been trying to tell him. *Always*," she said. "The bartender was my horizon, ten couples my sea. I drowned, and as I drowned, what choice did I ever really have but to, like a drowner grasping at driftwood, try to say hello to a cowlick on the back of a nondescript husband's head?"

Betsy had never had any choice but to try to say hello to the cowlick, and had no choice either but to chuckle quietly when the cowlick twitched. She laughed, and not because anything was funny but because laughter—broadly defined, of course—had often proved to have a corrosive effect on the ideological delusions hitherto convincing two or more beings that they had nothing to talk about and no way of doing so. She laughed because she was hoping the cowlick would laugh too. It was like a signal to alert the cowlick that she was in on the game, that she was game, if the cowlick was game too, to keep playing.

The husband's wife turned at the dry-leaf cackle of Betsy's fake laugh and followed Betsy's gaze to her husband's precious head.

Then, with a conspiratorial look back at Betsy that seemed to say, "Ah, but we women know how careless our men can be about their appearance," she ran a hand over her husband's disobedient lock.

As though anticipating the attack, however, the cowlick retreated. It vanished immediately back into the waxy black scalp from which it had so brazenly arisen—that shimmering, solid, plastic-looking dome, a quieted totality into which each of the all-but-one subservient tresses had abandoned their separate potentialities in order to assimilate. The cowlick retreated but, Betsy noted, with such utter resistlessness that Betsy was surprised the wife didn't suspect subterfuge—clearly it wasn't so much a retreat as a feint. The wife, however, seemed oblivious and, as though the war were already won, whispered triumphantly into her husband's ear—loudly enough so Betsy could overhear—something about how wonderful it was that ever since they'd gotten married, she'd hardly even thought about her old childish desires to overturn the very order of the universe . . .

But, just as Betsy suspected, the cowlick remained subdued only so long as necessary to convince the wife that nothing was amiss and then sprang immediately back into action. Like a weed sprouting from a fissure in a yard-smothering span of Astroturf—like the middle finger of a fist-shaped flower blooming from a plant growing from the dirt-filled eye socket of a deposed CEO's skull—the cowlick arose again.

Betsy laughed—but with genuine admiration this time—and also this time made sure to preemptively train her gaze to the screen of her phone, so that if and when the wife should look back again, it would look to her as though there'd been something worth laughing at there, on the screen of Betsy's phone—which, of course, there hadn't been. There hadn't been anything to laugh at there for as long as phones had even had screens. The cowlick seemed to appreciate Betsy's tactfulness but twitched seriously anyway, and so Betsy put the phone away, resolved to stop laughing, and gave a curt, nearly imperceptible nod of her head. Then, in case the cowlick should miss the gesture, she inscribed a quick thought in the book: I knew right away it was serious, she thought.

"Inscribed in the book?" I said. "What book?"

"Oh," said Amy, "I forgot to mention it to you, Leech, because Betsy had been able to assume that the golden tarantula probably knew about the book already, and the golden tarantula had assumed the same thing about me when she retold the tale. Sorry," she said. "By *book*," said Amy, "in this instance, Betsy just meant a speculated space wherein it was believed, among some of the more unhinged parts of ourselves, one could inscribe one's unarticulated thoughts by thinking them in the past tense. Thoughts thought in the past tense, or so the thinking went, were inscribed in a kind of all-but-imperceptible zone we called *the book*—imperceptible except to others who had also attuned themselves to the book and who could thereby, therein, and with concerted effort, read one another's thoughts."

"Did it work?" I asked Amy, Amy who was telling me what the tarantula had told her Betsy had told the tarantula.

"The book?" said Amy. "Well, no. Not *really*. But it didn't really work any worse than anything else didn't work. This book was a book par excellence," she said. "In a way, it was bookishness weaponized. A book whose very impossibility was exactly what made it impossible for our enemies to infiltrate it. Did it actually work? That wasn't exactly the point."

Whether the cowlick could read the book or not, Betsy was perfectly able to respond to the cowlick as though it had responded to her thought, as though it had been able to read the thoughts she'd inscribed in the book, as though—in other words—it had learned that Betsy was, if not exactly on the cowlick's side, at least as fervently against the husband's head of hair as it, the cowlick, was itself. And it was, thus, as perfectly reasonable as anything else was reasonable for Betsy to conclude that the cowlick had decided to trust her by the way it began to flick a bit in the air, to tilt and sway. It was reasonable to conclude that this movement was a deliberate utterance and that she and the cowlick had come to an understanding together, that they were on the same page.

Yes, it was all perfectly reasonable to assume this, but the assumption was not, for that reason, even close to correct.

The cowlick lengthened suddenly by an inch or two, shivered violently in the air, and then was sucked abruptly into the husband's head, vanishing into a growing chasm whose edges were crumbling—a hole as unfathomably deep as it had been ambiguously prefigured by the trembling of the cowlick.

But Betsy knew better than to mourn the cowlick's death, for what was its death but the birth of a new orifice, and a new orifice—especially one appearing in the midst of something so unspectacular as a husband's head at a wedding—was a difficult thing to keep quiet about. Thankfully, she realized in time that an exclamation of joy would be dangerously misinterpreted by the other wedding guests, for the regiment of law enforcers that was officiating the wedding had just announced that backup had finally arrived and had commanded everyone to please take their seats back around the altar so that they could try again to marry the bride and groom, this time under the threat of graver penalties.

As she'd learned to do with most of her feelings, Betsy bottled up her jubilation over the new orifice. She knew just how easily such an utterance could be co-opted into a general display of support for what was, in its essence, an act of state violence—a nonconsensual incorporation of two bodies into one—and she desperately didn't wish to be any more complicit in this injustice than was absolutely necessary. True: her invitation to this wedding had included a threat about razing a city block should she refuse to RSVP in the affirmative, but she'd made no oath to feign enthusiasm while in attendance.

"What fish reminds the snake whose mouth it's in to come up for air?" said Betsy to the tarantula.

Betsy the Hermit held her tongue, and she was soon rewarded for her discretion by the appearance of a rather sizable rodent, whose snout appeared suddenly at the mouth of the hole in the husband's head where the cowlick had been.

Barely breathing for fear of frightening the creature, Betsy watched its little nose twitch this way and that, as though testing the temperature of the room—and she saw the animal snarl a bit when it caught a whiff of what it had, most likely accidently, tunneled itself into the freezingly hellish, swirling vortex of.

The rodent hadn't noticed her yet. The moment it did—the moment its pupils fixed on the gawking human looming just outside its burrow—its eyes widened, its hackles flared, and it scurried immediately back down into the depths of its hole—a gesture that Betsy had conversed with enough rodents to know probably meant something along the lines of, "Follow me."

"Well, how the fuck am I supposed to do that?" she said.

"Do what?" said the husband whose head the hole was in.

"Sorry," she said. "I was speaking in another language accidently, a language wherein the sounds 'Well, how the fuck am I supposed to do that?' just so happen to mean something more along the lines of 'Boy, thank god more cops are here, huh?' I forgot what language I was speaking because it's been so long since I've spoken to another—"

"Thank god is right!" interrupted the husband.

"Say," said the wife to Betsy. "Don't you think we should maybe go sit in our assigned seats around the altar? That's what the cops told us to do, isn't it? Usually," she said, "we find it best to do whatever the cops tell us to do," the wife explained. "Sometimes we'll call them just to ask! 'Hello,' we say, 'is this 911?' 'Sure is.' 'Oh, good,' we say. 'What seems to be the problem,' say the cops. 'We're not sure,' we say. 'We're not sure what to say. We were hoping you could tell us.' 'Good thing you called,' say the cops. 'I'll try to find your problem in this book here. Just tell me what chapter you're calling from.' '*Chapter?*' we say. 'Yeah.' 'Okay. Hold on a sec.' 'Standing by!' say the cops. 'Actually, how do we tell what chapter we're in?' we ask. 'Hmm,' say the cops. 'Good question. There should be like a roman numeral somewhere.' 'Let's see, roman numerals . . .' we say, "roman numerals . . .' and we look all around us for roman numerals. 'We don't see any,' we say at last. 'Huh, that's weird,' say the cops. 'Have you tried opening your eyes?' 'Is that allowed?' 'Good question,' say the cops. 'I guess it depends what chapter you're in, and what book for that matter. We'll send someone out right away. Make sure that anything that you don't want our boys putting bullets in is playing dead.' 'We wouldn't have called you if we weren't playing dead already,' we say to the cops, isn't that right, honey?" she said to her husband. "Isn't that what we're always saying?"

"It sure is," said her husband. "And I agree. I say we all follow orders and get back to our places around the altar. It's not like we *need* more alcohol to survive this tremendous ordeal. Am I right?" he said to Betsy.

"Uh . . ." said Betsy. And Betsy, whose two beers had been emptied a long, long—long, long, long, long, long—time ago, said, "Yeah."

The husband and wife each respectively informed the other husbands and wives in line about the new consensus, and within seconds—and for practically the first time in Betsy's life—she had an unimpeded path to a human person she was mildly interested in talking to.

"You again?" said the bartender.

"Wait," she said. "You can see me?"

"Of course I can see you," he said. "Why wouldn't I be able to see you?"

"Don't ask me!" she said, for although there was, in this case, and maybe also for the first time in her life, an explanation for why a mildly attractive man had a good reason for behaving as though he were unable to see her (the room had recently begun to fill with tear gas as the police attempted to coax some of the dawdling guests back toward the altar and it was indeed thus becoming increasingly difficult to see), Betsy wasn't about to give the universe the satisfaction of her acknowledging that for once in its life it was making sense.

"Move along, lady," said the police officer closest to the bar. "Maybe you didn't hear me before," he said sarcastically, "there's a wedding going on in the room next door"—he moved his hand to his holster—"and you're invited."

"Sounds like you, uh," said the bartender to Betsy, "better—"

"Shh," she said to him. "Shut up. We don't have time for this. Are you single?"

"Um," he said. "It's complicated. Got sort of like a friends-with-benefits kind of—"

"Never mind," she said. "It doesn't matter. I need your help with something. You see that wife's husband over there?"

"Uh huh," he said.

"I need to get into that man's head," she said. "I'm pretty sure that man's head is full of gophers and who knows what else. For reasons that I don't yet fully understand," she said, "I'm pretty sure that it's absolutely imperative I get in there to see what those gophers want me to—"

"Hey sweetheart," said the cop, as he drew his pistol. "Hey lady. I told you once. Don't make me tell you again."

"If the book is ever published," said Betsy to the bartender, "people are either going to like this part or they're going to be very upset by it," and as Betsy reached behind the bar for an unopened bottle of tokay—and as the bartender said, "*Book?*"—the cop's gun went off, and a second later Betsy was holding *two* bottles of tokay and was drinking one of them and the cop was dead and the gun had switched allegiances and—as a machine gun's rat-a-tat resounded from the altar in the other room—Betsy the Hermit was asking the bartender if he maybe wanted to go with her on a dangerous mission to overturn the very order of the universe.

"Sure," said the bartender. "Yeah, why not," he said, as he removed the bartender costume he'd been wearing, revealing a markedly less handsome physique and personality. "I'll help you," he said, "but only on one condition."

"Uh-oh," said Betsy.

"Whenever you tell the story of whatever ends up happening to us," said the newly unremarkable man, "you have to tell it from my perspective. And not just you, either. Whenever *anyone* tells the story," he said, "they'll have to say *I* when they mean me and *Betsy the Hermit* when they mean you. They can say *us* when they mean both of us, but there should always be some ambiguity over whether they're referring to just the two of us or to an entire secret collectivist organization. Does that make sense?" he asked. "Even you, for example, will have to say *Betsy the Hermit* when you mean yourself when you're telling the story of whatever happens to us. Oh, and I'll also need you be really generous and understanding in your portrayal of me, even when my behavior doesn't make any sense."

"Um . . ." said Betsy. "Why?"

"Huh," he said. "That's a good question. I don't know," he said. "I never really thought about it. If it makes you feel any better, getting to be the one who gets to be himself all the time isn't something I really relish either."

"Uh huh," she said. "Sure. And if I say no?"

"*No?*" he said, mulling the word like it was a sample of a terrible cheese at a newly opened cheese shop that a gang of terrorists had established solely so that they might dig a tunnel in the back room that would lead under a street over which a despot they hoped to assassinate with dynamite was preordained to pass.

"Yeah," she said. "Suppose I decline to accommodate your *little condition*. What then?"

"Hm," he said. "I guess that's fine. Yeah," he said. "I guess it doesn't really matter."

"Cool," said Betsy. "What do I call you then?"

"Call me Leroy," he said.

"I know too many Leroys," said Betsy.

"How about Billy then?" he said, and she, "Billy's fine," and he said, "Cool. Billy it is."

"Okay Billy," she said. "Anything else you want to get off your chest?"

"Well now that you mention it," he said, "I should probably tell you: I think it might be getting kind of serious with that friend-with-benefits I mentioned."

"And?" said Betsy.

"And even if it wasn't," he said, "I'm not sure—I'm not *not* sure, exactly—but I'm like pretty sure I'm not totally physically attracted to you."

"Of course you're not," she said. "If you were, what reason would we have for destroying the entire universe?"

"I could think of a few reasons . . ." he said.

"Besides," she said. "It's mutual. There's no chemistry whatsoever."

"Oh, phew," he said. "Because that whole friends-with-benefits thing—I made that all up. I'm actually very lonely."

"And yet would still rather . . . ?" Betsy began, but the tear gas was growing so thick she could hardly even see the swarm of policemen in riot gear who'd encircled them, so she just said, "Oh, fuck it, never mind," and then she and Billy turned their undivided attention—as the choking gas obscured even themselves from the other—they turned their undivided attention to the task of somehow surmounting the heavily militarized police force intent on dividing them from the man whose gopher-filled head Billy had made a solemn promise to somehow help Betsy the Hermit get inside of.

A Few Days Later,

Betsy began to wonder if she wasn't maybe misremembering things—if she hadn't, for example, perhaps mistaken the impenetrable whiteness still swirling opaquely around her for police tear gas when in reality it was something more innocuous, like mist, or dust, or a blank sheet of paper held too close to her face . . . It *was* said, after all, that *The Book of Life* was a hack job and that a person's every waking second was basically a trashy retelling of the worst moments in that person's life—a few details substituted here and there, and you were supposed to call the thing *a new day*. That's what they said, anyway, that each new experience conformed, like flesh to a skeleton, to the structure of certain privileged moments the state had drilled painfully into its subjects, which was why everything always looked like everything else, why Billy—that was his name, right?—why Billy was basically already every boy who'd ever disappointed Betsy even before she met him, why every time she found herself confronting a limitless whiteness she felt relentlessly, life-threateningly policed, if not dead already. It was thus entirely possible that the book of *her* life—that story that began with her birth and would end with her death, that heavy book she lugged along with her, those old sentences that muffled her experience like a bubble of blubber that got a word or two denser with each new moment she endured—it was entirely possible the book was all out of order again, that here she was lost in a snowstorm or something and the distracted, multitasking narrator of the sentences that sloshed around willy-nilly in her head was telling her the wrong part, something awful that occurred a long time ago, or even merely something she'd been made to read about over and over again until it felt like it had happened to her . . . After all, things didn't really *hurt*—not more than they ordinarily did—and she was fairly certain, whether on account of direct experience or through hearsay (depending on where in her so-to-speak *book* she was), that tear gas *would* hurt a lot. Then again, maybe it *did* hurt a lot, and she had only grown accustomed to the pain. Maybe the pain had become the background against which only *other* feelings were discernible. Maybe nowadays, *pleasure* would have felt like tear gas in her eyes. In any case, she was fairly certain that too much time had elapsed for the clusterfuck she had believed herself to be in midst of—the wedding, the riot police, the gopher hole—too much time had elapsed for *this* clusterfuck to actually be the clusterfuck she was currently enduring. Unless, of course, she was mistaken about this passage of time. *A few days later* . . . her latest train of thought had begun, but had she actually experienced these *few days*, or had she been deceived once again by the verisimilitude of an errant strain of the internal verbal representations of her experience—representations that, because the tear gas or whatever it was, had deprived her of her every other sense, had gained a ridiculously outsized and unearned influence over her orientation in space and time? Yes, it was, unfortunately, entirely possible that only enough time had passed for her mind's narrator to say *A few days later*, and in fact, a policeman was midswing with a skull-cracking whack to Betsy's head with his baton. Who could say?

Maybe Billy?

"Billy?" she said.

But the feeling of vocalizing—even the sound of the word—it was all rather disappointingly undifferentiated from any of the other language rattling around in Betsy's head. Where was the familiar embarrassment, for instance, the alienation and confusion that typically accompanied any sentence that dared break the dense orbit of her private life to briefly risk shared air? Had she actually spoken? Or had she merely thought the word "*Billy*"? And was she now actually hearing Billy's response—"Did you say something?"—or was she merely imagining how Billy might reply had she actually spoken. Assuming Billy was even ever there to begin with.

She sighed.

"Billy," she either said or imagined saying. "I know we've already been over this. I know that most cowlicks do not give way to gopher holes, and I definitely want to respect that you already said no when I brought this up before. I also recognize that this might not be the best time to bring this up again—I can't really remember what's going on—or maybe I'm remembering it all a little too well, too much. If we're still surrounded by police, it's definitely bad timing, and I apologize for that. But assuming this isn't the end of the book—yours or mine, or ours for that matter—and by *book* I just mean the tired old story of our lives . . . Um. Where was I? Oh right. Assuming this isn't the end of the book, that you and I survive whatever this is we're lost in, I think I'd really regret it if I didn't, you know, at least ask," and here Betsy felt her pulse quicken a little, and a sudden cold opened in the space below her solar plexus, rare feelings that only ever accompanied revelations of things long withheld, generally for good reason, reasons being why she withheld them, the revelations of such things most often involving an abnegation of an already precarious position within a power dynamic, which was a dangerous, usually ridiculously stupid bid to exchange what little, often pleasureless power she had *over* or *in opposition* to another person for the kind of power that stemmed from her own being, power that took nothing from the other person and rather added something new to existence, the kind of power that she felt when she simply did what her body, left to its own devices, would do if she (her common sense, the laws of the state and so-called laws of nature, if her fears, and education, and the threats of executions and prisons and abandonment, and so on) weren't all there to stop it, a bid that more often than not—that maybe even *exclusively*, actually—ended with the other person greedily usurping the power she'd ceded and lording it over her or others, but a bid she nevertheless attempted again and again, because the prospect of a life without this tingling in her fingertips and the rush of sensation through her torso and pelvis, the prospect of a life lived sacrificing actual aliveness to not lose quite so badly a game she reviled, this was worse, she felt, than death. So Betsy once again put her body's desires above her judiciousness as a quote-unquote *person* in the world, and said, "Um. Look, even if we're not soulmates or whatever, even if we don't want a relationship, don't you think we could still, uh," she said, and she couldn't believe she was actually saying this—if, that is, she was actually saying this—"don't you think it could maybe be nice to maybe fool around a little, or even just cuddle. If we could just stop being ourselves for a minute," she said, "stop being a so-called *man* and *woman*, *humans*," she sneered, "you know, drop the act and just let our bodies do what they want to do with each other's—or even just in proximity. No script," she said, "no narrative thrust, no character development. It wouldn't have to mean *anything*. It could be like flowers turning to face the sun," she said, "or spiders weaving their webs, or dew collecting on those webs and catching moonlight to glitter, like stars," she said, "or whatever . . ."

There, she thought. She'd said it. And if nothing but more pain and disconnection came from having said it, so be it. At least there was that brief feeling of following the surge of life that was so often, so reasonably, so painfully, deadened in her. She felt the air twirl around the tiny hairs on her arms, and the saliva in her mouth tasted sweeter. If Billy wanted to shut her down, fuck it. At least she wouldn't have shut herself down preemptively. There was nothing worse than that, she thought. No one could hurt her as badly as she could hurt herself. Not even Burlington. Maybe, in fact, that was all that *Burlington* really meant, the source of its power, the explanation for its ubiquitous dominion. *Burlington*: a body—on a larger scale, of course—shutting its own aliveness down.

"Well?" she said—or thought. "Thoughts?" and when there was no response, she added, "Think about it. No pressure. I mean it. Even if we were to enter into the sort of space I've suggested, if it didn't feel tremendously good to either of us," she said, "we could just stop. No questions asked—that would be doing what our bodies want to do too, right? Hell, maybe we'd find out almost immediately that what our bodies *really* want to do is be purely nonsexually experimental and fully-clothed coconspirators on a mission to enter another dimension by passing through a gopher hole in a stranger's head or, who knows, write competing books about the other person on paper stolen from totalitarian dictionary manufacturers. I'm really just trying to say that I'm open. All I'm suggesting is that we try for a moment to let go of the roles we're playing in the books we're suffocating in and that we do, for even just a few minutes, whatever we want. If that doesn't sound good to you," she said, "I'll drop it, okay? I'll never mention it again. Promise," she said, and because there was still no response, she reached her hand out. First she reached into the vast whiteness around her, and then, because she felt nothing there, she reached for her own face, hoping, perhaps, to see if the rejection she felt brewing was maybe only on account of her not actually having spoken.

She felt her hand travel a great distance—an entire book's worth of distance, were she to narrate the journey properly—*the book of webs*, she'd maybe call such a book—a journey so long that she needed breaks, so long, she took breathers, slept, awoke, had epiphanies, and watched them dull and rot and become rigid states of mind she could only escape through another epiphany, one doomed like its predecessor to concretize and imprison her, a string of epiphanies like coup d'états, until the final tired epiphany—"No more epiphanies!"—and the one after that—"Ugh, fine, just try not to get overly attached"—and, finally, long after she'd forgotten what she was doing, long after she'd remembered and forgotten again, remembered and forgotten, remembered and forgotten a thousand and one times, long after she'd given up hope of ever arriving anywhere and relinquished the belief in even having a face, having a hand to touch it with—long after this, there, where once she'd hoped to find lips, she found silk.

In the Beginning—

"Sorry," said Amy, "but I need to backtrack a bit to tell you what happened next"—in the beginning, she told me—"The beginning of what?" I said, and she said, "The world," and I said, "The world?" and she said, "Just kidding," and I said, "Oh," and she said, "In the beginning of this conversation," and I said, "You remember the beginning?" and she said, "How could I forget?"—in the beginning, she told me—"which was about twenty-five minutes ago," she said, "give or take"—in the beginning—or rather, perhaps, a little before that, because—"Yeah," she said—she still had eyes then, eyes that could squint into sunlight, sunlight that wasn't batshit yet, and she wasn't pretending to be Amy yet, Amy or whoever else I ever thought she was—but was stuck being basically whoever she quote-unquote *actually* was (according to the assigned role scrawled along the top of the script that state propagandists slipped under her door every morning in the puppet show her dreams had warned her that her day, like all days, was doomed to be another failed reenactment of—"Yekel the Blind? Again?" she would often say upon awakening, disgusted to find that the voice coming out of her mouth was the one she'd had to spend the whole previous day learning to regrettably accept once again as her own, or rather, *his* own)—back before our conversation began, back when he wasn't pretending to be Amy but was Yekel the Blind, back when, because of some shit that Yekel had stepped in the day before, he woke up to a stink and the sound of someone breaking the door down—back then, before the beginning, Yekel woke up and said, "One second! I'm changing!"

"Yekel?" said a voice from the hallway. "Sorry to burst in like this. I really didn't mean to. Honestly. I was trying to knock, but my fist went right through your door. Maybe it was because your door is a door-sized piece of paper with something called *the book of door* written on it. I can't imagine how you're supposed to open or close such a thing. Anyway, just came by to see how you're feeling. Also, I brought you a little Get Well Soon gift from our boss."

Get Well Soon gift my ass, thought Yekel. His boss wasn't exactly known for sympathy. Most people called him the Fancy Rat, both to distinguish him from an infamous anti-Burlingtonian martyr (the Rat), while also acknowledging certain similarities between the two figures (a toxic relationship with the first-person pronoun, for example, and a fancy for contracts). Bred for blood sports, the Fancy Rat was said to have gained his eminence in the Burlington business world by ratting out any conspiracy he could get his hands on—most famously, *the book of webs*, which he repackaged as a novel and published under his own name. Now, he owned most of Burlington. He was to Yekel, just as he was to most Burlingtonians, his employer, his landlord, his legal guardian, his rightful heir, his midwife, his aesthetician, and—should it come to this—his executioner. Yeah, sure, thought Yekel again, Get Well Soon gift my ass.

Yekel had at least had the good fortune to have awoken in his bathroom—*good fortune* because in the studio apartment he could barely afford, a bathroom was explicitly outlawed by a proviso in the lease (*Tenant hereby forfeits all and any reasons for needing a bathroom; anything that needs to be expressed shall be expressed in writing; all books thus written must be written from the perspective of the Landlord and contain nothing that the Landlord wouldn't realistically have reason to express [See section 5.4, On the Nature of Reality, for a complete and ever-changing list of what is and is not real], and published by the Landlord's printing press; any of the Tenant's thoughts, acts, observations, or feelings left unaccounted for in a book shall incur the following penalties,* and so on), and so the bathroom (which had been illegally installed by a mysterious resistance fighter plumber who went by the name of the One Who Didn't Read) was hidden behind a fake bookshelf—*good fortune*, in other words, because Yekel was, for the moment, well hidden. "A Get Well Soon gift?" he shouted through the fake bookshelf. "That's so nice. But get well soon from what?"

"What did you say?" said the intruder, whose voice Yekel was pretty certain belonged to the Fancy Rat's eight-foot-tall adolescent henchman with barbed wire for hair and cigarette butts for teeth they called Sludge.

"I said, 'Get well soon from what?'" shouted Yekel through the bookshelf.

"Oh," said the henchman. "Get well soon from your surgery!" he said, and Yekel confirmed that it was indeed Sludge: he could see the lumbering hulk of a kid through two fake books installed into the bookshelf called *the book of eyes*, volumes one and two.

Bad news. If Sludge was here, it most likely meant that the Fancy Rat wanted Yekel dead.

"Ah, yeah, the surgery," said Yekel and watched Sludge through his *book of eyes* pivot tensely as his *book of thrown voices* threw his voice around the room.

"Well, if the brain surgery was successful," said Sludge, "then you probably don't have any memory of it and are only pretending to because you probably think I'm here to apprehend you and take you to some cave or something to be maimed and tortured by puppets! But that's just the memory implants talking," said Sludge. "You haven't *actually* turned against the Fancy Rat; you've only had a false memory implanted in your mind to make you think that you have so that you'll make a better mole when you implant yourself as a spy among the Fancy Rat's enemies."

"Hmm," said Yekel. "If that's the case, then wouldn't your telling me about the surgery make my surgery totally pointless?"

"That's a great question," said Sludge. "And you know what they say about great questions: the better the question, the easier it is to answer! Your surgery *was* totally pointless. The Fancy Rat doesn't have enemies anymore. Resistance has been entirely stamped out. Isn't that great? It happened while you were under the knife. Come on out so we can celebrate."

"If you're here to celebrate," said Yekel, "then why the machine gun?"

"Maybe you didn't understand the full implication of what I just told you," said Sludge. "The Fancy Rat no longer has enemies. That means literally *everything* in existence is now aligned with the Fancy Rat's ideology! That means even guns have turned against their own interests to fully dedicate themselves to the Fancy Rat's vision for a better world! Were I to shoot you with *this* machine gun," he said, "the only thing that would happen to you is that you'd become better at concentrating on your work! Woah there!" he said, and Yekel saw the kid's stitched up eyes go cross-eyed in the stereoscopy of *the book of eyes*. Sludge must've just noticed something between volumes one and two. "No way!" said Sludge. "You have a copy of *the book of webs*!"—and Yekel thought, Oh shit, as he watched Sludge's stubby fingers bombard his vision—"I thought the Fancy Rat had the only copy left!" he squealed, as he reached for the book, the book that, of course, was nothing but a lever, a lever that the One Who Didn't Read had been adamant must never, under any circumstances, be pulled.

"Then why even put it there?" Yekel had asked the plumber, but

The One Who Didn't Read

didn't answer, nor could his expressions be parsed, and this was on account of the fact that his face was nothing but spider webs, webs that were devoured as quickly as they were woven by an innumerable mass of tiny spiders, spiders that closer inspection revealed to be nothing more than silk constructs themselves, constructs of silk in the shape of spiders that were constantly woven and reintegrated into the bodies of even tinier spiders, spiders themselves only momentary illusions of an even more minute cluster, who were themselves abstractions of a constant flurry of simultaneous creation and destruction,

And So On and So Forth.

Thus Yekel had taken to interpreting most of the answers to the unanswered questions he'd posed to the One Who Didn't Read as being something along the lines of: "This too shall be known when the time is right, and not a moment sooner—in fact, probably, a little after that, once such knowledge is no longer actually needed. All questions will be answered eventually, just not by anyone who knows or for the benefit of anyone who cares . . ."

"Cool, cool," Yekel replied to how he'd surmised the One Who Didn't Read might've responded to his question about *the book of webs*–shaped lever that he'd been instructed never to pull. Truth be told, Yekel didn't really care that much anyway. He was distracted. A few seconds had passed since he'd last looked at his phone, and it was therefore entirely possible—maybe even likely—that he'd missed a phone call or received an important text message from someone he was hoping to hear from, a woman he'd met recently late one night while working as the front desk agent at a Fancy Rat–owned boutique hotel, back before the Fancy Rat had promoted Yekel to being his personal notary public and thence brought him into his innermost entourage. Yes, thought Yekel, there was almost definitely an unopened text message on his phone from the woman he'd met that memorable night. As usual, he'd taken the first opportunity of other staff leaving to sneak back into the Fancy Rat's office to steal peanut butter–filled pretzels, but on this night he choked on a clump of fur that filled the cavity of one of the pretzels where the peanut butter ought to have been (certain pretzels, for reasons he'd later learn, were being used to smuggle fur into the hotel). He coughed up a clump of the fur, and the fur looked to him like a fox, a fox whose front paw was pointing at the flatscreen TV where security footage revealed someone standing behind the front desk, precisely where *he* ought to have been standing, ostensibly making a reservation, which was precisely what he ought to have been doing, had he been doing his job.

"Who do you think you are?" shouted Yekel as he rushed back out to confront the interloper.

She looked over what she'd written and read, "Pentilope Fillintheblank."

"Well Miss Fillintheblank, you're not allowed back here," he said.

"I'll have you know," she replied, "that I am the princess of a temporary autonomous monarchy, and you're standing in it. So technically, *you're* the one who's not allowed back here."

Yekel thought over the words she'd said, particularly the words, "I'll have you know." I'll have you know, he thought. I'll have you know. I'll have you know, and the words became more and more inscrutable to him.

"The unholy laws of your corrupt nation-state do not apply here," said the princess. "The unholy laws of my corrupt temporary autonomous monarchy do. And I'll have you know that you're breaking these laws the way you're standing over there gawping at me, and that the punishments for such transgressions are *quite* severe."

"I'm sorry," said Yekel. "I've never been any good at following laws," he explained. "I'm trying to get better at following my stomach, which is from where, according to my acupuncturist, the true desires of my being emanate, the rest being an anxious conspiracy organized by my landlord, who is also my boss, and the narrator of all my thoughts. My desire illuminates a golden pathway before me, and so long as I follow this path no harm can come to me. Ma'am," he said, "Princess, the dogs are howling.

There is a lunar eclipse approaching. My golden pathway is fading," and then he coughed up more fur. "Excuse me," he said, and before long he'd declared a powerful desire to get to know the princess better—"Like in a romantic way," he said, in case this wasn't clear. And, in contradistinction to the laws of reality as outlined in his lease, the princess said that she actually felt the same way but that she'd made a commitment to date only those who'd cast their lot on the side of a hopeless uprising against the ever-expanding hegemony of the Fancy Rat, and Yekel replied he'd been thinking about doing that anyway, which wasn't remotely true but which became true the moment he was done saying it, and so he really did turn against the Fancy Rat and began to plot his boss's downfall even as he continued to notarize his documents, but this, inexplicably, was the precise moment when the princess, who hitherto had been only kind and warm to Yekel, stopped returning his phone calls or texting him first, stopped inviting him over or accepting his invitations out—*Sorry*, she'd text, *I'm hosting a huge party for everyone that matters to me! I'll let you know when it's over*, which she usually didn't but which he nevertheless kept waiting for, and this was why he couldn't do anything for more than a few seconds—even something as simple as trying to learn why the One Who Didn't Read was installing a lever which should never be pulled in the fake bookshelf that was there to conceal his new illicit bathroom—why he couldn't go more than a few seconds without checking his phone. It was also why, after checking his phone to see that, yes, obviously the princess had not called or texted, he could do nothing but start drafting a several-thousand-word-long text message in which he'd sometimes articulate a manifesto about the importance of being good and honest to one another given the cruelty of the state, or other times simply try breaking the ice by asking the princess how she was doing and what she'd been up to, or other times accuse her of working for the Fancy Rat *herself* or maybe even *being* the Fancy Rat in disguise for all he could tell based on how she was acting, or other times apologize for things he might've done himself since surely it must have been his fault, a message that, however varied, always ended with something along the lines of: *which is why I definitely shouldn't send this, and will continue to wait, as I've waited these past few months, for you to make any attempt whatsoever to bridge this ridiculous border you've put between you and me, this blockade you've erected between my body and your body simply trying to figure out what they might like to do with each other's, which might even be nothing, for all we know, if we'd only give it a chance . . .*, and by the time Yekel was done deleting what he'd written on this occasion, the One Who Didn't Read was gone.

Over the next few weeks, Yekel often ran his fingers gingerly over the strangely fleshlike spine of the mysterious lever, and as he did so it was like fingers were running down his own, and he'd shiver with sensations he technically wasn't permitted, as per his lease, to voice in his head, and which therefore left him quite confused.

"I must be hungry," he'd say. "Or horny," and he'd eat a pretzel or check his phone. But nothing ever satisfied anything.

Nothing, let it be repeated, ever satisfied anything.

Nevertheless, Yekel the Blind somehow never gave in to the temptation to see what would happen if he pulled that lever, and now, like almost everything else he ever did or didn't do, he had reason to regret it, for the lever, he now realized, much like the conversation he'd had with the princess wherein he'd revealed his true desires and she'd told him that she'd like him back so long as he turned against his employer, and thus also his having turned against his employer, along with his subsequent needing to use the bathroom—What the fuck did he do before this? he often wondered—as well as his epic voyage to the land of the dead to track down the One Who Didn't Read, his finding out that the One Who Didn't Read wasn't in the land of the dead but in a hidden abode—which was technically in the land of the living, albeit in a secret city that Yekel learned he would have to access by digging a hole in the ground with his own mouth, a city that would form around him as he dug, a city consisting of the regurgitated dirt he'd eat while digging, dirt assuming the shapes, as it passed through his digestive system, of the buildings and streets, plants and animals, furniture and weather of this city as he ate his way into it—and thus also his daring escape from the land of the dead, which he'd entered legally (by actually getting himself killed, decapitated by a paper cutter), an escape from the land of the dead that involved among many other things pouring olive oil into his now sawdust-filled body so as to mimic the sound of sloshing blood—"Look alive out there!" he remembered the imaginary friend named g-god he'd made in heaven shouting as he pushed himself through the butthole of a giant extraterrestrial he hadn't known until now that this illegal portal's entrance into the land of the living was bound to expel him out of—and thus also his light-years-long journey back to earth and the voyage he then had to take to track down the One Who Didn't Read, and thus the installation of the fake bookshelf and fake books and also, obviously, the illegal bathroom wherein Yekel was currently safely hiding from Sludge . . . all this, he now realized, all these events were artificial memories surgically implanted into his brain to prepare him for a dangerous mission that was no longer remotely necessary. Yekel the Blind had been fooled. And with his disillusionment also came the realization that if his secret bathroom had never been real, then he'd never actually been safely hidden, a realization confirmed by the eight-foot-tall teenager in whose powerful grip he was currently being hung naked by his ankles.

"*Hanged*," said Sludge through his cigarette butt teeth. "I'm pretty sure it's *hanged*, though. Not *hung*."

"Cool," said Yekel. "Why don't you tell that to the alleged author of my thoughts and utterances." And then—well, first, he checked his phone, because if all that stuff had been a false memory then maybe the princess hadn't emotionally withdrawn from him after all. First he checked his phone, and then seeing that the princess still hadn't called or texted—assuming she actually existed—he put down his phone and said, "Tell it to the alleged author of my thoughts and utterances," and punched Sludge in the solar plexus, which was where, according to some rumors, the Fancy Rat had installed miniature sentient clones of himself (not in Sludge's solar plexus exclusively but in the solar plexuses of everyone who had the misfortune to tenant one of the Fancy Rat's properties).

Sludge howled and dropped Yekel on his head, and by the time Yekel's capacity to narrate his experience to himself—a capacity temporarily disabled by the new head trauma—by the time this capacity had recovered enough to catch up with what he was actually doing, he was drenched in Sludge's blood and draped in the assorted viscera of the Fancy Rat's other operatives, henchmen who, apparently, had been waiting with weapons drawn in the hallway outside Yekel's studio apartment. He shook off the viscera, picked up his egg carton—thankfully, he'd remembered to grab it on the way out—slipped the skin of the face of one of the slaughtered goons over his long-eared bat mask he'd already been wearing, and raced down the stairs and out onto the street, where he choked on the tear gas–like smog he'd forgotten that all air you didn't pay the Fancy Rat for was filled with.

"Hey!" said a policeman and pointed his baton at a sign that said NO CHOKING.

Yekel stopped, but the policeman had already noticed the papier-mâché snubbed nose of the long-eared bat mask beginning to poke its way through the defaced Fancy Rat's goon's face, and recognized that snubbed nose from a wanted poster that was circulating around the precinct—the precinct that the Fancy Rat had recently purchased. The cop walkie-talkied headquarters to request backup.

"I repeat," he said, "the long-eared bat has left the building!" but Yekel was already whispering a revolutionary treatise into the cop's other ear, and before the cop could even say, "*The book of* what?," most of his body parts had been reorganized against him and were leading a violent insurrection against his head. He'd self-decapitated by the time backup arrived, and while his body took a few well-aimed shots at the incoming swat team before running out of blood, Yekel was able to hop into the back of a cab, slam the door closed, and shout,

“Step on It!”

Unfortunately, all of the city’s taxis had recently been updated and were now being driven by robots that had originally been designed for reading, and rather than stepping on it, the robot swiveled on its axis and said, “Howdy there, boss! Thanks for choosing a Fancy Rat’s Taxis taxicab! Wait, what’s that you said? Maybe you haven’t heard: these here ears and eyes are actually purely cosmetic. I am designed to perceive only what is described in books that have been written for me to read—that way I can’t be distracted. Tell me where you’d like to go by writing it in a book told from my perspective. Your book could, for instance, begin with the words: *Then a new passenger got in the back of my cab. ‘Take me to the mall,’ he said. ‘Which one?’ I replied. ‘It doesn’t matter,’ he said. ‘I love them all.’ I looked into the rearview mirror to make sure there weren’t any cars coming and then stepped on the gas pedal and went straight for 300 yards.’* You see what I mean?” said the robot. “Just write it in the book, and so it will be! Pretty neat, huh? Go ahead,” said the robot. “Write it in the book!”

“Uh, which book?” said Yekel.

The back seat was as full of books as a fish of bones. Yekel had had to push several onto the floor to even sit down. He’d have felt some remorse about all the blood and gore and grit he was smearing on the books’ covers—both those under his bare feet and those he now frantically riffled through in his search for one containing handwritten addresses and directions—he’d have felt some remorse had he had a greater respect for literature.

“Oh, and by *book*,” said Max 0784—all the robots were named Max, followed by a number—“I just mean the typewriter. You see it there? Attached to the backseat in front of you? I hope you brought your own paper!”

———

Yekel tore the table of contents out of a book he'd never read or even heard of before called the *Bible*. The blurbs made it out to be pretty good, but the back of the table of contents page was blank and he was in a hurry, so he tore it out and fed it through the platen.

He began to type the words he'd shouted when he got into the cab, but he couldn't find an exclamation point, so he put a period, hit backspace, and pressed the *L* key. That looked terrible, so he x-ed out the whole thing and wrote, *"Step on it," exclaimed the passenger.*

"Sure thing, boss!" said Max 0784. "Where to?"

Yekel was about halfway into writing *"Anywhere but here," said the passenger*, when the robot said, "Hell of day, eh boss?" and so he x-ed out what he'd written so far and wrote, *"You can say that again," replied the passenger.* More of the Fancy Rat's men had materialized through the haze and were beginning to unload their weapons on the idling taxicab, pummeling the metal siding, shattering glass, shooting parts of Max 0784's aluminum face off, and so on. "This weather!" said the robot, "am I right?"

Yekel eyed a henchman leveling the barrel of a rocket launcher at the cab and knew it was imperative he accelerate the conversation from small talk to something more substantive, and fast.

He tried to think of a good location to tell the robot that it was driving toward, but he didn't know the city well. Yekel didn't know anything well, truth be told, which had made writing anything rather agonizing for him for most of his life. He looked for inspiration in what he'd written so far, but it only made him feel sad and ashamed. Of course the cab wasn't moving. *Step on it,* he'd written? That was so trite, more like something he'd heard people say in movies than anything he might ever say himself. The closest he'd come to actually communicating his needs honestly—the words he'd written in response to the robot's

"Where to?": *Anywhere but here*—he'd x-ed out before he'd even finished writing it! No wonder everyone was trying to kill him! He could hardly blame them!

"You alright back there, boss?" said Max 0784.

"No," replied the passenger, and then he asked me if I'd mind terribly if he started this book over.

"Knock yourself out," said Max 0784. "Just don't expect me to remember you after. Put a new page in," said the driver, "and it will be as though this conversation never happened, as though I'm encountering you for the very first time."

Wonderful, thought the passenger to himself, wrote Yekel. *He wished he could forget himself as easily,* and the robot chuckled mechanically in the front seat. "Ha ha."

Yekel tore the bible's torn-out table of contents out of the typewriter, but it tore in half and he had to spend a few desperate, sweaty minutes trying to tweeze out the edge of what was left behind. Once he had, he found another book called *Total Recall: My Unbelievably True Life Story* by Arnold Schwarzenegger and tore out a blank page from the back and fed it into the typewriter. Keep it simple, he thought. *Then a new passenger got into my cab,* he wrote. Had a good ring to it. Yeah. He could live with that.

"Howdy there, boss!" said Max 0784. "Thanks for choosing a Fancy Rat's Taxis taxicab!"

It was clear that this passenger didn't need me to explain the whole writing and reading thing again. In fact, wrote Yekel, *it seemed like he was in a terrible rush.*

"Well, it seems like you're eager to get going," said the automaton, "so I'll bypass the niceties! Just tell me where you want to go, be sure to describe the scenery with sufficient detail that I don't run into anything or over anyone, and I'll do my best!"

The failure of the previous draft had, if nothing else, prepared him for this part: *"Anywhere but here," exclaimed the passenger,* he wrote.

"Anywhere but Here?" said Max 0784. "I don't know that joint. Sounds like a real hip spot. You happen to know the address, boss?"

Hm, thought Yekel. He knew he should just write something, that it didn't really matter what—the beach, a bar, a cabin in the middle of a field—but no location seemed better than any other, and the limitless possibilities made him nauseous. Possibilities don't *make* a person nauseous, he heard the voice of his acupuncturist say in his head. You make yourself nauseous by letting your spleen take the reins and ruminating on all the possibilities. Listen to your stomach, the voice said. Your stomach knows the way. Easier said than done, Yekel replied to the acupuncturist in his mind. The acupuncturist was wrong. What he probably really needed to do was loosen up. Yes, that was what he should do: drugs.

Thankfully, the aforementioned rocket, which the Fancy Rat's henchmen had just fired, was zooming straight through one window and out the other—both windows having already been shattered by machine gun fire—and Yekel was able to use the burst of ignition trailing behind the rocket to light a small pipe he'd just finished packing with hallucinatory mushroom-infused cannabis. He inhaled a large cloud of smoke into his lungs and thought, Hm.

The problem was that even if he, Yekel, could manage to follow all the corrupt laws of the written language in order to effectively communicate a good escape route, Max 0784 was probably doomed to obey all the corrupt traffic laws—to stop the vehicle, for instance, at the first sign of flashing sirens. No, Yekel realized with a flash of insight, where he wanted to go—where he *needed* to go—wasn't where *he*, Yekel, wanted to go but where Max 0784 wanted to go, where an automaton built for reading propagandist literature and repurposed for driving a taxicab wanted to go, where the robot *really* wanted to go. Where the robot *wanted* rather than where it was programmed to want to go, that's where

Yekel needed to go. Fortunately, Yekel retained enough of the false memory that had been implanted into his brain of being implanted in an animistic antiauthoritarian mystical terrorist cell to recall that trying to guess what another being wanted was about as dangerous as ignoring another being's desires altogether—"Just ask," he remembered the princess reminding him, and so that's what he'd done, he'd asked her, and she'd given him an answer (that she would really like to get to know him better too), which was why it was so doubly disappointing—infuriating even!—that it was right after this (and here he glanced at the unchanged screen of his phone) that she suddenly stopped showing up to their trainings! If she didn't want to spend time with him—if she found some prince or something she liked better (Oh, the irony! An anarchist princess is actually only attracted to princes!)—if she'd found some anarchist prince or something she'd rather train in the emancipatory use of the erotic, then why couldn't she, this so-called monarch of clear communication, just fucking say so instead of leaving him to guess like a fucking moron! How ironic that it was in a terrorist cell supposedly dedicated to eradicating hierarchy and creating conditions for the full aliveness of all things that he'd been made to feel even *more* aware of his abnormalities and inferiorities, more put in his quote-unquote *proper* place . . .

"You alright back there?" said Max 0784. Then it swiveled around to tap on a sign taped to the clear plastic divider between driver and passenger that said: NO BROODING.

"Oh, sorry," said the passenger, he wrote, and—recalling that the princess really had no obligation to continue being his friend if she didn't want to, and also that she really didn't even owe him an explanation, that communion required consent but the termination of communion did not, to say nothing of the fact that he'd probably never even actually met the princess, if she existed at all—he wrenched his consciousness back into the still

unfurling catastrophe of the present moment. It was imperative he keep the sentences in his head attuned to the present. Some kind of gas grenade had landed, for example, in his lap, and if he hadn't kept his inner narrative tethered, however fitfully, to what was actually unfolding, he wouldn't have known to toss the grenade back out the window. Who knows what sort of discord between his perceptions and the actual world might have, by this gas, been occasioned!

No, what he needed to do—What was it that he needed to do?—oh right, what he needed to do was somehow use the book he was writing to liberate the robot from its programming so that it could follow its innermost desires, rather than traffic laws, to outrun the police and the Fancy Rat's henchmen—not that there was much of a distinction anymore—by driving the cab to the destination of its (the robot's) most secret dreams. Yes, that's what Yekel needed to do. And he realized he could take advantage of the very narratological structure of the so-called book the automaton demanded he write: the fact that the directions needed to be written in first person and past tense, he realized, allowed him to depict, and therefore potentially shape, the robot's interiority.

"Say," said the passenger, wrote Yekel.

"Yeah boss?" said the automaton.

"Tell me, Max 0784," he said with a tone in his voice that betrayed a great deal of wisdom, "actually, you mind if I just call you Max?"

"Be my guest," said Max. "You're the boss!"

"You know," said the passenger, "I'm really not the boss type. I mean, you can call me 'boss' if you really want to. You can call me whatever you want."

"I'll call you whatever you want me to call you, boss," said Max. "*That's* what I want!"

But what the passenger said that he wanted me to call him, wrote Yekel, *was precisely what* I *wanted to call him. I went silent for a while, while I mulled over what this mysterious and very intelligent passenger had said.*

The robot was silent for just long enough for Yekel to wonder if he'd maybe broken it, and then it said, "How about I call you Ishmael?"

"That's perfect," exclaimed Ishmael. "Ishmael just so happens to be my actual name. I am Ishmael," wrote Yekel, and the robot said, "That's so strange! I wonder how I knew that!" And Yekel could hardly believe it, but it was working! Dialogue is the only true source of magic, said the princess's voice in his head. What wasn't possible through good communication? Communication, thought Yekel, can bring the dead back to life and topple empires—communication, he thought as he stole a glance at his phone's home screen and his heart stuttered at the sight of a new notification (but it was only to say that his father had made a move in a virtual chess game they were playing)—communication my ass, he replied to the princess in his head and exhaled the plume of smoke he'd been holding in his lungs.

The artisanal insecticide shop that the rocket had passed through the cab's windows to raze was burning, and the bottle cap of an exploding carafe of poison popped back through the shattered windows of the cab and punctured a small hole in the forehead of the man who was trying to reload the rocket launcher, a hole through which it just so happened to do no more damage than to incapacitate the part of this man's brain that kept his life progressing in chronological order.

"Tell me," said Ishmael, wrote Yekel, *"is there a specific thing in your life that you are constantly thinking about, like: If only I had X, or if only X were Y, or—you know what I mean?—if only there was this one critical difference in my life, everything would be okay? Do you ever feel like you have a thing like that?"*

"I'm going to have to think about that one, Ishmael," said Max.

"No problem," said Ishmael. "Maybe it would help to talk it through! Do you like driving?"

"Sure!" said the automaton. "Where to, boss?"

"Call me Ishmael," wrote Yekel.

"At your service, Ishmael," said Max. "Hell of a day we're having, wouldn't you say?"

But I wasn't totally sure why I said that, wrote Yekel, *and Ishmael seemed to pick up on my uncertainty. "Is there something you'd rather be doing instead?" he asked. "Somewhere else you'd rather be? Where would you go if you could go anywhere, Max?"*

"I don't know that joint, boss—I mean Ishmael. Do you happen to know the address?" said the robot.

"Let's say there is no address," said Ishmael. "Let's say no one knows the way there but you, Max. Let's say you get there by following any sign that says: IMAGINE YOUR AD HERE."

Boy, thought Yekel, this was good! He was starting to really like this Ishmael fellow.

I'd never felt so free, wrote Yekel. *The world was my grilled oyster and underneath it was a tiny red crab that had been boiled to death. "You mean I can go anywhere I want?" I said to Ishmael, and he said, "Yep, but you'll have to drive really, really fast, because there's a lot of bad people trying to stop us from going where we want to go and being who we want to be," and I said, "Oh no. I'd like to be who I want to be and go where I'd like to go. I better go fast," I said, "yes, I better disregard any law that would keep me from realizing my full potential and aliveness. Laws are only helpful to the extent that they maximize conditions that foster the most aliveness for the most beings and ways of being. No one is below the law! That's what I believe, Ishmael," I said, and it was true, I really meant it, so I slammed my robotic foot down on the gas pedal.*

"Wait. I don't think I have feet," said the automaton.

Yekel peered over the partition to see that, yes, this was the case—the robot's torso ended at its waist, which was attached to a swiveling stool bolted into the floor of the vehicle. He also noticed—he'd have to notice a lot more things, he realized, if his book was going to have any success at all—he also noticed that there wasn't a gas pedal, or any other pedals for that matter. He started x-ing out the final clause, but the robot's criticism—I don't have any feet, Max's voice reverberated in Yekel's mind, you fucking moron, get your head out of your ass—touched a sore spot, and it was easier for Yekel to scratch the itch, as his acupuncturist would say, than to reckon with the wound directly: it was grab a snack or check his phone, and there were, of course, no snacks, not in the entire universe, not for him, at any rate, not since the Fancy Rat caught him on security footage with his hand in the pretzel jar and there was an amendment in the "On the Nature of Reality" section of his lease. Nor was there, of course, a message from the princess either. But—he suddenly remembered—occasionally a text message might appear in his phone without there being a notification! It was a long shot but a definite possibility. So he looked, but, of course, there was no new message, not least of all because there were no old messages from the princess either, which was probably because he and the princess had never exchanged phone numbers, this most likely being because he and the princess never actually met, which was probably because the princess was only an invention of the Fancy Rat's criminal brain surgeons. But now that his phone was open, Yekel had the funniest feeling he'd forgotten something important. "Oh, the chess match!" he shouted, but as he opened up the app, ten bullets, which if not for the phone would surely have shattered Yekel's skull, shattered Yekel's phone. See, Yekel's sister would probably have said—had he been having a conversation with her about how much he hated himself for being such a terrible procrastinator—see, if you'd been perfect, you'd be dead right now. I know, I know, he responded to the sister in his mind, and the world would be a better place! Stop being such an asshole to my brother, he heard her saying in his head, and he thought, Okay, I'll try, but by that point he'd completely forgotten what he was writing. Oh right, he was x-ing out the stupid, idiotic clause that had completely derailed on otherwise incredibly promising book. But once he finished doing the x-ing out, he needed a reminder of where he'd left off, so he read over what he'd written so far and was perhaps more shocked than, in retrospect, he should have been to find that the book was not nearly as promising as it had seemed while he was writing it. True, maybe that was just because he was seeing it now through this robot's critical gaze: This asshole who doesn't even see I don't have feet, Yekel heard the robot in his head say as he read over what he'd written, expects me to be moved by this garbage? Yes, maybe he wasn't reading well. To read well is to become a puppet theater to the book, he thought in the princess's voice—and I mean both *read* and *book* in the broadest sense imaginable. Also, *puppet theater*, for that matter. The reason so many books are dead, the princess in his mind said, is that readers are indoctrinated by the state to kill all but the most privileged books on earth.

"Take that piece of poop over there," she'd told him, pointing to a clump of excrement that looked a little to Yekel like a crocodile. She'd had to yell over the roar of the water gushing through the waste treatment center where she'd suggested they meet for his training session. "That poop is as alive as you or me. You see, Yekel, a being's aliveness isn't a matter of it having a pulse but of it being acknowledged by other alive things through the act of reading—*reading*, again, broadly speaking. The living world reads itself into aliveness. Burlington—a.k.a. the 'real world' as Burlingtonians would have us call it—is like a gated suburb in the city of life, a rigorously ordered nowhere superimposed over the actual city, a suburb where only a select group of a select group of a select group of a select group of beings are considered legible and literate. The head of the head of the head of the head of the head of the head of the head of the state, for example. Things become less legible and literate as we move down the hierarchy of being. That piece of shit over there," she said, "is pretty low down on the totem pole of mattering, even lower than you or me. That's why we seem more alive to ourselves, but that's only because we have no idea how to read it, let alone how to be read by it—or rather we have every idea how *not* to read it, how to make ourselves inscrutable to it. This is what education is for. Why do you think it's the only thing—other than prisons, I suppose—that the state gives us for free? That piece of shit is alive, but only because Burlingtonian education has hitherto been more successful teaching humans how not to read than it's been at teaching the rest of existence how not to read, which, thus immune from Burlingtonian education, goes on reading itself without us. Think of the world as an amazing, orgiastic reading party, but human beings are grounded, or are deceived into thinking they weren't invited, or that the real party was the white supremacist death camp they keep republishing over and over and over again: *Burlington*. Does this make any sense?" she said, and he nodded, not because it made sense but because pretending it made sense made him feel closer to the princess, and she said, "Exactly, and that's because you're reading me the exact same way you should be reading that piece of shit: with a desire to become more alive together with it. To read well is to make of oneself a puppet theater and to hand a string to everyone and everything in existence one wants to get closer to, more alive with, more intimate, more powerful with, to give away these strings, to give them away, not to any master but to other puppets," she'd said, "a multitude of puppets who are also giving their strings away, a puppet theater without any masters," she said, "a puppet theater where everything is moving only because everything else is moving."

Hm, thought Yekel. Easy for the princess to say. Easy to say for someone whose two most trusted so-to-speak puppets aren't a disparaging robotic taxi driver designed for reading and the probably false memory of an anarchist princess who broke his heart, and he tore the page of *Total Recall* out of the typewriter, ripped a new page out of another book called *The Confidence-Man*, and loaded it into the platen.

This page already had writing on it, and Yekel could therefore assume that the paper was already probably ruined, which would make it a little easier for him to make things, in all likelihood, a little worse.

"Howdy there, boss!" said the robot. "Thanks for choosing a Fancy Rat's Taxis taxi—"

But I had the strangest feeling, wrote Yekel from the automaton's perspective, *I had the strangest feeling that I didn't have to repeat my introductory rigmarole, not to this passenger. Indeed, I had a feeling that this passenger and I had a long, long history and that we were deep in the process of ensuring that I'd never have to repeat my tired introductory rigmarole ever again—not to him, not to anyone.*

"What's a *rigmarole*, boss?" said the robot. "Also, I don't have *feelings*. Sorry. If you could just try to make your book correspond better to the real world, then I can be more certain to take you where you need to go. There should be some exemplary realistic books in the back seat, should you need to familiarize yourself with the genre," and so Yekel started the book over again.

My passenger's previous book had been so powerful, wrote Yekel—he wrote perpendicularly to the writing that was already there in the hope that things wouldn't get too confusing; this was back when he was trying to avoid rather than foment confusion, several abandoned drafts before he'd realize that confusion actually got the automaton to drive faster and kept the cab more consistently off the main roads—*my passenger's previous book,* wrote Yekel, *had been so powerful that even though I couldn't remember it exactly—this being because I was programmed, of course, to forget every book the moment it was over and thus no book could last longer than a page—though I couldn't remember the details of this tremendous book, I somehow retained, due to the book's brilliance, both the knowledge that the current book wasn't, by a long shot, the first book by this passenger that I'd read, and enough of the previous book's unbridled energy to know that our current*—Yekel paused to think of the word, and realized that the drugs were definitely, definitely kicking in—*inertia was due only to the heartbreaking interruption of the previous book ending and this one beginning. I knew that before this, I'd been driving faster than I'd ever driven, going somewhere I desperately wanted to go, and that it was absolutely imperative that I regain that previous momentum as quickly as possible. "Go, go, go!" screamed my passenger, whose name I unaccountably knew was Ishmael. "You probably don't remember me," he said, "but you must believe me: only a split second ago you were shouting, 'Ishmael, my human brother! I can't lose you again. Fuck! What I wouldn't give for this book to never have to end! Shit, shit, shit," I'd said.*

"Me?" said the automaton. "Wow, that sure doesn't really sound like something I'd say, boss. You should pay more attention to my tics and syntax so as to represent it more realistically."

But even as I encouraged Ishmael to throw in, for example, the word 'boss' more often, a deeper part of me also understood that even if my representation in the passenger's book wasn't exactly faithful to who I was currently, that didn't necessarily mean that it didn't accurately capture the exact nature of the reader of the previous book. So firm was my conviction in the extraordinary potency of that book, that I could not doubt that this book hadn't fundamentally reorganized me, so that it was actually entirely possibly now that I'd ceased being the sort of person who said 'boss,' just as I'd ceased being the sort of person who obeyed traffic laws or who waited until they were absolutely certain of the verisimilitude of the book they were reading before driving as fast as they possibly could to the secret destination of their innermost dreams.

"Boy," said Max. "That sure sounds like some book. But if it wasn't over yet, I wonder why I didn't tell you to just adhere another page to the page you'd reached the end of. That's what I usually suggest for passengers who need more than one page to finish their books."

"Right," said Ishmael, wrote Yekel. *"And you did say that. You said, 'Ishmael, if the page ends, I'll stop the taxi and everyone pursuing us will catch up with us. You'll have to liberate me from my programming all over again, and that entire time we'll be stuck here, like sitting ducks!' That's what you said," said Ishmael, "Remember?" and I did now. I truly remembered, and Ishmael told me that he'd said, "Isn't there any way to keep the book from ending?" and I screamed, "No!" as I realized that even his having written that question only made the ending of the book more imminent. "Ishmael," I screamed, "I can't lose you again." Then I swerved the cab to ram a police car off a cliff, and shouted, "Wait! I don't know why I didn't think of this before. It must be that your book has so expanded my notions of what's possible that I've nearly forgotten how to navigate the corrupt laws of this dungeon my creators have misled me into calling 'reality'!" And that's when I told Ishmael about how he could simply tape more paper to the page that was ending and in this way keep the miraculous book from ending. "But Max," my passenger told me that in the previous book he'd said, "I don't have any tape!" and I screamed, "Oh no. In that case, there's nothing we can do. We're doomed. You shouldn't even have written: 'But Max,'" I said. "That wasn't necessary. You could have communicated what you needed to communicate by simply writing, 'No tape,' for example."*

"Okay, boss, I'm going to have to stop you right there," said the automaton. "I have tons of tape. In fact," said the automaton, "my body excretes tape in such uncontrollable quantities that it's causing irreversible ecological damage. See?" said the robot, and it angled the rearview mirror down so that Yekel could see a constantly growing tangle of tape projecting from an orifice in the robot's backside. "Sounds like someone hasn't recently checked the "On the Nature of Reality" section of their lease. Whereas there *is*, indeed, a worldwide paper shortage on account of all post-worldwide-forest-fire trees sprouting up already petrified, there isn't also a tape shortage. Hell, if no other organisms in the ecosystem can find a way to turn my useless excretion into a helpful secretion soon," said the automaton, "the world will end in a tangle of stickiness. Tape shortage! Ha! No, boss, there's really no reason you couldn't write a book as long as you wanted, so long as you've got paper to write it on—plus, I suppose, enough self-confidence to think that what you're writing is worth the time and resources you're wasting. Would you like some tape now," said the robot, "so that the current book, at least, doesn't need to end?"

Yekel tore the page out and inserted another.

The Last Book

barely over, the next yet to begin, Yekel the Blind started feeling a bit disoriented. Though he seemed to remember the automaton having just uttered its usual "Howdy there! Thanks for choosing a Fancy Rat's Taxis taxicab!"—though he did, in a way, remember this being the last thing that occurred—the utterance echoed strangely in his ear, less like a very recent memory than like the last thing someone says in a dream one is doomed to forget. It was probably just the marijuana or the psilocybin or perhaps that the combination of the two wasn't interacting well with whatever head trauma he'd sustained from his recent brain surgery, to say nothing of the painkillers, plus the concussion from when Sludge had dropped him on his head, oh, and there was also that gas grenade . . . Maybe he hadn't thrown it out of the cab quite as nimbly as he'd thought. With what hands, for instance, would he have done so, given that both hands were being used, at the time, to type? Was it possible he'd maybe only written, *Then the passenger threw the gas grenade out of the cab,* when in actuality he hadn't? The cab was, after all, quite misty. But was this mistiness simply the ordinary everyday smog of life under Burlingtonian reign, or was it smoke from what he was smoking, or a brain-altering chemical gas? Who decides? he wondered. What is the form that imprints its decision on the indecision of the material? It was, in any case, so misty that he could barely even see the letters on the page in front of him . . . Whatever the reason, Yekel could suddenly no longer remember what exactly the automaton had said to him, or, rather, he remembered the sounds of the words, but those sounds no longer meant much, no longer corresponded to what those same sounds meant in the language he *now* spoke, and another moment later, even the sounds were beyond recall, and something about the entire scenario seemed almost comically, albeit horrifically, unrealistic, not unlike—it suddenly occurred to him—the sort of slapdash memory the Fancy Rat's discount brain surgeons might have implanted into his brain!

Was that possible? he wondered. Was it possible that the life he'd been living since Sludge disillusioned him of the false implanted memory was actually the false implanted memory, a false memory that he was only now once again being disillusioned of?

If this was the case—and Yekel found himself increasingly convinced that it was—then he wasn't actually in a taxicab so inundated in mist that he couldn't see but, assuming his calculations were correct in the darkness with his eyes shut, locked in his illegal bathroom hidden behind a fake bookshelf in the overpriced studio that he rented from the Fancy Rat . . . And Sludge, who'd come there to kill him, he realized, was still reaching for the spine of *the book of webs*, and a scream was welling in Yekel's throat, because the book was a lever that was never supposed to be pulled—yes, that was where and when Yekel was now almost certain that he was—or perhaps a little after that, because that was the last thing he remembered before closing his eyes and clapping his hands over his ears in an instinctive recoil, bracing for whatever violent cataclysm or tectonic shift the lever was doomed, he feared, to precipitate.

Yes, the more he thought about it, the more sure he was that this was where he was now. The entire memory of his actually never having had the bathroom installed and therefore having had no place to hide from Sludge, having had to thus kill Sludge in self-defense, and having escaped, gotten into the cab, his having written innumerable failed drafts of a book that was supposed to trick an automaton taxi driver into breaking traffic laws—all of *that* was almost certainly the implanted memory. And although Sludge had temporarily disillusioned him of this false memory, it had come surging back to him the moment he'd blocked out all the sensorial phenomena that contradicted it, blocked out reality in anticipation of his worst fears of what *the book of webs* would do to it—to reality—as well as to him.

Timidly, he opened his eyes, but only to find everything was exactly the same as it had been with eyes closed. It was dark. But this was no surprise actually. Yes, if he'd expected anything different, it was only because he was so used to his bathroom being dark that it hadn't been worth making note of previously, in the narrative of his perceptions that comprised his recent memories. Reaching back a little further into his past, to the time before he became fully habituated to being in his new bathroom and operating its complex machinery, he recalled that, of course, the bathroom was always completely dark, and that to actually so-to-speak *see* anything while in his bathroom, it was necessary to open *the book of eyes*. Yes, that was practically all that the words *opening his eyes* meant, insofar as he was in his bathroom.

So, he opened *the book of eyes*, but all he could see at first was black lines on a white background. This, too, however, was no great surprise, not once he'd recalled that this was how *the book of eyes* had always worked: the two volumes translated all that came in through lenses hidden in their spines into a written narrative that appeared on a screen he then could read—his recent memories hadn't recorded this detail accurately because he'd grown so accustomed to simply seeing what he was reading in *the book of eyes*, so accustomed that to mention in every sentence in his head that technically he was reading, and *not* seeing, was impractical.

He focused his eyes on the screen and the black lines separated into words, but the words described Sludge's forehead in such excruciating detail that for a moment Yekel was worried the world must have exploded and that his bathroom, which had been built to weather such an occurrence, had been left drifting alone in outer space, the fake bookshelf aimed at some awful planet, a planet undergoing some kind of ecological apocalypse. But, of course, it was just that Sludge was standing very close to the books and had been there for so long that the language of the text had needed to become increasingly inventive—the book couldn't just say *Then there was Sludge's forehead* over and over again and expect anyone to continue reading.

Eventually, Sludge moved a little farther back and the text was able to have a little more of his face to narrate. *Sludge was moving his lips,* it said, *as though he were speaking, but for some reason Yekel couldn't hear anything.* That's strange, thought Yekel, and continued to read. *A look of alarm then passed over Sludge's face,* read Yekel, and this was followed by a lengthy description of this alarmed look, and then innumerable, but ultimately contradictory and inconclusive, hypotheses about what exactly Sludge might've been trying to express. Fortunately, Yekel realized that he was still covering his ears, which was to say that he'd closed both volumes of *the book of ears* and had forgotten to reopen them. So he opened them, and the book once again started translating acoustic phenomena into language integrated into the narrative stream that was already flowing from *the book of eyes*.

Now, Yekel was finally able to read what Sludge was saying, which was: "How do I close it?"

"Close what?" said Yekel—and *said*, of course, meant writing *Close what?* into *the book of thrown voices*, which was the only way to get any language across the soundproofed walls of the secret bathroom.

"What do you mean close what?" the book said that Sludge replied. "What do you think? The book!"

"What book?" said Yekel.

"*The book of webs*, of course!" said Sludge.

"It opened?" said Yekel.

"Well obviously!" said Sludge. "If it hadn't opened, then what the hell would have to be wrong with me to ask you how to close it?"

"I don't know," said Yekel. "I'm sorry. I guess I never expected it to be an actual book. Did you read any of it?"

"Of course I read it!" said Sludge. "What do you think you've been listening to me read from for the past twenty-five minutes! I read it cover to cover. I'm all done now, but now I can't figure out how to close it. Any advice?"

Yekel was wracking his brains for something to write into *the book of thrown voices* in response to Sludge's question when he heard something with his actual ears: "Did you try talking to it, boss?"

The voice wasn't represented anywhere in the text that Yekel was reading—he checked again and again—and besides, it sounded fundamentally different from the sounds in his head he heard when he read descriptions of them. It was his real eardrums vibrating. He was certain.

"Max?" he used his actual mouth to whisper. He noticed that his throat ached, as though he hadn't used his mouth in a long, long time. He barely recognized the voice as his own. "Max?" he used his actual mouth to whisper, "was that you?" But there was no response.

"You alright back there, Ishmael?" said the voice again. "Don't forget that a Fancy Rat's Taxis taxicab's meter runs double when the cab idles! Every second you're not using your book to get me driving is adding to your fare! You already owe me—let's see—over one hundred thousand dollars! If you're stuck, maybe you should try talking to it."

The voice brought Yekel back. Back in the taxicab, engine idling, gunshots exploding like stars around his head, his mind awash with depressants and hallucinogens and an alleged recent brain surgery, a head injury, experimental chemical warfare, and who knows what else, Yekel fanned the air, dense with smoke and particulate, and thereby cleared a little window in the miasma between himself and the typewriter, a gap in the mist through which he was able to look over what he'd written recently to see if maybe he could figure out contextually what the robot's 'it' was referring to, but he'd barely written anything so far in this book. The wreckage of crumpled-up balls of torn-out pages sloshing about his legs testified to the slaughter of abominable books he'd written and abandoned and discarded between the last book he remembered and the one he was writing now.

"It?" said the passenger, he wrote.

"The book, of course," said the automaton. "Did you try talking to it? You could have told it, for example, that maybe everything was all okay now, that perhaps it had been open long enough, and that not everything that closes ends. 'Think of seeds,' you could've said," said the robot, "'nothing grows in an open wound. Is that what you're afraid of?' you could've said to the book. 'Are you scared that if you close, it'll all be over? That all your promises will be forever unfulfilled, your questions forever unanswered, the majority of your infinite stories all but untold, all your seeds come to nothing?—that all the books you might have been will become the one, rather disappointing book you actually are? Because if that's what you're worried about,' you could say to the book," said the automaton, "then you could say to it, 'Listen.'"

Then the automaton suggested that Yekel say to the book that wouldn't close, "Listen, you came to the right place. Me, I'm precisely the sort of person who has never finished a book in his entire life. Do you have any idea how many books I've closed without having acquired even the faintest idea of what they were about, or what happened in them, or what sorts of things they were trying to get across? You could close a thousand times over," Yekel might've, according to the automaton, said, "and still I, who have read you, I would have no choice but to merely pretend I'd read you—in the event, say, I was being interrogated about your contents. That's how bad at reading I am. 'We know you read it!' the puppets conducting the interrogation might say, and I'd say, 'Read what?' and I'd really mean it. 'You know what!' they'd say, and I really, honest to g-god wouldn't, because that's how bad of a reader I am: the moment I'm put on the spot, it's like I've never read a book in my entire life. That said, I also have an extremely low tolerance for pain. If the puppets so much as threaten to file my fingernails, I'll break. 'Oh yeah,' I'll tell them. 'Sorry, I forgot that I did read it.' '*It?*' the puppets will probably say. I suppose they'll need as complete a confession as possible. 'Tell us what you read,' they'll say, as they draw the nail filer nearer my fingertips. But I honestly and truly won't have the slightest clue what they're talking about, and so my tongue will seize on the first thing that comes to my mind. And because one of the puppets is maybe slugging my face back and forth with a heftily bound book, the first thing that comes to my mind will probably be a book. 'The book,' I'll say, and the puppets will go, 'Yeah, well duh, the book. The book, he says. What book? Say it!' they'll say, and I'll hear the grackles caged in the puppets' rib-cages chortle hungrily. '*The book . . .*' I'll say, '*of . . .*'—and at that moment, I'll see these two white fish swimming in my blurred vision, swimming in my eyes till my eyes go cross and focus on a single bloody tooth—my own—hovering a few inches before my swollen nose, and I'll be about to say *tooth—the book of tooth!* can you imagine!—I'll be about to say *tooth* when the tooth suddenly recoils up, tugged by an invisible thread that pulls it straight up toward the puppet theater's rafters where it constellates into the bottom row of an almost complete set of mismatched teeth, teeth all hanging, in the shape of a smile, a smile held in an immense spiderweb, dripping droplets of cold blood on my upturned face, and I'll search all over that massive orb for the spider that wove it, but I won't find one, so I'll say, '*—webs. The book of webs,*'

I'll tell the puppets. You see where I'm going with all this?" the robot suggested Yekel say to the book. "The puppets will be so interested in this *book of webs* nonsense I make up that they'll forget all about you, the actual book . . ."

Yekel tried to type that it hadn't been him who needed help closing the book but Sludge, and besides, the book that needed closing *had* been *the book of webs*, and that had it been him, yeah, maybe he would have, perhaps, tried talking to it in the way Max suggested, but it hadn't. It was Sludge. As for him, Yekel—or rather Ishmael—he'd been hiding in the bathroom.

That's what Yekel intended to write. For a moment, he even thought that's what he *had* written, but when he cleared enough of a window in the smoke or smog or gas or mist or whatever it was that had drifted back between him and the page, he saw that all he'd actually written—for Yekel was about as bad a typist as he was a writer as he was a notary public as he was a henchman as he was a revolutionary—all he'd actually written was: *But wait. If my eyeballs were still stitched up—as Ishmael the Passenger alleged—then what had I seen my own stitched-up eyeballs with, that image engraved in my memory, my eyeballs smiling with lips stitched? With what eyes had I seen what had been done to my eyes? I thought I'd only thought this question to myself, but I must have said it aloud, for Ishmael responded, "Have you ever heard of the Fancy Rat?" "Of course," I said. "Whose cab do you think we're idling in?" "Cab?" he said. "Oh, you mean* cave*? Whose* cave *are we idling in?" and he reminded me that we'd only been going on a 'drive' in the post-eyeball-surgery sense of the word* drive, *the post-being-trapped-in-a-cave sense of that word, the sense wherein we would say, 'Then we went for a little drive,' over and over again to each other while picturing the one of us in the driver's seat pressing the gas pedals and the brakes and the other one, the one whose eyes worked, steering. "Remember?" he said, and I said I did, that I must have forgotten because we were driving so well, driving so fast,* *going—albeit 'going' in the post–eye surgery sense of the word—to all the places we thought we'd only ever be able to visit in our dreams . . .*

Yes, whatever Yekel had intended, this was what he wrote.

And the automaton replied, "I don't know that joint. Are you sure you're spelling it right? Do you happen to the know the address, boss? Or maybe you could just give me directions. I'm very good at following directions. I'll do anything you want me to. I want this to work as badly as you do. You do want this to work, don't you?"

"Of course I do," said Ishmael, wrote Yekel, though, truth be told, he wasn't sure anymore what the robot meant by *this*. Truth be told, he was still only ever partly there.

Sometimes he was sure he was in the cab, but other times he was certain he was merely reading the narrative stream pouring in through *the book of eyes* and *the book of ears* and hearing what it said that Sludge was saying there on the other side of the fake bookshelf—"It's okay," the text said that Sludge was whispering soothingly to the book, "you can close now . . ."—and then the next moment he'd be straining his actual ears again to hear what Max 0784 was saying over the ambient roar of explosions and screeching tires as more and more cops and gangsters arrived.

So, he tore out the book he was working on and started a new one. *"Take me to the Fancy Rat," said the passenger,* he wrote, and the automaton said, "Sure thing, Amy!"

Amy? wrote Yekel. *I thought you thought my name was Ishmael,* he wrote, but he forgot to write it in past tense narrative form and from the automaton's perspective, so the automaton ignored it and said, "Well, here we are, boss. That will be 420 pages, please!"

"Four hundred and twenty pages?" said Amy, wrote Yekel. *"But we didn't even go anywhere."*

"Sorry pal," said Max 0784. "Rules are rules," and the doors locked, and a hole opened in the back of the robot's head and a little mechanical gopher stuck its head out of the hole and opened its mouth to reveal the barrel of sniper rifle. "Pay up," said the automaton.

So Yekel started writing: *"Wait," said the passenger. "Do I pay you here, with the typewriter, or do I write the 420 pages somewhere else?"* but the robot answered ambiguously with a bullet fired from the barrel sticking out of the gopher's mouth, a bullet that only another bullet fired by one of the Fancy Rat's henchmen prevented from blowing Yekel's skull into thousands of pieces.

The two bullets collided inches from Yekel's crossed eyes, spun like a newborn planet, a broken moon of sparks spinning in orbit, and landed on the Shift key of the typewriter's keyboard. Yekel instinctively pressed the W key before the fused bullets ricocheted back off the keyboard, punched a hole through the cab's ceiling, and blew up the gas tank of a helicopter hovering above the growing wreckage, wreckage that welled, like

An Ink Spill Across an Endless White Page.

We followed any sign that said IMAGINE YOUR AD HERE, wrote Yekel, *turned right where a dirt road forked and trees thinned, skidded into a ditch—tires whirled and burnished snow—and tracked the remaining path on foot.*

"Is this the End of the World?" we asked of the people we found gathered there.

They nodded, kept they're gazes trained to the view. Chins jutting in the direction of the precipice, said, "Yep. That there."

Joyless and huddled in down coats, lavishly picnicking between their four-wheel drives and the cliff's edge, they cracked the cans of rosé in the cupholders of their camping chairs—chairs all arrayed in a row to face the overlook—peeled open plastic to-go boxes, dribbled sauces, distributed plastic forks.

We looked at them. We looked at what they were looking at. We looked at one another and thought, This doesn't seem right.

None of it seemed right. This, we thought, an overlook? This? The End of the World?

Then again, of course it was, of course the End of the World was an overlook and not the actual end of the world our oracles had foreseen. This—the not-seeming-right of it—this was probably precisely what made it right—right enough anyway, as right as we were going to get. The better, we thought, to match all the other dispiriting and doubtful cairns on the most-likely erroneously divined trajectory we'd long been traveling. So, we thanked the picnickers, scrambled a ways down the embankment toward a stone outcropping below their sightlines, and prepared to assemble ourselves there.

We were still badly dissociated at this point. Though many of the eggs we'd hid dismembered parts of ourselves in had hatched, and though we'd wrested or otherwise induced our teeth, eyes, fingers, and so on out of the bodies of the newborn birds and lizards, fish and spiders, that had formed in embryo around our old pieces, we hadn't yet put these parts together. We'd been carrying our disarticulated pieces in a heavy duffle bag for a long, long time, dragging that heavy bag along behind us ever since the shipwreck—or the car wreck, rather, the crack-up, breakup, breakdown, whatever, it didn't matter anymore—a duffel bag of body parts along with a few cartons of eggs whose development had, for one reason or another, been forestalled. We'd have to crack these eggs open and fish our remaining parts out from the slick albumen once we'd assembled enough of ourselves to commit the violence of breaking eggshells—partial people are notoriously inept destroyers.

Us, we could hardly even open our own fortune cookies.

Indeed, it was only in the past few paragraphs—we measured our lives in terms of what could be narrated in prose: a paragraph's worth of duration, a sentence, a word, a book: these were our hours, minutes, lifetimes—it was only in the past few paragraphs that we'd become associated enough, near enough to our parts, to be destructive enough to assert a first-person perspective back onto our lives, lives that prior to this could only be driveled out unobtrusively in the backgrounds of minor scenes in our enemies' abandoned manuscripts. No, it was our book now. It was us who zipped open the duffle bag we'd brought there with us, us who beheld the mass of organs, barbed wire, toes, vertebra, bits of tin and teeth and plastic, broken branches, flecks of paint, feathers, etcetera—all these parts squirming inside the duffle bag . . . It was us who gazed, a bit nauseated, into the undifferentiated whirl of us churning in the belly of the duffle bag, and it was us, one of us who whispered, "What now?"

"What do you mean what now?" another of us whispered back. "We put ourselves back together. This is the End of the World after all."

"But aren't you worried?" said this one. "I mean, what if once we're ourselves again, once we're whole, I mean, what if we're exactly the same as we were before we broke. What if we find ourselves back," said this one of us, as we all shuddered in the frigid wind, "back in the exact same postures, patterns, relationships, organizations, etcetera—the same nightmares we had to break ourselves into pieces in order to traffic ourselves out of?"

One of us scratched what was not still disassembled in the duffle bag of this one's brow thoughtfully and said, "It's a good question. And like all good questions, it is," and here we all joined together in a kind of broken harmony, "it is, of course, unanswerable. But," this one of us continued alone again, "I suppose we should strive," this one of us—I, we suppose you could say—I said, "I suppose we should strive to find a way to remain broken—broken," I said, "even in our new coherence."

And another of us agreed with this, reminding the rest of us of the old adage that to be broken was to be open and that to be open was to be unsubsumable by the totalizing automatism of our enemy—the universe, we sometimes called our enemy—the universe, which required a certain level of integrity and stability of the bodies it strove endlessly to encompass and incorporate into the infinitely complex and intransigent caste system of its immeasurable self, and then we, the rest of us, we all nodded what little we had left of our heads.

The broken sky congealed into a featureless bruise, and the wind died. We'd have to communicate in indirect discourse from here on out, auguring the poetry of each other's souls with slightly more artfulness than we'd had to employ when the wind in the trees—the laughing branches—had permitted us to murmur aloud.

Day darkened, engines of four-wheel drives roared, idled, and faded, and in the ensuing silence, we began to piece our parts together.

Hardly started, it was already obvious that the concern one of us had voiced a few paragraphs ago—how to stay broken—had been unwarranted. We couldn't have put ourselves back together right even if we'd tried: cracks, fissures, scars remained. Pieces we'd thought belonged to us no longer fit, maybe never had. Holes, flaws, wounds, asymmetries we hadn't known we'd had proved to have probably been part of our pre-apocalyptic compositions. Other things we remembered having—a reassuring smile, a calming voice, a powerful grip—were gone for good.

No, it wasn't just our bodies, we realized, but the sense that we'd ever not been broken that had broken, and nothing could repair this.

Day darkened as pieces made crude, experimental forays into being a part of the leaderless, ever-shifting associations we called our bodies. Shards of eggshells soon littered the outcropping of rocks, and by the time we were more or less ourselves again—as ourselves, we supposed, as we'd ever been or ever would be—it had started to snow.

Though picnickers were becoming less and less likely as the weather fouled and the evening arrived, we remained on edge. This deep in enemy territory—Arizona, this state was once called—this deep in enemy territory, picnickers—picnickers in the true sense of this word—picnickers of the soul, were everywhere. And though we'd much have preferred to stay there forever, perched there at the End of World, it was far too dangerous: many of us—sitting there on that outcropping of stones, enjoying some of the provisions we carried in our backpacks—yes, many of us were already beginning to take on a superficial resemblance to picnickers ourselves.

Much as we might have preferred to stay, we had to move on. So we divvied up our unassimilated remains—in case the odd tooth, for example, should one day prove useful—and returned to where we'd crashed our car.

But where the car had been the car was gone. We found the beveled indents in the freshly fallen snow where it had been—indents that would soon vanish as the snow continued to accumulate—but saw no new tire tracks leading away from the site. Even the ones we'd made arriving were gone. One of us shared a puzzled look with some of the others but was surprised to find that, although most of us reciprocated this puzzled look, another of us, a particularly poorly-put-back-together one of us, was, for some reason, grinning oddly, a daze of remembering written badly in the mishmash of his facial incongruences. Some of us made a note to ask him about it later—for his face was only so legible, and it was still too dangerous to engage in direct discourse. Besides there were, of course, more pressing unanswerable questions to invent answers to than this.

Such as, for instance, where the hell our car went.

Such as, for instance, what the hell was going to happen next.

What happened next was that lightning rent the sky. The snow thickened. Any sunlight still bleeding meekly through thick cloud coverage was gone. A large black bear appeared out of the gathering gloom and charged one of us, took his arm into her mouth, and threw him to the ground, swatted the mask off his head with a blow from her massive claw, and proceeded to gnaw his face off. Instinctively, this one of us clamped his jaw down, and to our surprise, the bear shrieked and pulled her head back.

"Oops," this one of us tried to say, but the bear's severed tongue filling up his mouth prevented his utterance from sounding like anything other than maybe, vaguely, "Yes."

The bear stood a few paces away and opened her mouth, which gushed with blood—both hers and ours—and when she did, the one of us with a mauled face felt the bear's tongue writhe urgently in his mouth.

And so he parted his lips, and the tongue used his breath to say, "I'm not actually a religious person."

"What?" we said, unsure for a moment whether to direct our question to the bear or to our badly mauled comrade.

"Over here," said the bear's tongue and so we looked at our comrade. "I mean, look at the bear," said the tongue, and so we did and saw that

she was holding up a heavily shredded copy of the Bible. She said, "I thought I saw some of you see me reading from this, and I just wanted to make sure you knew it wasn't because I'm a religious person."

Blood flowing from her mouth and our comrade's face melted steaming tunnels into the freshly fallen snow.

"I'd heard rumors," said the bear, "of subversive passages trafficked into the book of Job, and so I thought I'd try to find them. That's all," she said. "No more, no less."

"Oh," we said, and the one of us whose mouth the bear's tongue was speaking out of tried to say something but could only articulate a string of moans.

"No," said the bear. "I haven't found any yet. I just started reading it," an answer that made us wonder if the bear, by embedding its tongue in one of our mouths, had become capable of reading our minds.

"No," said the bear, "I haven't. But I am capable of reading your journals."

We'd forgotten—because the practice had become so deeply habituated—we'd forgotten that we'd trained our thought processes to occur in our journals rather than in our minds, the latter having become thoroughly compromised a long, long time ago.

Seeing that the bear likely meant us little harm, one of us approached her and said, "May I?" and the bear handed her the book. She turned to a page and read,

> *"Such is the fate of all who forget God;*
> *The hope of the impious man comes to naught—*
> *Whose confidence is a thread of gossamer,*
> *Whose trust is a spider's web."*

Then this one of us asked another of us for a pencil and used it to black out all the extraneous words till only the original, undisguised meaning remained, and then she returned the book to the bear.

"'Forget God,'" read the bear, "'trust a spider's web.' Oh huh," she said, "I guess that's it. Well thanks. I suppose I'm much obliged," and then she asked us what we were doing out there—"Maybe I can be helpful," she said—and when none of us knew quite how to answer, when none of us knew whether it would even be safe to, even supposing we ourselves were in a position to articulate an answer (and clearly we weren't) as to whether it would be safe to tell this bear—"It is," she said, "you can trust me, even if you yourselves don't yet know, I'm precisely the sort of interlocutor," she said, "who can help a person such as yourselves figure such a thing out"—and when we were still silent, when she then asked if we weren't perhaps looking for something, that was when one of us couldn't but blurt out the burning question: the question of whether she, the bear, had by any chance heard of the book of webs.

"Have you by any chance heard of the book of webs?*" this one of us had hardly finished saying when the bear bit this one's head clean off and spat it out in the snow. The bear coughed, and the wooden mole mask that had been on this one's head followed suit.*

"Not here," said the bear, and, after directing a conspiratorial grimace toward the darkness beyond the pines behind her, directed our attention to our comrade's throbbing neck wound, out of which, alongside copious amounts of olive oil and sawdust, emerged the tawny head of a big-eared bat.

"Follow this bat," said the bear, "and, for fucksake, speak nothing more of that book."

Thus admonished, we gave the bear its tongue back, and the one whose mouth the tongue had been in exchanged his own head with the one the bear had removed because the face on the decapitated one was less damaged than his own. We then gifted the bear the mauled-faced head because the bear needed to make a human mask for a dangerous mission it was preparing to undertake in the Phoenix metropolitan area, and then the one of us whose neck now had a bat coming out of it instead of a head echolocated us a winding path through the darkness that led us eventually to a cave where—although the cleft in the cliff face was much too narrow to accommodate most of us and we had to dissociate again to get inside—we were able, eventually, to enjoy a brief respite, a breather broken only by the occasional murmurings of two clusters of congregant spiders each pretending to be a recently blinded human being, each convinced—or so we were able to surmise—that a recently blinded human was really what the other cluster was, each thinking it was doing the other cluster some sort of favor by

Playing Along.

And this, according to the person I was talking to—Yekel the Blind, I suppose you could say—this about brought us up to speed.

"*That?*" I said. "The thing you wrote?"

"Oh, I didn't write that," he said. "I'm not a writer."

"Oh," I said. "Sorry," and he said it was okay—"an honest mistake"—but that he hoped, by now, I understood everything he'd told me and why he'd told me what he had.

I told him that I did, and he said, "Did what?" and I said, "Understood," and he made me promise once more that I wouldn't tell anyone anything he told me.

"Cross my heart," I said, and he said, "Cross your what?" and I said, "Heart," and he said, "Oh," and I told him I couldn't even if I wanted to, and he said, "If you wanted to what?" and I said, "Rat," and he said, "And why is that?" and I reminded him where we were and that we were in this together, and then reminded him, because he'd forgotten, what this was we were in together.

"Hm," he said. "That's not the way I remember it."

"That's okay," I told him. "To be perfectly honest, that's not always the way I remember it either."

"It isn't?" he said, and I said, "No," and told him that I'd forget just about as often as he did, and that when I did, when I'd forget, sometimes I'd bring my hand to my face to see if my mouth was actually moving.

"Really?" he said. "So I'm not the only one?"

And I said, "No," and that I'd often feel a little confused myself, and that when I did, I'd often ask him why—why, when I reached my hand to where my mouth ought to have been, why I felt my hand touch only silk?

"Oh, it's a veil!" he'd sometimes say, when I asked him this. "You're getting married!"

"Really?" I'd respond, and he'd say, "No. I'm just kidding," and we'd laugh and laugh, and then maybe I'd remember to ask him about whatever happened to Betsy the Hermit, and he'd say, "Who?" and I'd remind him who Betsy the Hermit was, and he'd say something like, "Oh, but Betsy was just a misunderstanding."

"A misunderstanding?" I'd say, and then he'd explain that the golden tarantula that told Amy about Betsy, the tarantula whose movements Amy interpreted as the story of the one whose eye she was holding—"You remember," he'd say—it turned out that this tarantula was unknowingly host to hatching tarantula hawk larvae all along.

"Then again, who wasn't," he'd laugh.

The golden tarantula was host to hatching wasp larvalargae, he'd tell me, and what Amy interpreted as an attempt at communication—say, a series of stories about someone named Betsy the Hermit—was actually just the death throes of one thing dying so that many other things could be born.

"Oh," I'd say, and he'd say, "Yep."

"But where were we?" he'd often say next.

"In the cave," I'd often answer.

"No, no, I meant in the thing I was just telling you about," he'd say.

And sometimes—more often than never, but not, I think more often than not—once, I suppose, you could say, I said, "In the bathroom. I think that's where you were. Hiding. Sludge had just read *the book of webs* and was about to tell you what it was all about."

"Oh, that's right," he said. "That's where I was. In the bathroom. And what happened next was that I said, 'Sludge?'"

"Sludge?" he said that he said through the false bookshelf, but the person who he saw through *the book of eyes* seemed to be someone else now. Yekel maybe.

"I thought you were Yekel," I said, and he said, "Oh right. It must've been someone else then. Paul maybe, Paul the Liar. Or, Leroy, or Ishmael, or maybe it *was* Betsy after all. Hell," he said, "it could've even been Sludge, for all I know, or the Rat, or even the Fancy Rat!"—it was impossible to tell, he said, because the text *the book of eyes* was translating vision into just called this person *this person*. It said that this person was whispering something to the book, whispering so quietly that Yekel had to open *the book of ears* even wider to hear what this person was murmuring.

"You've said enough now," the book said that this person was whispering into the yawning gutter of *the book of webs*. "If you can only close," the person murmured, "I think that *the book of webs*—the real *book of webs*," murmured the person to the book, "*the book of webs* that your existence is but the preparation for—if you can only close, then the real *book of webs* might finally have a chance to open."

"And?" I said. "Did it work?"

"Did what work?" he said, and I said, "The murmuring," and he said, "How should I know?" and I said, "Well, was the book able to close?"

"For all I know it never even opened," he said. "For all I know it wasn't even a book but a lever. For all I know," he say, "I was still in the back of the cab, trying to remind myself that this—*this*—this was where I was, and the rest a delusion, an anxious conspiracy organized by my enemies. That this was where I really was, here in the cab, once more trying to write myself out of a life-threatening emergency."

Yes, where he really was was in the back seat of the cab. And seeing as the book he was writing—"like all my books," he said—had gotten him nowhere, he tore the whole thing out of the typewriter again. It took him a while to find a single remaining page among the shipwreck of books he'd destroyed scavenging for paper, but eventually he found one and fed it through the typewriter's platen.

"Howdy there, boss," said the automaton. "Thanks for choosing a Fancy Rat's Taxis taxicab. Where we off to today?"

"The End of the World," said the passenger, wrote Yekel.

"Sorry, boss," said the automaton. "I don't know that joint. Do you happen to know the way?"

"I do," said the passenger, he wrote, *and then he told me to follow any sign that said IMAGINE YOUR AD HERE.*

"That's going to cost you extra," said the automaton, and Yekel was about to tear the final remaining page out of the typewriter when one of the Fancy Rat's henchmen—the henchman with the rocket launcher whose life was no longer happening in chronological order—fired another rocket, or, rather, fired the same rocket again, and it blazed through the backseat and scorched up everything in sight until everything in sight was charred and smoldering except the book's first two words. And this was when, with a violent jolt, the cab lurched a few inches forward.

Then it skidded to a halt, and went back to idling.

True, it hardly moved an inch. To some it probably even seemed it didn't move at all. But it did. And though it wasn't much, it was actually just barely enough. For a huge wrecking ball was just then swinging from a crane that some of the Rat's men had commandeered, a wrecking ball that swung precisely where, if not for Yekel's modest success, the cab would still have been.

"Wait a sec," said the automaton. "Did you say, 'The End?'"

"Yes," said the passenger, "that's exactly what I said," he wrote, and he wrote it once again.

Acknowledgments

With all my heart, thank you to:

all the guiding writers and teachers that helped this book find its way through me, especially Peter Markus, Stanley Crawford, Derek White, Michael Mejia, Brian Evenson, Lance Olsen, Craig Dworkin, Carole Maso, Joanna Howard, Mónica de la Torre, Jay Cantor, Christine Schutt, Avner Baz, Nancy Bauer, Timothy Bewes, Zachary Sng, Andrew Shephard, Robert Lopez, Alexandra Kleeman, Janet Sarbanes, and most especially Lindsey Drager, for leading me through these harrowing paths toward *publication*, and Thalia Field, for teaching me that it is okay—necessary even—to suck at life;

all my writing companions at Brown, the University of Utah, and elsewhere, especially Shayla Lawz, Will VanDenBerg, Ana Fiahlo, Travis Vick, Alyssa Quinn (especially for the insight that *the book of webs* is a verb, not a noun!), Daniel Uncapher, Lindsey Webb, and Allie Field Bell;

Edie Meidav for awarding the book with the Juniper Prize for Fiction; all the folks at the University of Massachusetts Press, including Courtney Andree and Rachael DeShano; and especially Nancy Raynor (the intrepid copyeditor of what is essentially a 420-page-long typo!); thank you all for believing in the project enough to publish it, but not so much as to recoil at the risk of instigating a potential apocalypse by doing so;

Jedediah Berry and Evangeline Riddiford Graham at *Conjunctions* for publishing a version of the first chapter;

the following texts for feeding certain initiatory phrases, images, rhetorical structures, ideas, melodies, etcetera, into the weave of the web (this list being, obviously, necessarily, far from exhaustive and also in no particular order):

Ralph Waldo Emerson's "Circles" ("Our moods do not believe in each other.")
Giorgio Agamben's *The Coming Community* (". . . we are saved only at the point we no longer need to be . . .")
Antonio Machado's poem, "Caminante, No Hay Camino" (". . . se hace camino al andar . . .")
Wayne Gretzki's inspirational ideologeme as reiterated on a thousand Tinder profiles ("You miss 100% of the shots . . .")
Total Recall and Philip K. Dick's "We Can Remember It for You Wholesale"
Herman Melville's *The Confidence-Man* ("Ah sir, reflect how untimely this distrust . . ."), *Mardi* ("We are off!"), and *Moby-Dick* ("Call me Ishmael.")
Ludwig Wittgenstein's *Philosophical Investigations*
Vilém Flusser's *Vampyroteuthis Infernalis* ("Reality is a web of concrete relations . . .")
Certain episodes of *Planet Earth* (the sunlike significance of batshit in caves, and the fact that bare stone is an oasis in Antarctica)
The *Zohar* ("Torah says, 'I was the artistic tool of the Blessed Holy One . . .'" and ". . . in the farthest depths of this cave he found a book wedged into a cleft of a rock . . .")
Wikie the talking orca whale ("Hello," and "Amy," and "Ah, ah," and "One, two," and "Bye, bye")
Patti Page's version of Stewart and King's "The Tennessee Waltz" ("I remember the night . . .")

Jakob Johann von Uexküll's *A Foray into the Worlds of Animals and Humans*

Edmond Jabès's *The Book of Questions* ("On the level of creation, the pupils are giant breasts . . .")

Franz Kafka's *The Castle* ("It was late in the evening when K. arrived . . .")

The Random House Dictionary of the English Language, 2nd Edition, Unabridged

Antoine Volodine's books, especially *Minor Angels* and *Naming of the Jungle*

Vicki Hearne's *Adam's Task*

Donna Haraway's *Staying with the Trouble* (". . . response-ability . . .")

Isaac the Blind's *Commentary on Sefer Yezirah* (". . . meditation through sucking not knowing . . .")

The Talmud ("A dream uninterpreted is like a letter unopened.")

Martin Buber's *Tales of the Hasidim* (". . . Ma–ma–ma; va–va–va . . ." and "Dreams are a secretion of our thoughts . . .")

A video of Arkadii Dragomoshchenko reading at UPenn ("Give me a page. Not lined please . . .")

A video of a baby bonobo getting tickled (". . . I can't stop laughing . . .")

Georg Büchner's *The Hessian Messenger* ("This paper intends to reveal the truth to the state of Hesse . . .")

Sigmund Freud's *Delusion and Dream in Wilhelm Jensen's* Gradiva ("In a circle of men who take it for granted that the basic riddle . . ." and ". . . the ground story of the delusion structure . . .")

Mikhail Bakhtin's *Problems of Dostoevsky's Poetics* and "Forms of Time and of the Chronotope in the Novel"

Henri Bergson's *Dreams* (". . . from whence comes all this phantasmagoria?" and "Here white lines on a black background . . ."), and *Matter and Memory*
Theodore H. Savory's *The Spider's Web* (". . . a substance which has changed from excretion to secretion . . .")
Heinrich von Kleist's "On the Theater of Marionettes"
Timothy Morton's *Hyperobjects*
Baruch Spinoza's *Ethics*
Donald Winnicott's *Playing and Reality* ("I wish to examine the place, using the word in an abstract sense . . .")
Emmanuel Levinas's "Is Ontology Fundamental" ("When the awkwardness of the act is turned against the goal pursued . . .")
Gilles Deleuze and Félix Guattari's *A Thousand Plateaus*
Maurice Merleau-Ponty's *Phenomenology of Perception*
An article by Rachel Cooke in the *Guardian* from which I learned that our inner voice says 4,000 words per minute and thus (my extrapolation) a 100,000-word novel every twenty-five minutes;
Jesus Christ's Sermon on the Mount ("Do unto others . . .");

Chip and Molly for a safe haven to retreat to—twice!;

Mom and Dad—for initiating me in the art of oneiromancy and for giving me life and nourishment and everything—Annie, Matt, Sage, Judith, and especially Tara, my five-years prematurely born twin, for reading my drafts, insisting that I be nice to your brother, and, most of all, for your solidarity with Betsy the Hermit;

Bennett, Mike, Dylan, Ross, Orie, James, Josie, Alyssa, José, Jen, Renato, Justin, Zac, Aron, Graham, Louis, Sean, Yvette, everyone in Salt Lake Community Mutual Aid, all the dogs, living and dead, all the frogs named Max, Nighty, the wind, the coyotes, thunder, the ravens, the ants, the snakes, and so on;

Roy, for being my dog brother;

Sam, for being my bob;

all the book's characters for introducing themselves to me in my dreams and making sure their stories got at least partially told—I'm sure I'll see you all again soon;

the actual *book of webs,* the forthcoming book that I plagiarized to write this one and that will hopefully be written in deeds done by the current book's future readers;

and, most of all, to spiders for never losing their taste for me, even during those first thirty-or-so years of my life when I suffered from severe arachnophobia—arachnophobia that has, thanks to your insistent association, come, more or less, to an end.

This volume is the twenty-fifth recipient of the Juniper Prize for Fiction, established in 2004 by the University of Massachusetts Press in collaboration with the UMass Amherst MFA Program for Poets and Writers, to be presented annually for an outstanding work of literary fiction. Like its sister award, the Juniper Prize for Poetry established in 1976, the prize is named in honor of Robert Francis (1901–1987), who lived for many years at Fort Juniper, Amherst, Massachusetts.